"YOU'VE MADE A TRAGIC MISTAKE, MY LORD. A MARRIAGE BETWEEN US WILL BE DISASTROUS."

"Why do you say that?" Richard asked.

"Because I believe it," Keely said, her violet-eyed gaze pleading for his understanding. "In case you hadn't noticed, I'm different from Ladies Jane and Sarah and all those other women."

"I noticed." Richard planted his hands on either side of her head as she pressed her back against the oak tree. Leaning close, he added, "I don't desire those other women, else I would have married one of them."

His intimate nearness and his clean masculine scent assaulted her senses. Keely felt him with every tingling fiber of her body and was quite certain he could hear the frantic pounding of her heart.

"I—I have secrets," she said, trying to discourage him. "I cannot share them."

"Dark secrets?" he teased, tracing a finger down the length of her silken cheek. "Beauty, your heart is pure and as easy to read as an open book. Besides, I'm partial to ebony hair and violet eyes. . . ."

Oh, why would he not heed her warning? An experienced man of the world, the earl should know that appearances could be deceptive. . . .

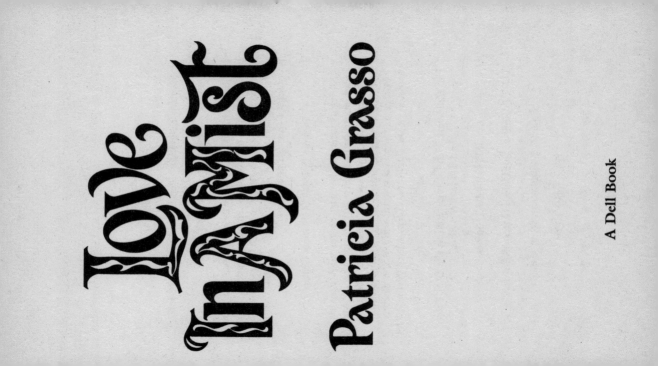

Love in a Mist

Patricia Grasso

A Dell Book

Published by
Dell Publishing
a division of
Bantam Doubleday Dell Publishing Group, Inc.
1540 Broadway
New York, New York 10036

ISBN: 0-440-21669-9

Printed in the United States of America

Published simultaneously in Canada

December 1994

10 9 8 7 6 5 4 3 2 1

OPM

Dedicated to Noralee Murphy, whose knowledge of all things magical is surpassed only by her generosity in sharing that special expertise with me

And to Percy, my pretty boy who possesses the gentle soul of a saint

And to Pip, the orphan boy whose "great expectations" brought him into my heart and my home

Chapter 1

Wales, August 1575

 Dark gray clouds, changing afternoon into twilight, hovered over the lush green land. A flash of lightning brightened the sky and then vanished as quickly as it had appeared.

Eighteen-year-old Keely Glendower stood at the window and watched nature unleashing her forces. The gathering storm outside the keep mirrored the storm brewing within her. Worry troubled Keely's delicately chiseled features; her aching sadness mingled with constricting fury, making breathing difficult.

Her beautiful mother was dying young.

Keely sighed raggedly, brokenly. Her heart railed against what her mind knew to be true. Her gentle mother was dying.

Megan Glendower Lloyd lay in the bed across the chamber, slowly bleeding to death from a final, futile attempt to give her husband a second son. There was nothing to be done but await the end.

"Is she dead yet?"

Keely whirled around at the sound of that voice. Her skin prickled with loathing at the sight of her stepfather.

Baron Madoc Lloyd filled the doorway. Tall and muscular, the baron could have been a handsome man except for the revealing coldness in his gray eyes.

Keely stared hard at him. Her startling violet-eyed gaze judged him guilty of murdering her mother.

"Am I a free man?" Madoc asked in a loud voice.

Keely flushed with appalled anger, pointed an accusing finger at him, and opened her mouth to speak. Before she could utter a word, a spectacular bolt of lightning zigzagged across the sky outside the window behind her, and a deafening boom of thunder reverberated in the chamber.

"Hex me not," Madoc cried, crossing himself. He slammed the door shut.

Keely started to go after him, but the voice from the bed stopped her.

"Leave him to the divine forces," her mother said.

Keely hurried across the chamber and sat on the stool where she'd been keeping a lonely vigil beside her mother's sickbed. In spite of her sadness, Keely managed a smile for her mother.

"What Madoc desires most will kill him in the end," Megan told her. "Trust me, for I have seen it."

Keely nodded. Whatever her mother saw came to pass. Always.

"There was a time when Madoc loved me beyond reason," Megan said, her voice soft with remembrance, "but my heart belonged to your father. And still does."

That bit of information surprised Keely. Her mother had always refused to answer her questions about her real father, and so she'd stopped asking. Keely hoped her mother would say something more now. She'd waited a long, long time to learn about him. And now perhaps the waiting was over.

"You resemble me, but your violet eyes are his," Megan went on. "Each time I looked into your eyes, I saw him. Madoc could never forgive you for being *his* daughter."

"We'll speak more of this after you've rested," Keely said, realizing her mother was wasting what little reserve of energy she had left.

"My beloved daughter," I stand at the gateway to the Other World and will soon be gone," Megan told her. "By the time the cock crows, I will have begun the Great Adventure."

Keely opened her mouth to refute her mother's impending death.

"Do not deny what I have seen," Megan said. "It is Lughnasadh, the time of marriage and divorce, and I will finally be free of Madoc. . . . Fetch my sickle."

Keely hurried across the chamber to her mother's chest. She returned in a moment, sat on the edge of the bed, and offered her mother a tiny golden sickle used for cutting mistletoe from the mighty oak trees.

"Upon my death, that golden sickle passes to you," Megan said. Then she removed the only piece of jewelry she'd ever worn and gave it to her daughter.

From a heavy chain of gold hung a dragon pendant. A blaze of sapphires and emeralds, lit by glittering diamonds, the pendant was the head of a dragon. One ruby rose flamed from its mouth.

"Wear this always. The magic of its love will protect you," Megan said. "Your sire wears the dragon's tail."

Keely placed the necklace over her head and touched the dragon where it rested against her chest. "Will you tell me his name?"

"Robert Talbot."

A smile of pure joy lit Keely's face. She had waited so many years to hear her father's name, and now she knew.

"Walk among the powerful, but find happiness where the birch, the yew, and the oak converse," Megan said. "Trust the king who wears a flaming crown and possesses the golden touch. Beware the blacksmith."

A chill danced down Keely's spine. "The blacksmith?"

"Go to your father when Madoc exiles you," Megan said.

"That will never happen as long as Rhys lives," Keely assured her. She wanted her mother's final hours to be without worry.

"Though he does love you like a sister, Rhys is only your stepbrother and must obey Madoc or be disowned," Megan said. "I know these things because I have seen them. Promise to go to your father."

"I swear it," Keely said, then planted a kiss on her mother's cheek. "Where will I find this Robert Talbot?"

A soft smile touched the dying woman's lips. "Robert Talbot is the Duke of Ludlow."

Keely paled several shades. "The *English* Duke of Ludlow?"

Megan merely smiled at her.

"I'm a blasted Englishman?" Keely cried, appalled.

"Englishwoman," Megan corrected, patting her daughter's hand.

Disturbed by her mother's incredible revelation, Keely stared into space. She'd been bred to despise all that was English, but that tainted blood flowed through her own veins. Oh, Lord! Where did she belong? Here in Wales, the land of her birth? Or in England, the land of her enemy? Nowhere?

"Teach your children the Old Ways," Megan said.

Keely gave Megan her full attention. Thinking only of herself when her mother lay dying was horribly selfish. Thoroughly English.

"I will be with you again at Samhuinn," Megan promised. "Give me your hand."

As Keely watched, Megan drew an imaginary circle in the palm of her hand and said, "Remember, my child. Life is a circle with no beginning and no ending. You are born, you live, you die."

With one finger, Megan circled Keely's palm a second time. In a soft, chanting voice, she said, "You are born, a child, a young woman, an old woman . . . you die."

Again, Megan circled her daughter's palm and chanted, "Born, grow, die. *Reborn*."

The hand holding Keely's went limp and fell away. Keely gazed at her mother's serene expression and knew she had passed into the Great Adventure.

Keely kissed her mother's hand. She leaned down, buried her face against her mother's chest, and wept.

Gradually, her sobs subsided and then finally ceased. Still, she rested against the comforting solidness of her mother.

What would become of her now? Keely wondered. She

had lost not only her mother but her home. Though she'd lived her entire life at her stepfather's holding, Keely knew she was no Lloyd and had never felt that she belonged there. Now she was alone in the world.

Perhaps not. Her stepbrother Rhys loved her like a sister, as did her cousins Odo and Hew. And now there was Robert Talbot, the man who sired her.

Slowly and wearily, Keely stood up and went to her mother's table. She returned with a bouquet of oak leaves and mistletoe and a hooded white robe. Her mother's lavender scent clung to it, nearly felling Keely with aching loss. Placing the bouquet in her mother's hands, Keely kissed her cheek and whispered, "Until we meet at Samhuinn."

Keely shrouded her mother's empty shell with the white ceremonial robe. She touched the dragon pendant, gleaming against the crisp whiteness of her linen blouse, and prayed its magic would give her the inner strength she needed.

After taking a deep breath to steady herself, Keely left the chamber and walked down the torch-lit corridors toward the great hall. She stepped inside and nodded at her mother's women, who hurried away to prepare the body for burial.

Keely stood alone inside the doorway and scanned the crowded hall. Rhys wasn't there; but Odo and Hew, her loyal cousins, saw her stricken expression and hurried toward her.

Seated at the high table, Madoc looked up from his mug of ale and saw her.

"Well, she took her sweet time dying," he drawled in a voice slurred with drink.

Keely stepped back a pace as if she'd been struck. Her flawless complexion paled to a deathly white. All around her sounded the shocked gasps of the Lloyd clansmen and retainers.

How dared Madoc speak of her gentle mother in that despicable manner! Intending to set him straight, Keely started toward the high table, but her cousins reached her in time to prevent the confrontation.

Odo and Hew were larger than most men and possessed in brawn what they lacked in intelligence. Standing on either side of her, the brothers held her arms and warned her to silence.

Odo, the older of the two, nodded in the baron's direction. "Baiting him will serve no purpose."

"Where is Rhys?" Keely asked.

"He rode out earlier to go raiding," Hew answered. That surprised and hurt Keely. "You mean, he went raiding even though my mother was near death?"

"He had no choice," Odo told her.

"Madoc ordered it," Hew added.

Keely stared with barely suppressed rage at her stepfather, who sat like a king at the high table.

"Where's my supper?" Madoc demanded, banging his fist on the table. "Bring more ale. I cannot celebrate my freedom without ale. And I want Elen with the big teats to serve me."

Keely's violet gaze cursed him, but heeding her cousins' advice, she turned away, her ebony hair swirling around with her movement. Keely left the great hall and headed for the kitchen. Like two gigantic hounds, Odo and Hew followed behind her.

"Greetings, Haylan," Keely called, crossing the kitchen to the middle-aged cook.

"I'm very sorry for Megan. Such a wise and gentle soul," the older woman said, hugging her. "'Tis the baron's loss, though I doubt he realizes it."

"Grief makes Madoc hungry," Keely told her, blinking back tears. "Serve supper promptly, and be certain Elen attends the baron."

Haylan nodded and then shouted, "Elen!"

Answering the call, a pretty serving girl appeared and hurried across the kitchen toward them.

"Deliver this to the high table," Haylan ordered, handing the girl the bowl. She yanked the girl's bodice down a couple of inches, saying, "Cleavage comforts a grieving man. Be kind to the baron."

"I hope my kindness will kill him," Elen said with a grimace.

"You know my mother's last wishes," Keely said, turning to her cousins. "When supper is done, clear the hall for the deathwatch. I'll return then." With that, she left the kitchen.

Three hours later, Megan Glendower Lloyd lay in state inside the torch-lit great hall, her simple wooden coffin resting on trestles. Wrapped in her white robe, Megan appeared to be sleeping.

Keely walked into the nearly deserted hall. With her ebony mane cascading to her waist in pagan fashion, she wore her own white ceremonial robe and the blazing dragon pendant. In her hands she carried a fresh bouquet of oak leaves and mistletoe.

Odo and Hew stood beside the bier and waited for her.

"Have you seen to the grave?" Keely asked.

"Dug where you wanted," Odo answered.

"And the cross?"

"Carved to your order," Hew replied.

Keely nodded with grim satisfaction and placed the bouquet across her mother's chest. Then she sat on a wooden bench beside the bier.

Odo and Hew sat down on either side of her. Faithful Haylan walked in, carrying her own stool, and sat with them in silence. Finally, Madoc arrived and took a seat on the bench next to Odo.

"Keeping the watch means losing a good night's sleep," Madoc complained.

"It's the least you can do to honor a loving wife who died trying to give you another son," Keely shot back.

"Megan was never a loving wife," the baron grumbled, his voice filled with bitterness. "Her heart always belonged to him. Never me."

Keely froze. He spoke of her father. Had Madoc known him? Keely opened her mouth to question her stepfather but felt her cousins' hands touch her forearms, warning her against rash speech.

An hour passed. And then another.

"I'm thirsty," Madoc announced, breaking the silence as he rose from the bench. "I'm in need of something fortifying. I'll be back."

He left the hall and never returned.

Father Bundles arrived in the crowded great hall an hour before dawn. As he made his way through the mob of clansmen and retainers, the old priest muttered under his breath about the earliness of the hour. Burying a body in the middle of the night was barbaric, he thought. And that was before he saw Keely.

Keely looked like a pagan princess in her flowing white robe. Around her neck hung a wreath fashioned from oak leaves and mistletoe.

"Shame on you for wearing that to Megan's funeral," Father Bundles scolded her. "You'll be needing my absolution before the sun sets this day."

Keely arched a dark brow at him. "I honor my mother's memory, Father Bundles. If you want to waste time in sermons, we'll forgo the funeral mass. The choice is yours."

"'Tis blasphemy," Father Bundles said. He scanned the crowded chamber. "Where are Baron Lloyd and Rhys?"

"The baron is sleeping off the effects of his drinking," Keely told him, "and my brother is busy plundering the English."

"'Tis an unnatural family," the old priest grumbled. "These friends have come to bury Megan," Keely said, gesturing toward the crowd. "Please begin the service."

With Odo and Hew acting as pallbearers, Father Bundles led the way from the great hall to the chapel. Keely walked behind the casket, and everyone followed her.

The old priest opened his mouth to pray, but Keely

called out, "Celebrate the short mass, Father. Megan desired a dawn burial."

Father Bundles's expression told Keely that Madoc would hear of her blasphemy. The short mass took exactly twenty minutes.

"Megan will not be interred in the Lloyd vault," Keely announced. "My mother wished to enjoy the rising sun for all of eternity."

Though he did look ready to explode, Father Bundles swallowed his fury. Expressing anger in the house of God was a terrible sin.

Keely pulled her hood up to cover her ebony mane and led the unusual funeral procession out of the chapel. Odo and Hew, carrying the casket, followed her. Behind them walked Father Bundles and then a piper playing a mourning lament. The baron's clansmen and retainers marched behind in silence.

Bright tentacles of orange light streaked the eastern sky as the funeral procession wended its way past the graveyard to a grassy incline where three gigantic oak trees stood together like old friends. The grave beneath one of those mighty oaks faced the rising sun.

"This is unhallowed ground," Father Bundles protested.

"Then you must bless it," Keely snapped, losing patience.

Ready to argue, Father Bundles glanced at Odo and Hew. Their great size, combined with their threatening expressions, made him reconsider.

Father Bundles recited a few prayers in Latin, sprinkled the grave with holy water, and hurried away. After offering words of condolence, everyone but Keely and her cousins dispersed.

Odo and Hew lowered the casket into the ground as the sun rose in all of its radiant glory. The air was hushed as if the world held its breath.

Keely closed her eyes, raised her arms toward the sun, and whispered, "Father Sun kisses Mother Earth." She looked down at the open grave. "Rest in peace, dear mother. Watch the light come into the world each day."

Odo and Hew refilled the grave and set the temporary marker, a Celtic cross carved from oak, into its place. Later, the stonecutter would place the permanent cross there.

"Rhys should have been here," Keely said, her disappointment obvious.

"He'll be furious with Madoc," Odo remarked.

"My earliest memory is of Mother and me sitting beneath these oaks," Keely said, tears welling up in her eyes. "We sat here every day, no matter the season or weather, and she taught me the Old Ways. I'm alone in the world now."

"But you have us," Hew protested.

"And don't forget Rhys," Odo added.

And Robert Talbot, Keely thought. But she said with a sad smile, "Thank you for your loyalty, cousins."

Brushing the tears from her cheeks, Keely knelt beside her mother's grave. She removed the oak and mistletoe wreath from around her neck and placed it over the cross, whispering, "Send me a sign, Mother."

A sudden gust of wind blew the hood off her head, and falling oak leaves fluttered around her. Keely closed her eyes and murmured, "Until Samhuinn."

Unnerved, Odo and Hew looked at each other. Those two fearless warriors of many a raid made a protective sign of the cross—just to be sure.

By the time Keely and her cousins returned to the great hall, clansmen and retainers were crowded inside eating their morning meal. Looking tired and none too happy, Madoc sat at the high table. His complexion was ashen, and his head rested on one hand.

Father Bundles stood beside him. The old priest appeared in a high agitation as he talked and gestured toward the hall's entrance.

"Aye, Father," Madoc agreed in a loud voice, his gaze

sliding to his stepdaughter. "Megan raised her daughter to be as heathen as she."

Heedless of consequence, Keely advanced on the high table. "Do not foul my mother's memory by slandering her good name, you sniveling son of a—"

"Curse and rot you!" Madoc shouted, banging his fist on the table, stopping Keely in her tracks. "I am the lord here. Never speak to me in that disrespectful manner again."

Knowing her stepfather was all bluster, Keely arched one ebony brow at him. "Your grief makes you cranky," she said. "Perhaps a mug of ale will revive your good humor." She threw him a contemptuous look and added, "A lord? More like a drunken snake masquerading as—"

Leaping out of his chair, Madoc banged his fist on the table again. Rage reddened his complexion.

"You are naught but a bastard witch!" Madoc shouted, advancing on her.

Odo and Hew stepped in front of Keely like two fierce hounds protecting their mistress.

"Stand aside," Madoc ordered.

"You must go through us to get to her," Odo announced.

Madoc couldn't credit the insubordination he was hearing. He glanced from one hulking brother to the other and said, "Your combined brains are no bigger than a rooster's balls."

At the insult, Odo and Hew growled low in their throats. Madoc wisely retreated several paces.

"You are not of the Cymry," Madoc said to his stepdaughter. "Take your few possessions and leave Wales."

"The blood of Llewelyn the Great and Owen Glendower flows in my veins," Keely cried. "I am a true princess of Powys and Gwynedd."

"You are the Princess of Nowhere," Madoc sneered in a voice that carried to the far corners of the hall. "That blazing dragon pendant and those violet eyes mark you the uncherished by-blow of an Englishman."

Everyone in the chamber gasped audibly and fell silent.

"Megan is dead," Madoc went on. "Seek out your English father. Begone from my land." Turning his anger on clansmen and retainers, he warned, "Show your backs to this simpering bastard, or be outcast yourselves."

Keely turned on her heels in a swirl of white robe and ebony hair and marched proudly out of the hall. Before following her outside, Odo and Hew growled as menacingly as they could at the baron, who leaped back another pace.

When her cousins joined her outside, Keely said, "I never thought Madoc would—" She broke off with a sob, and tears streamed down her cheeks.

"He wouldn't dare if Rhys was here," Odo said, putting a comforting arm around her.

"Madoc lies," Hew added.

Both Keely and Odo stared at him blankly.

"You never simper," Hew explained. "At least, I never saw you simper." He looked at his brother and asked, "What does *simper* mean?"

Odo cuffed the side of his brother's head. "What does it matter, you blinking idiot?"

Hew shrugged. "I guess you don't know either."

In spite of her predicament, Keely smiled at her two giants. "I thank you for being faithful cousins," she said. "Odo, please prepare Merlin for traveling. Include a bag of feed for her. Hew, ask Haylan to pack a food basket for me. Enough to get me to England."

"We're going with you," Odo said.

"Sharing my exile is unnecessary," Keely said, refusing to let them give up their home.

"We insist," Hew said. "Besides, nothing is forever."

"The three of us will return to Wales one day soon," Odo added.

"Then I accept your offer," Keely agreed, grateful for their company. "My father lives in Shropshire."

"Who is he?" Odo asked.

"Robert Talbot."

"Talbot does sound like an English name," Hew remarked.

Keely looked at him. "The renowned Duke of Ludlow is most assuredly an Englishman."

"The Duke of —?"

"Your hearing is keen. The Duke of Ludlow sired me," Keely said, already turning away. "Now let's not waste any more time. Meet me at the stableyard in one hour."

With her few possessions neatly folded inside her leather satchel, Keely spared a final glance at her sparsely furnished chamber and then hurried outside. The stableyard was conspicuously deserted except for Haylan, Odo, and Hew. Apparently, the Lloyd clansmen and retainers were too fearful of incurring the baron's anger to see her off. Keely didn't blame them for keeping their distance from her. If Madoc was capable of outcasting his own stepdaughter, he could do the same or worse to them.

When she stood in front of Haylan, Keely pasted a bright smile onto her face. "Thank you for everything," she said quietly to the older woman. "Especially for your loyalty to my mother."

"Megan was a great lady," Haylan replied. "The same as you'll be one day."

Keely hugged the woman, saying, "Please tell Rhys not to follow me. I'll write him after I've settled into my new home with my father."

Haylan nodded and then looked at the two giants standing there. "Protect the girl with your lives."

Odo and Hew bobbed their heads in unison.

Fighting back tears, Keely gave Haylan another quick hug and then mounted Merlin. Odo and Hew mounted their own horses.

"Wait!" a voice called.

Keely turned and saw Father Bundles running into the stableyard.

"I'm sorry for this trouble I've caused you," the priest said when he reached her side.

"There's no need to apologize," Keely told him. "At the moment of my conception, the wind whispered my destiny to the holy stones. What is happening was meant to be."

Father Bundles refrained from lecturing her about the sinful folly of her religious beliefs. "I'll celebrate a mass each day for the repose of Lady Megan's soul," he promised.

"Thank you, Father," Keely replied. She believed in the significance of the Christian rites no more than her mother had, but to insure the peace of mind of people like the priest, they'd always pretended otherwise.

"God protect you, child," Father Bundles said, blessing her with the sign of the cross.

Without another word, Keely and her cousins rode out of the stableyard. Though an aching sadness settled around her heart, Keely never once looked back for a final glimpse of her former home. Her destiny lay in England: Megan had seen it, and what her mother saw came to pass. Always.

Leicester, England

The sun rode high in a cloudless blue sky that sultry day in mid-August. Unusually hot summer weather gripped the land and its people.

A solitary horseman reached the crest of a grassy knoll and felt a rejuvenating surge of relief at what he saw. After journeying for long days beneath that scorching sun to catch up with Queen Elizabeth on her annual summer progress, the Earl of Basildon had arrived at his destination. Before him rose Kenilworth Castle, the home of Robert Dudley, the Earl of Leicester.

Tradition linked the ancient castle with the reign of King Arthur, but Richard Devereux knew better. The great house actually began as a Norman fortification. Henry V added a summer house on the shore of an artificial lake, and Dudley built his own block of buildings in the light high-windowed style so popular in these modern times.

"I can't believe Elizabeth gifted the son of a traitor with all this," Richard muttered to himself. To the Dudley family, loyalty was like the weather—subject to change without warning.

Eager to put his travels behind, Richard spurred his horse forward and galloped the remaining distance to the great house. He reached the inner courtyard and leaped off his horse, then tossed the reins and a coin to a waiting stableboy.

"Be sure to treat him well," Devereux ordered.

"Aye, my lord," the boy said with a toothy grin.

"I wondered when you'd arrive," a familiar voice said.

Richard turned toward the voice and offered his hand to Baron Willis Smythe, one of his closest friends. "I don't suppose Dudley's saved me a chamber?" he asked.

"Accommodations are cramped," Smythe replied. "Luckily, I've saved you a cot in mine."

The renowned Earl of Basildon and Baron Smythe walked together toward the main building. The myriad females they passed—high-born ladies no less than lowly serving wenches—paused to admire the perfect picture of virility the two friends presented.

Both men enjoyed magnificent physiques—broad shoulders, tapered waists, and well-muscled thighs shown to best advantage in the tight hose they wore. But all similarities between them ended there.

The taller green-eyed earl sported a thick mane of burnished copper hair and moved with a predator's grace. The heavier black-haired baron had deep-set blue eyes and moved in a lumbering gait.

Given their pick, those perusing females would undoubtedly have chosen the earl who, as everyone knew, was richer than the pope. Baron Smythe usually lacked funds, though his intense gaze promised rewards more valuable than gold.

"Both Lady Mary and Lady Jane have been pestering me about your arrival," Willis Smythe said as they entered the main building's foyer. "How will you juggle two mistresses in the same house without getting yourself into trouble?"

There was no reply. Smythe turned when he realized his friend had paused.

Richard stood in the middle of the foyer and watched a passing young lady. When she recognized the earl, the blond-haired beauty stopped, curtsied in his direction, and smiled winsomely. After undressing her with his smoldering emerald gaze from the top of her head to the tips of her slippered feet, Richard winked suggestively at her.

"Lady Sarah is looking especially lovely," Richard remarked, watching her walk away.

"Is she destined to become your next mistress?" Willis asked. "Or will that greatness elude her?"

Richard glanced sidelong at his friend. "You know, Will, I never dally with unmarried women."

"*Devereux!*"

Richard turned at the sound of his name and waited as the Earl of Leicester approached them.

"Welcome to Kenilworth. The queen is resting after the morning hunt," Dudley said. "Shall I have your arrival announced?"

"I'd prefer to wash the dust from my face before I see Her Majesty," Richard replied. "Tell Burghley I'm here with important information."

"Not bad, I hope."

"On the contrary, quite good."

"What is it?" The words slipped out of Leicester's mouth before he could bite them back.

Richard stared at him, a stare that told the older man the information was no business of his.

"Housing the royal retinue does create a crowding

problem," Dudley said, recovering himself. "Smythe and you will share a chamber."

"I understand," Richard replied, his intense dislike of the pompous earl evident in his polite expressionless response. Without another word, he turned his back and walked away with Willis Smythe.

Had he glanced back, Richard would have caught a deadly expression etched across his host's face. The Earl of Leicester, possessive of the queen's affection, harbored no fondness for the Earl of Basildon. In fact, the older man eagerly awaited the arrogant upstart's comeuppance.

"Here we are," Willis said, opening a door.

Richard followed him inside and looked in disgust at the closet posing as a bedchamber. "I should have known Dudley would see me ensconced in the worst chamber at Kenilworth. Call a servant, will you?"

Smythe opened the door and hailed the first passing servant. "You, girl, get in here!" he barked an order.

A pretty serving girl stepped nervously into the chamber. Richard read the anxiety in her expression and smiled to put her at ease.

"I'd like something light to eat and a pan of warmed water for washing," Richard said, his voice a soft caress, soothing the girl's worry. "Would that be possible?"

Mesmerized by the handsome earl's smile, the girl stared at him and said nothing.

"Miss?" Richard prodded, pressing a coin into the palm of her hand.

"I'll take care of it right away, my lord," she said, recovering herself, then hurried away to do his bidding.

"Whenever I order a servant, the service is poor," Willis complained. "But when you give an order, the wenches trip over their own feet in their haste to please you. Why is that, I wonder?"

"You haven't been paying attention," Richard said, removing his dusty doublet and tossing it aside. He sat on the edge of the cot and yanked his boots off. "A world of difference lies between a simple request and an order."

"What do you mean?" Willis asked, sitting on the opposite cot.

"Give a woman what she wants, and in return she'll move mountains to please you," Richard told him. "Reading a woman's secret desire is so incredibly easy. For example, most serving girls yearn to be treated like a lady, while most of the noblewomen I know—like Lady Sarah—yearn to be ravished like common wenches. Follow that one simple rule, my friend, and the gentler sex will adore you."

Willis grinned and folded his arms across his chest. "What happens when you finally meet an unreadable woman?"

Richard shrugged. "I'll probably marry her and make her my countess."

"What if she's a commoner?"

Richard cocked a copper brow at him. "England's wealthiest earl can marry whomever he pleases."

"With the queen's permission, of course."

"Never fear. I can handle Elizabeth."

"Is there a chance the servants jump to do your bidding because they know your purse is fat?" Willis asked, his voice tinged with envy.

Richard smiled at the other man's tone and tossed him a full bag of coins. "Try both approaches," he suggested.

"Let me know the outcome."

"Do not deny the queen loves you because your business ventures fill her coffers with gold," Willis said, irritated that his wealthy friend could afford to toss a bag of coins away with cavalier disregard for what others needed.

Feigning surprise and dismay, Richard replied, "I thought Elizabeth loved me for my devilish good looks and dashing charm."

Willis burst out laughing. He stood then and crossed the chamber, saying, "I'm off. I'll see you later." Before he could get out the door, two serving girls rushed past him. One carried a pan of warmed water while the other offered the earl a platter piled high with food. Casting his friend a bemused glance, Willis Smythe shook his head and quit their chamber.

Two hours later, the Earl of Basildon, dressed severely in black except for the white lawn ruff around his neck, emerged from his chamber and headed for Dudley's study, where he'd been summoned to attend the queen. He knocked on the door and entered at the sound of the answering call. Robert Cecil, Lord Burghley, sat alone at the desk.

"So you've finally arrived—and only six weeks late," Burghley said by way of a greeting. "If you'd delayed any longer, you could have met us at the gates of London."

"Is she very angry?" Richard asked, sitting down in the chair opposite him and placing a small package on the desk. "I have good news, and an idea that will make the three of us richer than the pope."

"Putting business before pleasure is a respectable habit," Cecil remarked. "She'll forgive you for that."

"I acquired that habit from England's finest," Richard replied, referring to the years he'd been fostered in the other man's household.

Burghley nodded at the compliment. With a smile he said, "I suppose Dudley gave you the worst chamber possible."

"No, Dudley gave Smythe the worst chamber," Richard replied. "He saved none for me."

Burghley frowned at the mention of the baron's name. "I thought I'd advised you to terminate your friendship with Smythe," he said.

"Why do you dislike him?" Richard asked. "Willis fostered in your household too. Is it because he hasn't a gold piece to his name?"

"We've had this conversation a hundred times before," Burghley replied. "My reasons have nothing to do with his lack of funds. I believe Smythe is untrustworthy, and I harbor suspicions about his involvement in his father's and his brother's deaths. You know that, Richard."

"I cannot believe Will murdered his family to inherit that piddling title."

"Greedy men murder for less. Do not forget that he squandered the inheritance that—"

The door opened suddenly. The two men shot to their feet and bowed as the queen entered.

Tall and slim and red-haired, Elizabeth Tudor was still a stunningly handsome woman at the ripe age of forty-two. She wore a low-cut gown in lady blush silk that bore a fortune in gold braiding and pearl embroidery. Spectacular diamonds glittered from her throat, fingers, and hair. When she moved, Elizabeth sparkled as brilliantly as a dancing sunbeam.

The queen made herself comfortable and gestured Burghley to sit. She left Richard standing like an errant child awaiting punishment while she looked the uncomfortable earl up and down.

"The prodigal courtier arrives," Elizabeth said. "Your extreme tardiness does irritate Us."

"Forgive me, Majesty," Richard apologized, bowing deeply. "Though I yearned to be in your company, your business interests held me prisoner in London."

"You sound like Cecil. Too many years in my dear Spirit's household have made you an overly serious young man," the queen replied, pleased with his artful apology. "Sit down, dear Midas. Tell Us what you have touched and turned into gold these past weeks."

"I've received important information from the East," Richard said. "My sister Heather writes that Sultan Selim is dead. Prince Murad is now sultan. His mother and his wife favor trade with England."

"Your sister married whom?" Elizabeth asked.

"Prince Khalid, the sultan's cousin."

"Ah, yes. I remember now. All three of your sisters possessed the incredible impertinence to marry without Our permission."

"Flighty girls," Burghley interjected. "Nevertheless, each of the Devereux chits have proven themselves to be loyal Englishwomen, especially the youngest sister."

Richard flicked his mentor a grateful glance and continued, "I have a scheme that will make the three of us rich."

"My dear Midas, you are already rich beyond avarice," Elizabeth teased.

"Then you can be certain that I am incorruptible and do this for you," Richard quipped. His expression became animated as he explained his plan. "Grant me a royal charter for my latest venture, the Levant Trading Company, and we will share the profits. Eastern diplomacy moves slowly. I calculate three years will see us fully operational."

"And what share goes to the Crown?" Elizabeth asked.

"The lion's cub deserves the lion's share of fifty percent," Richard answered. "Burghley and I will split the other fifty, and England will prosper with this powerful ally."

"Seventy percent," the Queen insisted.

"Sixty," Richard shot back.

"You have a deal," Elizabeth said with a smile. "Cecil, you will see that he gets the charter without delay."

Richard opened the package he'd brought with him, saying, "The sultan's mother sends this humble gift to show her good faith."

The humble gift was a fan. Its feathers were a billowing rainbow of hues set with diamonds, and its hilt a mass of emeralds, sapphires, and rubies.

"And this comes from the sultan's wife," Richard added, producing a nosegay of porcelain flowers also set with priceless jewels. "We'll need to send reciprocal gifts. Heather informs me this is the way of eastern diplomacy."

Impressed with her newest trinkets, Elizabeth examined them closely and asked without looking up, "And how shall we reward your sister's loyalty?"

"Her loyalty needs no reward," Richard replied.

"Though she begs me to send her a litter of piglets."

"Why piglets?" Elizabeth asked.

"To raise for the slaughter," Richard explained, a smile lurking in his voice. "My sister is a remarkable woman. She loves pork but hasn't tasted it in nine years, since it's forbidden to Moslems. Heather feels certain her husband couldn't refuse her a gift from England's queen."

"How cunning," Elizabeth complimented his sister. "You have served Us well, Richard. Is there anything else you wish to discuss?"

Richard hesitated for a fraction of a second and then began, "About my tour of duty in Ireland—"

"You're much too valuable to serve abroad," Burghley interrupted, earning himself a censorious glance from his protégé.

"Request denied," the queen said.

"But Your Majesty—"

"Peers of my realm may not serve abroad unless they have an heir."

"Then I request permission to produce one," Richard said.

"What? Shall you visit the market and purchase a son?" Elizabeth quipped.

Burghley chuckled, a sound that few people ever heard.

Richard flushed hot with embarrassment. "I request permission to marry and produce an heir," he amended. "My dear boy, protocol requires you to select a bride first and then ask Our permission," the queen explained as though speaking to a child. "Whom did you have in mind?"

"I have an interest in the virtuous and lovely Morgana Talbot, Ludlow's daughter," Richard lied, hoping he'd happened upon a suitable name. One woman was much the same as another. Besides, marriage was a business venture, and love was unnecessary to sire an heir. He needed to get to Ireland to help protect his oldest sister's family from the greedy vultures governing there. Perched in Dublin Castle, those corrupt English birds of prey awaited the opportunity to swoop down upon the proud Irish nobility and seize whatever they could. Only a rich man like himself stood beyond temptation's reach. Otherwise, civil war was inevitable.

"Do you love Us so little that you would leave Us to take a wife?" Elizabeth asked.

"Lady Morgana's simple prettiness could never compare with your beauty," Richard assured her, then gifted her with one of his boyish smiles. "You hold my loyalty, my admiration, and my heart in thrall. Morgana Talbot is merely a poor substitute for you."

"Impertinent flatterer." Elizabeth tapped the top of his hand with her fan's jeweled hilt.

Richard flicked a glance at Burghley, whose hand covered his mouth to hide a smile.

"Get Talbot's permission and then court the chit," Elizabeth told him. "You are a financial wizard and a born courtier. We cannot understand what you find so appealing about war."

"I worry for my sister Kathryn," Richard admitted. "She writes that Ireland is in turmoil."

"Tyrone's countess," Burghley explained to the queen.

Elizabeth sighed. "We find that We sent wolves to govern in Ireland."

"By the way, Kathryn writes that she is suffering a severe roofing problem," Richard added. "But her husband's request to import lead has been ignored."

"Lead can be made into ammunition," Burghley said. "Send Richard's brother-in-law whatever he needs," the queen ordered. To Richard, she added dryly, "You've a sister in Scotland. No special request from her?"

"None at this time," Richard lied. He was not about to tell the queen that his Scots brother-in-law barraged him with requests to aid in having Mary Stuart released from her English captivity. Even Brigette's three oldest sons now wrote him beseeching letters asking that their queen be returned to Scotland. For all his family loyalty, Richard dared not push his queen too far.

The queen stood, indicating the audience had ended. "Well, then, Our subjects await Our presence in the hall." At that, she breezed out of the chamber with Burghley.

"And if Devereux should produce an heir?" Burghley whispered to the queen as he escorted her to the banquet hall.

"I care not if the pup produces a hundred sons," Elizabeth replied, flicking a sidelong glance at her minister. "I refuse to allow one of my most valuable courtiers to run off to Ireland and get himself killed."

Burghley nodded, satisfied.

Richard followed behind them and stood in the entrance to the banquet hall. The gift-giving ceremony was about to begin.

Elizabeth sat regally in the castle's most comfortable chair, set upon a raised dais. The Sheriff of Leicestershire approached, bowed formally, and presented her the usual silver-gilt cup filled with gold coins.

"It is a remarkable gift," Elizabeth said, looking at the cup and its contents. "I have but few such gifts."

"If it pleases Your Majesty, there is a great deal more than gold in it," the sheriff replied.

"What might that be?" the queen asked, a puzzled smile on her face.

"The hearts of all your loving subjects," he answered.

"We thank you, Mr. Sheriff," Elizabeth said, sincerely pleased. "It is a great deal more indeed."

Watching her, Richard was filled with admiration and love for Elizabeth. In spite of her womanly vanity and difficult temperament, a more magnificent monarch had never sat upon England's throne.

"You always wear that pained expression as if you walk about with a pike stuck up your—"

Richard whirled around to find the Earl of Leicester standing beside him. He stared stonily at the queen's longtime favorite.

"Her Majesty's summer progress should be a time for gaiety," Dudley said. "Don't you ever laugh? Smile, at least?"

"Ah, Leicester, laughter indicates empty-headedness," Richard told him, "and smiling hides deceit." With that, he turned to leave the hall.

"Departing so soon?" Dudley asked, his voice laced with sarcasm. "We shall miss you."

"Shropshire and a bride await me," Richard said, surprising the other man. He walked away, the unusual sight of a speechless Leicester bringing the hint of a smile to his lips.

Chapter 2

 Keely soaked in a tub set up in her rented chamber at the Boar's Head Inn, near Ludlow Castle in Shropshire. The dreary chamber, only slightly larger than a closet, had a single window overlooking the cobbled innyard, but the room was tidy and clean, as were the linens on the cot.

Would her father acknowledge her? Keely asked herself for the hundredth time.

By God's holy stones! He would acknowledge her, Keely answered herself, and she conjured their poignant reunion scene in her mind.

With graceful dignity she would walk across Ludlow Castle's great hall. Robert Talbot, sitting in a chair in front of the hearth, would rise at her entrance and clutch her against his chest. He'd call her daughter; she'd call him father. Together they would shed tears for the loss of Megan. Then her father would promise to love and protect her, erasing the pain of the eighteen years they'd missed.

Such a perfectly heartwarming picture. *Too perfect.* Troubling thoughts intruded upon that perfect day-dream.

Where would she go if Robert Talbot turned his back on her? Keely wondered. He'd abandoned her mother all those long years ago. How had Megan possessed the blind faith that this irresponsible English lord would love his natural daughter and proclaim their kinship to the world? After all, she was merely his bastard.

And Rhys! She hadn't even had a chance to bid her beloved brother a final farewell. What had Rhys done upon discovering her gone, outcast by Madoc?

A knock on the door interrupted her thoughts, and Odo's voice rang out, "Are you ready, little girl?"

"I need a few minutes more."

Keely stepped out of the tub and toweled herself dry. She dressed in a skirt of soft lightweight wool, the same violet color as her eyes, and a white linen blouse with a deep scooped neck and long full sleeves that gathered at the wrists. She pulled her black leather riding boots on, and slipped the jeweled dragon pendant over her head. It glittered against the crisp whiteness of her blouse.

Keely brushed her hair and plaited the ebony mane into one thick braid. She opened the door and said to her cousins, "Please come in.

"Did you bathe?" she asked, inspecting them up and down. When they bobbed their heads in unison like two overgrown children, she added, "I must say, you do look handsome."

"You're looking fine yourself, little girl," Odo returned the compliment. "Are you ready to meet your father?"

Though her stomach churned at his words, Keely squared her shoulders with determination. "Ready as I'll ever be," she said.

"Should we take our belongings with us?" Hew asked.

"We'll fetch them later if there's a need," Keely replied. She smiled at them, to bolster her own courage as much as theirs, then grabbed her cloak and headed for the door. Odo and Hew followed her out.

The ostler had Merlin and her cousins' horses saddled and waiting in the cobbled innyard. Flanked by Odo and Hew, Keely mounted her horse and started down the road toward Ludlow Castle.

A timeless beauty shrouded the village and countryside of Ludlow. Overhead the sun shone in a clear blue sky, and from the west blew a gentle summer breeze. Delightful thatched-roof cottages dotted the heavily forested, sparsely populated horizon. Colorful wild flowers—dark pink bull thistle, blue chicory, orange and pink day lily, goldenrod, pale pink marjoram—blazed in wanton disarray.

And then Ludlow Castle, gray and forbidding, loomed before them like a primeval beast cast in stone. Keely's breath caught in her throat. Anxiety tightened her stomach into a mass of knots, and her heart pounded frantically. For the first time in her life, she felt true fear. Dealing with so many uncertainties was a less than placid business.

Keely forced herself to take several deep calming breaths. A coward she might be, but no one else would know it.

"The ducal flag waves from that tower," Odo said, pointing toward it.

"Then the duke is in residence," Hew added.

"I don't feel very well," Keely said, losing her nerve, trying to turn Merlin around. "We should return tomorrow. I'm certain I'll be feeling better by then."

"You've come this far and must go all the way," Odo said, his horse blocking her retreat.

Reluctantly, Keely nodded. She wanted nothing more than to bolt all the way back to Wales, but forward was the only path left open to her.

Since England was a land at peace with itself, Keely and her cousins rode across the permanently lowered drawbridge, through the outer ward, and into the inner courtyard. No one stopped or questioned them until they entered the main building.

"State your business here," The man, apparently a high-ranking servant, blocked their entrance to the great hall.

"Who are you?" Keely asked. Oh, lord! She hadn't meant to sound so haughty. Bastards had no business being arrogant.

"I am Mr. Dobbs, the duke's majordomo," the man informed her in a lofty tone of voice. "And you are?"

"Lady Glendower," Keely answered with a tentative smile. "I have urgent business with the duke."

Dobbs looked down his long nose at her and noted her common attire. The chit didn't appear to be any kind of lady that he'd ever seen.

"His Grace is busy," Dobbs said, trying to usher them outside. "Come back another day."

Though her courage was slipping away, Keely stood her ground. If she left now, she'd never return.

"My business with His Grace takes precedence over any other," Keely insisted. "Please inform him of my arrival."

The majordomo opened his mouth to order them away, but a woman's voice sounded from inside the hall, "Who is that, Dobbs?"

Dobbs turned toward the voice and answered, "A young woman who insists she has business with His Grace."

"Bring her to me," the lady said.

The great hall was like nothing Keely had ever seen. The enormous chamber had a high-beamed ceiling and two gigantic fireplaces. Colorful banners hung from the rafters, and vivid tapestries adorned the walls.

Keely stared at the owner of the voice, a blond-haired and blue-eyed angel. Perhaps a year or two younger than Keely, the woman wore an ice-blue silk gown that showed her figure to best advantage. A rather plain stern-looking older woman stood beside the angel.

"My lady, I present Lady Glendower," Dobbs introduced them, placing special emphasis on the word *lady* in front of Keely's name. "Lady Glendower, I present Lady Morgana, His Grace's daughter."

Morgana Talbot gave her full attention to the petite intruder. She quickly assessed the other girl's delicate beauty—shining ebony tresses, flawless ivory complexion with a hint of roses upon her cheeks, and curvaceously slim figure.

With a start, Morgana realized the girl's eyes were violet—the same rare color of her father's. Her gaze fixed on the blazing dragon that appeared to be the missing half of the pendant her father always wore. Could this girl be her father's by-blow?

Keely knew the angel standing in front of her was her half-sister. Were there other siblings? Noting her sister's expensive gown, Keely glanced down at her own sad attire and felt ragged. She was, in truth, the poor relation.

Each sister saw in the other the very qualities she lacked. In that instant, natural enemies were born.

"Lady Glendower," I present my companion, Mrs. Ashemole," Morgana Talbot introduced them.

Keely nodded at the older woman.

Mrs. Ashemole looked her up and down. Her expression told Keely that she failed to pass inspection.

"His Grace is away," Morgana said. "Could I be of assistance?"

"The ducal flag flies over Ludlow," Keely answered.

"You misunderstand. My father is visiting friends," Morgana said with an insincere smile. "What business do you have with him?"

"I'm afraid 'tis a private matter," Keely replied. "I'll return in a few days."

"No!"

Keely stared in surprise at the blonde.

"His Grace is an important man who cannot grant interviews to anyone who wishes," Morgana insisted. "State your business, and I will relay the message."

"Thank you, but I'd rather not," Keely said, turning away.

"My father hasn't seduced you with promises of a position, has he?" Morgana asked.

Shocked, Keely whirled around and stared open-mouthed at her sister.

"Seducing beautiful women is my father's favorite hobby," Morgana lied.

Keely blanched and stepped back as if she'd been struck.

Had coming to Ludlow Castle been a mistake? No—Megan had never been wrong about the things she "saw." Something here was amiss. Keely could almost see frightened hate leaping at her from her half-sister.

"I apologize for intruding upon your day," Keely said stiffly. "I will return another time."

"Whom shall I tell His Grace to expect?" Morgana asked.

Keely forced herself to give her sister a serene smile. "Tell His Grace that his daughter came to call."

"Fraud," Mrs. Ashemole snapped. The word sounded like a curse upon her lips.

From behind her, Keely sensed Odo and Hew start forward. She held her hand up to stop them.

"Dozens of my father's bastards live between Shropshire and London. Of course, he never acknowledges them," Morgana said, her voice filled with venom, so at odds with her angelic expression. "Dobbs!"

The Talbot majordomo, apparently eavesdropping, rushed into the great hall.

"Throw this bastard off my property," Morgana ordered.

Dobbs looked at Keely and hesitated, then started toward her. The terrifying sight of the two Welsh giants advancing on *him* stopped the servant in his tracks.

"No need to trouble yourself, Mr. Dobbs," Keely said, maintaining her poise. "I can find my own way out."

Blinded by tears, Keely fled the hall and flew down the stairs. She nearly toppled a young man over in her haste to escape the humiliating rejection she felt.

Fifteen-year-old Henry Talbot, the duke's only son and heir, quickly stepped aside for the beautiful vision racing toward him. Who was she? A new servant? Staring after her, Henry decided he'd like to practice his latest and most satisfying hobby—lovemaking—with her.

Henry started up the stairs again and saw two giants bounding down them. Leaping out of their way, the boy pressed his back against the wall. If they were the vision's guardians, he'd never sample her charms.

Checking the top of the stairs, Henry verified that no one was about to trample him. His path was clear, and he headed to the great hall, where his sister was in a dangerously high rage.

"How dare that slut march as bold as you please into this hall?" Morgana was complaining as she paced back and forth in front of the hearth.

"Calm yourself, my lady," Mrs. Ashemole said. "The wench is a fortune-hunting fraud."

Morgana whirled around and frowned at the older woman, saying, "She wouldn't dare show her face here again." From the corner of her eye, the blond beauty spied her younger brother walking toward them, and she added with a smile that didn't quite reach her eyes, "Mrs. Ashemole, please leave me to visit with my dear brother."

Henry snorted with contempt as the older woman left the hall. His sister's smiles always meant trouble for someone—usually him.

"Ashemole can be so tedious," Morgana said. "Though I do admit the woman is uncommonly loyal."

"Ashemole is well paid for her loyalty," Henry replied.

"Who was your lady visitor?"

"The slut was no lady," Morgana snapped. "The minx had the audacity to march into our hall and demand to speak with Father."

"She certainly was pretty."

"I suppose, in a common sort of way."

Suppressing a smile, Henry glanced sidelong at his sister. That she gave the other girl that much praise surprised him.

"What did she want?" he asked.

"The chit was bent on telling Father that she is his long-lost daughter."

"Do you think she really is—?"

"Between those violet eyes and that damned dragon pendant, there's little doubt who sired her," Morgana interrupted him. "How like Father to scatter his seed far and wide."

"Violet-eyed like father," Henry echoed. "Why didn't you call him?"

"Why bother him with such a trivial matter as one of his by-blows?" Morgana countered. "Besides, do you actually want to share your home with a base-born wench?"

"Bastards cannot inherit," Henry said. "What harm could she do us?"

"It's bad enough the Countess of Cheshire is sniffing after Father," Morgana complained. "We don't need someone else trying to steal our inheritance."

"*My* inheritance," Henry corrected her.

"Of course. Whatever you say."

"Where Lady Dawn is concerned," Henry said, "Father is the one doing the sniffing. I've never seen such big—"

"Humph! You men are all alike."

"And what does that mean?"

Pointedly ignoring his question, Morgana steered the subject to her favorite topic of conversation—herself. "As for myself, I cannot decide between Richard Devereux and Willis Smythe. Which one should I marry?"

"I don't care who is unfortunate enough to win your hand," Henry said, his expression pained.

"Your attitude is unbecoming of the future Duke of Ludlow," Morgana scolded him. "Though Devereux is an earl and one of the richest men in England, Baron Smythe's devilishly handsome face does attract me."

"Marry Devereux, and take Smythe for your lover," Henry said in growing disgust. "Where's Father?"

Morgana shrugged. "Probably lying abed with Lady Dawn," she said in a nasty tone. "Why do you ask?"

"Because, you idiot, he needs to be told about—"

"Keep your lips shut about her," Morgana threatened, "or you'll regret it!"

"Father has the right to know he sired another child," Henry insisted. Then: "Besides, I'd like to meet this other sister of mine."

"If you tell Father about this, I'll tell him about that pretty maid you've been—" Morgana broke off, unwilling to say the words. Instead, she gave him an arch look and finished, "I know what you've been doing, and I know Papa ordered you to leave Ludlow's maids alone. You've already sired two bastards. How many do you expect Father to support?"

"You win," Henry agreed reluctantly.

"Do you swear it?"

"I swear I won't tell Father about this other child of his."

"I knew I could depend upon you," Morgana said, then planted a kiss on his cheek before turning to leave the hall.

Alone, Henry wiped his contaminated cheek with his sleeve and sat down. Though he'd sworn to keep his lips shut, he hadn't promised not to tell their previously unknown half-sister where to locate their father when he traveled to London.

"Dobbs!" Henry shouted. When the servant appeared several moments later, he ordered, "Send a man to follow those three who just left Ludlow. Tell him to try the Boar's Head. 'Tis the only inn for miles. Then I'll need parchment, quill, and one of my father's couriers. Hurry, man."

Bereft of hope, Keely leaped onto Merlin and galloped out of Ludlow Castle's inner courtyard. Once outside the castle's outer curtain, she slowed the mare to let her cousins catch up, and they rode in silence.

Madoc had been correct, Keely thought. She *was* the Princess of Nowhere.

No longer did the rustic scenery appear idyllic to Keely. The area's sparse population mirrored her desolation; the thatched-roof cottages appeared to be hovels; even the myriad wild flowers, swaying in the gentle breeze, mocked her loss.

Somewhere between Ludlow Castle and the Boar's

Head Inn, Keely's aching pain changed to simmering anger and then boiling rage. The Duke of Ludlow had impregnated her sweet mother and then abandoned her. For that he would pay dearly. But how? Revenge against one of the most powerful peers of the realm seemed impossible.

Causing another's fear is wrong, Keely heard her mother's patient voice scolding her.

Keely's rage left her then as quickly as it had come, leaving her depleted of energy. Her baser impulses— caused by the tainted English blood that flowed through her veins, no doubt—would be kept under rigid control. Surrendering to such negative forces would certainly destroy her.

"What shall we do now?" Hew asked as the three of them ate dinner at a long table inside the inn's common room.

"Keely will wait a day or two," Odo answered, "and then she'll try to see her father. This time we'll go to Ludlow at suppertime when the duke's certain to be about."

"I cannot return to Ludlow," Keely said, shaking her head sadly. "That girl—my half-sister—doesn't want me there."

"Perhaps the lady was being cautious," Odo suggested.

"I saw in her eyes that she recognized me for who I am," Keely disagreed. "My existence threatens her."

"You're the duke's daughter," Odo said, "the same as she is."

"Not quite the same," Keely corrected him. "I am the duke's bastard."

"I say let's go home," Hew said. "Rhys will protect you from Madoc."

Keely's expression mirrored her unspeakable sadness. "The Princess of Nowhere is a woman without a home," she replied in an aching whisper. "Sharing my exile is unnecessary. I want both of you to return to Wales."

Odo reached out and covered her hand with his own. Hew placed his hand on top of theirs.

"We're all three of us in this together," Odo insisted.

"I couldn't have said it any better," Hew remarked.

"'Course you couldn't," Odo told him. "'Cause you're a blinking idiot."

Keely smiled at them and would have spoken, but the inn's door opened, drawing their attention. Dressed in the Duke of Ludlow's livery, a ducal courier entered the common room. He scanned the nearly deserted chamber and then advanced on them.

Reaching their table, the Talbot man-at-arms asked, "Are you the woman who visited Ludlow Castle this morning?"

Nervous, Keely worried her bottom lip with her teeth and nodded.

The courier produced a rolled-up parchment and handed it to her.

Confused, Keely stared at the man for a long moment and then at the missive in her hand. She opened it slowly and read. Then, raising her violet gaze to the courier's, Keely smiled.

"Is there any reply?" the man asked, his tone softening at the beauty of her dazzling smile.

"Please tell him I said thank you."

The courier nodded and, without another word, left the inn.

"Let me see the message," Hew said.

"You can't read," Odo reminded him.

"Nor can you," Hew shot back.

"Never said I did," Odo countered. "Well, little girl, are you holding good news in the palm of your hand?"

"I have a brother Henry," Keely told them. "He says *our father* will return to his London residence the third week of September. He's certain I can speak to him there without interference from the Lady Morgana."

"That is good news, indeed," Odo said.

"Are we going to London now?" Hew whined. "I

never thought I'd live to see the day I journeyed straight into the heart of our enemies."

"Of course we're going to London," Odo said, cuffing the side of his brother's head. "Keely has a need to meet her father."

"Escorting me to London is unnecessary," Keely told them. "I'm certain I can find my way."

"Do you think we'd let you travel alone?" Odo asked.

"You won't get rid of us that easily," Hew added.

"I'd never want to rid myself of either of you," Keely said. "Well, then. Have we enough coins to cover our expenses?"

"Now, little girl, don't start worrying about trifles," Odo ordered. "Get yourself upstairs and take a long nap. We'll be leaving this afternoon."

Keely smiled and rose from the bench. Leaning down, she gave both men a peck on the cheek. "I love you dearly," she announced, making them blush.

As soon as she disappeared up the stairs, Hew glanced at his brother and asked, "Well?"

"We've very few coins," Odo verified. "No need to worry, though. We'll reach London and survive until the third week in September. Something is bound to turn up."

The inn's door swung open again, and a tall, well-built man entered. His arrogant demeanor and expensive-looking clothing positively screamed "rich nobleman." The lord walked over to the innkeeper and said in a loud voice, "I require a decent chamber for no more than an hour and a hot bath to accompany it. I will, of course, pay your regular daily rate. How far is Ludlow Castle?"

"Thirty minutes up the road, my lord," the innkeeper answered. "Please, follow me. I'll show you to my best chamber."

Watching the nobleman climb the stairs behind the innkeeper, Odo leaned close to his brother. "Something just turned up," he whispered.

Hew snapped his head around and stared in horrified

dismay at him. "Are you thinking what I think you're thinking?"

"What the blazes are you jabbering?" Odo asked, cuffing the side of his brother's head. "Speak English."

"Highway robbery is a hanging offense," Hew warned in a low voice.

"Consider it raiding," Odo advised. "Anyway, hanging is a quicker death than starving."

"We'll never get caught," Hew whispered, his expression suddenly clearing.

Odo's gaze narrowed on him. "How can you be so sure?"

"We carry the carnelian stones," Hew answered, pulling one of the smooth brandy-colored stones from his pocket and holding it up. "Keely said the magic in these stones will protect us from harm. Megan taught her such things."

Odo closed his eyes against his brother's abject stupidity and successfully squelched the urge to strike him. "I know the perfect place in the road to meet our friend," he said, rising. "Let's go."

Hew looked at him blankly. "What friend?"

This time Odo did cuff the side of his brother's head and growled, "You blinking idiot."

"Ohh," Hew exclaimed in understanding, then followed his brother outside.

An hour later, Odo and Hew were ready to embark upon their "raiding." The unmasked would-be raiders hid in the dense woods along the road and waited for their intended victim, who even now approached at a leisurely pace toward Ludlow Castle.

Closer rode the nobleman.

He was almost abreast of their hiding places.

Odo signaled Hew to ride. They bolted into the road in front of and behind the man. Startled, his horse reared. In the movement the black-clad nobleman lost his hat, revealing a flaming mane of copper hair. He reached for his sword but stayed his hand on its hilt when he felt the tip of a sword touch his back.

"Who dares to accost the queen's man?" the Earl of Basildon growled, his voice and his expression telling them they were beneath his contempt.

"Those traveling this road are now required to pay a tax," Odo told him. "We are the tax collectors."

"Give us whatever coins you carry, my lord high-and-mighty," Hew added.

Richard Devereux raised his copper brows at their demand. "You dare attempt to rob the Earl of Basildon?"

"We're not *attempting* anything," Odo shot back. "We're *doing* it. Hand me your sword, hilt first, and then the dagger."

Richard remained motionless, silently refusing.

"Make haste," Hew snapped. "Or you'll regret it."

Richard slowly drew his sword. As he started to hand it over, he kicked his steed's flank, and the horse danced sideways. Richard slipped his booted foot out of the stirrup, kicked Odo's horse, and swung the sword hilt into the side of the other man's face.

"Run!" Hew shouted, losing his balance, sending his brother bolting for escape.

Hew toppled off his horse and fell with a heavy thud in the road. Desperate to escape the Englishman, Hew scrambled to his feet and staggered into the woods. Within mere seconds, strong hands grabbed him from behind and tackled him.

Richard raised his fist to strike, snarling, "I want to see your pained expression when you swallow your teeth."

Suddenly, he groaned and collapsed. Dead weight.

"Did you kill him?" Hew asked, staring up at his brother.

"Gave him a love tap is all," Odo answered, lifting the earl so that Hew could slide from beneath him. "He'll be waking from his nap soon enough."

"And sounding the alarm," Hew said, touching his

neck as though he already felt the noose tightening. "We must slow him down."

Odo considered the problem for a long moment and finally said, "Stealing his horse will give us the time we need to collect Keely and leave the area."

"Are we adding horse-thieving to highway robbery?" Hew groaned.

"Cheer up," Odo replied. "The English can only hang you once."

The two Welshmen began divesting the earl of his valuables. Before leaving, Hew pulled one of the magical carnelian stones from his pocket. He placed it in the palm of the earl's left hand and closed his fingers around it.

"So Keely won't scold us if she ever discovers what we've done," Hew explained, catching his brother's questioning look.

"Take his boots too," Odo ordered. "Walking barefoot to Ludlow will give us plenty of time."

Odo and Hew mounted their horses. With the earl's horse in tow, they disappeared into the safety of Shropshire Forest.

Some time later Richard opened his eyes, stared up at the clear blue sky, and then sat up slowly. He reached for the back of his aching head and looked around in confusion. Where was his horse? And boots?

"Bloody buggers," he swore.

He glanced at the brandy-colored stone clutched in his left hand. Was this their payment for stealing his possessions? Beside him on the ground sat his hat.

With the stone in one hand and the hat in the other, Richard got to his feet. The stone would forever serve as a reminder of the villains and what they'd done to him.

If ever I get my hands on them, Richard promised himself, *I'll make them wish they'd died in infancy.*

With that, Richard began the most humiliating task of his life—the walk to Ludlow Castle. "Ouch!" He reached down and dislodged a jagged stone from between his toes, then straightened and started walking again.

The bastards had taught him an important lesson, Richard decided. When he finally reached Ireland, he would always remember to guard his back. But lesson or no, the villains would pay for their crime against him.

So busy was Richard planning the myriad forms his revenge could take that he arrived at Ludlow Castle in record time. Only the Talbot men-at-arms' laughter yanked him out of his wholly satisfying daydream of revenge.

Richard marched proudly across the lowered drawbridge, through the outer bailey, and into the inner courtyard. Though his face flamed with hot embarrassment, the Earl of Basildon pretended deafness to the shouts of laughter he evoked in passing.

"What the bloody hell are you doing, Devereux?" The growl belonged to Robert Talbot.

Richard turned toward the growl and arched a copper brow at the Duke of Ludlow's imposing figure. "I've come to court Morgana, Your Grace."

"You walked barefoot from Leicester?"

"I've been robbed, you blockhead!" Richard shouted, shaking his hat at the duke. None but one still dared laugh at the earl.

A throaty chuckle drew their attention. "Why, Tally," drawled the Countess of Cheshire, "Devereux has the cutest pair of—" The duke's hand snaked out and covered her mouth, leaving her thought unfinished.

"I do apologize for the inconvenience. Of course you're welcome to my wardrobe," Robert Talbot said as he escorted the earl inside. "We'll catch the culprit and hang him—you can be certain of that."

"Search the area for two giants," Richard said.

"Giants?" Talbot echoed, unable to credit what he was hearing.

"I mean, two rather large men," Richard amended. "They spoke with an accent, probably Welsh."

"Most unusual," Talbot replied.

Morgana Talbot stood in the entrance to the great hall and watched her father and a barefoot Earl of Basildon disappear down the corridor. "What's happened?" she asked the passing countess.

"Devereux has come to court you," Lady Dawn answered, giving her a feline smile. "The earl has very attractive toes, if that sort of activity appeals to you. I heard from Lady Mary *and* Lady Jane that the Earl of Basildon has more to offer than meets the eye."

Morgana Talbot's gaze narrowed on the other woman, but her curiosity overruled her animosity toward the voluptuous countess. "What does he have to offer me?"

"Devereux sports a freckle on the tip of his—" With that, the Countess of Cheshire chuckled throatily and strolled into the great hall to await the men's return.

Chapter 3

English hedges and gardens misted with purple Michaelmas daisies and their strange fragrance wafted through the air, announcing the full Harvest Moon and the autumnal equinox, when day and night balanced perfectly. London's Christians prepared their Saint Michael's Day feast, and the farmers in the surrounding countryside prepared to celebrate their Harvest Home.

Others prepared themselves for a different kind of observance. They knew Saint Michael's true identity—the pagan saint previously known as the Sun God.

Early evening, the quiet time before twilight, drifted from east to west across England. In the midst of a secluded oak grove on top of Primrose Hill stood three people, two giants and a petite dark-haired woman.

"Now, little girl, I don't like this," Odo said.

"You'll be burned as a witch if anyone sees us," Hew added. "I don't doubt we'll be burned as warlocks with you."

"These kings and queens of the forest will protect me," Keely said, gesturing to the oak trees. She donned her white robe over her violet wool skirt and white linen blouse, then drew its hood over her head to cover her ebony mane, adding, "Robbing that lord in Shropshire has placed us in grave danger. Whatever harm we cause others returns to injure us tenfold."

"Damn," Hew muttered. "We said we're sorry,"

"How many times are you going to scold us, little girl?" Odo asked. "We did leave him that carnelian stone for protection."

Keely's lips quirked, but she gave him no answer. Instead, Keely took the eight rocks that Odo held out to her and said, "Madoc Lloyd wounded my soul. Failing to observe Alban Elued, the Light of the Water, will make the wound fester and poison me."

Keely walked to the center of the oak grove and used the rocks to make a large circle, leaving the western periphery open. Between each of the rocks, she set wild berries of elder, whortles, sloes, and damsons.

"Will you join me?" Keely asked her cousins. "Safety lies within the circle."

Both Odo and Hew shook their heads. Protecting her from possible intruders required alertness.

Keely entered the circle from the west and closed it behind her with the last rock, saying, "All disturbing thoughts remain outside."

After walking to the center of the circle, Keely turned in a clockwise circle three times until she faced the west and the declining sun. She closed her eyes, focused her breathing, and touched the dragon pendant, its sapphires, diamonds, and ruby sparkling in the dying sunlight.

Keely shivered as a ripple of anticipation danced down her spine. She loved the rituals her mother had taught her; however, without Megan's special talent, Keely felt uncertain about their effectiveness.

"The Old Ones are here," watching and waiting," Keely spoke in a soft voice into the hushed air. "Stars speak through stones, and light shines through the thickest oak." Then, in a louder voice, "One realm is heaven and earth."

Keely walked clockwise around the inside periphery of the circle and collected the wild berries, then set them down beside her in the center, the soul of the circle. "I store the good and cast out the useless. Thanks be to Mother Goddess for the fruit of the earth. Thanks be to Esus, the spirit of sacrifice embodied in these majestic trees, giving us food to eat, air to breathe, wood to house and warm us."

Keely paused a long moment, conjuring in her mind

what came next, gathering the proper emotion much as nature gathers its forces. She turned around three times, opened her arms to implore, and called in a loud voice, "Spirit of my journey, guide me to hear what the trees say. Spirit of my ancestors, guide me to hear what the wind whispers. Spirit of my tribe, guide me to understand what the clouds foretell."

Keely gazed toward the setting sun and then closed her eyes. "Open my heart that I may see beyond the horizon."

Long moments passed. And then it happened; images floated across her mind's eye . . . .

Misty darkness. A sinking feeling in the pit of her stomach. Unseen evil lurking near. Then the warm feeling of security. Strong, comforting arms as solid as the mighty oaks surrounding her. Welcoming arms. Protecting arms . . . .

The image dissolved into the reality of Primrose Hill.

Keely opened her eyes and touched the gleaming dragon pendant, praying, "I, invoke the power of my mother's love living inside this dragon to protect me and mine."

Watching and listening with rapt attention, Hew whispered to his brother, "I'm no coward, but she's giving me the creeps."

"I know what you mean," Odo agreed, unnerved enough to look over his shoulder. "I feel like these trees are itching to grab me."

Both men started toward Keely at the same time, but stopped short when she spoke.

"Breaking the circle is forbidden," Keely warned without looking, gesturing them away. Closing her eyes, she ended the ceremony: "I thank the goddess and these oaks for passing their wisdom through me."

Feeling sapped of her energy, Keely slowly walked to the western periphery of the circle and picked up the rock, breaking the enchanted circle. She removed her robe and folded it, then retrieved her satchel.

"Did you hear what the trees were saying?" Odo asked.

"I did," she answered.

"And what the wind whispered?"

"Yes."

"There's no wind today," Hew said.

"The wind is always with us," Keely told him.

"I didn't hear it."

"You blinking idiot," Odo said, rounding on his brother. "Of course you couldn't hear it. The wind *whispered* in her ear."

Keely smiled at her cousins and then studied the sky. The western horizon still flamed with the dying sun, but the eastern horizon darkened into a deep muted shade of slate blue.

"Did you see beyond the horizon?" Hew asked.

Keely nodded, hoping she'd interpreted the signs correctly, wishing she'd been blessed with a smidgeon of her mother's talent. "We must return to London and stay hidden within our rooms until dawn."

"Why?" Odo asked.

"Safety sits inside that tavern," she answered.

"Safety's a person?" Hew blurted out.

"Perhaps," Keely said with an uncertain smile. "I did feel his arms protecting me."

"Whose arms do you mean?" Odo asked.

Keely shrugged. "I couldn't see his face."

"Probably me," Hew said.

"What makes you think so?" Odo asked. "I'm stronger than you."

"You bloody well are not," Hew shot back.

"Am—"

"*Not!*"

Keely giggled. She loved these fierce brothers who felt duty bound to protect her.

"What are we hiding from?" Odo asked her.

"You mean *whom*," Keely corrected him. "Day and night are in balance, but Father Sun is waning. After today, the lord you robbed in Shropshire will be unable to find us."

"I've a fondness for my neck," Hew said, touching his throat. "How do you know we'll find safety at the Royal Rooster? Did you understand what the clouds foretold?"

"The answer to that lives in tomorrow," Keely replied. "The trees and the wind and the clouds bade me return to that tavern."

Hew snorted. "Well, I never heard a thing."

Odo cuffed the side of his brother's head. "Lest you forget, Keely has the gift. Don't you, little girl?"

"Well, Megan had the sight," Keely hedged. Her small white teeth worried her bottom lip before she admitted, "I've never actually experienced such, but I do feel in my bones that something remarkable is about to happen."

"That's good enough for me," Odo said.

"Hiding in our rooms sounds reasonable," Hew agreed. "We'll be less than spit in the wind if that lord catches us, and I don't need the second sight to tell me so."

"We've other problems as well," Keely said as they mounted their horses. "The gold from selling that lord's horse won't keep us long in London. Perhaps we can get employment at the tavern if my father refuses to acknowledge me."

A silent depression settled over them as they entered London proper. Even at this late hour of twilight, the narrow streets and lanes teemed with scurrying people, the city's inhabitants seeming to be part of a neverending race. The cramped buildings and lanes closed around Keely until she felt as if she were suffocating.

Taking deep calming breaths, Keely rode with her cousins through Cheapside Market and past St. Paul's Cathedral. Finally, they turned their horses up Friday Street, where the Royal Rooster Tavern was located.

So far from home, Keely thought, feeling overwhelmingly isolated in spite of her cousins' company and the hundreds of people she passed. No demand hereabouts for a Druid priestess with dubious talent nor an impoverished Welsh princess. *Taffy*, as these insulting Englishmen labeled the Welsh.

Keely hoped she'd correctly interpreted what she'd seen on Primrose Hill, and that the Royal Rooster Tavern offered refuge from the lurking evil she'd sensed. Surely that lord's power to catch them would diminish with the waning sun.

If she'd known how wrong she was, Keely would surely have bolted to Wales and braved her stepfather's wrath. At that very moment, the object of her thoughts sat inside the Royal Rooster Tavern and waited for the appearance of the two gigantic highwaymen who'd robbed him of his dignity.

The Rooster's common room was surprisingly spacious, large enough for the hearth and a bar. On the left side of the chamber, near the narrow stairway that led to the second-floor bedchambers, was the hearth. The bar stood in the corner on the opposite side of the room. Tables and chairs were positioned around the chamber.

Richard Devereux sat facing the tavern's entrance at a table near the bar in the far corner of the room. With him was his friend, Willis Smythe. The two men drank ale and talked.

"If I'd known you were treating me," Willis was saying, "I would have insisted we sup at an establishment frequented by a better class of people."

"The fare is exceptional here," Richard replied.

"For the past two weeks, you've been avoiding the snickers at court," Willis teased. "The longer you stay away, the harder it will be to return."

"The queen's financial interests have kept me busy of late," Richard said.

Willis smiled and couldn't quite contain his chuckle of amusement.

"Losing one's dignity is no laughing matter," Richard added. "And if you value that handsome face, you'll refrain from repeating the story again. Burghley mentioned that you've been telling anyone willing to listen."

"I'm sorry," Willis apologized, wearing an unrepentant grin.

"The owners of the Rooster are friends of my sister Brigette," Richard said, changing the subject. "Bucko passes along whatever he overhears the city's merchants discussing."

"A countess befriending tavern keepers?" Willis echoed, surprised.

Richard shrugged. "Years ago, Brigette quarreled with her husband, ran away to London, and found temporary employment here as a serving wench until they reconciled."

Willis burst out laughing. "Even better. A countess masquerading as a tavern wench?"

"As I recall, Iain wasn't laughing at the time," Richard said dryly.

"Your brother-by-marriage shares a trait with you," Willis remarked.

Richard raised his copper brows at the other man.

"No sense of humor?"

"Apparently, you possess enough good humor for both of us," Richard said. "Besides my humiliation, what's the latest gossip at court?"

Willis paused a long moment as if thinking and then said, "Rumor has Lady Morgana Talbot and you almost betrothed."

Richard rolled his eyes. "You would do well to follow my example. Find yourself an heiress. What else is happening?"

"A certain Signor Fulvio Fagioli, recently arrived from Italy, is creating havoc with the ladies," Willis told him. "Muscles and charm make an irresistible combination, you know . Fagioli brought a new device with him from Italy. It's called a fork, and—"

"Here we are, my lords," a woman said, setting two bowls of steaming stew in front of them on the table.

"Greetings, Marianne," Richard said, looking up at the proprietor's wife. He reached for her hand and kissed it in a courtly manner.

Marianne giggled. She was a handsome well-endowed woman with warm brown hair, shot throughout with strands of pale blond and gray. Shrewd intelligence shone from her hazel eyes.

"Madame Jacques, I present Baron Willis Smythe," Richard said, making the introductions.

Taking his cue from his friend, Willis kissed the woman's hand and said, "The pleasure is mine, madame."

"Breedin' does tell, don't it?" Marianne said, clearly impressed. "We've not seen ya for a while. How's that sister of yours?"

"Brie's well," Richard answered, "but she's been cursed with a daughter as temperamental as she."

Marianne smiled and shook her head in sympathy. "I can't laugh too hard at Brie's misfortune. My own daughter Theresa mostly makes me miserable."

"My condolences," Richard replied. He lowered his voice and said, "I'm here to catch two thieves and need your help. Are two men of gigantic proportions staying at the Rooster?"

"You mean the ones with that violet-eyed woman?" Marianne asked.

"A violet-eyed woman?" Richard echoed, surprised. The only person he'd ever met with that unusual eye color was the Duke of Ludlow.

Marianne nodded.

"Their names?"

"Glendower, I think. Or Lloyd."

"Dumb *taffy*," Willis muttered.

"The swine robbed me along the road to Ludlow Castle," Richard told Marianne.

"Snatched the boots off his feet and stole his horse," Willis added. "The earl walked barefoot all the way to Ludlow Castle."

Marianne burst out laughing. Willis Smythe joined her. Richard struggled against an embarrassed blush but lost, one of the disadvantages in being born a redhead. People had been laughing at him ever since he'd run into those two giants in Shropshire, and he didn't like it one bit. The stinking Welshmen would pay dearly for his humiliation.

"Want me to call the Watch?" Marianne asked.

Richard shook his head. The Watch would see the villains hanged at Tyburn, but exacting his own revenge would be much more satisfying. Besides, Richard didn't want to see the woman hanged, in the unlikely event that she proved innocent of her companions' crime.

"How did you know they were here?" Willis asked him.

"Those blockheads sold my horse to my man, Jennings," Richard answered.

Willis grinned. "They stole your horse and then sold it back to you?"

"Precisely."

"Are you going to arrest them?" Willis asked.

"The woman's presence changes my plans," Richard said with a shake of his head. "I'll have Beagan and a few of my men keep them under surveillance."

"Here they come," Marianne whispered out of the side of her mouth. "I'll leave ya now."

"If you dare turn around," Richard warned his friend, "I swear I'll strangle you with my bare hands."

Willis grinned and proceeded to watch his friend stalk his prey with his gaze.

The sight of Keely hit Richard with the impact of an avalanche. His eyes widened, mirroring his shock, as he stared at the petite ebony-haired beauty walking through the tavern with those two giants. Even dressed in common attire, she appeared irresistibly lovely, much lovelier than any of the acclaimed beauties at court.

Richard watched her take a seat at a table across the room. Suddenly, revenge was the farthest thing from his mind. . . .

Safe at last, Keely thought as she entered the tavern. Odo led Hew and her to a table in the corner near the hearth.

Sitting between them, Keely suggested, "Let's forget about supper and go directly to our chambers."

"You haven't eaten all day," Odo admonished her.

"You're too skinny as it is," Hew added. "Besides, I'm famished."

Keely gave in with a nod of her head. She was jumpier than a frog in a pond, her nerves fairly crackling with tension. Keely knew in her Druid bones that something remarkable was about to happen. She felt as if she stood on the edge of a precipice—or possibly even the brink of disaster.

"What'll it be, folks?" Marianne greeted them with a smile. She set mugs of ale in front of Odo and Hew and a goblet of mulled wine for Keely.

"Five bowls of stew," Odo ordered.

"Five is it?"

"We're hungry," Hew said.

Keely reached for her goblet of wine and took a sip. Its warmth soothed her badly frayed nerves. As she set the goblet down, Hew slumped in his chair and his hand tugged at her sleeve.

Glancing up at his horrified expression, Keely realized that trouble had somehow found them. "What is it, cousin?"

"That lord we robbed is sitting over there," Hew whispered.

"Where?" Odo exclaimed, half rising out of his chair to scan the crowded chamber.

"Don't look," Keely ordered in a loud whisper.

Odo and Hew instantly dropped their gazes.

"Where is he?" Keely asked.

"The red-haired man, dressed in black, at the table nearest the bar," Hew answered.

Keely glanced in that direction. On the opposite side of the common room at the table nearest the bar sat two English lords. Deep in conversation with his friend, the red-haired Earl of Somewhere seemed unaware of their presence in the tavern.

"What should we do?" Keely asked.

"Sit still," Odo said. "He won't notice us in this crowd."

"That's right," Hew agreed. "As long as we call no attention to ourselves, he won't notice us."

Keely suffered a powerful urge to slide beneath the table and hide. Afraid to look across the room, she fixed her gaze on the wine goblet. Uncomfortably, she felt the lord's intense scrutiny—or was it her imagination?

Unable to endure the uncertainty another moment, Keely summoned her courage and forced herself to look across the room. The lord appeared deep in conversation with his friend, yet she couldn't shake the feeling that he watched them.

Keely's gaze slid to the earl's dark-haired companion. A disturbing image of lurking evil shrouded in dark mist formed in her mind and made her shiver.

When the two men stood abruptly, Keely's lips formed a silent perfect O. Odo and Hew were caught and would be hanged. If only she'd been blessed with her mother's unworldly talent, she would have correctly interpreted her vision and her cousins would not be coming to this tragic horrifying end.

The earl stood and called a friendly farewell to the tavern's owner, then turned to follow his companion to the door. His gaze flicked past them and then returned to Keely. She watched in growing horror as the earl changed direction and advanced on their table.

"No weapons," Keely whispered to her cousins. "We'll talk our way out of this."

Though she tried to appear casually unconcerned, Keely was unable to tear her gaze from the approaching earl. His copper hair was the brilliant radiance of Father Sun, and his disarming emerald eyes the green of her beloved forests in springtime. His features were ruggedly, handsomely chiseled and his lips sensuously formed. Walking toward their table, he moved with a hunter's predatory grace. Holy stones! The man was a pagan god sprung to life before her eyes.

"Trust the king who wears a flaming crown and possesses the golden touch. . . ."

Keely gave herself a mental shake to banish her mother's prophecy. This was no king, no pagan god, merely a man. And an odious English earl to boot.

Stopping at their table, Richard ignored Odo and Hew and gazed down at Keely, who stared through large violet eyes back at him. Richard smiled then and turned the full force of his charm on her.

"My lady," he greeted her with a slight incline of his head. Taking her hand in his, he bowed low over it and said without taking his gaze from hers, "Like a siren's song, your rare beauty called across the chamber to me."

Keely blushed furiously. She didn't know whether to be flattered by his outrageous compliment or insulted by his arrogant boldness. No man had ever spoken such intimate words to her—and no man had ever possessed a smile as radiant as his.

"Richard Devereux, the Earl of Basildon, at your service," Richard introduced himself, gazing deeply into her violet eyes, fully aware of his effect on her. "And who might you be?"

That smile could light a whole castle, Keely thought as she stared into his incredible emerald eyes. She couldn't seem to find her voice.

"My lady?" Richard prodded.

"I am—" Her voice came out in the high-pitched squeak of a nervous soprano.

Richard grinned.

Keely blushed and cleared her throat. "I am Lady Keely Glendower," she finally managed to say.

"A pleasure to make your acquaintance, Lady Keely," Richard said. He glanced at Odo and Hew who, certain they were about to be arrested, squirmed in their seats.

"I sincerely hope, my beauty, that neither of these gentlemen claims you as his wife."

"My cousins," Keely replied. "Odo and Hew Lloyd."

Richard shook hands with each of them in turn and then remarked, "You do seem vaguely familiar. Have we met somewhere before?"

"Impossible," Keely spoke up, drawing his attention from her cousins. "We've only just arrived from Wales."

"Are you in London for business or pleasure?"

"Neither. My cousins are escorting me to my father's home. You see, my mother recently passed on to the Great Ad—" Keely broke off, shocked at what she'd almost revealed. "I'm to live with my father in London."

"Who is your father?" Richard asked.

"An Englishman."

Richard's lips quirked. "I gleaned as much. I only ask because I might know him."

Keely forced herself to smile as winsomely as she could. "Many Englishmen crowd London's lanes."

Though he considered himself an expert at prying information out of people, Richard realized with a start that she hadn't actually answered his question. He tried again, asking, "Will you be staying long at the Rooster?"

Keely shook her head. "In the morning I will present myself to my father."

"Lady Keely, your uncommon beauty has given me great pleasure," Richard said, bowing over her hand. "I'm quite certain we shall meet again." Without another word, the earl quit the tavern.

Keely stared at his retreating back—his magnificently

masculine back. For her cousins' sake, she sincerely hoped they'd never meet again. And yet—

Keely sighed. Dreaming about things that could never be was useless.

"He's gone," Odo said.

"We're safe," Hew added. "You can stop shaking now."

Keely managed a faint smile. Though she hadn't eaten since the previous evening, the sight of the stew set before her made her stomach churn. "I don't feel well," she said. "I'm going upstairs. Enjoy your supper."

Clutching her satchel, Keely stood up and made her way through the crowded tavern. On shaking legs, she climbed the stairs to the second floor and walked the length of the corridor, then entered her chamber.

Without bothering to light a candle, Keely crossed the dark chamber to the cot and pulled her ceremonial white robe out of the satchel. She wrapped the hooded robe around herself as if it could offer her protection.

Keely looked at the cot and sighed. Between the earl's unnerving appearance and the frightening prospect of confronting her father, Keely knew that sleep would elude her that night.

She lay down on the cot anyway, and her thoughts traveled through space and time to Wales. Memories of her childhood and her wonderful mother crowded into that tiny chamber. Keely recalled that, no matter the season of the year, Megan and she would wander the woodland surrounding the Lloyd estate and study the special divinity of nature. Each afternoon they would sit together beneath the mighty oaks where her mother passed the Golden Thread of Knowledge to her.

Tears welled up in Keely's eyes and spilled down her checks. Surrendering to her sorrow, she wept until sobbing exhaustion put her to sleep.

Keely awakened during those hushed magical moments before dawn. Her chamber held the crisp bite of late September's early morning chill. Wrapping herself in her white ceremonial robe, Keely wandered to the room's tiny window. The eastern horizon blazed with orange light as dawn quickly approached.

Her gaze dropped from the sky's oceanic horizon to the narrow lanes below. *Civilization?* Keely thought. How could these English even breathe? She felt as though London's crowded conditions were suffocating her.

Keely's thoughts drifted to the man she would meet that day. What kind of man had sired her? Could she really find happiness as an English lord's daughter? It seemed a preposterous notion, yet her mother had seen it.

Bright streaks of orange light crept higher over the horizon. The rising sun, different each day of the year, seemed especially inspiring on this fateful morn. Was that a good omen?

Keely drew the hood of her robe up and covered her head. If only she could be outside to *feel* the rising sun. "Myrddin, greatest of Druids, guide my words," Keely began her greeting of the dawn. Trying to get closer to the rising sun, she pressed the palm of her hand to the window pane and chanted, "Father Sun kisses Mother Earth. . . . Father Sun kisses Mother Earth."

After completing this morning ritual, Keely sat down on the edge of the bed and tried to concentrate on the impending meeting with her father. Unfortunately, a certain copper-haired earl paraded across her mind's eye instead, and that made her think of the danger threatening her cousins. The Earl of Basildon had remarked that Odo and Hew looked familiar; it would be only a matter of time before he realized that her cousins were the culprits who'd robbed him.

Keely pondered her dilemma. According to her mother's teachings, she could cast the magic circle and beg a favor. A single favor—anything more insulted the Goddess's generosity.

Keely sighed. She had planned on asking for her father's acknowledgment, but now her cousins faced life-threatening danger—the earl's retribution. Her choice was no choice at all.

Fetching her satchel, Keely withdrew a black cloth bag and emptied the holy stones it contained into her hand. From these she chose nine: one white agate for spiritual guidance, two dark carnelians for courage and protection, two rose quartzes for healing, two black obsidians for positive power, and two purple beryls for breaking bad luck. Then she pulled her tiny golden sickle from the satchel.

Keely walked to the center of the room and made a makeshift circle with the stones, keeping only the white agate and the golden sickle in her hands. Entering the circle from the west, she closed it with the agate and said once again, "All disturbing thoughts remain outside."

Walking clockwise around the inside of the circle, Keely pointed the golden sickle toward its invisible periphery and fused it shut. She walked to the center of the circle, faced the east, and whispered: "Stones of power, love, and lore, I do implore. . . . Spirit of my journey, spirit of my ancestors, spirit of my tribe—aid my cause. Keep Odo and Hew safe from harm. Let Richard Devereux drink without injury from the River of Forgetfulness." Bowing her head, she added, "I give thanks to these holy stones, my venerable spirits, and this sickle of gold."

Keely walked to the circle's western periphery and picked the agate up, breaking the enchantment. She gathered the rest of her stones, put them back into the cloth bag, and sat on the edge of the bed to meditate on her father and await the appointed time.

At noon, Keely and her cousins dismounted in the front courtyard of Talbot House, London's most magnificent mansion. Keely looked up at the sun riding high in a cloudless blue sky. She knew that forever afterward, the midday sun would remind her of the day she finally met her father.

"Maybe we should have left our belongings at the tavern," Odo remarked, remembering what had transpired at Ludlow Castle.

Keely shook her head. "If Robert Talbot refuses to acknowledge me, we will return to Wales."

"Are you certain?"

"My mind is set."

"I hope that earl we robbed doesn't live nearby," Hew said, glancing around nervously. The tavern's proprietor had already informed them that all of England's nobles kept residences in the Strand, London's most elite section.

"Harbor no fears on that account," Keely told them. "I've invoked the Goddess's power for your protection."

"Too bad you didn't ask her to make us invisible," Hew muttered.

"Why, cousin," Keely said with a smile, "I never thought of an invisibility shield."

"No dallying," Odo said. "Time to meet your father, little girl."

Keely paled at his words but nodded. She was as ready as she'd ever be. Together, she and her cousins entered the duke's mansion. Surprisingly, no one stopped or questioned them. Inside the main foyer, servants hurried past them while a couple of men-at-arms stood near the wall on their left and talked together.

When they tried to enter the great hall, a servant blocked their path and demanded, "Who goes here? What is your business?"

"We want the duke," Odo replied.

"Is there a problem, Meade?" a man's voice called from inside the hall.

Meade glanced over his shoulder and said, "No, Your Grace." Turning back to the three intruders, he snapped, "The duke has guests and cannot be disturbed. Now, get out!"

Keely's heart sank, and her bottom lip quivered in her valiant struggle to control her aching emotion. She was being turned away. Again.

"We've traveled many miles to see his high-and-mighty," Odo growled at the man.

"We aren't leaving, you turd," Hew added.

Keely stifled a nervous, horrified giggle. "You mean *toad*," she whispered.

"He means *turd*," Odo said.

"Take your doxy and leave," Meade ordered, pointing a finger toward the door, "or I'll call the guard."

"Call all the guards you want," Odo said, lifting the hapless servant by his neck and flinging him into the hall, where he crashed on the floor.

A woman screamed.

A man cursed.

A third voice boomed, "What is the meaning of this?" With Odo and Hew marching in front of her and blocking her view, Keely walked into the great hall. The scene wasn't exactly as she'd envisioned, but she'd made it inside.

"Are you the Duke of Ludlow?" Odo demanded.

"Yes."

At that, the Welsh giants stepped aside, and Keely found herself standing only inches before a powerfully built, middle-aged nobleman. His startling violet eyes and thick ebony hair matched hers.

"Are you Robert Talbot?" Keely asked in a small voice. The nobleman paled, and his eyes clouded as though he were caught in the midst of remembered pain. "Megan?" he asked in an aching whisper, one of his hands reaching toward her. "Is it you?"

"My name is Keely," she told him. Oh, why did he seem so tortured? He had, after all, deserted her mother. Duke Robert shook his head as if to clear it. His imagination was playing a cruel prank on him. Megan had been dead these past eighteen years.

"Where did you get that?" the duke asked, dropping

his gaze to the dragon pendant, glittering against the crisp whiteness of her linen blouse.

"My mother gave it to me," Keely said. Her hand shielded the pendant. It was her mother's legacy to her, and she'd rather die than let anyone take it away, sire or not.

"And where did she get it?"

"My sire *gifted* her with it," Keely told him, her violet gaze locking meaningfully on his. "Eighteen years ago."

"What is her name?" the duke asked, looking as if he'd seen a ghost.

"Megan Glendower."

"Does your mother still live?" he asked, unable to mask the eager, hopeful tone in his voice.

Keely shook her head. "She's been dead these past two months."

Duke Robert closed his eyes against the rush of tears welling up in them, and an anguished moan escaped his lips. He took several deep calming breaths, cleared his throat, and gave her a wobbly smile. From beneath his shirt, Duke Robert pulled his own pendant. Diamonds, emeralds, sapphires, rubies, and gold formed the dragon's lower body and tail.

"This is your pendant's mate," he said, his violet-eyed gaze searching hers for any sign of the love that already swelled in his heart for her.

Determined to save herself from the heartache of another rejection, Keely flicked a glance at the pendant and feigned indifference, saying, "Yes, I see."

"Child, I am your father," Duke Robert announced.

"Her father?" sounded another voice.

"Damn," Odo muttered behind Keely.

"Double damn," Hew echoed his brother's sentiment.

Keely turned toward the owner of that strangely familiar voice and froze. There stood the earl whom her cousins had robbed. "Triple damn," she murmured, realizing her magic had failed her.

Ignoring the earl's outburst, Duke Robert looked

around at the crowd of curious spectators lingering about and shouted, "Get the hell out of my hall!"

The Talbot retainers and men-at-arms tripped over each other in a mad scramble to obey their lord. Almost instantly, the hall emptied.

"After eighteen years," Duke Robert said to Keely, "what have you to say to your father?"

"I have no father," she replied, her voice tinged with bitterness, her gaze never wavering from his. "You sired me, nothing more. If Megan hadn't made me swear to present myself to you, I would be far away from here now."

Her insolence brought an instant reaction from the duke, but not the one she would have expected. Something flickered in his intense gaze, and then his chiseled lips split into a broad grin.

"Chessy, did you hear that?" Duke Robert called to the voluptuous woman standing beside the earl. "She's got my proud spirit, don't she?"

"I can see that she does, Tally," the woman agreed with a smile and a nod of approval.

The pride in the duke's voice touched Keely's heart, and for the first time since her mother's death, she felt hope and optimism stir within her breast. "I hope your man is uninjured," Keely said. "Odo and Hew are indebted to you," he said.

"Oh, Tally," gushed the woman. "How utterly heart-warming."

Duke Robert glanced at his majordomo who, at that very moment, was limping out of the hall. "I believe Meade will survive." He turned his attention on the giants. "For delivering my daughter to me, I am forever indebted to you," he said.

"Come, child," Duke Robert held his hand out. "Meet my friends."

Keely looked at the outstretched hand for an excruciatingly long moment. Finally, she smiled shyly at the duke and placed her hand in his.

"I present Lady Dawn DeFey, the Countess of Cheshire," Duke Robert said.

Though she appeared to be in her early thirties, youthful beauty still clung to the countess. Auburn-haired and brown-eyed, Lady Dawn was voluptuous of figure. When she smiled as she did now, two adorable dimples decorated her cheeks and made her look even younger. She wore a red and gold brocaded gown, more suitable for a court gala than an afternoon in front of the hearth. Diamonds and gold draped her neck, earlobes, and fingers.

"I am pleased to make your acquaintance, my lady," Keely said, curtsying. "You were aptly named for the day's most beautiful moments."

"Tally, the dear child is as sweet as an angel," Lady Dawn complimented her. "So much pleasanter than that bitch you sired. . . . Take my advice, Devereux. Look to this daughter instead of the other."

"Morgana cannot help the way she is," the duke said in defense of his absent daughter. "She takes after my late wife's family. You'll see, my dear. She'll come around."

Duke Robert turned Keely to his other guest. "I present my neighbor, Richard Devereux, the Earl of Basildon."

"The kindest of fates have brought us together," the earl said with an easy smile, stepping forward to kiss her hand. "I knew we would meet again, my beauty."

Keely's hand trembled in his. Her head spun dizzily, and her stomach churned in response to the topsy-turvy spinning.

"I think I'm going to be sick," Keely cried as the world inside the hall became unfocused, and she found refuge in a faint.

"She's swooning," Richard said. He caught her before she hit the floor and lifted her into his arms.

"Oh, dear!" the countess cried.

"This way, Devereux," the duke ordered. "Carry her upstairs."

Richard followed Duke Robert out of the hall, past the

surprised retainers who'd been eavesdropping in the foyer, and up the stairs to one of the bedchambers. Behind them marched Lady Dawn, Odo, and Hew. At the countess's order, the two Welsh giants waited in the corridor.

Setting Keely down on the bed, Richard stared at the face that had haunted his dreams the previous night. She was even more exquisite than he remembered—her beauty and fragility reminded him of a rare exotic butterfly.

Keely regained consciousness slowly. When her eyes fluttered open, she found the earl's vivid emerald gaze fixed upon her and worry etched across his features. Keely looked at Duke Robert's expression of concern and tried to rise.

"Stay down and rest a moment," Richard said, his hands gently pressing her back onto the bed.

Keely did as she was told.

"Do you have any pain?" Lady Dawn asked, sitting on the edge of the bed.

Keely shook her head, but the movement made her stomach churn. She covered her mouth with her hand.

"Was it something you ate?" Richard asked.

"No, your presence at the tavern last night ruined my supper."

His emerald gaze narrowed on her. "Breakfast, then?"

"I had none," she answered.

"Child, when did you eat last?" Duke Robert asked.

"Twas supper, the day before yesterday."

"Silly chit," Lady Dawn said, relieved the malady was so easily cured.

Keely watched the countess cross the chamber, open the door, and call for Meade. Within minutes, the servant appeared, listened to her softly spoken instructions, and then left to do her bidding.

"You'll feel better shortly, my dear," Duke Robert said.

"Lady Dawn has ordered a light lunch for you," the earl told her.

"Afterward, you'll sleep," the duke added. "You're not to rise from that bed until tomorrow."

Keely realized they were being kind, but she felt so conspicuous lying on the bed while the earl's intense gaze devoured her. In truth, he appeared hungrier than she.

"I'll see you out," Duke Robert said, drawing the earl's attention.

Before leaving, Richard smiled at Keely. "I'm certain you'll be feeling better soon," he said.

"What about my cousins?" Keely called as the two men reached the door. "Odo and Hew need me."

"Your cousins will enjoy my hospitality for as long as they wish," Duke Robert assured her.

Keely's gaze slid from her father to the earl, whose expression had become unreadable. She nodded once and lay back against the pillows.

"Keely is well. 'Tis only hunger that made her faint," Duke Robert informed Odo and Hew, who still waited in the corridor. "Return to the hall, and Meade will provide you with a meal and a place to perch."

"Thank you, Your Grace," Odo said, his gaze fixed warily on the earl.

"Aye, 'tis kind of you," Hew added. "I mean, considering the fact you're English and all."

Odo cuffed the side of his brother's head and apologized. "He's an idiot and don't know any better, Your Grace."

"I understand," Duke Robert replied, struggling against a smile as the two Welshmen hurried away. Turning to Richard, he said, "You will excuse me, Devereux? I want to sit with my daughter while she eats."

Richard nodded, glanced at the closed bedchamber door, and asked, "May I have your permission to call upon Lady Keely?"

Duke Robert chuckled and slapped his shoulder in camaraderic. "I had the same reaction the first time I set my eyes on her mother," he said. "However, I know of your reputation with the ladies. Are your intentions honorable, boy?"

"I never toy with unmarried innocents," Richard replied. "I must marry and sire an heir, and a blood bond between the Talbot and Devereux families appeals to me."

"Then I suppose you'll soon be asking for my blessings on your impending nuptials to her," Duke Robert said, only half joking.

"'Tis a bit premature for that." Richard cocked a copper brow at the older man. "Keely looked at my face and fainted, but I may be able to persuade the lady to change her opinion of me."

Duke Robert snaked out his hand and grabbed the earl's arm. "I warn you, Devereux. If your intentions prove less than honorable, I shall be forced to kill you."

"I understand, Your Grace." At that, Richard retraced his steps down the corridor and disappeared downstairs.

Duke Robert paused before entering the bedchamber, and a grim expression appeared on his face. Running a hand through his hair, he leaned back against the wall.

What the bloody hell am I to do now? Duke Robert wondered as remorse wove itself around his aching heart. *Which of the three children I love do I destroy?*

His firstborn, the miraculous product of the greatest love of his life, believed herself to be a bastard; but possessing a knowledge that no one else shared, Duke Robert knew otherwise. Megan Glendower and he had been legally wed, albeit in secret. Keely was his legitimate heiress.

And therein lay the problem. Though he longed to atone for the pain of the first eighteen years of Keely's life, Duke Robert couldn't bear the thought of naming his only son a bastard.

Duke Robert straightened away from the wall and

squared his shoulders. Henry was innocent of his father's unintentional bigamy and would not be punished for it.

With grim determination etched across his features, Duke Robert decided he would do whatever he could for Keely. He'd acknowledge her publicly, present her at court, and make the best possible match for her. Keely deserved a husband who would make her happy, and the wealthy Earl of Basildon appeared to suffer no qualms about her alleged bastardy.

Duke Robert relaxed. He would do whatever he could to further the match. With the Countess of Cheshire's assistance, he would see Richard and Keely wed before the bells rang the new year in.

Chapter 4

"Good morning, my dear."

At the sound of the faraway voice, Keely swam up from the depths of unconsciousness and opened her eyes. Is this a dream? she wondered, focusing on the unfamiliar chamber.

"'Tis time to awaken."

Keely turned her head toward the voice. Standing beside the bed, Lady Dawn smiled at her.

"Good morning, my lady." Keely pushed her ebony hair away from her face, rubbed her eyes, and stretched.

"What time is it?"

"Twelve o'clock."

Keely's gaze slid to the windows. Dim light filtered into the room. "Too bright to be twelve o'clock," she said.

"Twelve noon on a mostly cloudy day."

Keely snapped her gaze back to the countess. "That's impossible. I never sleep through the dawn."

"As you can see for yourself," Lady Dawn said, "there wasn't one today."

"Dawn always follows night," Keely replied.

"I suppose it does," the countess said, then chuckled throatily. "I cannot be certain, however, because I always sleep through it."

"Dawn is the most inspiring time of day," Keely told her, sitting up. "Would you like me to awaken you tomorrow morning to see it? Which chamber is yours?"

"The duke's chamber is mine," Lady Dawn answered, watching for her reaction.

"Then where does His Grace—?" Keely blushed scarlet. "Oh."

Lady Dawn swallowed a chuckle at the girl's embarrassment. "Does it bother you that I share your father's bed?" she asked baldly.

If possible, Keely's blush deepened even more. "Do you love him?"

"Very much."

"In that case," Keely said, "sharing his bed doesn't bother me at all."

"I do believe we shall become great friends," Lady Dawn exclaimed, pleased to have one ally in the Talbot household. "Here's a tray on the table, and the chamber pot is behind the screen over there. As you can see, the bath in front of the hearth is steaming. I'll return shortly with a gown."

"Please, do not trouble yourself on my account," Keely said.

"Nonsense." The countess turned to leave. "I'm delighted you're here."

Alone, Keely decided to invoke the power of the gods to protect herself. She was, after all, a stranger in this household. Who knew what unseen forces were at work here?

Slipping her chemise off, Keely walked to the window. She closed her eyes and pressed the palm of her right hand to its pane in an attempt to get closer to nature's forces outside.

"Great Mother Goddess, fierce guardian of all your children, I do need your protection," Keely implored softly. "Join with me and make me bold. Blessings to all spirits who rush to my aid. Between us then is this bargain made."

After bathing and donning her chemise, Keely wrapped herself in her white ceremonial robe and dragged a chair close to the window. She sat down and watched the clouds break apart. Sunlight kissed the earth below. *A good omen?*

Keely decided to concentrate on Odo and Hew. Her cousins needed someone to protect them from their own lack of judgment, but each time she tried to visualize them, her powers of concentration failed her. Instead, the Earl of Basildon's handsome image flitted across her mind's eye.

In spite of the threat he presented, Keely felt strangely safe. She knew with her Druid's instinct that he'd never harm her. It was there in his disarming smile and the gleam in his eyes. If he'd wanted to see her cousins hanged at Tyburn Hill, the earl would have done so already. Unless . . . dared she hope that her forgetfulness spell had worked?

Keely's thoughts drifted to the earl's physical attributes. His fiery copper hair resembled a blazing sunset, and his emerald eyes reminded her of the forests in springtime. Like a pagan god sprung miraculously to life, the earl's perfectly proportioned physique more than pleased the eye. As long as she lived, Keely would never forget her first sight of him walking toward her in that tavern.

Without thinking, Keely caressed her lips with her fingertips. How would his sensual lips feel if pressed against—?

Holy stones! Keely jerked herself up straight, shocked by where her thoughts had roamed. The earl was a dangerous, despicable Englishman. Anathema to her. Wasn't he? Keely knew she wasn't as sure about that as she would have been a few days ago. Brooding about her uncertainty, she stared out the window.

Lady Dawn returned a few minutes later. In her hands she carried a violet and gold brocaded gown with matching slippers.

Keely had never seen so fine a gown in her life. "Those aren't mine," she said.

Lady Dawn smiled. "The gown and slippers belong to Morgana, your younger half-sister."

"I can't wear another's clothing," Keely refused, though she was unable to hide the longing in her expression as she stared at the beautiful gown.

"Your father bade me choose something pretty for you to wear," the countess told her.

"Won't Lady Morgana be angry that I've borrowed her gown?" Keely asked.

"Of course. That's what makes this whole affair so enjoyable."

"Then I couldn't."

"Your father is trying very hard to please you," Lady Dawn said, giving her a reproving look. "Would you repay his kindness with churlishness?"

Keely sighed. His Grace had invited her into his home. In good conscience she could hardly rebuff his intended kindness.

"The violet in the gown almost matches your pretty eyes," the countess coaxed. "Besides, the Earl of Basildon plans to call upon you today."

"But why would he wish to do that?" Keely gasped, surprised.

"Apparently, Devereux is quite taken with your beauty," Lady Dawn answered. "Your father gave him permission."

"Well," Keely hedged, gazing longingly at the offered gown and slippers. "If you really think I should—"

"I do," Lady Dawn said. "I'll even help you with your hair."

"A countess shouldn't perform such a menial task."

"Consider me an aunt," Lady Dawn said expansively, then frowned. "No, that won't do. I'm much too youthful to have an eighteen-year-old niece. Think of me as your older and wiser sister."

Suppressing a smile, Keely donned the gown and then slid her feet into the matching slippers. With joy lighting her face, she looked at the countess and said, "I cannot believe it. They fit perfectly."

"What a beauty you are," Lady Dawn said with an approving smile. "Would you like to see yourself?"

Keely nodded, eager as a young girl.

Lady Dawn opened the chamber door and beckoned

her to follow. They slipped into a chamber two doors down the corridor. Leading her charge across the chamber, the countess said, "This is your father's chamber."

Richly appointed, the enormous chamber sported Persian carpets covering the floor and colorful tapestries decorating the walls. Filtered sun lit the room through the high windows. Behind a screen stood a pier glass.

When Keely stepped in front of it, her mouth dropped open in surprise. Was that beautiful young woman really her?

The brocaded gown had a form-fitting bodice and a low-cut square neckline. Its long tight sleeves ended in a point below her wrists.

Keely looked *and felt* like a princess. Her smile was pure joy until her gaze touched the exposed swell of her breasts above the most daring neckline she'd ever worn. The dragon pendant glittered against the flawless ivory of her skin and drew attention to the crevice between her breasts. Uncertainly, Keely worried her bottom lip with her teeth.

Lady Dawn chuckled at her expression. "I'm quite certain Morgana never looked that lovely."

"Perhaps my own clothing would suit me better," Keely said. "The bodice is too bold, don't you think?"

" 'Tis virginal by court standards," the countess disagreed. "Come, my dear. Your father wishes to speak with you."

Pleased that she needn't wear her own drab clothing, Keely followed her out of the room. They retraced their steps down the corridor and went downstairs.

"Thank you, my lady," Keely said before entering the deserted great hall where her father awaited her.

The countess gave her an affectionate hug and then left her there.

Seated in front of the hearth, Duke Robert stood at her entrance. His gaze swept over her from the top of her head to the tips of her feet. Then he started across the hall to greet her.

Disconcerted by his stare, Keely dropped her gaze and enchanted her father with the perfect picture of demure femininity. She looked up shyly when he reached her side.

"You are as lovely as your mother," Duke Robert said, his voice husky with remembrance. "Sit over here with me."

"Thank you for the loan of the gown, Your Grace," Keely said, placing her hand in his.

Duke Robert noted her formality but ignored it. Instead, he escorted her to one of the two chairs in front of the hearth and then sat down in the other.

Keely folded her hands in her lap and stared at the floor. She felt awkward. For eighteen long years she had yearned for a father, but now that she had him, she didn't know what to say. Her father was a stranger to her.

Keely stole a glance at him and caught him staring at her. Breaking their silence, she said, "And thank you for inviting me to stay here last night."

"This is your home," Duke Robert said.

"A house is not a home," Keely replied, gazing at the crackling fire in the hearth instead of at him. "A home is people who love me and whom I can love in return."

"I love you," he told her.

"You cannot possibly love me," she disagreed, daring a sidelong glance at him. "You don't even know me."

"You are the seed that sprang from my loins," Duke Robert replied, his words making her cheeks pinken. Good Christ, how many years had it been since he'd seen a sincere blush color a woman's complexion? "When you become a mother, you'll understand how I dare profess my love so easily."

"If you say so, Your Grace," Keely mumbled, staring at the hands she was wringing in her lap.

An awkward silence descended on them. Though it hurt her to do so, pride made Keely refuse the duke's offer of love. He'd abandoned her mother and her. Erasing a lifetime of pain proved impossible.

"I understand your reticence, child," the duke said. "I ask you, as your father, to grant me the opportunity to earn your love."

"You *sired* me," Keely corrected him, unaware of the accusation in her voice. "You never fathered me."

Never forget that he hurt Megan, she reminded herself. *Never forget that the English, especially their lords, cannot be trusted.*

Duke Robert stood and paced back and forth in front of the hearth while he tried to organize his thoughts. He realized his daughter's wounds were deep and that each word he uttered needed to be chosen with care.

To avoid looking at her father, Keely peeked at the great hall. She'd been much too nervous the previous day to give any particular attention to her surroundings.

More impressive than Ludlow Castle's, this hall sported two massive hearths, one at each end. Overhead were heavy-beamed rafters, from which hung myriad Talbot banners. Brass sconces and vivid tapestries, most depicting the hunt, decorated the walls. One tapestry was different from the others, its motif being a maiden and a unicorn sitting together.

Keely rose from the chair and walked toward it. Something about that particular tapestry called out to her, and she had a powerful urge to touch it. Closing her eyes, Keely placed the palm of her right hand against the tapestry. She could feel her mother's spirit in it, and the faintest of smiles touched her lips.

Standing close behind her, Duke Robert spoke with a catch of emotion in his voice, "Megan made it for me. That tapestry and the dragon pendant are all that I've had of her for eighteen years. Now I have you."

Keely turned around slowly but kept her back pressed to the tapestry. She needed the assurance of her mother's presence. Gazing unwaveringly into his violet eyes, so like her own, she said, "You did love her. I'm sorry for your loss."

"I've lost more than Megan. I lost the immeasurable

pleasure of watching *you* grow from infant to woman," Duke Robert said. "In spite of what you think of me, I am your father and have your best interests at heart."

Keely wet her lips, gone dry from nervous apprehension. If the duke and she were to establish a familial relationship, it had to be based on truth.

"I have a confession to make," Keely began, then hesitated for a long uncertain moment before continuing. "I am a pagan."

Amazingly, Duke Robert smiled at her announcement. "Everyone at court behaves like a heathen," he said.

"Excepting Elizabeth and Burghley, of course. Why, you cannot imagine what goes on there."

"I mean, I believe in the Old Ways," Keely tried to explain. "Like Megan, I am Druid."

"Whatever you are can never change the fact that I am your father," Duke Robert said, surprising her. "I want the chance to know you."

Dumbfounded, Keely could only stare at him. Where was the blistering lecture on the dangers and evils of her outrageous beliefs? How could this seemingly kind-hearted man have impregnated and abandoned the woman he loved? Why did he invite her, a virtual stranger, into his home and his heart? Was he a fool? Or was she?

"Will you give me your trust, child?" the duke asked.

Keely lifted her chin a notch. "You have a very poor record on that account, Your Grace," she answered.

Duke Robert's lips twitched. Damn if the girl hadn't inherited his pride and his courage along with his violet eyes and his ebony hair. "Then will you give me a chance to earn your trust?" he asked.

Keely hesitated. The reason she'd traveled to England had been to place herself in his guardianship. Her mother had wanted it so. Finally, she nodded and answered, "Yes, Your Grace."

"That title is too formal between father and daughter," Duke Robert said, a smile of relief appearing on his face. "My other children call me Papa."

Keely had always yearned to speak that word, but the years of suffering proved impossible to dismiss so easily. Though causing another's pain violated everything she believed, Keely couldn't stop herself. The duke had abandoned her pregnant mother and, in so doing, had sentenced the babe—namely, her—to a pain-filled childhood. Her need to hurt him as he'd hurt them proved too strong to resist.

Steeling herself against the hope shining at her from his violet eyes, Keely replied, "I cannot do that, Your Grace."

Her words hurt herself as much as him. Keely felt her heart break at the expression of misery that crossed his face. But how could his pain match what she'd endured for eighteen years?

Duke Robert recovered quickly. He drew her into a sideways hug and planted a kiss on her temple. "Whenever you are ready," he said, "I'd be proud to have you call me Papa."

A lump of raw emotion formed in Keely's throat. Her bottom lip quivered. Two fat teardrops brimmed over her eyes and rolled down her cheeks.

"We'll have none of that," Duke Robert said, gently brushing her tears away. "The brightest of futures awaits you in England, and the misery of the past eighteen years will soon begin to fade."

"I'm too different," Keely whispered. "I'm Welsh and don't belong here."

"You're almost as English as I am," the duke said, gently tilting her face up and gazing into violet eyes that mirrored his own. "I loved your mother and planned to marry her, but my father convinced me that she had died."

"If you truly loved her," Keely asked, "why didn't you return to Wales and verify her death?"

"At the time, I had no reason to doubt my father's

word," Duke Robert answered, his gaze skittering away from hers. "Wouldn't you believe what I told you?"

"No." The word fell between them like an ax. He was hiding something, Keely felt it in her bones and saw it in his eyes. Megan had believed his words of love—but could she?

"Child of my heart," the duke said, his embrace tightening, "I love you as dearly as my other children. Fortune has gifted me with a second chance, for whenever I look at you, I feel that Megan is near."

Keely studied his face. That he'd truly loved Megan and believed her dead, what misery had *he* suffered through the years?

"Megan sent you to me," the duke went on. "You will consider this your home."

"Odo and Hew—" Keely began.

"Your cousins are welcome for as long as they wish," Duke Robert interrupted. "They're at the stables right now. Would you like to see them?"

"Oh, yes. May I?"

"This is your home, child. You may wander wherever you will. By the way, Merlin is an excellent piece of horseflesh but"—Duke Robert chuckled—"*a female*."

Keely beguiled him with a winsome smile. "I know."

"How you remind me of Megan," Duke Robert said, a wistful tone in his voice. He planted another kiss on her temple. "One last question."

Keely nodded.

"Under what circumstances did you meet young Devereux?"

"The earl introduced himself to me at the tavern where I was staying."

"That's all there was to your meeting?"

Keely cast him a bewildered look. "What else could there be?"

Duke Robert read the innocence in his daughter's expression and relaxed. The Tudor court's most notorious rake hadn't touched her. *Yet.* With luck, the two would be married before that happened.

"Run along and visit your cousins," Duke Robert said, relinquishing his hold on her.

Surprising him, Keely reached up and planted a kiss on his cheek, murmuring, "Thank you, Your Grace."

Keely left the hall and headed for the main foyer where she spied the duke's majordomo, Meade. The hapless servant still limped.

"Good day, my lady," Meade greeted her, opening the door.

"The same to you," Keely replied. "Please, sir, can you tell me which way to the stables?"

"At the end of that path on the left."

Keely nodded but lingered a moment longer, saying, "Meade, I hope you won't mind some advice. Rub evening primrose oil on your ankle. Then mix feverfew herbs with cider and drink it. Your pain will vanish in no time at all, and your limp will disappear."

"Thank you, my lady," Meade said with the hint of a smile on his usually somber face. "I shall try it."

Odo and Hew grinned with relief when they saw Keely and stood to greet her.

"Are you feeling better?" Odo asked.

"Yes, thank you. Much better," Keely returned their smiles. "And you?"

"Your father has himself an excellent cook," Hew answered, patting his belly. "We've stuffed ourselves so full, we can hardly move."

"The duke sired me," Keely corrected him. "He never fathered me."

"Now, little girl—" Odo began but clamped his lips shut when she frowned at his intended lecture.

Oblivious to their byplay, Hew scratched his head in puzzlement. "Ain't a sire the same as a father?"

"Idiot," Odo muttered. He reached out and cuffed the side of his brother's head, then turned to Keely and asked, "What are we going to do about that earl? He lives next door."

"There's nothing to fear," Keely replied, sounding more confident than she actually felt. "I cast a spell of forgetfulness upon him, and I do believe you'll be safe so long as you remain on His Grace's property. Where's Merlin? I want to see her."

Odo and Hew led Keely inside the stable. In one of the stalls on the right stood Merlin, who nickered a greeting and nudged her mistress.

"Have you been a good girl?" Keely crooned as she stroked the horse's neck. The sight of the pretty mare that Rhys had given her filled Keely with a longing for home. Turning to her cousins, she said, "I wish to leave this place and return to Wales."

"Madoc is there," Hew reminded her.

"Rhys will defend me against him," she countered.

"Now, little girl, you can't leave yet," Odo argued. "You've just found your father."

"The duke is a stranger to me." Tears welled up in her eyes. "I don't belong here."

Nor anywhere, Keely thought to herself.

"Give him and yourself a chance," Odo said. "You'll settle in."

"Well, will you stay here with me?"

"For as long as you want," Odo agreed.

"Forever," Hew added, brushing a tear from her cheek. "The duke has some fine-looking oak trees in his garden."

"I must meet them," Keely said, visibly brightening. She hugged Merlin and kissed her cousins' cheeks, then left the stables.

Autumn painted vivid colors within the perfect setting of the duke's garden. Besides nature's orange-, gold-, and red-leafed trees, an army of gardeners had landscaped the grounds into a rainbow of seasonal shades. Chrysanthemums in a variety of hues adorned the manicured garden, along with white baby's breath, purple flowering cabbage, pink sweet alyssum, marigold, snapdragon, and fairy primrose.

Keely sighed deeply at the glorious array. Autumn excited her because of Samhuinn, the beginning of the Druid cycle of life when the gates of Samhuinn, the beginning of the upon the past and the future. The thin veil between this earthly world and the beyond lifted for exactly three days. This Samhuinn was especially important because Megan had promised to return to her then.

After wandering around and touching each oak as a means of introducing herself to it, Keely sat down on a stone bench. The duke had immediately accepted her for what she was. Why was she unable to accord him the same respect? Harboring a grudge was so unlike her.

Since that horrible, long-ago day when she'd been only five years old, Keely had yearned for her true father. It seemed like only yesterday. . . .

Having finished weaving her very first oak-leaf wreath, Keely dashed across the courtyard toward her father. How proud he would be when she presented him with the wreath!

"Papa!" Keely called, pushing through the crowd of Lloyd clansmen in the courtyard. "I've made you a gift!" She held the wreath out to him.

"Never call me Papa," Madoc growled, brushing past her. "You're his bastard."

Hurt and confused, Keely hung her head. Tears spilled over her eyes and streamed down her cheeks. What had she done wrong this time? Why didn't Papa love her?

A long shadow fell across her path. Keely looked up and saw twelve-year-old Rhys. "Are you still my stepbrother?" she asked.

"Never mind him," Rhys said, crouching down to be eye level with her. "I am and always will be your brother. May I wear your pretty wreath?"

Keely managed a faint smile, but her bottom lip

quivered with the effort. As if she were crowning a king, Keely lifted the wreath and hung it around his neck.

"Rhys," she whispered, "what's a bastard?"

Before he could answer, another voice beside her said, "And I'm definitely your cousin."

Keely looked around and saw twelve-year-old Odo crouched beside her.

"Me too," ten-year-old Hew added.

"You idiot." Odo cuffed the side of his brother's head. "If I'm her cousin, then you're her cousin."

"Well, you didn't need to hit me."

"How else can I knock some sense into that head of yours?"

"But you're rattling my brains," Hew protested.

"You ain't got none," Odo shot back.

Keely giggled, almost happy again. These overgrown cousins of hers acted silly, but she loved them all the more because of it.

"Make me a wreath," Odo begged.

"Me too," Hew added.

"I'm first," Odo said, reaching to cuff his brother. "I'm older."

Ducking his brother's hand, Hew countered, "But I'm handsomer."

Keely looked at her brother. "Do you love me?" she asked, searching his eyes for the truth of the matter.

"Yes, very much." Rhys crushed her against his chest and hugged her tight.

Keely rested her head against his shoulder and saw Madoc frowning at them across the courtyard. The name he'd called her echoed in her mind. Bastard . . .

"Tears, my beauty?"

Startled, Keely snapped her head up and stared into vivid emerald eyes. "What are you doing here?" she demanded.

Richard raised his brows at her impertinence. "I live here. Remember?"

"No, you live—" Keely cringed inside at her outrageously rude behavior.

"Over there," he supplied, gesturing to the adjacent estate.

"His Grace is inside," she said.

"His Grace?" Richard cocked a brow at her. "So formal a title for your own father?"

Discouraging further conversation, Keely turned her head away and feigned disinterest, but her heart pounded frantically within her breast. The earl presented a threat to her cousins, but Keely was worried for her own peace of mind at the moment. His male beauty nearly blinded her. A woman could cheerfully drown in the fathomless pools of green that were his eyes.

"When we met at the tavern," Richard asked, "why didn't you tell me Ludlow was your father?"

"I considered my father's identity no business of yours," Keely replied without bothering to look at him. With luck, he'd go away.

"My lord," Richard said, lifting one booted foot and resting it beside her on the bench.

"What?" Keely snapped her head around and nearly swooned at the incredible sight of his well-muscled leg and thigh perched so disconcertingly close to her.

"You should have said, 'Twas no business of yours, *my lord.'"

"You may be *a* lord," Keely told him, "but you aren't *my* lord."

If she hadn't been speaking so impertinently to him, Richard would have applauded her spirited wit. After all, few men at the Tudor court dared speak to the queen's favorite in that rude manner.

Instead of becoming angry as he knew she expected, Richard smiled benignly. "I've brought you a welcoming gift," he said. He offered her the single perfect orchid that he held in his hand.

Keely gave him a bewildered smile and reached for it. When their fingers touched, an unfamiliar but wholly exciting sensation raced throughout her body. It was gone in an instant.

Surprised by his kindness, Keely stared at the orchid. No man had ever given her such a wonderful gift as a perfect flower. With the exception of her brother and cousins, no man had ever given her any gift. She'd never even had a suitor. Madoc's hatred of her served to discourage those who might be interested. Besides, no man would marry her without a dowry, and everyone knew her stepfather had no intention of offering one.

"'Tis beautiful. Please forgive my bad manners," Keely apologized, feeling churlish. "Your sudden appearance frightened me."

"Then you must forgive me," Richard replied, his voice a soft caress. "Never would I intentionally frighten or hurt you in any way."

His words did nothing to calm her fears. Keely couldn't seem to drag her gaze away from his. A thousand airy butterflies took wing in the pit of her stomach, and her hands in her lap trembled.

"I always thought only Englishmen and Madoc behaved rudely," Keely remarked, unaware of the insult she'd leveled on him. "I see that I carry that flaw inside me."

"Who is Madoc?" Richard asked, cocking a brow at her.

"My stepfather." Keely bit her bottom lip for a long moment. "Would you care to sit with me?" she finally invited him.

Richard gave her an easy smile and sat down beside her, so close his thigh teased her gown. The lady was definitely attracted, Richard concluded, but nervous because of the fact that those two blockheads robbed him in Shropshire.

What the bloody hell was he thinking? Richard frowned ferociously. He'd been the innocent victim, not the damned perpetrator of that crime!

"Is—is something wrong?" Keely asked in a small voice.

Richard gave himself a mental shake, then took her hand in his and kissed its sensitive palm. "You look especially lovely today, my lady," he complimented her.

Keely blushed and cast him an ambiguous smile.

Was she shy? Richard wondered. *Or sly?*

His gaze dropped to the gentle swell of her breasts above the low-cut bodice of the gown. When his eyes lifted to hers, she looked disgruntled. A man would have had to be blind to miss the displeasure stamped across her delicate features.

Richard had the good grace to flush, though amusement lit his eyes and made them glitter like emeralds. Never had he met a woman with such modesty. Even the queen's virginal maids-of-honor were less restrained than this beauty.

"I was admiring your dragon pendant," he lied. "A most unusual piece."

Keely's expression cleared. She touched the pendant and said, "'Tis my mother's legacy to me."

Holding her gaze captive with his own, Richard purposefully pasted his best smoldering look on his face. He knew how effective that particular expression was with women.

Keely felt a melting sensation in the pit of her stomach. Within mere seconds the simmering heat became a raging boil, but her instinct for survival surfaced quickly. Keely tore her gaze from his and remarked, "How lovely the trees dress in autumn, especially the oaks. You know, they're powerful huggers."

"I beg your pardon?" Richard couldn't credit what he'd heard.

"I—I was admiring His Grace's garden," Keely explained, too late realizing what she'd almost revealed about herself.

"You have the most delightful accent," Richard said.

"You're the one with the accent," Keely differed, giving him an unconsciously flirtatious smile.

"We English have a phrase that best describes you Welsh," Richard said, returning her smile. "*Daffy taffy.*"

Keely lost her smile, and one perfectly arched ebony brow shot up in a perfect imitation of *his* irritating habit. "We Welsh have a term that best describes English half-wits like you—*gifted.*"

Richard shouted with laughter, not only at what she'd said but at her irreverent lack of regard for his august rank. Imagine, insulting the queen's favorite earl!

For her part, Keely could only stare at him. His good humor in the face of what she considered a devastating insult surprised her.

"I'm wounded," Richard said, his eyes sparkling with unmistakable merriment. "Your sharp tongue slices me to pieces."

"What a happy soul you are," Keely replied. "Finding humor in the most unlikely places."

"Dudley should hear this."

"Who?"

"Robert Dudley, the Earl of Leicester," Richard answered as if that explained it.

Keely stared at him blankly. "I've never heard of the man."

Richard gave her a lopsided grin. "I'm beginning to like you more and more."

"I like you too," Keely replied, her lack of guile a refreshing change from the women at court. "Could we perhaps be friends?"

Richard nodded. He wanted more than friendship from this beauty, but he was wise enough to keep that thought to himself. Richard knew with a predator's instinct that unlike the other ladies of his acquaintance, Keely would fly away in fright if he moved too quickly. Besides, he needed time to investigate her part in her cousins' crime against him.

Feigning nonchalance, Richard stretched his legs out

and drew a brandy-colored stone from his pocket. He rolled it around in the palm of his hand and glanced sidelong at Keely.

"Unique, isn't it?" he remarked, catching her wide-eyed stare.

She nodded and looked away. "The carnelian stone protects its owner from harm. Where did you get it?"

"I found it in Shropshire and keep it for luck," Richard answered. Slyly, he added, "Your cousins—"

Keely visibly jerked into alertness, and Richard realized she knew about the robbery. Before or after the fact? he wondered.

"Your cousins seem vaguely familiar," he went on.

"Yet I cannot place where I've seen them."

"My cousins rode with me from Wales," Keely replied.

"I'm sure you never saw them before that night at the tavern."

Richard smiled, nodded, and dropped the subject. He didn't want her thinking that he recognized her cousins.

"Since you're newly arrived in England, please let me take you on a tour of London's most interesting sights."

"Without a chaperon, that would be improper," she objected.

Richard raised her hand to his lips. He gazed into her violet eyes and said in a husky voice, "Your beauty does incite me to impropriety."

His lips on her hand and his intimate words conspired against her. Keely was neatly caught by his disarming emerald gaze.

As a devastatingly lazy smile spread across his features, Richard moved closer, and slowly his mouth descended to claim her parted lips. Keely closed her eyes, and their lips touched in what would have been her very first kiss, but—

Honk! Honk! Honk!

Startled, both Richard and Keely leaped away from each other. She whirled around and saw a fat white goose with an orange beak waddling across the lawn toward them. Around its neck hung a gold collar inlaid with emeralds and diamonds. Lady Dawn, accompanied by two young boys, walked several yards behind the goose.

"Hello, Anthony," Richard called, then whispered out of the side of his mouth, "The countess's pet goose."

Keely stifled a giggle. "The goose is not for supper tonight?"

"Eat Anthony?" Lady Dawn cried. "Swallow your tongue, child!" She turned to her pages and ordered, "Bart and Jasper, return Anthony to his room."

As the boys led Anthony away, Richard stood and offered his seat to the countess. He bowed over Keely's hand, saying, "I look forward to our next meeting, my lady." His eyes promised her they'd begin exactly where they'd stopped.

"Sup with us this evening," Lady Dawn invited him.

"Unfortunately, I'm obligated to attend the queen," Richard refused. "Perhaps tomorrow?"

"You're always welcome at Talbot House." Lady Dawn drew Keely to her feet, saying, "The dressmaker is here to take your measurements, my dear. Tally is sparing no expense on your behalf."

"Enjoy your day," Richard said, turning away. He started across the lawn.

"The earl gifted me with this orchid," Keely told the countess.

Lady Dawn chuckled. "In the language of flowers, when a man gives a woman an orchid, he means to seduce her."

Staring at the earl's retreating back, Keely crimsoned with offended embarrassment. Richard chose that moment to turn around, sweep them a deep bow, and wink at Keely. Then he disappeared down the walk that led to his own estate.

"Nicely done," the countess complimented her. "Devereux will soon be eating from your hand. At least asking for it in marriage."

"Marriage?" Keely echoed in a shocked whisper.

"I do so love weddings," Lady Dawn drawled, hooking her arm through Keely's as they turned to the house. "I've been the bride three times already, but I will especially enjoy planning this one. The marriage of the decade, unless the queen decides to wed."

Holy stones! Keely thought in growing dismay. She'd only been at Talbot House for one confusing day. Already the earl had her bedded, and the countess had her wedded to him. How would she ever survive this land of eccentrics?

One hour at a time, an inner voice whispered. *Or else you'll go mad within a week.*

Chapter 5

Keely tossed and turned on the stormy seas of worry and awakened before dawn from the fitful sleep that had finally overtaken her. Autumn's chill nipped the air inside her chamber, but she ignored it. Instead of stoking the embers in the hearth, she wrapped herself in her white ceremonial robe and padded on bare feet across the chamber.

A steady rain drummed rhythmically against the window. Keely's head pounded in time with the beating of the rain. Worrying about Odo and Hew was literally making her sick. She couldn't live indefinitely with this danger threatening her cousins.

The earl knew he'd seen them somewhere. It was only a matter of time before he remembered the specifics.

Honesty is the best policy, Keely thought. The earl had said he'd never intentionally hurt her. Hanging Odo and Hew at Tyburn Hill would certainly cause her a great deal of pain. Should she confess to the earl and beg his mercy? What if he arrested her cousins? How could she live with that on her conscience? This was all her fault. If Odo and Hew hadn't been concerned for her welfare, they would never have resorted to robbery, would never even have journeyed to England.

Keely decided she would ask the Great Mother Goddess for guidance. If she envisioned a suitable ending to her confession, she would speak without delay to the earl.

Using her magic stones, Keely made a makeshift circle in the center of her chamber and left the western periphery open. She entered from the west and used her last stone to close the circle, saying, "All disturbing thoughts remain outside."

Keely fused the invisible periphery shut with her

golden sickle and then turned in a clockwise circle three times until she faced the west again. She dropped to her knees, closed her eyes, focused her breathing, and touched her dragon pendant.

"The Old Ones are here, watching and waiting," Keely whispered. "Stars speak through stones, and light shines through the thickest oak. One realm is heaven and earth."

After pausing a moment to gather the proper emotion, Keely opened her arms and implored, "Spirit of my journey, guide me to hear what the trees say. Spirit of my ancestors, guide me to hear what the wind whispers. Spirit of my tribe, guide me to understand what the clouds foretell. Hearken, spirits, to my call. Open my heart that I may see beyond the horizon."

And then, it happened. Images floated across her mind's eye. . . .

A warm room filled with books. An even warmer smile on the earl's face. The warmest feeling of security . . . strong, comforting arms. Welcoming arms. Protecting arms . . .

The image faded and dissolved into the reality of her bedchamber.

Opening her eyes, Keely touched her pendant and prayed, "I invoke the power of my mother's love, living inside this dragon, to protect me and mine. I thank the Goddess for passing her wisdom through me."

Keely walked to the western periphery, lifted the magic stone, and broke the enchanted circle. She removed her ceremonial robe and folded it, then went back to bed and yanked the quilt up to her chin.

Keely's path was clear. She would visit the earl that day and beg his mercy for her cousins and herself. Somehow, they would make restitution.

* * *

An hour before noon, Richard sat at his desk in Devereux House's richly appointed study and frowned at Willis Smythe. Richard's head pounded from the deadly combination of too late a night and the frustrating financial records he'd wasted the morning poring over. The thought of the reports due the queen by the following day staggered his mind.

"Why do you squander your money?" Richard asked, irritated. "Whoring and gambling produce no profits. I'll gift you with a two percent share in my Levant Trading Company, but the profit on only one percent will be paid to you. I'll reinvest the other percentage for a greater yield."

How generous, Smythe thought snidely as he relaxed in his chair and stretched out his legs. He took a healthy swig of his ale and remarked, "My father and my brother always saved. Both died before they could enjoy the fruits of their labor."

Richard recalled Burghley's warning to him at Kenilworth Castle: *"Untrustworthy . . . involved in his father's and his brother's deaths . . . squandered the inheritance."* Richard gave himself a mental shake. Willis and he had fostered together and were as close as brothers. Unless proven wrong, Richard refused to give credence to those slanderous rumors.

"Should I toil from sunrise to sunset and die without any pleasure?" Willis was asking.

Richard cocked a copper brow at him. "Pleasure-seeking is your vocation, Will. Are you so determined to leave nothing for your son?"

"I have no son."

"My point is that you will father a son one day."

"Worry about fathering your own son," Willis shot back. "Getting that tour of duty in Ireland is impossible without one. By the way, how goes your courtship of Morgana Talbot?"

"After spending a week in her company at Ludlow, I realized that marrying Morgana would be too great a sacrifice," Richard replied. "Unless, of course, misery excited me."

"An heiress is a possession I could use," Willis said.

"Mind if I try my hand with her?"

"Be my guest," Richard answered, inclining his head.

"The duke's other daughter interests me."

"Talbot sired only one daughter."

"As of a couple of days ago, His Grace claims two."

"How can that be?"

"Do you recall the woman with those two thieving Welshmen at the Rooster?" At the other man's nod, Richard went on, "That wench is actually a lady, albeit His Grace's by-blow from a Welsh gentlewoman. He's acknowledged their relationship, and I mean to pursue her."

"A bastard?" Willis exclaimed, then hooted with derisive laughter. "Imagine, England's wealthiest earl courting a bastard! Elizabeth will never consent to the marriage. Why not take her as your mistress? Better yet, let's both take her as *our* mistress. Consider the pleasurable hours—"

Richard stood so abruptly, it startled the other man into silence. "I can handle Elizabeth," Richard said. "If you don't mind, Willis, I have a mountain of reports due the queen tomorrow morning. I won't be futtering any woman if I lose my head. No pun intended."

Oblivious to his friend's anger, Willis rose from his chair. He reached out to shake Richard's hand just as a knock sounded on the door.

Jennings, the earl's majordomo, entered and said, "My lord, Lady Glendower wishes an interview. Will you see her?"

A surprised smile appeared on the earl's face. "Escort Lady Glendower here."

"You have the Devil's own luck," Willis remarked.

"Luck has nothing to do with success," Richard told him.

And then Keely stepped into the study. She wore a

gown created in rose cashmere, enhancing the bloom on her cheeks. A matching shawl covered her more interesting charms. Alluring yet simple.

"Welcome, my lady," Richard greeted her. The two men started across the study toward her.

Keely smiled as winsomely as she could and flicked a glance at Willis Smythe. "I'm sorry to intrude," she said, losing her nerve. "I can return another day."

"Lady Glendower, I present Baron Willis Smythe," Richard made the introductions. "Will was just leaving."

The baron smiled at her; Keely felt a ripple of fear dance down her spine. When he bowed over her hand, she nearly shrank back. Oh, why hadn't she foreseen his dark threatening presence?

Smythe turned to Richard. "I'll see you at court," he said, then quit the chamber.

Keely heard the door click shut behind her. As she stood five steps inside the room, her gaze appraised the chamber.

The study reeked of masculinity. Near the windows on one side of the room sat an intricately carved desk fashioned from sturdy English oak. Rows of books lined two walls from floor to ceiling, and the fourth wall sported a hearth where a fire crackled. Perched in front of the hearth were two comfortable-looking chairs.

Almost hesitantly, Keely looked at Richard. The earl, dressed severely in black, appeared the picture of casual elegance as he watched her through his disarming emerald eyes. His black silk shirt conspired with his form-fitting breeches and boots to give him a rather dangerous look. The only splashes of color in his appearance were his fiery red hair and his emerald green eyes.

Holy stones! Keely thought, dropping her gaze. She'd never seen such a sinfully magnificent man. Had coming here been a mistake? Too bad she needed his mercy instead of his arrogance. He seemed to possess plenty of that.

Good God! Richard thought as he stared at her. Never

had he seen such an adorable creature. Though she was a penniless commoner, she did possess the bearing of a countess. Did His Grace know she was here? Richard doubted it.

Long silent moments stretched between them. Disturbed by his intense presence, Keely kept her eyes downcast and wished he would say something.

Taking a deep breath, Keely gave the earl's chest a tentative smile which brought an answering smile to his lips. She tipped her head back to look up at him, for at six feet and two inches, the earl was more than a foot taller than she.

"What do you have to say for yourself?" Richard asked by way of a greeting.

"I—there is a matter of some importance that we need to discuss, my lord."

Richard cocked a brow at her. "*My lord?*" he teased.

"I thought I was merely *a* lord."

Embarrassed, Keely dropped her gaze and reminded his chest, "You already accepted my apology for that rudeness."

"So I did," Richard agreed, then glanced in the direction of his desk. He just had to finish the queen's reports, and if he insisted that the young lady wait to speak with him, she'd be in his company that much longer.

"Unfortunately, you've arrived at a bad time," Richard told her. "I'm obligated to finish the reports on my desk. The queen expects them in the morning. If you don't mind waiting, why not dine with me?"

"I'd like that," Keely accepted, glad for the reprieve. An English earl with a full stomach should be more amenable.

"Do you read?" Richard asked, gesturing toward the book-lined walls.

Lifting her chin a notch, Keely said, "We Welsh possess many fine talents."

With a smile Richard said, "Sit in front of the hearth, and I'll bring you a few books."

While Keely settled herself in one of the chairs, Richard selected several books on various subjects. He set them in a pile on the floor and handed her the one on top, saying, "This is a particular favorite of mine called *Lives of the Saints.*"

"Trying to instill moral fiber in me?" Keely quipped, taking the book from him.

Richard gave her an easy smile. "If it bores you, choose another."

Keely rested the book on her lap and opened it. Holy stones! she thought in surprised dismay. *Lives of the Saints* had been written in a foreign language—and she could barely read English. Was this his idea of a joke?

Unamused, Keely flicked a sidelong glance at the earl, who now seemed oblivious to her presence. If he'd intended to enjoy a laugh at her expense, she was going to disappoint him. Keely decided she would pretend to read.

She tried to give her full attention to the gibberish in her lap but cast an occasional glance at the earl. Her occasional glances lengthened into appraising stares. Keely unconsciously surveyed his charms—fiery copper hair, emerald jewels for eyes, handsomely chiseled features.

Keely sighed. The earl was a maiden's dream and infinitely more interesting than *Lives of the Saints.*

Resting her head back against the chair, Keely closed her eyes. Anxiety for her cousins had taken its toll. Warmth and safety enveloped her and lulled her into a peaceful sleep.

"Bloody shit," Richard muttered, flinging the quill down in disgust. He'd just tallied the same column of numbers for the tenth time and reached his tenth different total. It was her fault. He looked at his guest. Her presence was as distracting as hell.

Deciding he needed a break, Richard poured himself a whiskey, a gift from his Scots brother-in-law. He sipped it, then grimaced against its potent taste and coughed to alleviate the burning sensation. How Iain actually enjoyed this rot was beyond him.

With cup in hand, Richard stood and wandered across the chamber to stare at his sleeping guest. Lady Keely was an enchanting puzzle, and learning her secrets was an irresistible challenge.

Richard tried to imagine Morgana Talbot cuddled into his chair but couldn't. All he saw was Keely with her shining ebony mane, thick fringe of sooty lashes, and flawless ivory complexion. God, he wanted her—*badly.*

Richard glanced toward his desk. Duty called—no, screamed—for his attention. He needed those figures totaled by the time he reported to the queen in the morning.

Lifting the discarded book from Keely's lap, Richard struggled against a shout of laughter. His guest had been reading *Lives of the Saints* upside down. Apparently, reading Latin was not numbered among her many fine talents.

Reluctantly, Richard returned to his desk and the troublesome column of numbers. Whenever he glanced in Keely's direction, he felt a chuckle of laughter bubbling up. Imagine, the saints and their lives turned upside down.

As dinnertime neared, Jennings knocked and entered. Before the man could utter a word, Richard gestured for him to be quiet and pointed at the chair where Keely slept.

"Should I hold dinner back, my lord?" Jennings whispered.

"Give me a couple of minutes to awaken her," Richard said. "Set a table up in here."

Jennings nodded and left.

Richard crouched beside Keely's chair and whispered close to her ear, "Time to awaken, my lady." When her eyelids fluttered open, Richard felt as if he were drowning in those glorious pools of violet. Like a delicate but heady wine, her beauty intoxicated his senses.

"Dinner is about to be served," he said, inhaling deeply of her fragile scent. "I hope you're as hungry as you were tired."

Embarrassed at being caught sleeping, Keely blushed and dropped her gaze. How could she have fallen asleep in this man's house? In his very presence, no less! Did he enjoy magical powers that she hadn't foreseen?

"Smudges of fatigue circle your eyes," Richard said.

"We must discuss—"

"After dinner," he said.

Ever the consummate courtier, Richard escorted his guest to the table set for two and assisted her into her chair. Gazing across the table at her, Richard decided that Keely was one of those rare women whose beauty need never be enhanced. No matter her circumstance, she was simply perfection.

A bouquet of flowers sat in a vase on the table. There were baby's breath, a single red rose, and violet blue blossoms that she failed to recognize.

"'Tis the last rose of summer," Richard said, seeing where her gaze had fallen.

"I do love roses," Keely told him. "I once had a cat who loved them with baby's breath."

"Their perfume attracted him."

Keely gave him a puckish grin. "I believe 'twas their taste Percy found irresistible. He ate them."

Richard grinned. His gaze on her warmed considerably.

Keely reached out and touched one of the violet blue flowers, asking, "What is it?"

"*Nigella damascena.*"

Keely looked at him blankly.

"Known in English as love-in-a-mist," Richard told her.

"What a beautiful name," she said with a soft sigh. "I love flowers and plants and trees." *And mist,* she added to herself.

"The flower's beauty withers when compared to yours, my lady."

Keely blushed furiously. No man had ever voiced such a thought to her. Peering at him from shyly lowered eyes, she felt like the ignorant *taffy* that, she was quite certain, he thought she was. How did she dare sit across the table from a noble of Queen Elizabeth's court, an experienced man of the world? And then she thought of Odo and Hew. *Hanging at Tyburn Hill.* That kept her from bolting out the door.

Several mouth-watering dishes sat on the table between them. There were oysters in parsley sauce; thin slices of baked ham, sprinkled liberally with cinnamon and served with a sharp mustard sauce; a side dish of peas and baby onions; and rissoles of fruit—dried fruits and nuts enclosed in a batter and fried in oil. Goblets of wine sat beside their plates.

"Will that be all, my lord?" Jennings asked.

Richard looked at his guest and raised his brows in a silent question.

"Well, I—I would prefer milk instead of wine," Keely admitted.

"Bring the lady a goblet of milk," Richard ordered his man, then cast a pointed look at the other servants, who immediately left the study. "I usually dine in the hall but thought the privacy here would be more comfortable for you."

Keely peered at him from beneath her sooty lashes. Though she appeared serene, her nerves tingled in a wild riot. How exactly did an impoverished Welsh princess converse with a wealthy English earl? In truth, they had nothing in common.

Keely lifted the goblet of milk and drank. When she set it down, she looked like a young girl with a delicately tiny white moustache. She wasn't a child, however, as evidenced by her sultry violet eyes with their heavy fringe of ebony lashes.

Richard dropped his mesmerized gaze from her incredible eyes to her invitingly full lips. He suffered a sudden urge to lick the milk off her upper lip. And then—

Keely's tongue flicked out and licked the milk away. Performed in embarrassed innocence, her gesture was blatantly sexual. And as seductive as sin.

Richard closed his eyes against the temptation and swallowed a groan of need. His arousal rode him hard, and he struggled for control of himself.

"Eat the ham," Richard ordered, sternness masking his desire.

Keely refused with a shake of her head.

"You need the nourishment," he insisted. "A summer's breeze could knock you over."

"I despise pork," Keely told him. "Never touch it."

Richard, who'd eaten and enjoyed everything ever set before him on a table, was unable to comprehend such a peculiar dislike. He lifted a slice of ham off the platter and offered it to her, coaxing, "Just a little."

"Please, I can't."

"Give me one good reason."

"I have an aversion to pork," Keely said, looking him straight in the eye. "So would you if you'd been killed by a wild boar."

Richard stared at her in bewildered surprise. What the bloody hell was she talking about?

"A wild boar killed me once," Keely tried to explain. "In another life, that is. Which is why—" She broke off, shocked at what she'd revealed about herself.

"Another life?" Richard echoed.

"I have lived many times before." Keely gave him that ambiguous smile of hers, then reached across the table and touched his hand. "And I think you have also lived before."

Richard's first instinct, which he successfully squelched, was to yank his hand away and tell her she was mad.

His second instinct, which he controlled with a bit more difficulty, was to laugh in her face.

His third instinct, which he acted upon, was to use her eccentricity to his own best advantage. He cast her a devastating smile and covered her hand with his own. In a husky voice, Richard told her, "I do feel as if I've known you for a long, long time."

Keely dropped her gaze. Her hot blush was redder than the last rose of summer mingling in the vase with the love-in-a-mist flowers.

"Please, may I have my hand back?" Keely asked in an embarrassed whisper.

"Certainly." Feeling in control of the situation again, Richard smiled inwardly. Her shyness proved her virtue and pleased him. She was unlike any woman of his acquaintance. Soon, he decided, he'd unravel the mystery surrounding her and discover all there was to know about her.

At the meal's end, Richard escorted Keely to one of the chairs in front of the hearth and then sat in the other. He stretched his long legs out and looked at her.

"Did you enjoy *Lives of the Saints*?" Richard asked, his eyes sparkling with suppressed merriment.

"Actually, I found their lives too revolting to read," Keely answered. She didn't want him questioning her about a book she was unable to read.

"Really?" Richard raised his brows at her.

"Martyrdom holds no appeal for me," she elaborated. "Senseless torture and meaningless suffering disgust me."

Richard nodded and turned his gaze toward the hearth, seemingly lost in his own thoughts. From the corner of his eye, he caught a furtive movement and saw his guest furtively moving her booted feet as if she couldn't get comfortable.

"What's wrong with your feet?" he asked.

"They hurt without my stockings."

"For God's sake." Richard stood abruptly and turned toward her.

Keely shrank back in her chair.

Richard knelt in front of her and yanked her boots off, then shocked her even more by massaging her right foot. "You should have worn your stockings," he scolded her without looking up.

"I—I couldn't find them," Keely said in a small voice.

"I was in a hurry and never expected to be here this long."

Switching to her left foot, Richard gazed into her eyes and teased, "Relax. I'm not going to bite your toes off."

"Your biting my toes is the least of my worries," Keely replied, rueful laughter tingeing her voice.

Richard grew serious and said, "Tell me your worries, sweetheart."

The time for confession had arrived.

"'Twas Odo and Hew who robbed you in Shropshire," Keely blurted out.

"I know," Richard said as a smile of admiration for her honesty spread across his features.

Extreme agitation rendered Keely deaf to his words and blind to his smile. Her defense of her cousins came out in a rush: "Robbing you was an accident. You happened upon the wrong place at the wrong time and behaved so uncooperatively. If only you'd been the least bit amenable—Odo and Hew worried for my continued survival. And—and they left you the carnelian stone for protection. No harm done, then— *What did you say?*"

"If highway robbery weren't so serious an offense, Richard would have laughed at her surprised expression. "I said, I know Odo and Hew robbed me."

"How?" Keely cried.

"Your cousins are incompetent blockheads," Richard answered. "First they left their faces unmasked, and then they sold my horse to my own man."

Keely became suspicious. "Why haven't you arrested them?"

"Is that what you want?"

"*No!*"

"I'd planned on seeing them hanged," Richard admitted. "But then you walked into the tavern with them."

"I don't understand."

Richard leaned close, his handsome face merely inches from hers. "I'd never do anything to hurt you," he said again in a husky whisper.

Ever so gently, he drew her into his embrace. Mesmerized by his intense gaze, Keely was caught by the unfamiliar and wholly irresistible gleam of desire in his emerald eyes.

Richard's face hovered above hers for the briefest moment and then descended as one of his powerful hands traveled to the back of her head and held her immobile. Their lips touched in a kiss.

When Keely relaxed in his arms, Richard's lips on hers became ardent and demanding, stealing her breath away. His tongue persuaded her lips to part, then explored and tasted the sweetness of her mouth.

And then it was over.

Richard drew back and studied her dazed expression. He traced a finger down her silken cheek and rubbed his thumb across her lips. "'Tis past time to run home, dearest. Your beauty could corrupt the morals of a saint," he said. "Rest easy that your cousins' secret is safe with me."

Keely blushed. Now that she'd let him kiss her, how would she ever face him again? The earl seemed so relaxed and casual about what was to her one of life's milestones: her first kiss.

Richard reached for her boots, intending to help her, but Keely was faster. She plucked them out of his reach and said, "I'll carry them."

Standing, Richard cocked a copper brow at her. "You're going to walk barefoot?"

"I love the feel of Mother Earth beneath my feet," Keely said, rising from the chair.

Richard couldn't credit the fact that she was still blushing. Unless——"I'll escort you home," he said.

"That's unnecessary," she refused. "I've wasted enough of your time, my lord."

"Moments shared with you are no waste of time," Richard said smoothly. "In fact, you've brightened my day immeasurably. And I'm *a* lord. Remember?"

Keely smiled in spite of her embarrassment. "I appreciate your understanding." She padded on bare feet across the study, but when she would have disappeared out the door, his voice stopped her.

"Keely?"

She turned around. "Yes?"

Richard closed the distance between them and stood in front of her. "Thank you," he said.

Keely gave him a bewildered look. "For what, my lord?"

With one hand, Richard gently tipped her face up and gazed into the most disarming eyes he'd ever seen. "For gifting me with your first kiss."

"How could you know?" Keely moaned in mortification. And then it came to her. She was an incompetent kisser. To make matters worse, kissing wasn't something a virtuous lady could practice.

"You are incredibly sweet," Richard said reassuringly.

"You could tell by my taste?" she exclaimed, relieved.

Richard struggled against a shout of laughter. He gave her a quick kiss and let her go.

Instead of returning to his desk, Richard sauntered to the window and watched her run across the lawns to Talbot House. Somehow, he'd known she'd be magnificent. Keely Glendower was a seductive angel, a rare woman of courage and integrity. Most worthy of becoming his countess. Despite her illegitimacy, she possessed the noble qualities he desired in a wife. He would enjoy both his blood bond with Talbot and his tour of duty in Ireland.

Humming a bawdy tune, Richard headed for his desk.

The sooner he finished his work and reported to the queen, the sooner he could return and demand Keely's hand in marriage. That the lady might not desire his hand in marriage never entered his mind.

Chapter 6

"You did what?" Odo exclaimed.

"I visited the earl yesterday," Keely repeated. "I begged his mercy for robbing him."

"Do you want to see us hang?" Hew cried, touching his neck as if he already felt the noose tightening.

"You blinking idiot," Odo said, cuffing the side of his brother's head. "Harming us is a thing Keely could never do. Could you, little girl?"

Keely shook her head and looped her arm through Hew's. "There's nothing to fear," she assured him. "I've set matters straight. The earl was surprisingly understanding. We couldn't stay here indefinitely with that hanging over our heads."

"Don't say the *H* word," Hew whined.

Hiding a smile, Keely turned to Merlin's stall and stroked the mare's forehead. She took an apple from her pocket and gave it to the horse.

"Well, little girl. What did the man say?" Odo asked.

"Richard swore your secret was safe with him," Keely answered. "He promised he'd never do anything to hurt me."

" 'Richard,' is it?" Odo remarked, suspicious.

Keely ignored his comment.

"Can the earl be trusted to keep his word?" Hew asked.

"He'll keep his solemn word or suffer the consequence of deceit," Keely told them. "But I do not completely trust any Englishman, so never venture onto his property."

"We won't," Hew replied.

"Who accompanied you to the earl's?" Odo asked.

"No one did."

"Did he *try* anything?"

Keely arched an ebony brow at him and feigned ignorance. "Like what?"

"You know what I'm talking about," Odo said.

"Try what?" Hew asked.

Odo slapped the side of his brother's head and then turned on Keely. "I'm waiting for your answer, little girl."

Recalling the earl's passion made Keely blush. "Twas merely a kiss."

"I should have killed that good-for-nothing in Shropshire!" Odo said.

"Hush! 'Tis wrong to voice such evilness," Keely scolded him. "Richard played the part of a proper gentleman. Yes, he's English, but better than most, and I won't listen to you malign him. 'Twas an innocent kiss."

"What's wrong with kissing?" Hew rounded on his brother. "You done more than—"

"Shut your mouth in front of the girl," Odo snapped, reaching out to hit him.

Hew sidestepped to safety but did as he was told.

Keely swallowed a giggle. "Caution is advisable," she said. "What you need is an invisibility shield."

"This stable is too busy," Odo warned. "Someone's likely to catch you mumbling those incantations."

Keely pressed her cheek against Merlin's, then turned around, saying, "His Grace and Lady Dawn are closeted with a business associate in the study. The gardens will be deserted at this hour of the day, and I know the perfect spot for privacy. Let's go."

Keely led the way out of the stable and down the path to a secluded area of the garden that bordered one side of the Talbot mansion. Here several oak trees stood guard.

"The crisp smell of Samhuinn permeates the air," Keely said, pulling her woolen shawl closer around her shoulders. "That wondrous night is fast approaching."

"I don't smell nothing," Hew whispered.

"Me neither," Odo agreed.

Keely looked up at the sky. The dying sun blazed like molten fire in the west, while the eastern horizon darkened into a deep indigo. Autumn's vibrant colors of red, gold, and yellow swirled around her.

"All things are possible with the help of the Mother Goddess," Keely told her cousins. "But be warned. I am working without the requisite candles and herbs. Do not tempt capricious fate by placing yourselves in front of the earl. Understand?"

Odo and Hew bobbed their heads in unison.

Keely wished she had her bag of magic stones and ceremonial robe, but she didn't want to chance returning inside to get them. Instead, she gathered eight stones at random and made a makeshift circle, being certain to leave the western periphery open.

"Will you join me?" Keely asked, glancing at her cousins.

Both men shook their heads.

Entering the circle from the west, Keely set the last stone down and said, "All disturbing thoughts remain outside."

Keely walked to the center and covered her head with her shawl. She turned three times in a clockwise circle until she faced the west again, then closed her eyes and focused her breathing.

"By the powers of Mother Earth and Father Sun, control of our lives returns to us," Keely implored. "With invisibility shield and armor tight, we win this battle to be free of fear."

Keely walked to the circle's western periphery and lifted the stone, breaking the enchantment. Then she kissed the stone and tossed it over her left shoulder.

"All will be well," Keely said as she walked toward her cousins.

" 'Tis nearly suppertime," Odo replied. "Get yourself inside, little girl."

Keely nodded but placed the palm of her hand against Hew's cheek, asking, "Feeling better, cousin?"

Hew grinned and bobbed his head.

"Run along, then. I'll go to supper in a few minutes."

Alone, Keely advanced on the oak tree. She placed the palms of her hands against its bark and whispered, "Your power is mighty, my friend. I knew you'd be marvelous to touch."

Stepping closer until her whole body touched it, Keely wrapped her arms around the oak's trunk—as far as they would go—and hugged it. "From the first moment I saw you, I knew we'd be friends."

As Keely was invoking the universe's unseen powers, Richard Devereux sat inside the Duke of Ludlow's study. He reached across the desk and accepted the offered goblet of Madeira malmsey, then leaned back in his chair and stretched his long legs out.

"Here's yours, my dear," Duke Robert said, handing Lady Dawn her goblet of wine. He looked at the earl and asked, "What's on your mind, Devereux?"

"With great reluctance, I must risk offending you, Your Grace."

Duke Robert stared without expression at the younger man and waited for him to continue.

"My interest in Morgana has permanently waned," Richard told him. "I do regret any hurt this causes."

"That's the best news I've heard this week," Lady Dawn remarked, earning a censorious glance from the duke.

"Until death do us part' can be a long, long time," Duke Robert said. "No man should marry a woman he doesn't want."

"'Tis most understanding of you," Richard replied, setting his goblet of wine on the desk. He stood then and wandered across the study toward the window. "I am requesting Lady Keely's hand in marriage."

"I knew it!" Lady Dawn exclaimed, clapping her

hands together. "What a striking couple Richard and Keely will make. Don't you think so, Tally?"

"I have no objections to the match," Duke Robert admitted.

Richard glanced over his shoulder and smiled at the sight outside the window. The object of his desire was playing an unfamiliar game with her cousins. That two gigantic warriors would attend Keely, gamboling in a circle like a young girl, touched his heart. Their loyalty to his intended wife was admirable. Richard could almost sympathize with their reason for robbing him.

"Are you listening?" the duke's voice penetrated his thoughts.

Richard turned around and smiled sheepishly. "I was admiring the view, Your Grace."

"True love does make people behave strangely," Lady Dawn said.

Duke Robert rolled his eyes but refrained from commenting on his beloved's observation. "I approve of the match," he said, "but the final decision is my daughter's. I would never force any of my children to the altar."

"I foresee no problem," Richard replied. "When she visited me yesterday, Keely seemed quite attracted to me."

"Keely visited you?" Duke Robert echoed, surprised.

"We dined together," Richard explained. "Despite my somewhat tarnished reputation, I assure you 'twas an innocent meal."

"Chessy, be a love," Duke Robert said. "Tell Meade to fetch Keely."

Richard glanced over his shoulder, saying, "You'll find Lady Keely in the garden . . . *hugging a tree.*"

The duke bolted out of his chair and hurried across the room. He reached the window in time to see his daughter give the oak tree a quick kiss.

Richard turned a stunned expression on the duke.

"'Tis a Welsh custom," Duke Robert lied. "Kissing an

oak insures good luck to the household. Kindhearted of her to think of my welfare."

Richard relaxed and smiled with amusement. "Very loving, indeed, Your Grace."

Keely stopped short when she walked into the study. What was the earl doing here? she wondered, beginning to panic. Had he decided to tell her father that Odo and Hew were guilty of highway robbery? How could she have believed an Englishman's word? The whole damned race had no honor.

Smiling, Richard crossed the chamber and kissed her hand, then gazed deeply into her violet eyes—*her angry violet eyes.* What had upset her? He hadn't even spoken yet.

Giving her hand an intimate squeeze, Richard asked, "What game were you playing in the garden?"

Keely froze. "P-playing in the garden?"

"You were twirling in a circle while your cousins watched."

"Cousins?"

"Odo and Hew, remember?"

"Yes, I remember," Keely said, evading his question.

So much for invisibility shields.

"Sit over here, dearest." Richard escorted her to one of the chairs. "Your father has something important to tell you."

"Is Madoc dead?" Keely asked, her expression hopeful. If that happened, she could return posthaste to Wales. Duke Robert's lips quirked. "I've had no news from Wales, my dear."

"Your father consents to our marriage," Richard told her. "If you'll have me, sweetheart."

Keely snapped her head around to gape at the earl. "Marriage?" she squeaked, shocked.

"Oh, what fun we'll have planning the wedding," Lady Dawn gushed with glee. "'Twill be the marriage of the decade."

"What do you say to the earl's proposal, child?" Duke Robert asked.

Keely looked from the earl to the duke. Was her father trying to get rid of her? She had no desire to wed, let alone with an an Englishman. She knew that a woman's problems sprang from that ruthless creature called man. Megan's miserable life proved that beyond a reasonable doubt. The daughter had learned hard lessons from the mother's mistakes. Keely would not be forced into a marriage, but for Odo's and Hew's sake she needed to extricate herself from this coil very, very carefully. The earl could still have a change of heart regarding her cousins' secret.

"'Tis exceedingly flattering to be considered for such an exalted position," Keely said politely. "However, I cannot possibly accept."

Unused to having his desires thwarted, Richard refused to believe what he'd heard. Rejection was unthinkable. "What did you say?" he asked.

"Any woman would feel proud to call you her husband," Keely went on, "but I traveled to England to find my—His Grace. I couldn't possibly marry at this time and leave him."

"You'd be living next door, child," Duke Robert said with a smile. "Devereux is England's most sought-after bachelor, and a woman without a man is incomplete. Besides, younger girls than you are happy mothers made. Isn't that true, Chessy?"

Keely remained determined. "If—if you'd like me to leave, I can return to W—"

"What the bloody hell is wrong with me?" Richard snapped, losing control for the first time in his well-ordered adult life. How dare this little nobody refuse the renowned Earl of Basildon!

"You're English," Keely said as if that explained everything, her anger rising to meet his.

"You're almost as English as I am."

"I'm Welsh!"

"A woman in your position should be grateful for any offer, much less dare to refuse England's premier earl."

Keely paled at his insult. She knew what he meant. She'd heard that same epithet hurled at her before. The earl merely phrased himself more politely than most. For some strange reason, she'd expected better from him.

"Watch your words, Basildon," the duke growled in his daughter's defense.

Keely rose from her chair and faced the earl. "Of what position do you speak?" she challenged, her voice and her expression filled with contempt.

Richard glared at her. "Your position as a noble bastard."

"Enough!" Duke Robert shouted, banging his fists on the desk.

"All dragons do breathe fire," Keely said, finding her voice through her pain. Without another word, she walked in graceful dignity to the door.

In an instant Richard was after her. "I'm sorry," he apologized, grasping her forearm to prevent her escape.

"I—I didn't mean what I said."

It was then that Keely gifted the earl with his second humiliating shock of the day. She raised her violet-eyed gaze to his and said coldly, "Remove your odious paw from my person."

"You aren't accepting my apology?" Richard asked in surprise.

"No."

Being rebuffed twice within the span of several minutes didn't sit well with Richard. "Do you realize any woman in England can be mine for the asking?"

"All but one." With her head held high, Keely quit the chamber.

Duke Robert cursed soundly, rose from his chair, and crossed the chamber. "I'll speak to her," he said, then disappeared out the door.

Uncertain where he'd gone wrong, Richard stared at the door blankly. The chit had rejected his proposal of marriage and refused to accept the first apology he'd ever given anyone!

"So that's the fabled Devereux charm," the countess purred behind him.

"Very funny." Richard turned around. "Tell me, Cheshire. When one offers an apology, isn't the other person required to accept it?"

"I don't actually know," Lady Dawn answered. "I've never apologized to anyone. Do you really want her?"

"Does it matter?" he asked.

"Poor Richard, bedding England's myriad eager has retarded your powers of seductive persuasion," Lady Dawn commiserated with his unusual predicament. "Trapping a vixen into marriage is easier than falling out of a tree. I could help you."

Richard cocked a copper brow at her. "How?"

"Trust me, darling," she replied, looping her arm through his. "The simpler the plan, the better 'twill work. Here's what we'll do. . . ."

Upstairs, Duke Robert knocked on his daughter's bed-chamber door and then entered. She lay curled on the bed, weeping with her face turned into the pillow. The duke crossed the chamber and sat on the edge of the bed, then gently gathered her into his arms.

"Weeping is no cure for calamity," he said. " 'Twill only make you sick, my dear."

"I—I w-want to g-go home," Keely sobbed, resting her head against the comforting solidness of his chest. "I don't b-belong here."

"Basildon overreacted to your rejection," Duke Robert said, stroking her back. "You cannot believe how distraught with remorse he is."

"No, I cannot believe that," Keely replied, then added in a small voice, "I don't usually weep when people call me a bastard."

Guilt coiled itself around the duke's heart. His daughter was no more a bastard than he, but the world would never know the truth of her birth. Her pain was his pain. How could he have ruined so many lives?

"Who called you that?" he asked.

"Madoc, my stepfather." Keely hiccoughed. "I've always felt as though I belonged nowhere. 'Tis what Madoc called me—Princess of Nowhere."

Duke Robert suffered the strongest urge to murder the despicable Welshman. Because of him, his firstborn, the child of his heart, had endured a childhood of indignities. If he ever chanced to meet the black-hearted villain—

Keely worried her lower lip and then gazed at him through violet eyes limpid with her tears. She had to confide in him. Because of her rejection, the earl would probably break his word concerning her cousins.

"I have a confession, Your Grace," she began.

Duke Robert kissed the crown of her head and joked, "What terrible crime have you committed, child?"

"Highway robbery, I'm afraid."

"What?"

"Odo and Hew, worried for my survival, robbed the earl in Shropshire, and—"

"Your cousins robbed Basildon?"

Keely nodded. "I'm afraid so. Richard promised that their secret was safe with him, but now—can you guarantee they'll remain free of the hangman's noose?"

"Yes." At her expression of doubt, Duke Robert explained, "Your father, dear child, is a powerful and influential peer of this realm."

"More powerful than the earl?"

"Considerably more powerful than that sour-faced pup," he assured her.

"Sour-faced?" she echoed, puzzled.

"Devereux walks through life like he has a pike stuck up his—" The duke cleared his throat. "At times, he wears a pained expression. 'Tis a nasty habit borrowed from Burghley."

"Richard is forever smiling and finding humor in the

most unlikely places," Keely disagreed. "At least, he did until today."

Duke Robert smiled. "Perhaps you bring out the best in him. And the worst." He gave her a hug. "Rest awhile. I'll send supper up later."

Keely smiled wanly. "Thank you, Your Grace."

"Remember, child. Whenever you're ready, I'll be your Papa."

Morning had almost aged into afternoon by the time Keely awakened. Opening her eyes, she stared out the window at a mostly cloudy day. Though his radiant face wasn't visible to human eyes, she knew that Father Sun was out there hiding behind those forbidding clouds.

Heavy-hearted, Keely was unable to prevent her thoughts from wandering to the earl. Richard appeared as glorious as Father Sun, a pagan god sprung to life, but what dwelt inside a man's heart was what mattered most. Though he'd sworn to keep her cousins' crime a secret, the earl had shown his English callousness by calling her a bastard. Unfortunately, even a bastard had hopes and dreams and feelings.

Keely sighed in dejection. She wished they'd met under different circumstances—another time, another place. The earl's world could never be hers. If she'd agreed to the marriage, he would regret making her his wife. She couldn't live without love. Besides, the English earl would never accept that she was a Druid.

Rolling over, Keely saw her breakfast tray and a bouquet of love-in-a-mist flowers on the bedside table. She sat up and noticed a second love-in-a-mist bouquet on the floor beside the table. A third perched on the stool, while a fourth sat on the floor in front of the hearth.

As Keely looked around the room, a soft smile touched her lips. Her bedchamber was a garden of love-in-a-mist bouquets.

"Time to awaken," Lady Dawn called, walking into the chamber. On the bed, she placed a violet wool skirt with a matching cashmere shawl and a white scoop-neck linen blouse. "As usual, I've chosen something lovely for you to wear."

"From where did these come?" Keely asked, gesturing at the flowers.

"The earl sent them this morning," Lady Dawn answered, "and I carried them in here myself so the servants wouldn't awaken you. See you in a bit, darling."

The countess breezed out of the bedchamber.

Keely stared at the love-in-a-mist bouquets. Apparently, the earl's apology had been sincere. Had he changed his mind about wanting to marry her? He didn't seem to be the type of man who'd accept a simple no for an answer.

Intending to complete her morning routine, Keely stood up and stretched, then crossed the chamber to the privacy screen. What she saw behind it made her dissolve into giggles. Sprouting from the chamber pot was another bouquet of love-in-a-mist flowers.

After washing and dressing, Keely sat on the edge of the bed and ate the bread, cheese, and milk that had been left there for her. She looked up from her meal in surprise when someone knocked on the door.

"Enter," she called.

The countess burst in. Behind her walked the earl's majordomo.

Carrying a silver tray, Jennings marched across the chamber and announced, "For you, my lady."

A folded piece of parchment lay on the tray. Beside it sat a bouquet of Michaelmas daisies and violets.

Keely lifted the bouquet and inhaled its perfume. Then she reached for the note.

"In the language of flowers, violets are a token of love," Lady Dawn told her. "And the Michaelmas daisies mean farewell."

The earl was giving up, Keely decided. Was she relieved or disappointed?

The note had no salutation or signature. Written in a

bold flourishing script were the words: *Hurting you was never my intent. Please forgive me.*

The earl *was* sorry, Keely concluded. How much pride had it cost him to apologize to a bastard, albeit a noble one? Harboring a grudge was unthinkable.

Keely looked at Jennings and said, "Tell the earl my answer is yes."

"Very good, my lady." Jennings hesitated and then added, "The earl bade me tell you that he wished to apologize in person, but his injury prevents movement."

"Injury?" Keely and Lady Dawn echoed in unison.

" 'Tis his ankle," Jennings told them. "Sprained, I believe."

"You must visit the earl," Lady Dawn said to Keely, "and accept his apology in person, my dear."

Concern etched itself across Keely's features. "What is the earl doing for his sprain?" she asked. When the majordomo shrugged his ignorance, Keely said, "Tell the earl I will come to him at four o'clock and bring something to speed his recovery."

"Very good, my lady." Jennings left the chamber.

"May I ask Cook to prepare an ointment for the earl's ankle?" Keely asked the countess.

"What do you need?"

"A blending of swallow and peter oils."

"I'll take care of it myself," Lady Dawn said, then left the chamber.

Keely revised her opinion of the earl. The sight and the scent of the myriad love-in-a-mist bouquets cheered her. Richard *did* care about her feelings. His kindness and remorse proved that he was not a complete English swine. Apparently, the earl was a battleground for good and evil. She only hoped he wasn't beyond redemption.

By early afternoon, the sun had broken through the clouds. At four o'clock, as Father Sun was making his descent in the west, Keely left Talbot House and headed in the direction of the earl's mansion. In her hands she carried the bottle of swallow and peter oils.

As she slipped through the opening in the hedges and stepped onto the earl's property, Keely glanced across the manicured lawns to his gardens. What she saw stopped her in her tracks. Keely closed her eyes, quite certain she was mistaken, but when she opened them again, the startling sight was still there.

Three trees stood together like old friends. Keely recognized the shining whiteness of the sacred birch, the dark evergreen spikes of the sacred yew, and most sacred of all, the majestic oak. The rare sight of these three standing together nagged her.

Reaching for the memory, Keely pressed her index finger across her lips and closed her eyes. Then Megan's prophecy returned to her:

"Walk among the powerful, but find happiness where the birch, the yew, and the oak converse. . . ."

Keely shook her head, refusing to believe what stood before her eyes. Her mother could not have meant she'd find happiness here. That was simply too absurd to consider. Birch, yew, and oak abounded in the millions across the breadth of England and Wales. Why, there had to be hundreds of holy places where the three most sacred of all trees conversed together! She could never find happiness with an Englishman. At first opportunity, Keely decided, she'd return to this hallowed site and worship. Perhaps on Samhuinn Eve.

"Follow me, my lady," Jennings said when she'd gained the foyer. He started toward the stairs.

"Where are you taking me?" Keely asked.

"The earl is abed," Jennings answered. "His injury prevents his coming downstairs to greet you."

Keely flicked her tongue out and wet her lips, gone dry from nervous apprehension. It was logical, she supposed. He'd sprained his ankle, else he would have come to Talbot House. After a moment's hesitation, Keely nodded and followed the majordomo up the stairs.

Clad in tight black breeches and an unbuttoned black silk shirt that left his copper chest hair visible, Richard was reclining on the bed when she walked in. His copper hair blazed like a fiery sunset, and his cool emerald gaze was as refreshing as the forest in springtime.

Keely felt like swooning at the sensuous sight of a pagan god sprung to life. She longed to flee the chamber, but it was too late. She raised her gaze to his and was caught by his intense emerald gaze.

"Thank you for coming, my lady," Richard greeted her as his man set a stool next to the bed and left.

"Call me Keely."

"Then you must call me Richard." The warmth of his smile could melt mountain snow.

Keely answered his smile with one of her own, then crossed the chamber and sat on the edge of the bed to inspect his ankles. Holy stones! The man even had beautiful feet.

"There's no swelling," she said. "Which one is it?"

"Both."

Keely looked at him in confusion.

"I sprained the right one," Richard explained. "Then I twisted the left trying to hobble upstairs."

"This mixture will help." Keely poured some of the oil into her hand and passed him the bottle. Lifting his right ankle onto her lap, she began to work the oil into his skin—his beautiful skin. What she needed was a diversion from what she was doing.

"Have you changed your mind about my cousins?" she asked.

"Perhaps."

Keely snapped her head up, saw his smile, and realized he was teasing her. "You stole too," she teased him back. "You kissed me without my permission."

"What I did in the study could hardly be labeled a kiss," Richard told her. "Besides, if every man who stole a kiss from a pretty girl were condemned as a thief, there'd scarcely be an Englishman alive." His gaze narrowed on her. "You'd like that, wouldn't you?"

Keely remained silent, but the hint of a smile flirted with the corners of her lips.

"If you kiss me with passion now," Richard baited her, "I'll consider your cousins and myself even."

"Extortion is against the law," Keely reminded him.

"Let's begin a life of crime," Richard suggested, leaning forward. "Robbery and extortion could be our specialties."

Keely gave him a withering look.

"Well then, tell me about yourself," he said.

"There's nothing to tell."

"I have three older sisters," Richard told her, thinking she'd reveal more of herself if he did. "Kathryn is the oldest at thirty, followed by Brigette at twenty-eight and Heather at twenty-six."

"I always wished for a big family, especially a sister," Keely admitted. "Tell me about yours."

"My sisters tormented me without mercy and had absolutely no respect for a fledgling earl."

Keely laughed. "Do they also attend the court?"

"Sadly, none of them live in England."

"Tell me how they tormented you."

Richard cocked a copper brow at her. "Might you be looking for ideas?"

Keely smiled and set his right foot on the bed. She lifted his left foot onto her lap and began massaging oil into his ankle.

"Your name is quite unusual," Richard remarked.

"*Keely* means 'beauty.'"

"Appropriate. *Richard* means 'powerful ruler.'"

Keely smiled at that. He did possess the arrogance of a king. "How old are you?" she asked.

"I became twenty-five on the sixth day of May."

"We are direct opposites," Keely told him. "You were born a stubborn bull, while I am a deadly scorpion."

"You're too delicate and gentle to be dangerous," Richard disagreed.

"Spoken with all the arrogance of a man." Keely set

his foot aside, then removed herself from dangerous temptation by wandering across the chamber to gaze out the window.

Twilight's muted shades of dusky violet, deep indigo, and black velvet washed across the horizon. Dusk was Keely's second favorite time of day.

The fog off the Thames crept closer and closer to the house. The heavy shroud of mist clung to the earth like a lover.

"What do you see?" Richard asked, reclining against the pillows on his bed.

"Beyond the horizon," Keely answered without thinking.

"What excellent eyesight you have." Laughter lurked in his voice.

"Seeing beyond the horizon requires *heart*, not eyesight."

"The Thames is probably impossible to see through the evening fog."

"I see dragon's breath, not fog," she replied.

"Where's the dragon?"

"Nearer than you think."

Keely turned away from the window and realized with a start that the earl had removed his shirt. Mesmerized by the fiery copper hair covering his chest, Keely wished she had the courage to march across the chamber and run her fingers through it. Would those strands of fire be hot to the touch?

"Do you like what you see?" Richard asked in a husky voice.

His question startled Keely. Her gaze flew to his, while her cheeks pinkened into a becoming blush. Keely tried to think of a jaunty reply, but her mind remained humiliatingly blank.

"I really should be leaving," she said.

Richard nodded but fixed a pitiful expression onto his face and asked, "Before you leave, could you rub a little more oil into my ankles?"

Keely hesitated for a fraction of a second, then gifted him with a beguiling smile and returned to sit on the bed. She poured a bit of oil into her hand and began massaging his right ankle.

"Sunset is my favorite time of day," Richard said conversationally.

Keely looked at him in surprise. "Sunrise is mine. Dawn fills my heart with hope."

"Are you awake that early?"

Keely nodded. "I love to greet the dawn."

"Do you know that every sunset is different?"

"As is every sunrise."

Sitting so close that their bodies were merely a hairbreadth apart, Richard gazed at her upturned face. "Your eyes are the most startling shade of violet," he told her. "A man could lose himself in their mysterious depths."

Keely blushed and dropped her gaze. "Thank you for the flowers."

Richard gently tilted her chin up and waited until she raised her gaze to his. "You do remind me of a princess," he whispered.

Keely stared at him unwaveringly as his face slowly inched its way to hers. The sight of his sensual lips descending to claim hers made her heart flutter with anticipation.

Her eyes closed. Their lips met. His mouth felt warm and gently insistent on hers.

"So sweet," he murmured, his breath mingling with hers.

The intoxicating feel of his mouth and the husky sound of his voice made Keely melt. Strong arms encircled and drew her against the solidness of his body as her arms entwined his neck.

Keely reveled in these new and exciting feelings and returned his kiss in kind.

Encouraged by her ardent response, Richard deepened the kiss. His tongue flicked across her lips, which parted for him like a flower blossoming in the heat of the sun. In an instant, his tongue invaded the sweetness of her mouth—probing, exploring, tasting.

Keely shivered in his embrace as she surrendered to his masterful possession. Losing herself in his drugging kiss, she stroked his tongue with her own.

Ever so gently, Richard pulled her down on the bed. His lips left hers and rained feathery light kisses on her temples, eyelids, and throat. When his mouth returned to hers, his kiss was all-consuming.

Swept away on wings of unfamiliar yearning, Keely never felt him pushing her blouse and chemise down, baring her pink-tipped breasts to his heated gaze. Richard flicked his tongue lightly across one of her nipples and suckled gently, igniting the essence of her womanhood into a blazing inferno, sending flames of molten sensation coursing through her body.

Keely burned with white-hot desire. As if from a distance, she heard a woman's moan of pleasure. *Her own.* Beyond reason, she molded her young body to his. . . .

As Keely succumbed to the earl's seduction, the Countess of Cheshire donned her cloak and left Talbot House. She strolled leisurely down the path to the stables, but before she reached the stableyard, she began to run.

"Tally, where are you?" Lady Dawn called.

"Here!" The voice sounded from inside one of the stables.

Lady Dawn rushed inside. Duke Robert, Odo, and Hew were inspecting the hooves of one of his horses. This was even better than she had planned.

"I found this in Keely's chamber," the countess said, waving a piece of parchment in the air. "You'll be interested in reading it."

"Later, Chessy," the duke snapped without looking up. "Can't you see I'm busy?"

The countess curled her lip at his back. "'Tis important."

"I'm listening. Read it."

"Very well," Lady Dawn said sweetly. She opened the parchment and began in a sultry voice, "'My dearest beauty.'"

The three men stopped what they were doing and looked at her.

Pleased that she had an attentive audience, the countess read with feeling: "'Losing my temper was unforgivable, but can you fault me for wanting you in my bed forever? What we shared the other day was paradise. Come to me, my darling. I long to feel your silken—'"

"Where is she?" the duke demanded.

Lady Dawn fixed a frightened expression on her face.

"V-v-visiting the earl."

Duke Robert dashed out of the stable, with Odo and Hew hard on his heels. A smile of satisfaction appeared on Lady Dawn's face, and then she hurried after them. She wouldn't miss this for all the diamonds in England.

"You can't go up there," Jennings insisted, blocking the stairway as the three gigantic men tried to rush past him.

As if he were no bigger than a gnat, Duke Robert lifted the man and tossed him across the foyer. With the duke in the lead, the avenging horde of three flew up the stairs.

"Devereux!" Duke Robert shouted, barging into the earl's bedchamber.

"No!" Keely cried as her father and cousins crashed into the room.

Richard leaped off the bed and protectively blocked her from view, giving Keely a chance to cover her bared breasts. Though courageous by nature, Richard possessed a healthy instinct for survival, which made him step back a pace. He'd expected only the duke to discover him in this untenable position. Was three-against-one Cheshire's idea of a joke?

The angry intruders advanced on Richard. Three fists aimed for his handsome face. Duke Robert's fist reached it first, hitting the earl's right cheekbone, sending him whirling to the left. Odo's fist met the earl's left cheekbone there, and Richard whirled back to the right. Hew's fist caught his face dead center, sending him sprawling to the floor.

"*Richard!*" Keely dropped to her knees beside him. She gently cradled his head against her chest and glared at her rescuers. "I'll never forgive you for hurting him."

Too dazed to move, Richard grinned stupidly at her and murmured, "Hello, Beauty."

"Prepare yourself for a wedding, Devereux," Duke Robert growled. "I'll be speaking with the queen in the morning."

"I can't marry him!" Keely cried.

"You'll marry Devereux," her father threatened, "or I'll be forced to kill him."

The Countess of Cheshire arrived at that moment. She wrapped her cloak around Keely's shoulders and helped her rise.

Duke Robert lifted his future son-in-law to his feet and warned, "Report to the queen in the morning, or I'll brave the Tower by shackling and dragging you to the altar." With that, the duke gestured to the countess and the Welshmen, then followed them out of the room.

"Please, I don't want to marry," Keely pleaded as the countess led her down the corridor to the stairs. She looked back to see Richard following them. Even in the corridor's dim light, his face appeared battered, but his step was spritely.

No limp, registered in Keely's mind. *Nothing wrong with his blasted ankle.*

A defeated sob escaped Keely. The earl had purposely stolen her virtue in order to force her to the altar. If only her father and her cousins hadn't discovered her in that untenable position, she could have denied losing her innocence. Oh, why had the Mother Goddess forsaken her? Would she ever find happiness or a place where she could belong? Or would she always be an outsider?

"If Devereux doesn't make you happy," Duke Robert

promised in a poor attempt to offer comfort, "I'll cut his heart out with a dull blade."

His words brought tears to Keely's eyes. She didn't want a husband who made her unhappy. Nor, for some strange reason, did she want Richard hurt for ruining her life.

"Devereux is richer than the pope," the countess told her, offering her own special brand of comfort as they started down the stairs. "Consider the jewels and the gowns that will be yours."

"I don't want jewels and gowns," Keely sobbed.

"Swallow your tongue," the countess snapped. "What is it you want?"

"I want only love."

The heart-wrenching sound of her sobs drifted to the top of the stairs where Richard stood. He smiled in spite of the pain it caused his swelling face. He wanted the exotic beauty in his bed and a tour of duty in Ireland. The Duke of Ludlow was about to gift him with what he desired.

"Jennings, I need you!" Richard shouted, holding the palms of his hands to his throbbing face.

"Coming, my lord," the majordomo called. "As soon as I lift myself off the floor."

Chapter 7

Autumn wore its most serene expression early the following morning. Clear blue skies kissed the distant horizon, and gentle breezes caressed the land, promising an incomparable day of rare perfection.

Oblivious to the paradise around her, Keely worried her full bottom lip with her teeth as she sat between Duke Robert and Lady Dawn. Their canopied barge wended its way down the Thames River toward Hampton Court, situated twelve miles southwest of London.

Keely would have enjoyed her first excursion on the river, but nervous apprehension blinded her to the idyllic passing scenery. She could hardly believe she was floating down the Thames to meet the English queen and beg permission to wed the conniving earl.

Richard Devereux was the last man in the world Keely would choose for a husband. His handsome face and courtly manner did attract her, but he was too arrogant, too smooth, and much too English for her peace of mind.

Keely would refuse to become trapped in a loveless marriage. She'd already suffered a near loveless childhood. There had to be a way to prevent this fiasco. How could she survive in the land of her enemy if she were married to a man who didn't love her?

"Accompanying you to court is unnecessary," Keely ventured in a small voice, glancing sidelong at her father, "as is marriage with the earl."

"I told you several times, the queen may wish to meet you before agreeing to the union," Duke Robert replied, clearly irritated. "My mind is set. I will debate the point no further."

Oh, why wouldn't he listen to reason? Keely thought, aggravated. She'd always yearned for a father but had never realized how overbearing one could be.

"You absented yourself from my life for eighteen years," Keely reminded him in an accusing voice. "How do you dare drop into it now and order me about?"

"*You* dropped into his life," Lady Dawn defended the duke. "English children obey their parents."

"I'm Welsh," Keely snapped.

"'Tis enough," Duke Robert ordered, his voice rising with his annoyance. To Keely, he added, "Your cousins agree with my decision."

"I apologize to both of you," Keely said, hanging her head in shame. "Fear incites me to disrespect and unkindness."

"There's naught to fear," the countess assured her, reaching out to pat her hand.

Duke Robert put an arm around his daughter and drew her protectively close. "Chessy will explain all that a bride needs to know so you needn't be nervous."

"I don't belong here," Keely cried, looking at him through eyes brimming with tears. "Everyone will laugh at me. The earl will grow to hate me. I'm nobody."

"Marrying the Earl of Basildon will gain you instant acceptance," Lady Dawn told her. "Why, the most popular courtiers will be seeking your company."

"Here we are," Duke Robert said as their barge stopped beside the quay.

Keely looked up. On what seemed like acres of manicured lawns stood Hampton Court, with its endless roofline of turrets, pinnacles, and chimney stacks. Trees, hedges, and shrubs grew as far as the eye could see.

"This has more the appearance of heaven than an earthly residence," Keely murmured, awed by the spectacular sight.

Duke Robert chuckled. "Old King Henry loved to impress. Hampton Court is his monument to himself."

The palace was a beehive of activity. Horses clattered

continuously through the courtyard. Tradesmen with carts of foodstuffs, purveyors of finery and jewelry, and noblemen with their families arrived and departed with hope in their eyes or disappointment etched across their faces.

Keely stared in wide-eyed wonder at the perpetual movement swirling around her. Hampton Court was a city unto itself, and its constant motion was dizzying.

"No one lives comfortably here," Duke Robert admitted.

"The nobles come for power," Lady Dawn said.

"Or its illusion," the duke added.

Walking between them, Keely looked from her father to the countess. This is their world, she thought. Megan could never have belonged here. And neither did her daughter.

"People come to court for wealth," the countess told her.

"Or the promise of it," the duke qualified.

"They come for advancement and fame."

"And often leave in disgrace because of the notoriety they achieve."

Entering the palace proper, Duke Robert ushered his ladies through a maze of corridors and long galleries. Servants, dressed in blue livery, carried trays of food. A squadron of grooms, their arms laden with firewood, scurried to deliver their loads to the yeomen who waited to lay fires in the hearths.

As Duke Robert escorted Keely and Lady Dawn through the labyrinth of Hampton Court, highborn men and their ladies called out friendly greetings to them and paused to stare at the young beauty who accompanied the duke and the countess. The courtiers' curiosity about her identity was apparent in their expression.

Fascinated by the noblemen and their ladies, Keely returned their stares. The women wore stiffened farthingales beneath their daringly low-cut gowns, and as many jewels as they could put upon their person. The men wore tight, knee-length breeches and brocaded doublets trimmed with lace and buttoned with jewels. Bright silk stockings, garters fringed with gold spangles, and leather shoes adorned with stylish rosettes accessorized their outfits. Some men even wore earrings and rouged their cheeks.

"I feel conspicuously out of place," Keely whispered, feeling like a sparrow set down in a cage of peacocks.

"Don't fret, darling. Natural beauty like yours startles their artificiality," the countess said, smiling and nodding at a group of passersby.

When they finally stood outside the audience chamber, Keely began wringing her hands in anxiety and asked, "What will we do now?"

"Relax," the countess suggested.

"And wait," the duke said.

Long silent moments passed. Keely glanced down the corridor and saw two men, dressed completely in black, advancing on them. In their somber attire, they looked as out of place as she felt. It was as if two hawks had invaded an aviary of canaries.

Keely realized with a start that the taller of the men was Richard Devereux, his two blackened eyes matching the bleak color of his clothing. Though she refused to forgive him for tricking her, the sight of his battered face made her wince inwardly. She wasn't worth what he'd suffered. Her fingers itched to touch his bruises and vanquish his pain with her magic.

As the two men neared, Keely dropped her embarrassed gaze to the floor. That she knew of their presence became apparent in the telling blush that pinkened her cheeks.

"Good morning, Your Grace," Richard greeted them.

"Basildon." Duke Robert nodded. "Burghley."

"My dear countess," Richard said, bowing over Lady Dawn's hand. He turned then to Keely, kissed her hand, and smiled, saying, "Rising early enhances your beauty, dearest."

Richard turned to his middle-aged companion and said without any trace of shame, "Lord Burghley, I present Lady Keely Glendower, Ludlow's natural daughter and, I hope, my intended wife."

The earl felt no shame about her bastardy, but Keely did. She lowered her gaze in embarrassment and dropped the lord a curtsy.

"Good morning, young lady," Burghley said, giving her an appraising stare. As if satisfied by what met his perceptive gaze, Burghley turned away and nodded at the guards in front of the audience room, then entered the chamber and left the four of them standing in silence to await the queen's pleasure.

Uncomfortably, Keely felt the earl's gaze on her. She leaned against the wall, closed her eyes, and implored the Mother Goddess to aid in the earl's recovery. Her lips moved with the silent chant.

"Are you praying the queen will refuse my suit?" Richard asked.

Keely opened her eyes and said, "My lord, I do pray for your health."

That admission brought a smile to Richard's lips. "You look especially lovely today. The pink of your gown enhances the maidenly blush on your cheeks."

Before Keely could respond, the audience chamber's door opened. Lord Burghley beckoned Duke Robert and Richard inside, leaving Lady Dawn and Keely waiting in the corridor.

"Relax, darling," the countess said. "You're the perfect mate for Devereux."

"Why do you say that?"

"Marrying you will give him the three things he desires most: you, a blood bond with your father, and a tour of duty in Ireland."

"What have I to do with Ireland?" Keely asked.

"Devereux has been forbidden to serve abroad until he sires an heir," the countess told her.

That information didn't sit well with Keely. Being used

to get a son smacked of Madoc Lloyd killing her mother with myriad miscarriages.

"The earl is a handsome man," Keely said. "Dozens of women would gladly marry him and produce his requisite heir."

"Those dozens of women are not you."

Keely made no reply. The countess was kindhearted but illogical. Beyond her physical body, a penniless bastard had nothing to offer England's premier earl.

"Here comes trouble," Lady Dawn announced.

Keely glanced down the corridor. Two young women were hurrying toward them.

"Lady Jane is married but desires bedsport with the earl," the countess whispered in Keely's ear. "Lady Sarah, the blonde, is angling to get Devereux to the altar."

The two fashionably dressed ladies greeted the countess deferentially. Both women spared a curious peek at Keely.

"We thought we saw Burghley and Basildon headed in this direction," Lady Jane said.

"Have you seen them?" Lady Sarah asked. "We have something important to discuss with the earl."

"I'm sure you do," Lady Dawn purred, "but both men attend the queen. Even now, the earl is requesting the Duke of Ludlow's daughter in marriage."

Lady Jane could not have cared less, but Lady Sarah was unable to hide her disappointment. "How lucky Morgana is," she said forlornly.

"Not Morgana, darlings. The earl desires a union with the duke's other daughter," the countess told them, enjoying herself immensely. "Allow me to present Lady Keely Glendower, the Duke of Ludlow's oldest and prettiest daughter."

Humiliated but proud, Keely managed a faint smile. She could read in their shocked expressions what they were thinking: *a bastard.*

"Congratulations," Lady Sarah said.

"My very best," Lady Jane added, appraising her newest rival's charms.

Without another word, the two young women turned and walked away. They wanted to be the ones to spread the news that England's most eligible bachelor was marrying a ducal bastard.

"A bit of advice, darling," Lady Dawn said, watching the women leave. "At court, friends come and go, but enemies tend to accumulate. Trust no one but your husband and your family."

While the countess was imparting her knowledge about life at court, tempers flared inside the royal audience chamber. Irritated with her enraged favorite duke, Queen Elizabeth frowned ferociously at him while Lord Burghley, her most trusted minister, simply shook his head in disgust at the whole sordid affair. Only Richard appeared relaxed and placid, though shockingly battered.

"Either Devereux marries her," Duke Robert ranted, "or I'll be forced to kill him."

"Spare Us your dramatics, Ludlow," the queen snapped. "More pressing problems than your bastard's tarnished reputation require Our attention."

At the royal reprimand, the Duke of Ludlow clamped his mouth shut.

"Basildon agrees to the match," Elizabeth continued, "but We want to see the chit first."

"Keely is waiting with Lady Dawn in the corridor," the duke said.

"And what has Cheshire to do with this nasty business?" the queen demanded.

Duke Robert flushed. "When Keely arrived, the countess happened to be visiting and offered to help me get her settled."

"How exceedingly kind of her," Elizabeth said dryly. "Tell Cheshire to attend Us also."

Duke Robert bowed and marched the length of the enormous chamber to the door, then beckoned them inside. Smiling, the Countess of Cheshire held her charge's trembling hand as they walked toward the queen. Keely, white with fright, and the countess swept deep curtsies when they reached the queen.

"Rise," Elizabeth bade them.

Keely looked up and became blinded by the queen's brilliance. Elizabeth's red-gold hair was the fiery color of the setting sun, and her sharp gray eyes resembled fine mist. She wore a bright yellow gown and a fortune in diamonds and pearls upon her person.

"She certainly has the look of you," Elizabeth remarked to the duke. To Keely, she said, "What have you to say in defense of yourself, child?"

Keely couldn't find her voice. How did a mere mortal converse with a goddess?

"Speak up," Elizabeth snapped.

The sharp command startled Keely. Her glorious violet eyes widened, and nervous tremors shook her whole body.

"I—I am honored to be in the presence of Your Majesty and regret this unnecessary annoyance to your peace," Keely said in a quavering voice. "I know you have important matters of state to ponder, and I apologize for wasting part of your valuable day."

"The chit may be a Welsh bastard," Elizabeth said to the duke, "but she's inherited your courtier's instincts." The queen looked at Keely and said, "Child, speak briefly and truthfully. Did my dear Midas compromise your virtue?"

"Your Majesty, I do freely admit that His Grace discovered his daughter and me in bed," Richard spoke up. "I am willing to wed her."

Too nervous in the queen's presence even to turn her head, Keely glanced sidelong at the earl. His bold words colored her complexion a vibrant scarlet. Stealing her innocence was bad enough, but how did he dare to announce their shame to the Queen of England?

"You randy, strutting cock!" Elizabeth shouted. "For

corrupting this innocent, I should make you shorter by a head."

Frightened, Keely opened her mouth to cry out, but Duke Robert was faster. He snaked his hand out and covered her mouth in a gesture to remain silent.

"I will spend the remainder of October at Nonsuch," the queen said. "Both of you will return to Hampton Court on the tenth day of November and be wed at the Royal Chapel. I want an end to this absurd business." She turned to the duke and asked, "What of your other daughter?"

"Morgana has a list of possible——"

"Marry the chit to anyone you want—excepting a Darnley cousin," the queen interrupted, rising from her throne.

Duke Robert dropped to one bended knee. "I have one final request," he said.

Elizabeth's gray gaze narrowed on him. "You're pressing your luck, Ludlow."

The duke's expression became even more determined. His violet gaze never wavered from hers.

"Well, get on with it," Elizabeth snapped. "What is it?"

"I beg permission to wed the Countess of Cheshire," Duke Robert said in a loud voice. "That is, as soon as Keely is settled."

"Cheshire's already nagged three husbands into the grave," Elizabeth replied, "but I care not if you wed the lowest scullery maid. This marriage foolishness gives me the headache." With those parting words, she stormed out of the chamber.

"Fornicating fools," Burghley muttered, leveling a disgusted look on the lot of them. He hurried after the queen.

"I will call upon you at Talbot House to negotiate the contract this afternoon," Richard told the duke. He smiled at Keely and kissed her hand, then quit the chamber.

Shock at what had transpired kept Keely's anger at bay and fixed her mind on the trivial. As they left the audience chamber, she asked the countess, "Why did the queen call the earl Midas?"

"'Tis her nickname for him," Lady Dawn answered.

"But what does it mean?"

"Midas was a legendary king whose touch turned everything to gold," Duke Robert explained. "So too does the earl possess the golden touch with his business ventures."

"Trust the king who wears the flaming crown and possesses the golden touch. . . ."

Megan's prophecy came rushing back to Keely, the significance of it nearly felling her. Had her mother seen the earl in her visions? Was he truly the man in whom she should place her trust? How could she ever be certain?

Swimming up from the depths of unconsciousness, Keely heard the voices as if they called to her from a great distance. Was she dreaming?

"She won't wake up," the first voice said.

"What should we do?" asked the second.

"Nudge her."

"But what if she's dead?" the second asked in a horrified whisper. Then: "Ouch! You needn't pinch me."

"She's not dead, you blockhead," the first voice said with authority. "Perhaps if both of us call her."

"Lady Keely," the women chimed in unison. *"Wake up!"*

Keely bolted up straight, startling the young women who cried out and leaped back a pace. Confused, Keely stared at their smiling faces and gazed at her surround-

"My lady?" whispered a woman's voice.

"Richard said her name is Keely," a second woman told the first.

"Lady Keely, time to awaken," the first called in a loud whisper. "Napping beneath an oak tree isn't at all the thing to do."

ings. She still sat on the grass beneath her favorite oak tree in her father's garden.

Keely rubbed her eyes and then looked at the women. Holy stones! Double images of the same woman stood in front of her. What was wrong with her vision? She looked at them again. *Twins.*

Dark-eyed brunettes, the women appeared to be a year or two younger than herself. The twins were mirror images, the only difference between them a tiny mole above one girl's upper lip.

"Who are you?" Keely asked.

"I'm May," the twin with the mole answered.

"And I'm June," the other said with a smile.

That told Keely nothing. Her gaze narrowed on them. "What are you doing here?" she asked.

May and June looked at each other and giggled.

"We're Richard's kinsmen," May told her.

"Kins*women*," June corrected her sister.

May gave June a censorious glare, then smiled at Keely and explained, "Richard—I mean, the earl—invited us to be your tiringwoman."

"*Women*," June corrected her sister again.

May reached out and slapped her sister's arm.

Keely burst out laughing. Their bickering reminded her of Odo and Hew, who always seemed to be arguing with each other.

"I do not require tiringwomen's services," Keely told them.

"We'll never advance in life if you don't," June whined in disappointment.

"Being chosen made us so happy," May said. "Our sister Spring—"

"Born on March the twenty-first," June interjected.

"—is Lady Brigette's tiringwoman," May finished.

"Who is Lady Brigette?" Keely asked.

"Richard's sister," the twins chorused together.

"Our sister April was Lady Heather's woman," June said.

"Lady Heather is also Richard's sister?" Keely asked.

"Yes," the twins chimed.

"We hoped to be yours," May said, wearing a down-cast expression.

Keely swallowed the laughter bubbling up inside her. Even by Welsh standards, these women were refreshingly candid. Leaning against the oak, Keely eyed them and remarked, "Four sisters named Spring, April, May, and June?"

"Mother named April for the month she was born," May told her.

"What about you?" Keely asked.

"Us too," June answered.

"But you're twins!" Keely exclaimed, making them giggle.

"I was born on the last day of May."

"And I was born on the first day of June."

Keely smiled at the delightfully bizarre sisters. "From where did you come?"

"Next door," they chorused.

Keely's smile became a chuckle. Their good humor and enthusiasm were contagious.

"Very well," Keely said. "You may be my tiringwomen."

The two sisters screamed with relieved delight, hugged each other, and jumped up and down with glee. Finally remembering themselves, they looked at their new mistress and smiled sheepishly.

"Forgive our happy outburst," June apologized.

"We'll be the best tiringwomen ever," May promised.

"*Women*," June corrected her.

"There she is," a masculine voice said.

May reached out and pinched her sister.

Keely looked across the garden and waved a greeting to Odo and Hew. "My cousins," she said to the twins, who stood gaping at the handsome giants advancing on them.

"We heard the happy news about your betrothal to the earl," Odo said, ignoring the two staring sisters.

"Why didn't you tell us yourself?" Hew asked, his hurt apparent in his voice.

Keely rose from the ground. She took a moment to brush the back of her gown with her hand, then leaned back against the oak and said, "I needed time alone to think."

"Why would you want to do that?" Hew asked, genuinely puzzled.

Odo cuffed the side of his brother's head. "You blinking idiot," he scolded. "The girl needed to ponder her forthcoming marriage."

May glared at Odo and then sidled up to Hew. She placed the palm of her hand against his head, asking solicitously, "Did he hurt you?"

Hew smiled, and there was no mistaking the gleam in his eyes when he answered, "I'll feel better if you stroke it gently."

Jealous of the attention being lavished upon his brother, Odo scowled darkly and then glanced at June, who smiled at him with adoration in her eyes. He returned her smile.

"You're very strong," she complimented him.

Odo grinned. He rolled his sleeve up and clenched his right hand, then held his fist against the side of his head and made the enormous muscle in his upper arm bounce up and down in a dance.

Keely and June clapped with enthusiasm.

Not to be outdone, Hew rolled his own sleeves up and made both of his upper arm muscles dance. All three women clapped their appreciation.

"I can touch my nose with the tip of my tongue," Odo bragged.

"I can wiggle my ears *and* touch my nose with the tip of my tongue," a voice behind them boasted. *"At the same time."*

Keely whirled around at the sound of that voice. With his hands resting on his hips, Richard stood there.

"Show Odo and Hew around Devereux House," Richard bade May and June. "Introduce them to my staff."

At Keely's nod, Odo and Hew followed the twins down the path that led to the earl's estate. Watching them walk away, Keely said, "My cousins are warriors, not servants."

"From what I just witnessed," Richard countered, "they don't behave like any warrior I've ever seen."

Keely flicked him a sidelong glance. Much to her consternation, the earl leaned beside her against the tree.

"They bested you in Shropshire," she reminded him.

"I would have beaten Hew," the earl told her, "but 'twas two against one."

"A testament to your virility," Keely replied, then regretted her choice of words.

Richard leaned dangerously close, so close that she felt his warm breath on her cheek, and promised in a husky whisper, "In no more than a month, my lady, you'll feel the full weight of my virility."

Keely blushed from the top of her head to the tips of her toes, but she refused any other acknowledgment of his sensual threat. "Do not let my cousins' lack of intelligence fool you, my lord," she warned. "Odo and Hew could get to the pope and live to tell the story. My cousins are near invincible as long as they understand and follow the orders of others."

"Mayhap they'll pledge themselves to me after we're wed," Richard replied. "I can always use a few more good men."

Keely arched an ebony brow at him in a perfect imitation of his irritating habit and said, "Odo and Hew are forsworn to me."

"Women in England do not keep men-at-arms," he informed her.

"I'll start a new fashion," she teased, giving him an

unconsciously flirtatious look. "'Tis no more unusual than the startling sight of men who rouge their cheeks."

Richard chuckled. "Would you care to see my muscles dance?"

Keely struggled against a smile but lost. She leaned back against the oak and gazed at him, marveling at how incredibly handsome he was—and how deceitful.

Steeling herself against the powerful urge to fling herself into his arms and press her lips to his, Keely asked with a tinge of censure in her voice, "And how are your injured ankles today? Dare we hope for a miraculous overnight recovery?"

Richard cast her a wicked devastating grin and then leaned close, so close his lips were only inches from hers. In a husky voice, he said, "I'm sorry, sweetheart. I yearned to be in your company again, but I couldn't control myself once you sat beside me on the bed. I had no idea your father would burst into my chamber. Forgive me?"

Keely sighed and glanced away. What else could she do but forgive him? The die was cast, and for better or for worse she would become his wife on the tenth day of November. Without bothering to look at him, she nodded once in acceptance of his apology.

"Then let's seal your forgiveness with a kiss," he suggested.

Keely snapped her gaze back to his. "Stealing my virtue does not give you leave to enjoy liberties with my person," she said tartly.

Stealing her virtue? Richard thought in disbelief as he stared down at her determined expression—an exquisitely beautiful, determined expression. Did she actually believe that what they had done on his bed amounted to a loss of virtue? Oh, what an innocent minx she was turning out to be!

"As I told my cousins," Keely said, "I came to sit beneath this oak and enjoy some peace. Then the world descended on me."

"Sit?" Richard teased. "You were kissing this tree the other day. By the way, you never did tell me. What was that game you and your cousins played?"

Keely blushed with surprised embarrassment. How much had he witnessed that day? Apparently, enough to make him wonder. What would the earl do when he discovered he'd married a Druid?

"Will you kiss my oak and bring us luck?" Richard asked, his green eyes lit with amusement.

"That sounds lascivious. Besides, only earls may kiss the oak tree today."

"I'd rather kiss you."

"I'd rather you didn't." Keely held him off with her hand. Then, "I have no need for a tiringwoman. Why, for the love of God, did you send me two?"

"The Countess of Basildon does need a tiringwoman," Richard told her. "Besides, I'm fond of both May and June. I couldn't ask the one without hurting the other. Thus, for the sake of familial peace, you'll make do with two."

Keely nodded, admiring his loyalty to his family, but her expression grew somber. With worry etched across her delicate features, she warned, "You've made a tragic mistake, my lord. A marriage between us will be disastrous."

"Why do you say that?" Richard asked.

"Because I believe it," Keely said, her violet-eyed gaze pleading for his understanding. "In case you hadn't noticed, I'm different from Ladies Jane and Sarah and all those other women."

"I noticed." Richard planted his hands on either side of her head as she pressed her back against the oak tree. Leaning close, he added, "I don't desire those other women, else I would have married one of them."

His nearness and his clean masculine scent assaulted her senses. Keely felt him with every tingling fiber of her body and was quite certain he could hear the frantic pounding of her heart.

Holy stones! she thought. How could she live the remainder of her life with this agitation? She'd be dead within a week.

"I—I have secrets," Keely tried to discourage him. "I cannot share them."

"Dark secrets?" he teased, tracing a finger down the length of her silken cheek. "Beauty, your heart is pure and as easy to read as an open book. Besides, I'm partial to ebony hair and violet eyes."

"Then marry His Grace," she replied, frustrated by his lack of caution. Oh, why would he not heed her warning? An experienced man of the world, the earl should know that appearances could be deceptive.

A sudden unfamiliar pang that Keely failed to recognize as jealousy shot through her. She narrowed her gaze on him and asked, "To what were you partial before ebony hair and violet eyes?"

Richard gave her a lazy smile. "Blondes, brunettes, and redheads."

"'Tis just as I suspected," Keely said. "You, my high-and-mighty lord, are partial to getting your own way."

Richard frowned at the censure in her voice.

"Are you in pain?" she asked, alarmed. "I know how to alleviate it."

Though he'd never traveled that road before, sympathy was an alternate route to a female's heart. "'Tis throbbing a bit," he lied.

"Close your eyes." Keely stepped perilously close and placed the palms of her hands against his temples. Trying to garner the needed concentration, she closed her own eyes, and her lips moved in a silent chant.

Without warning, Richard's mouth covered hers. His arms circled her body and yanked her against the hard muscular planes of his own.

Keely's senses reeled. Instinctively, she entwined her arms around his neck and surrendered to his warm insistent lips.

And then it was over as quickly and unexpectedly as it

had begun. Keely opened her eyes and saw his arrogant smile of satisfaction.

"I specifically told you I'd rather not kiss," she said, embarrassed by her easy capitulation to his sensual onslaught.

Richard grinned knowingly. "'Tis your own fault, sweetheart. You're too damned irresistible."

"Well, I'll forgive you this time." Keely knew that he knew she hadn't protested overmuch.

"Would you escort me to your father?" Richard asked.

Keely looked from his emerald gaze to his offered hand. She had the feeling his question was symbolic, somehow more significant than his casual voice implied. The earl was asking something more of her, something she felt powerless to refuse him.

Keely placed her hand in his. His fingers closed around it, trapping her in a pleasurable captivity. Hand in hand, they strolled in silence across the lawn to Talbot House.

"I believe His Grace awaits you in the study," Keely said when they entered the main foyer.

Richard smiled and kissed her hand, saying, "Until this evening, my beauty." He started down the corridor, but her voice stopped him.

"My lord?"

Richard turned around.

Keely gave him a mischievous smile. "Can you really wiggle your ears and touch your nose with your tongue?"

"Among other things." Richard winked at her. "I'll perform for you on our wedding night."

Hours later, Keely stood in front of the pier glass in her father's bedchamber and studied her reflection. A woman's betrothal was one of life's milestones, and though Keely felt she was stepping down the road to disaster, she wanted to look her best for the earl on this momentous occasion.

Her gown, created in violet velvet that matched her eyes, had a low-cut square neckline and a tight-fitting bodice. Around her neck glittered her mother's legacy to her, the jeweled dragon pendant. Making an unspoken statement about her pride in her Welsh heritage, Keely had brushed her ebony hair until it crackled and then let it cascade in pagan fashion to her waist.

Keely turned away from the pier glass but delayed leaving the chamber. Nervous and excited, she dreaded the actual moment when she would sign her life and her well-being into the earl's keeping. She closed her eyes and took several deep breaths, but the image of the earl's devastating smile flitted across her mind's eye.

In her secret heart, Keely knew she would ultimately succumb to his charm. She only hoped she wouldn't be too hurt when he became disenchanted with the outsider he'd married in a fleeting moment of foolishness.

Who am I trying to deceive? Keely scolded herself. Already infatuated with him, she'd be crushed when his affections wandered to those sophisticated women at court.

"Trust the king who wears the fiery crown and possesses the golden touch. . . ."

Had Megan seen Richard in her vision? Keely wondered for the hundredth time since leaving him in the foyer. Had her mother meant she'd find acceptance and happiness with him? Did he possess the strength of character to ignore the whispered murmurings of *bastard* when the queen's courtiers learned of her questionable background?

Keely walked into the great hall and stopped short. Holy stones! A hundred ducal retainers and men-at-arms lingered there, awaiting her arrival. Betrothals, like weddings and christenings, were joyous occasions; catching a glimpse of the happy event appeared to be foremost on everyone's agenda that evening.

Across the hall, Richard and Duke Robert sat in the two chairs in front of the hearth. With their backs turned to the hall's entrance, they were unaware of Keely's arrival. The countess perched on the arm of His Grace's chair.

Turning her head as the hall's occupants quieted, Lady Dawn spied Keely and smiled, saying, "Here she is."

Richard rose from his chair and turned around. His emerald-eyed gaze wandered appreciatively over her curvaceously petite form.

Keely felt like swooning as his smoldering gaze fixed on hers and then dropped to peruse her body. A high blush stained her cheeks. The earl was undressing her with his eyes! His gaze never wavering from hers, Richard sauntered across the hall. He lifted her hands to his lips and whispered in a husky voice, "You look good enough to eat."

Keely stared at him blankly.

"I'll explain what that means after the wedding," Richard said with a smile, then escorted her across the hall to her father and the countess.

Duke Robert rose from his chair and kissed her cheek. "You are breathtakingly beautiful, my dear," he complimented her.

"Good enough to eat?" Keely asked in innocence.

"'Tis what the earl said."

Duke Robert coughed and glanced at Richard, who had the good grace to flush. Lady Dawn chuckled throatily.

"The contract only needs our signatures," Duke Robert said as he led them to the table. He signed first and passed the quill to the earl, who signed with an exaggerated flourish. Keely took the quill from his hand but hesitated.

"Do you mind if I glance at it first?" she asked. Richard inclined his head and said, "Be my guest, sweeting."

Keely perused the document quickly. Though she could read the individual words, the meaning of all those legal terms was lost on her. "I—I would like something added," she said. "Would that be possible?"

Richard cast her a puzzled smile.

Duke Robert, unused to less-than-obedient females,

explained in a slightly irritated tone of voice, "The document is already drawn, child. We cannot—"

" 'Tis such a minor thing," Keely persisted. "We could squeeze it in here at the bottom."

"What would you like, dearest?" Richard asked.

"I want this document to stipulate that Odo and Hew are forever free of the hangman."

Richard cocked a copper brow at her. "Your cousins cannot possibly enjoy immunity for uncommitted crimes. I am agreeable for past deeds only."

Keely nodded. " 'Tis fair."

Richard made the necessary addition to the agreement and initialed it so there would be no chance of misunderstanding in the future. He handed the quill back to her. Instead of signing, she twirled the quill in her hands and worried her bottom lip with her teeth.

"Sign the agreement, dearest," Richard prodded.

Keely cast him an apologetic smile and then turned to the duke, saying, "Your Grace, may I have a private moment with you?" She flicked the earl a glance and added, "I promise I'll sign the document afterward."

Duke Robert and Keely walked five paces away. Standing on tiptoes, Keely whispered into his ear but kept her gaze fixed on the earl.

Watching them, Richard felt certain she was stalling. Even if he had to grab her hand and force her, the little minx would sign the betrothal contract before she left the hall.

Suddenly, Duke Robert's face split into a broad grin. He nodded once and escorted his daughter back to the earl.

"Devereux, my daughter has called my attention to something we men would consider insignificant," Duke Robert said. "Yet 'tis an important matter to every prospective bride."

"What might that be?" Richard asked, suspicious.

Duke Robert cleared his throat and struggled to keep

from laughing. "Keely believes you haven't properly proposed marriage to her. She'd like you to do so now—with *sincere* emotion."

"'Tis an oversight easily attended," Richard looked at Keely. "Come, my lady. Let us sit in front of the hearth."

Turning to guide her across the hall, Richard realized with a start that a hundred pairs of curious eyes watched their every step. Never in his wildest imaginings had he ever thought he'd be proposing marriage to a beautiful but eccentric half-Welsh woman for the pleasurable edification of an audience of ducal servants. And what the bloody hell could he do about it? Nothing!

Richard cast a sidelong glance at Keely. She appeared to be enjoying her moment of glory. Let her have her way in this, he decided. After they'd spoken their vows, all moments of glory would belong to him.

Keely sat in one of the chairs in front of the hearth and artfully arranged her skirt, then looked expectantly at him. Deeming she was ready, Richard knelt on one bended knee and smiled to hear the many female sighs elicited by the picture they presented.

Clasping her hands in his, Richard grinned broadly. "I ought to box your ears," he whispered through clenched teeth.

Keely's violet eyes widened at the threat. She couldn't quite control the horrified giggle bubbling up.

"If you dare laugh," Richard threatened, "I'll take you across my knee and give you the spanking you so richly deserve for putting me through this."

Keely instantly regained her composure.

"Lady Keely, a few rare people like yourself have elusive greatness thrust upon their shoulders like a mantle," Richard said in a strong voice that carried to the far corners of the hall. "Dearest lady, will you do me the honor of becoming my wife and my countess?"

Resounding applause erupted inside the hall.

Keely's own moment of embarrassment had arrived.

Unable to find her voice, she nodded her head in acceptance.

"Speak the words, dearest," Richard ordered. "These people await your answer."

"I will," Keely said in a voice as soft as a whisper.

"Louder."

"I will!"

Another round of applause erupted in the hall.

Ignoring their audience, Richard arose and offered her his hand, but when she stood, he yanked her into the circle of his embrace. His lips swooped down and captured hers in a long, slow, soul-stealing kiss.

The Talbot men-at-arms and retainers went wild, cheering and applauding and whistling their approval.

Richard gazed with budding love at her dazed expression and said, "'Tis time to sign the agreement."

Keely affixed her name to the document and then glanced at the earl. For better or for worse, she would become his wife.

Richard withdrew something from his pocket and held it up. "Your betrothal ring, beauty."

Keely gasped at what she saw. The exquisite ring was a gold band adorned with a row of eight priceless gems.

"What a beautiful trinket," Lady Dawn gushed.

"Well done, Devereux," Duke Robert said in approval. Richard had eyes only for Keely. "'Tis symbolic," he explained. "The jewels spell the word *dearest: d*iamond, *e*merald, *a*methyst, *r*uby, *e*merald, *s*apphire, and *t*opaz."

Taking her left hand in his, Richard slipped the ring onto her third finger and said, *"Por tous jours."*

"What does it mean?" she asked.

Richard cupped her chin in his hand. "For always."

Without forethought, Keely placed the palm of her hand against his cheek. She surprised him even more by planting a chaste kiss on his lips.

"Will you walk with me to the door?" he asked.

"You're leaving?"

"I regret I must attend the queen," Richard told her.

"I leave within the hour and will be gone for two weeks."

"Two whole weeks?" Keely cried.

Richard smiled. "Thank you, dearest."

"For what?"

"For that incredibly disappointed expression. Knowing you'll miss me cheers my heart."

"I won't miss you," Keely lied.

"Yes, you will. And you'll long to feel my lips cover yours. Like this——" Richard kissed her soundly, leaving her yearning for more.

Chapter 8

She missed him and longed to feel his lips cover hers.

Two weeks passed excruciatingly slowly for Keely. On the fourteenth day after Richard's departure, she sat on a stone bench in the duke's garden.

All around her, autumn was rapidly ripening. Though the afternoon sparkled with blinding sunshine, the wind's crisp bite foretold of the season's passing.

Keely pulled her cloak close around her shoulders and stared in the direction of Devereux House. Would the earl return home that day as promised? Or would her watching be in vain? What was he doing at that precise moment? Whom had he seen at court, and to whom had he spoken?

Those questions and a hundred others tormented Keely and stole her peace of mind. Nervous anticipation fluttered like butterflies' wings inside the pit of her stomach, and the thought of Richard sauntering across the lawns toward her fanned the embers of desire that had lain dormant since his departure.

When that insidious monster called insecurity reared its frightening head, Keely wondered in a near panic if the earl might already be regretting his betrothal to her. She looked at her betrothal ring with its row of precious jewels, and the sight of it cheered her flagging spirits.

"Por tous jours," he'd said. "For always."

Keely closed her eyes and tried to recapture his passionate kiss. It was no use. Reliving the past, however recent, was impossible. A world of difference lay between remembering the kiss and actually feeling his warm lips pressed to hers.

Still, Keely kept her eyes closed and contented herself

by conjuring the earl's handsome image. By now, his bruises would be healing, and—

"Hello, darling!" the Countess of Cheshire called from across the lawns.

Keely opened her eyes and stared in surprised dismay at the four people advancing toward her. Along with Duke Robert and Lady Dawn walked the blond-haired angel from Ludlow Castle, her half-sister, and an adolescent boy, probably her half-brother. Steeling herself against the expression of hatred on the blonde's face, Keely rose from the bench and waited for them to approach.

"Henry and Morgana, this is your sister Keely," Duke Robert announced. "Keely, here are your brother and your sister."

Because he'd done her an act of kindness by sending that message to her, Keely first turned to fifteen-year-old Henry, who'd inherited his father's ebony hair and had his sister's blue eyes. When he grinned at her, Keely returned his smile.

"I'm pleased to make your acquaintance," Henry said.

"My feelings mirror yours," she replied.

Unable to delay the inevitable, Keely turned to the glaring blue-eyed angel who'd had her thrown out of Ludlow Castle. "I've always wished for a sister," she said with a tentative smile. "I do hope we can be friends."

"Sneaky slut," the angel hissed, the vehemence in her voice forcing Keely to step back a pace.

"Mind your tongue, Morgana," Duke Robert warned, "or I'll banish you to your chamber."

"I refuse to share my home with your bastard," Morgana told him. "Get rid of her."

And so it begins, Keely thought as humiliation stained her cheeks. *Bastard* echoed through her mind. It appeared that the earl would be forced to face his folly sooner than she'd expected.

"I shan't hesitate to send you back to Shropshire," the duke threatened his daughter. "I'd suffer no qualms about locking you up until you're too old to wed."

"She's stolen my gown!" Morgana cried, stamping her foot.

"I apologize for borrowing your clothing," Keely said. "His Grace and the countess insisted I wear them. I'll change immediately and return it to you."

"Do you actually think I'd wear it now that you've touched it?" Morgana asked, her voice filled with contempt.

"Your sister is here to stay," Duke Robert said. "Guard your viper's tongue, and practice those genteel manners that I paid Ashemole to teach you."

"Give over, Morgana," the countess drawled, intent on using the girl's own petty outrage against her. "Keely will be leaving us in less than a month."

"I eagerly look forward to the day," Morgana shot back. "And of course, to your own departure as well."

Duke Robert reached out to give his shrewish daughter a well-deserved shake, but the Countess of Cheshire stayed his hand. She smiled at the girl and went in for the kill, purring, "Our dear Keely has managed to capture the Earl of Basildon's eye. Devereux and she will be married next month at Hampton Court. 'Twill be the marriage of the decade."

"You've stolen my intended?" Morgana shrieked.

"Your intended?" Keely echoed, shocked. She looked at the duke for confirmation, but he was busy frowning at the countess.

"Conniving bastard!" Morgana screamed. With her bejeweled hand, she lashed out at Keely and slapped her hard.

The force of the blow sent Keely reeling backward. She landed on the ground beside the stone bench.

When the other three rushed to her aid, Keely turned her head away and whispered, "I'm fine."

"Your lip is bleeding," Henry told her, offering his handkerchief.

Keely glanced sidelong at the linen and then at him.

"'Tis clean," he assured her. "I haven't used it."

That remark brought a tremulous smile to Keely's lips. She accepted his handkerchief and pressed it against her mouth.

"Shall I help you up?" Henry asked.

Keely shook her head and without turning around said, "I'm very sorry, Lady Morgana. I never intended to cause you pain." That Richard had courted her sister hurt Keely more than her bleeding lip.

"Keely did nothing wrong," Lady Dawn said. "'Twas the earl who demanded the match. Devereux adores her, probably because of her *gentle manner*."

"I cannot believe this is happening," Lady Morgana whined, tears welling up in her eyes.

"Go to your chamber," Duke Robert ordered. "Do not dare show your face until supper, or I'll take a belt to your backside."

"You're siding with *her?*" Morgana wailed. "She's poisoned my own *father* against me?"

"Do as I say." The duke's stern voice held a final note of warning that the irate girl failed to heed.

"I suppose the bastard couldn't wait to tell you how I had her thrown out of Ludlow," Morgana sneered.

"You threw her out of Ludlow?" Duke Robert roared, his face mottling with rage.

Realizing her mistake, Morgana stammered, "I—I d-didn't think you'd want to be bothered with one of your by-blows."

Without warning, Duke Robert slapped his daughter. He grabbed her upper arm and dragged her toward the mansion. Morgana's loud pleadings for mercy could still be heard after she disappeared from sight.

Henry chuckled, tickled that his sister had entrapped herself. The Countess of Cheshire cast him a feline smile and then headed back to the house.

But Keely wasn't smiling. She leaned forlornly against the bench as tears brimmed over her eyes and rolled down her cheeks.

"Are you certain you're uninjured?" Henry asked, helping her to rise. He sat beside her on the bench.

Wallowing in misery, Keely stared straight ahead. She struggled to maintain her composure but failed. A heart-wrenching sob escaped her throat. And then another. Finally, she hid her face in her hands and surrendered to her tears.

"Would you care to use my shoulder?" Henry asked, uncertain of what to do.

His chivalrous offer caught Keely by surprise. She stopped weeping abruptly, cast him a sidelong glance, and tried to smile. "I'm *very* happy that you're my brother," she said, then hiccoughed. "Thank you for the message you sent me."

Henry grinned. "'Twas nothing. Besides, foiling Morgana's plans brings me so much pleasure."

"Is my lip still bleeding?"

Henry slid closer and inspected her lip, then nodded and ordered, "Press the linen down hard."

Keely did as he instructed.

"So tell me, sister," Henry asked with a wicked gleam in his eyes, "how did you ever trap the elusive Earl of Basildon?"

"Brother, you've the gist of it wrong," Keely answered with a rueful smile. "That arrogant rascal trapped me."

"How did Devereux manage that?" he asked.

Keely shrugged and then related the events of her downfall that culminated in their father's unexpected entry into the earl's bedchamber. "How His Grace knew what was happening is beyond me," she ended her tale. "Only Lady Dawn knew where I'd gone, and even she had no idea the earl would be abed when I arrived."

How wondrously naïve his new sister was, Henry thought, struggling not to laugh in her face. "Never underestimate the Countess of Cheshire's intelligence because of the size of her—" He broke off and coughed, hiding the vulgarity he'd almost uttered. "You witnessed how skillfully the countess engineered Morgana into that revealing rage."

"No one can goad us into negative action unless we allow it," Keely disagreed. "Each soul bears the responsibility for its own fate. If she'd responded with kindness to my offer of friendship, Morgana would be enjoying this glorious autumn afternoon instead of weeping alone in her chamber."

"I'm positive Ashemole is consoling her." Henry gently pulled her hand away from her face and inspected her lip. "The bleeding stopped," he told her, then watching for her reaction, added, "Devereux must want you badly."

"I cannot credit that. I'm a Welsh nobody."

Henry gave her a lopsided grin. "Any mirror will tell you his reason."

Keely smiled. "Thank you for the pretty compliment, brother."

"Where are those giants of yours hiding?"

"Odo and Hew feel more comfortable at the stables," she answered, starting to rise. "Come with me, and I'll introduce you."

"Later," Henry said, touching her forearm to prevent her leaving. "First, please tell me about yourself."

"I lived at my stepfather's holding in Wales," Keely said. "When my mother passed away, I journeyed to England to find my natural father."

"Not only did you find Papa, you found Devereux, and the rest is history," Henry remarked. "What are the wedding plans?"

Keely shrugged. "The countess and, I suppose, the earl have it planned. All I need to do is attend. Did you know there are men at court who rouge their cheeks?"

"Bloody popinjays," the boy muttered.

Honk! Honk! Honk!

Keely and Henry looked in the direction of that sound. Eluding his keepers, Anthony the goose was waddling as fast as he could toward them.

"What do you think of the countess's pet?" Henry asked.

"Anthony lives better than most," Keely replied. "I especially love his emerald and diamond collar."

The honking goose stopped in front of Keely, who'd begun a practice of feeding him a treat each afternoon. She reached into her pocket and withdrew the slice of bread she'd saved from her dinner. Breaking it into small pieces, she fed the fat goose and then gestured to his keepers, Bart and Jasper, who leashed him and led him away.

"Friendship is wherever we find it," Keely said, glancing at her brother. "Even a goose or a pig or a tree can be a worthy friend."

Henry smiled. His sister was lovely and charming, but definitely strange. If he had to choose between the two, he'd take Keely over Morgana any day. Lovely, charming, and strange were more pleasant by far than selfish, shallow, and vicious.

"Will you be attending my wedding?" Keely asked. "Odo and Hew need someone to watch over them while the earl and I are busy with our guests."

"When is it?"

"The week after Samhuinn."

"What's that?"

"Samhuinn is what the church now calls All Hallow's Eve, All Hallow's Day, and All Soul's Day," Keely answered. "'Tis three days of potent magic, when the veil between our world and that of our ancestors draws aside. Those who are prepared can journey to the other world."

Henry snorted with disbelief. "Do you actually believe that people can leave this world and journey to—"

"The past and the future," Keely supplied. "'Tis a marvelous time when chaos reigns. Don't the English celebrate it?"

Henry's gaze narrowed on her. "How do the Welsh celebrate?"

"With feasts and disguises and pranks."

"Disguises and pranks?" he echoed, interested.

"Great fires are lit inside and outside the house," Keely told him, her excitement infectious. "The doors are thrown open, and a sumptuous feast is served."

"What about the disguises and pranks?"

"You must wear your clothing turned inside out and blacken your face with soot so evil spirits won't recognize you," Keely went on. "For three days, you may trick anyone you want. Without repercussions, I might add."

"I can hardly wait," Henry said, rubbing his hands together. A mischievous gleam lit his blue eyes. "Giving the fig is the only English tradition for All Hallow's Eve."

"What's that?"

Henry made a fist with his right hand and stuck his thumb up between his first and second fingers. "See," he said, holding his hand out. "'Tis a fig. Give it to family, friend, or lover on All Hallow's Eve. The fig means 'I like you.'"

"What is so special about that?" Keely asked. "I could do that any day."

"'Tis the English custom," Henry insisted. "You wouldn't give a friend a New Year's gift on Midsummer's Eve, would you?"

"No."

"We give New Year's gifts on New Year's and the fig on All Hallow's Eve. Understand?"

Keely gifted her brother with a beguiling smile and nodded.

"Pranking the Countess of Cheshire would be fun," Henry said, thinking of that lady's pendulous breasts heaving with her fright. "What do you say?" When she nodded, he added, "Lean close. We want no one to overhear us."

Keely and Henry bent their heads together and plotted pranks against the inhabitants of Talbot House. So intent were they on their outrageous schemes, they never heard the intruder's approach.

"Hello, beauty."

Keely snapped her head up at the sound of that voice, and before she thought to mask her feelings, she gifted the earl with a dazzling smile that told him how happy she was to see him. The butterflies' wings returned to her stomach, but Keely cared not a whit. The sight of the earl's handsome face cheered her.

"Did you miss me, dearest?"

"I might have, but the countess kept me busy."

"You wound me, sweetheart," Richard said. "Each moment at court felt as long as a day. I feared I'd expire pining for you."

Keely arched an ebony brow at him. "How fare the Ladies Sarah and Jane?"

"*Who?*"

Keely burst out laughing, more at his expression of feigned innocence than at what he'd said. How one man could be so devastatingly charming boggled her mind.

"Henry and I were plotting our Samh—I mean, our All Hallow's Eve pranks."

Henry stood up and offered the earl his seat on the bench beside Keely, then winked at him. "Congratulations on your forthcoming marriage, my lord," he said. "Any good hunting at court?"

"I've quit that sport," Richard replied, winking back at the boy. He looked at Keely and lost his good humor. "What's wrong with your mouth?" he demanded. "And your eyelids are heavy. Have you been crying?"

"I fell," Keely lied. "The pain brought me tears."

Richard surprised her by putting his arm around her shoulder and drawing her close. In a gently chiding voice, he said, "Do you see how much you need me to protect you, dearest?"

"No one could have protected her from the bitch's wrath," Henry said, earning himself a censorious frown. "Morgana smacked her."

"Henry." Keely's voice held a warning note.

"Give us a few moments of privacy," Richard said to

the boy, his irritation apparent. It was a command, not a request.

"Certainly." Henry turned to Keely and said, "I do wish you weren't my sister so we could practice my new hobby together."

"I can help you," Keely offered.

"Not with this hobby."

"Why can't I?"

Henry winked at the earl and then walked away, calling over his shoulder, "'Tis making love."

Keely blushed scarlet. She refused to look at the earl.

"Never lie to me again," Richard said, close to her ear.

"I despise liars."

"Telling the truth would only have created more problems," Keely tried to explain, her violet-eyed gaze pleading for understanding. "Besides, you neglected to tell me that Morgana and you had intended to wed. 'Twas by omission a lie."

"Morgana intended to marry me, but after passing the longest week of my life at Ludlow Castle, I had no such intention toward her," Richard replied. "Only a man enamored of misery would offer for that one."

Keely felt relieved. "Disagreeable people are usually unhappy. Try to be more sympathetic."

"Could you be jealous?" Richard asked.

"No. Of course not," she answered too quickly.

Richard raised his brows, a habit of his that was becoming more endearing to her with each passing day.

"What were Henry and you planning?"

"A special All Hallow's Eve celebration."

"And what might that be?"

"'Tis a surprise."

Richard planted a chaste kiss on the uninjured side of her mouth and coaxed, "Share it with me, dearest." Keely shook her head. "'Tis a secret between my brother and me."

Richard longed to press his lips on hers but controlled

the urge because of her injury. He contented himself with nuzzling her neck instead.

Keely wondered what to do as delicious shivers of delight danced down her spine. Should she allow him this liberty because of their betrothal? Or ought she to stop him—something she didn't want to do?

"Several reports await me," he murmured against her ear, "but I'll sup with you tonight."

"That's not a good idea," she tried to refuse. "Morgana—"

"Baron Smythe will keep her occupied," Richard said, brushing his lips against her temple. "Willis is interested in Morgana."

Keely suffered a chill feeling of dread at the mention of the black-haired baron. Worry etched itself across her delicate features.

"What's wrong?" Richard asked.

"I don't like the baron," Keely answered honestly.

"But you scarcely know him."

"'Tis a feeling I have—and trust."

"Woman's intuition?"

Keely didn't smile. "The aura of untimely death surrounds him like a shroud. The baron is a dangerous, untrustworthy man."

Richard chuckled. "Are you a fortune-telling gypsy?" he teased. "Or a witch?"

"I am a—" Unwilling to jeopardize their marriage, Keely broke off. She wanted this pagan god sprung to life, if only for a brief time.

"You're a what?" Richard prodded with an amused smile.

"A silly woman."

"Not so," Richard said, rising and kissing her hand. He cast her a purposefully smoldering look and whispered huskily, "You are as lovely as the legendary goddess Venus and as sweet as marchpane. . . . But, you are wrong about Willis."

Keely managed a smile. "I'm certain you're correct."

"Until supper, dearest." Richard turned and walked away. Almost home, he stopped short as he recalled Burghley's warning to him at Kenilworth Castle. Richard whirled around and retraced his steps back to the garden, but Keely had already vanished inside Talbot House. Was it merely coincidence that she'd used the exact words to describe Smythe that Burghley had?

Early evening's supper hour found Keely lingering in her bedchamber. Her reluctance to face her sister's hatred had imprisoned her there all afternoon, but delaying the inevitable was now impossible. Only the delivery of her new gowns cheered her flagging spirit.

Keely wore a pale gray velvet gown with an underskirt and an underblouse of ivory silk. Its subdued color reminded her of the mountain mists in Wales and matched her mood. The only splashes of bright color were the violet of her eyes and the glittering dragon pendant she always wore.

How humiliated she would be if Morgana hurled insults at her in the presence of the earl, Keely thought. Though it could be for the best. The earl needed to learn what marriage to a bastard meant. He'd either break their betrothal or arm himself against the gossip that would assuredly follow her through life.

Thinking of Richard reminded Keely that Baron Smythe would also be a supper guest that evening. Though she disliked the baron, she'd set her revulsion aside for the earl's sake. She started to worry her bottom lip with her teeth but stopped when a pinch of pain shot from her swollen lip up the side of her face.

Keely gave herself a mental shake and rubbed the palm of her hand across an imaginary wrinkle on the skirt of her gown. To forever hide from her sister's hatred would be impossible. She lifted her chin a notch, squared her shoulders, and left her chamber.

"Hello, beauty."

With his arms folded across his chest, Richard leaned

against the wall in the foyer. His emerald-eyed gaze swept over her petite form and gleamed with an emotion Keely failed to recognize.

"What are you doing?" she asked, surprised to see him loitering there.

"Waiting for you, of course."

Keely cast him a pleased smile. " 'Twas unnecessary. I know the way to the hall."

Richard raised his copper brows at her and said solemnly, "Brave knights always protect their ladies from dragons. I thought you would want me by your side when we enter *her* company."

"How gallant of you," Keely replied, warmed by his thoughtfulness. "How could you know what my feelings would be?"

"My heart is attuned to yours, dearest."

"My lord, you do possess the most outrageous tongue."

Richard gave her a wolfish grin. "After we're wed, I'll show you how truly outrageous my tongue can be."

Keely blushed. She had no idea what he meant, but her short experience with the earl had shown her that his words usually had secret meanings.

"You do blush prettily," Richard said, and planted a kiss on her flushed cheek.

Instead of escorting her into the hall, Richard led Keely to a small family dining chamber, where the others awaited them. Seated at each end of the table were Duke Robert and Lady Dawn. Morgana and Willis Smythe were already seated on one side while Henry sat on the other. Beside him two places were set for them. Keely sat down between Richard and her brother.

"Latecomers get no supper," Morgana announced. "They must wait until the next meal."

"I'll decide who eats and who doesn't," Duke Robert said sharply.

Steeling herself against her fears, Keely smiled as

warmly as she could at the baron. "Seeing you again is a pleasure, sir."

"Willis," he corrected, returning her smile. "You've injured your lip?"

Keely nodded. "I fell."

On either side of her, Richard and Henry cleared their throats to indicate their disapproval. Morgana's blue-eyed gaze shot steel daggers at them. For her part, Keely gave her full attention to her meal.

A medley of appetizing dishes were laid out on the table in front of her. Cabbage chowder was the first course, followed by roasted chicken with rice and almonds. Braised spring greens and golden leeks with onions accompanied the chicken.

"You look lovely in your new gown," Duke Robert complimented Keely.

"Like a tiny gray pigeon," Morgana added with a malicious smile.

"Or a pretty mourning dove," Richard said smoothly. Henry cleared his throat, and when he caught Keely's eye, he winked at her and said in a loud voice, "Lady Dawn, I would know all about the wedding preparations."

"'Twill be the wedding of the decade," the countess replied, ignoring the duke's warning frown. "Just think, Henry. Our darling Keely will be wed to England's premier earl, one of the queen's favorites, amid the splendor of Hampton Court."

"Elizabeth plans to make this a grand affair," Richard added, taking his cue from the countess.

"And I am honored to serve as your best man," Willis said, raising his wine goblet in a salute to his friend.

"Is the queen paying for it?" Morgana asked.

"The bride's father assumes the expenses," Duke Robert answered.

"Such fuss and bother for a bastard?" the blond beauty sniffed as if offended at the waste.

"Morgana." Duke Robert's voice held a note of warning.

Keely crimsoned but sat proudly erect in her chair. Though her sister's cruelty angered her, Keely refused to respond to it and thereby ruin the meal for the others. Besides, how did one refute the truth? She was, in fact, a bastard. Refusing to look at anyone, she kept her eyes downcast and folded her hands in her lap.

Both Richard and Henry reached over to give her hand an encouraging squeeze, but they caught each other's instead. Seeing their hands entwined across her lap, Keely giggled and placed *her* two hands on the table. Realizing their mistake, the man and the boy snatched their hands back.

"I hope I'm allowed to attend," Henry said to his father. "Keely needs someone to watch over her cousins."

Richard snapped his head around to stare at Keely. That she expected the two thieving giants to attend his wedding surprised him. In fact, the thought of those bumbling blockheads mingling at court filled him with dread.

Catching the earl's reaction, Morgana asked, "You actually intend to present those louts at court?"

"Odo and Hew are family," Keely told her. "Of course they will see me married." She looked at the earl for confirmation. "Won't they?"

"I never intended otherwise, dearest," Richard assured her, recovering himself. "May, June, and Henry will guard—I mean, keep them company."

"May and June?" Willis asked.

"Richard hired two cousins to serve as Keely's tiringwomen," Lady Dawn told him.

"Why does she need two?" Morgana whined, jealous.

"One will suffice."

"Dear Richard is twice as wealthy as any other Englishman, so Keely requires twice as many women," Lady

Dawn answered, confident in her nonsensical logic.

"Have you seen her betrothal ring?"

Keely instantly hid her left hand on her lap. Annoying her sister made no sense.

"Let's see," Henry said, yanking her hand high into the air for all to see. With great exaggeration, the boy inspected it, saying, "Diamonds, emeralds—"

"Papa," Morgana interrupted, enraged by her brother's baiting, "did you know that Henry's been futtering Ludlow's maids?"

Richard and Willis burst out laughing. The Countess of Cheshire chuckled throatily. Keely bit her lip to keep from laughing, then regretted doing so when she felt the pain. Only Duke Robert appeared unamused.

"'Tis an unfit topic for the table," the duke informed his daughter. Turning to his son, he added, "We'll discuss this later."

"Now, Tally," the countess drawled, coming to the boy's defense. "'Tis natural for boys to—"

"Chessy, the last thing I need is a castle filled with my son's b—" Duke Robert broke off. As far as the world knew, his own bastard sat at the table with them.

Morgana broke the uncomfortable silence that followed. "What made you decide to marry our dear, lamentably illegitimate sister?" she asked the earl.

"Devereux wanted her so badly," Henry blurted, "he tricked her into a compromising situation."

"How difficult could that have been?" Morgana sneered. "She probably inherited her mother's wanton habits."

As the duke reached out to slap his daughter, Keely leaped out of her chair so quickly, it toppled over. Glorious in her fury, she placed the palms of her hands on the table and glared with murderous intent at her sister.

"Heed my words," Keely warned the other girl. "I can and will bear the insults you heap at my feet, but speaking ill of my mother is quite another matter. Megan was the gentlest woman who ever walked upon this earth and would forgive whatever you said; however, Englishness taints my blood, and I am decidedly less forgiving than she. If you even whisper her name, 'twill be your final earthly act, for I will kill you. Understand?"

Shocked, Morgana could only stare at her.

"Answer my question," Keely shouted. "Do you understand?"

"Y-y-yes," the blonde stammered, bobbing her head up and down.

"Your continued good health depends upon your remembering that," Keely threatened. Then with her head held high, she quit the chamber.

Richard saw the tears that welled in Keely's eyes as she turned to leave the chamber. "Bloody hell," he muttered and went after her.

Slowly and deliberately, Duke Robert rose from his chair. His gaze never wavered from Morgana's as he walked around the table. Grasping her upper arm, the duke yanked her out of the chair and dragged her out of the chamber.

"More leeks, baron?" Lady Dawn asked with a feline smile.

His lips quirked. "No, thank you, my lady."

"Tell me, darling," she said, her gaze sliding to the younger Talbot. "However did you become interested in fluttering maids?"

Henry choked on his wine. . . .

Richard caught up with Keely in the foyer as she was about to run up the stairs. He reached out and grabbed her upper arm to prevent her flight.

"Leave me a—" Keely broke off when she saw who it was.

Richard flicked a meaningful glance at the curious servants, who understood his unspoken command and dispersed. "You mustn't let Morgana upset you. Spitefulness rules her tongue," he said once they were alone.

"The other courtiers will assume a similar attitude,"

Keely told him, her violet eyes glistening with unshed tears. She started to slip the betrothal ring off her finger.

"Don't you dare!" Richard ordered, staying her hand.

"Marrying me is a terrible mistake," she said.

"I'll be the judge of that." Richard drew her into the protective circle of his embrace and traced a finger down the side of her silken cheek. "You're merely upset with Morgana at the moment, and 'tis understandable."

Keely sighed and relaxed against him. "My lack of patience worries me as much as what she said. How can I ever atone for that sin?"

"You needn't worry about atoning for sins, dearest. You're a saint."

Keely gave him a lopsided smile. "Perhaps you'll add a chapter about me in *Lives of the Saints*?"

Richard planted a kiss on her cheek. "Go to bed, dearest. Remember, if you should execute Morgana, Queen Elizabeth is an intimate friend of mine. . . ."

Meanwhile, Duke Robert pulled Morgana down the corridor in the opposite direction from the foyer and kicked the library door open with his booted foot. Shoving his daughter into the chair in front of the hearth, he snarled, "Move, and I'll beat you within an inch of your life."

Duke Robert grabbed an old Bible from a bookshelf and thrust it into her hands, ordering, "Read this and reflect upon the error of your ways." Without another word, he stormed out of the chamber.

How humiliating to be treated so crudely in the baron's presence, Morgana seethed. This is the bastard's fault. She's stolen my gowns, my intended husband, and even my father's love.

Frustrated beyond measure, Morgana flung the Bible onto the floor. An old yellowed parchment fell from between its pages and fluttered to the floor. Without much interest, she picked it up and glanced at it.

"Oh, my lord," Morgana gasped in horrified shock. Hiding her face in her hands, she wept uncontrollably.

The library door opened. Willis Smythe crossed the chamber, glanced indifferently at the Bible on the floor, and knelt beside her chair. Putting a comforting arm around her, he said, "Don't cry, sweetheart. If you would only try to be civil to—"

"You don't understand," Morgana sobbed. "'Tis scandalous. Oh, whatever shall I do?"

"Once Lady Keely's wed to Devereux, no one will dare—"

"I don't give a fig about her!"

"Then what has brought you to this sorry state?" Willis asked in a soothing voice, his blue eyes shining with sincerity. "Trust me, gentle lady."

Morgana passed him the yellowed parchment and studied his expression as he perused it. Bewilderment crossed his face first, and then recognition.

"'Tis a marriage document," Willis said as he read. "That Duke Robert wed Lady Keely's mother upsets you?"

"Her mother is only recently dead," Morgana whispered, unable to meet the censure she was certain she'd see in his eyes. "Keely is my father's legitimate heir, while Henry and I—" She broke off, unable to voice the horrible truth.

"His Grace will never jeopardize Henry's inheritance," Willis assured her. "Your tragic secret is safe with me."

"Burn it," Morgana ordered.

"We dare not destroy it here," Willis replied, folding the parchment and putting it into his pocket. He drew her into his embrace. "Trust me to take care of it," he said.

Willis's mouth swooped down and covered hers in a passionate kiss. Then he pressed her head against his shoulder and stroked her back soothingly.

Never again would he be forced to scrounge for a coin, Willis thought. The means to insure his good fortune sat folded in his pocket.

"Trust me, dear lady," Willis whispered against the

blond crown of her head. "Your best interest is my sole concern."

"I do trust you, sir," Morgana said, relaxing against the comforting solidness of his masculine frame, "with all of my heart."

Chapter 9

I do love him with all of my heart.

That staggering thought hit Keely with the impact of an oak tree falling on top of her.

"Por tous jours," she whispered. "For always."

Keely stared out the window in her bedchamber and waited for sunrise. She shivered with the early morning chill, but duty was more important than physical discomfort. False dawn brightened the eastern horizon, heralding the sun's impending appearance.

When had the English earl become so important to her? Keely wondered. He'd weathered the previous evening's storm, but she knew better than most that a man's affection is as constant as the fickle moon. Would his tender regard for her survive the tempest at court?

Keely didn't trust him. Yes, the earl had kept his promise regarding her cousins, and he even appeared unashamed of her less-than-honorable beginnings. But Megan had trusted Robert Talbot and suffered for it.

"Trust the king who wears the fiery crown and possesses the golden touch. . . ."

Richard Devereux wore a fiery crown, and the queen called him Midas in honor of that legendary king with the golden touch. Was the earl the one whom her mother had seen? What if she gave him her trust and he proved unworthy? Would her life be endangered or merely her heart?

The turmoil in Keely's mind and heart made her yearn to sneak outside and feel the rising sun as well as see it. Keely needed a favor from nature's forces. She would ask the Mother Goddess to bolster the earl's inner strength.

Ignoring the poisonous tongues set against her would require patience and fortitude.

The solemn sanctity of that rare holy place in the earl's garden would insure a successful intercession. Where the birch, the yew, and the oak conversed dwelled powerful magic.

Without bothering to change out of her nightshift, Keely grabbed her ceremonial robe and wrapped it tightly around herself, then padded on bare feet across the chamber to the door. Excitement coursed wildly through the life's blood in her body. She hadn't properly worshipped since the evening before she'd met her father. No wonder her mind seemed cloudy and her heart heavy.

Pressing her ear against the door, Keely listened for footfalls in the corridor. There were none. She opened the door a crack and peered outside. No one was about, the hour still too early for the servants to rise. Steeling herself with a deep breath, she stepped into the corridor and closed the door noiselessly.

Hugging the wall with her back, Keely glided down the dimly lit corridor and then started down the stairs. Reaching the bottom, she saw that the path across the foyer to the door was clear. Unless an early riser loitered in the courtyard, she would escape outside undetected.

On tiptoes, Keely scurried across the foyer. In one swift motion she opened the door and flew outside. The courtyard was deserted.

Keely glided like an angel of the night through the heavy mist that clung like a lover to the earth. She stopped once to verify that no one watched her progress, then slipped down the path that led to the earl's estate.

Holy stones! Keely thought, stopping short. She'd left her golden sickle and magic stones behind. Keely glanced over her shoulder but then decided that forward was the only way to go. The duke's servants would be rising by the time she reached her chamber and retrieved what she needed. She'd never make it back here without being seen.

Towering above the mist, the three holiest of trees stood together like old friends. Keely smiled at the shining whiteness of the sacred birch, the dark evergreen spikes of the sacred yew, and most sacred of all, the majestic oak.

Keely pulled the hood of her robe up to cover her head and advanced on the holy place. Worshipping at nature's sacred shrine made her feel like the most fortunate of souls. As she walked toward the trees, Keely chose eight common rocks at random.

Casting the enchanted circle, Keely set the rocks in their proper places: northwest, north, northeast, east, southeast, south, and southwest. She entered the circle from the west and closed her with the last rock, saying, "All disturbing thoughts remain outside."

Reaching the center of the circle, Keely turned in a clockwise circle three times until she faced the east, where the sun was beginning to reach for the world. She closed her eyes and focused her breathing.

"The Old Ones are here, watching and waiting," Keely spoke into the hushed dawn air. "Stars speak through stones, and light shines through the thickest oak." In a louder voice, she called, "One realm is heaven and earth."

Keely paused to gather the proper emotion, then opened her arms and implored, "Spirit of my journey, guide me to hear what these trees say. Spirit of my ancestors, guide me to hear what the wind whispers. Spirit of my tribe, guide me to understand what the clouds foretell. . . . Myrddin, greatest of Druids, open my heart that I may see beyond the horizon."

Long moments passed. And then it happened—

Strong hands grasped her upper arms in a steely grip and whirled her around. Keely's hood fell off in the movement, revealing the ebony mane that cascaded to her waist. At the same time, her eyes flew open and focused on the earl's angry face.

"What the bloody hell are you doing?" Richard growled, giving her a rough shake.

"Breaking the sacred circle is forbidden!" Keely cried.

"You've ruined my—"

Richard's expression mirrored his shocked disbelief. Without warning, he scooped her into his arms and carried her across the lawns.

"I can walk," she protested in a small voice.

"Shut up," he snapped.

With Keely in his arms, Richard marched past his sleepy-eyed servants, carried her into his study, and slammed the door shut with his booted foot. He set her down in front of a chair and then shoved her into it.

"Why were you spying on me?" Keely demanded in the sternest voice she could summon.

"I'll ask the questions," Richard shot back. "Remember, my lady. You trespassed onto my property."

"Why, of all the—" Intent on escaping, Keely started to rise.

"Sit," Richard ordered, pressing her back on the chair. Keely wisely stayed where she was.

Richard stared hard at her for an agonizingly long moment. "Are you some kind of witch?" he asked finally.

"Surely you do not hold with such absurd superstitions," Keely replied.

"What I believe is unimportant," Richard snapped. "I want to know what *you* believe. Were you practicing witchcraft on my property?"

Keely looked him straight in the eye and answered honestly, "No. I would never do that."

His emerald gaze narrowed on her. "What exactly do you believe?"

"Has the Inquisition landed in England?" she countered.

"Answer my question." *Or else* was left unspoken.

"I—I was baptized a Christian," Keely hedged, dancing around the truth.

The lady is cunning, Richard concluded, but not quite as cunning as he. "You haven't answered the question, my dear. What are you?"

Realizing she had no choice but to tell him the truth, Keely lifted her chin a notch and met his emerald gaze unwaveringly. She uttered one word, a single word that sent shock waves crashing throughout his entire being.

"*Druid.*"

"Good Christ, I'm betrothed to a pagan!" Richard exploded.

"I do have certain knowledge," Keely boasted, her voice filling with arrogant pride.

Richard closed his eyes against her incredible stupidity and shook his head in disgust. When he looked at her again, contempt had etched itself across his features.

"Knowledge without common sense is a dangerous thing," he told her.

Keely opened her mouth to protest his insult, but Richard grabbed her chin in his hand and ordered, "Keep your mouth shut, and listen to me."

Like a general before his troops, Richard paced back and forth in front of her and delivered a stinging lecture. "You are the most foolish woman I've ever met—even sillier than my sisters—and lacking common sense enough to insure your own survival. Do you know how many people believe in witches? *Do you?* Thousands! Why, even the queen believes in the supernatural. Do you realize you could be burned at the stake? *Do you?* Frightened people always act first and ask questions later."

Keely gave him a serene smile. "My lord, none of us really dies. Our souls pass into the Great Adventure."

More stupidity, Richard thought. His words were falling on deaf ears. He needed a different approach.

Richard crossed the chamber to his desk and poured himself a dram of Scots whisky, then downed it in one long gulp. Now he understood why his brother-in-law enjoyed the drink. Like nothing else in God's universe, it fortified a man when dealing with that illogical creature called woman.

Richard turned around and returned to where Keely still sat, too nervous to move. He knelt on one bended knee in front of her and warmed her hands with his own. "Dearest, I do fear for your safety. Believe what you will, but flaunting yourself before an unforgiving society can be fatal."

Keely couldn't credit what she was hearing. "Do you mean you accept my beliefs?"

Richard forced himself to nod. "Most in this land are dangerously intolerant. Your beliefs must remain secret."

"Very well," Keely agreed. Both Megan and she had always carefully avoided offending others.

Richard visibly relaxed.

"What were you doing outside so early?" she asked.

"I wanted to watch the sunrise because I knew you'd be watching it too," he admitted.

That tender admission brought a smile to Keely's lips. "I never imagined you'd be cavorting in my garden and chanting incantations," Richard added, making her giggle. He stood and offered her his hand, saying, "I'll walk you home."

Relieved that she needn't keep her secret from him, Keely placed her hand in his. Together, they walked outside and headed down the path toward Talbot House.

"Now, then. I'm taking you on a tour of London this morning," Richard informed her when they reached the courtyard. "Be ready to leave at ten."

"I don't think—"

"Would you prefer passing the day in Morgana's company?" he asked, arching a brow at her.

"I'll be ready at nine," Keely said, and disappeared inside.

Richard turned to leave but spied the duke walking up

the path from the stables. Blood and dirt soiled the ducal shirt and breeches, but the man was smiling.

"My favorite mare has foaled," Duke Robert announced. He glanced at the door through which he'd seen his daughter disappear. "'Tis awfully early to be calling upon Keely," he remarked.

"I found my sweet betrothed cavorting around the trees in my garden," Richard said, watching for the other man's reaction. "She was mumbling incantations."

For one brief moment, Duke Robert seemed at a loss for words but quickly recovered. "Sleepwalking," he lied, his gaze skittering away from the younger man's.

"Sleepwalking, my arse." Richard gave him a lopsided smirk and shook his head with disapproval. "You know, don't you?"

Duke Robert nodded.

"How can you allow Keely to endanger herself? Forbid her—"

"I had no part in her sorry existence for eighteen years," Duke Robert interrupted. "Megan instilled her own strange—*but harmless*—beliefs in her daughter. We cannot change the past, Devereux. We can only look to the future."

"You're her guardian now," Richard reminded him.

"Would the pope renounce the Church of Rome?" Duke Robert countered. "I think not. Neither will Keely renounce what's been ingrained in every fiber of her being. My daughter would prefer death to straying from her chosen path. You know the Welsh have always lacked expediency. 'Tis their custom to die for what they believe in their hearts."

"Those who are different at court do attract attention," Richard said. "'Tis a fact that can be deadly as well as disgraceful."

"Keely needs a husband strong enough to keep her safe, even from the queen," the duke replied. "If you aren't capable of the task, step aside. I'll find another who is."

Richard bristled at the insult but said nothing.

"Is the wedding on or off?" Duke Robert asked.

"On." Without another word, Richard turned and marched back the way he had come.

Watching his retreat, Duke Robert smiled with satisfaction. "Pups like you think you know everything," he said to the empty courtyard. "Devereux, you're about to learn a hard lesson. When a woman pricks a man's heart, his independence and peace of mind become ancient history."

Autumn wore its prettiest expression when Keely stepped into the courtyard at the appointed hour of ten. Vanquished by the radiant sun, the early morning mists had evaporated, and a gentle breeze tickled her face and flirted with the bottom edge of her cloak.

Keely wore a violet wool skirt and white linen blouse beneath her black wool cloak. Her ebony hair had been parted in the middle, woven into one thick braid, and then knotted at the nape of her neck.

"Good morning again," Richard greeted her with an easy smile. "Your beauty does brighten my day."

Keely blushed and returned his smile. From beneath the thick fringe of her sooty lashes, she admired his stark masculine appearance. Dressed completely in black, the earl reminded her of a handsome bird of prey, much nobler than those rouged peacocks at court.

"You shouldn't be riding astride," Richard said, lifting her onto Merlin's back. "English ladies ride sidesaddle."

"We Welsh are not simpering Englishwomen," Keely replied. "I do love the feel of Merlin between my legs and would be unable to ride properly otherwise."

Richard flushed. Though spoken in innocence, her arousing words hardened his manhood. He stared at her, but Keely only gave him her ambiguous smile. Did she realize how graphically suggestive her words were? No woman of eighteen could be that naïve—could she? Turning their horses northeast, Richard and Keely rode at a leisurely pace down the Strand. Londontown lay to the east.

"Your lips look much better today," Richard remarked. Then: "Did you know Merlin is a female?"

"Yes. What is your horse called?"

"The horse has no name."

"Every creature needs an identity," Keely insisted. There was no mistaking the censure in her voice.

Richard flicked a sidelong glance at her. "You name him, dearest."

Keely looked at his handsome black horse while she considered the matter and then said, "Pepper."

Richard chuckled. "Pepper is no fitting name for an earl's horse."

"You require a name suitable for a man?"

Richard nodded.

"Let me see. How about Stupid?"

Richard snapped his head around and saw her mischievous smirk, then gifted her with that sunny smile of his. "Black Pepper, it is."

As they rode down the length of the Strand, Richard pointed to its places of interest. On the left stood Leicester House, separated from Arundel House by the Milford Stairs. On their right sat Durham House, where both Edward VI and Jane Grey had lived at separate times. Up ahead rose Westminster Hall and Abbey. Old King Henry lay there beside his beloved queen, Jane Seymour.

Richard and Keely veered to the right at Charing Cross and rode into London proper. Here the crowds of Londoners grew increasingly larger, forcing them to pick their way carefully down the narrow twisting lanes.

Many of the passersby paused to stare as they rode past, and Keely felt distinctly uncomfortable. She stole a peek at the earl, who appeared unaffected by the curious stares of London's commoners. In fact, he seemed oblivious to their very existence.

"Good health to Midas," one bold man shouted.

Richard flashed the well-wisher a smile, tossed him a coin, and called, "God save the queen."

Reaching St. Paul's Cathedral, Richard and Keely turned right onto the Old Change. At the end of that street, they went left onto Thames Street. Keely had no idea where they were going but followed the earl's lead.

"Our first destination lies just east of London proper," Richard told her. "The White Tower is England's most famous landmark. 'Tis a combination palace, garrison, and prison. Because the Tower reminds her of unpleasant days, Elizabeth never keeps court there. Though honoring tradition, she did sleep there the night before her coronation. I was very young at the time, but my parents attended."

At the end of Thames Street, the palace of White Tower loomed before them. Richard halted his horse and gazed at it, saying, "My own father stayed in Beauchamp Tower when Bluff King Hal became irked with him."

"He lived to repeat the story?" Keely asked, surprised. Even the backwoods Welsh had heard horrifying tales of the English monarchy and its fearsome Tower.

Richard smiled at her ignorance. "Dearest, the Tower has neither dungeon nor torture chamber. 'Tis exceedingly easy to escape if you possess the coins to bribe the guards or the courage to leap into the Thames."

"Your father escaped?"

Richard shook his head. "My father walked out the door, once Henry's anger had passed."

"What was his crime?"

"He married my mother without the king's permission."

Riding through the Middle Tower's gates—the castle's main entrance—Keely felt a chill of apprehension dance down her spine. "'Tis cursed here," she announced. "The Conqueror mixed dragon's blood with the mortar."

Richard cast her an amused look. "Dragons do not exist, except in lively imaginations like yours, dearest."

Richard dismounted and then assisted Keely, who stayed close to his side. An uneasy feeling of oppression pressed down on her. In spite of what the earl said, Keely knew in her bones that the cursed castle housed restless souls who were doomed for all of eternity. Who among these Christian English had the knowledge and the courage to help those poor lost souls find their way to the other side?

When two scarlet-clad yeomen rushed forward to attend their horses, Richard tossed each a coin. "We'll be attending the chapel service," he told them. "We require no escort."

An unearthly growl rent the air behind them. Keely panicked and threw herself into the earl's arms, crying, "Angry spirits haunt this place!"

Richard chuckled, though his arms did encircle her protectively. The yeomen looked at each other and smiled.

" 'Tis the lions in the Queen's Menagerie," Richard explained. "We'll view them on our way out."

Taking Keely's hand in his, Richard led her down the passage to the Lieutenant's Lodgings. "We'll go in here," he said, guiding her toward the door.

Keely did not hear him. Her attention had fixed on a gate a little farther down the passage. "What's that entrance?" she whispered.

" 'Tis known as Traitor's Gate."

Keely shivered. Bleak desolation overwhelmed her senses, and she resisted the earl's gentle pressure on her hand. "I cannot abide this place of hopelessness. Take me away from here."

"Dearest, only traitors need fear the Tower," Richard said with a reassuring smile. Apparently, the Tower's reputation had reached Wales. " 'Tis a castle, nothing more nor less."

"Each place has a spirit," Keely insisted. "I am more sensitive than you, and the souls trapped forever within these stone walls cry out to me. Ignorant Englishmen never see beyond the horizon."

"Dead is dead," Richard snapped, becoming irritated.

"No one can speak to us from the grave."

"How wrong you are, my lord."

"Are the Welsh ruled by unreasoning fear?"

"I am *uneasy*," Keely corrected him. "Lead the way. Perhaps I can guide a few of them along the path to the Great Adventure."

"Do *not* start chanting those infernal incantations," Richard ordered as they cut through the Lieutenant's Lodgings to the grassy inner courtyard on the other side of the building. When they emerged from the Lodgings a moment later, he said, "'Tis called Tower Green. That building ahead of us is the Chapel of St. Peter ad Vincula. The chaplain royal celebrates mass each day at eleven."

The atmosphere inside Tower Green was eerily hushed. The gray stone walls surrounding the inner courtyard seemed to trap silence inside, and a cool stillness pervaded the air.

Keely felt as though she'd stepped into another world; the noisy humanity crowding London's narrow lanes seemed a million miles away. A prickly sensation made the wispy strands of ebony at the nape of her neck rise. Peering around, Keely saw a dark-haired woman pacing back and forth outside the Lieutenant's Lodgings' windows.

"Who's that?" she whispered, looking up at the earl.

Richard glanced over his shoulder but saw no one. "Of whom do you speak?"

"That wo—" Keely looked over her shoulder. The woman had disappeared inside the Lodgings. "Never mind."

Passing the simple cobbled square, Richard debated telling Keely its sordid history but decided against it. His betrothed didn't seem to be enjoying their excursion, and he was beginning to regret taking her there. King Henry VII had commissioned the chapel, and it had been built in the early Tudor style. The floor was flagstone, and the pews a polished wood. Diffused sunlight streamed into the sanctuary through the windows and shone on the gleaming brass accoutrements. Above their heads, the ceiling was a rich Spanish chestnut.

The eleven o'clock hour boomed. Keely jerked to attention in alarm and looked around.

"Relax, dearest. There's naught to fear," Richard whispered. What in God's holy name disturbed her? he wondered. Since they'd ridden into the Middle Tower, Keely had been as nervous as a fledgling warrior in the midst of his first battle. Did her unease have anything to do with her strange religious beliefs? Richard fervently hoped not. At court, Queen Elizabeth required her nobles to accompany her to mass. He could make plausible excuses for his wife once or twice, but every day was simply out of the question.

As the strokes of the bell ceased, the chaplain swept in. Resplendent in the scarlet robes of a chaplain royal, he nodded at Richard and Keely, who were the lone worshippers in attendance that morning.

Matins began. The longer it went on, the more agitated Keely grew. Extreme apprehension filled every pore of her being as a heavy melancholy settled on her. The weight of a thousand souls seemed to implore her to help them. Couldn't the earl feel the unhappiness permeating the air? What about the chaplain? Was she the only one sensitive to the horrors of the past?

Keely sat statue-still, though her life's blood pumped wildly throughout her body. Her nerves tingled in a rioting panic, and perspiration beaded her upper lip. Her breathing became shallow gasps. Suddenly, she bolted to her feet. She tried to get past Richard, but he grabbed her wrist to prevent her flight.

"Let me go!" Keely cried.

The chaplain whirled around. He stared in surprise at the frantic noblewoman struggling to escape the Earl of Basildon.

With a strength born of desperation, Keely shoved Richard and flew past him out of the pew. She ran down the aisle, crashed through the door, and dropped to her knees on the cool damp grass. Keely bent her head and swallowed great gulps of reviving air.

"Darling, are you ill?" Richard asked, kneeling beside her.

Keely looked up and recognized the concern etched across his features. She shook her head.

Richard helped her stand and then drew her into his embrace. "You should have told me you were unwell!"

Keely leaned heavily against his comforting solidness, the reality of his flesh and blood body easing her panic. She glanced at the chapel and then at the cobbled scaffold. Finally, Keely turned her violet-eyed gaze on him and said in a voice that mirrored her misery, " 'Tis the saddest place in the whole wide world."

"I don't understand," Richard said, stroking her back in a soothing motion. "I hear mass in the chapel whenever I visit. I never intended to upset you."

"M-murdered queens lie buried beneath the chapel's flagstones," Keely said in a quavering voice. She turned in the circle of his arms and pointed toward one of the fortress's distant towers. "And over there—"

" 'Tis called Wakefield Tower."

"Two murdered princes lie together beneath it," Keely told him.

"You cannot know that," Richard said. "No one knows where Edward Plantagenet's sons were buried. Their uncle ordered the execution."

Keely stared at the Tower. "You are wrong. The Tudor usurper ordered their—"

Richard snaked his hand out and covered her mouth to prevent further speech. Keely looked into his eyes and recognized the fear he tried to mask with anger.

"Richard Plantagenet ordered the princes' execution," the earl insisted in a voice that brooked no argument. "Never express a different opinion. The princes disappeared nearly a hundred years ago. Stirring up old controversies can serve no good purpose. Do you understand?"

Keely nodded. The slaughter of the two young princes had been regicide at its most horrific worst. The Tudor usurper's granddaughter sat on England's throne. Labeling the founder of that dynasty a murderer of innocent children would be unappreciated.

Richard and Keely retraced their steps across the Tower Green. The farther they got from the chapel, the calmer Keely became. Before them stood the Lieutenant's Lodgings.

"Basildon!" a voice called.

Richard turned around and smiled at the middle-aged man walking across the Green toward them. "William Kingston, the Tower constable," he said. "I'll return in a moment." At that, Richard started across the Green toward the man.

Anxious to be away, Keely started to turn back to the Lodgings but stopped short. The woman she'd seen earlier stood no more than three feet away.

Spectacularly dressed, the woman wore a black velvet robe over a vivid scarlet kirtle. Her ebony hair had been caught up in a pearl-trimmed headdress. Though regally garbed, the woman wore clothing that was a shade outdated.

For some unknown reason, Keely felt compelled to drop her a curtsy. "Good day, my lady," she said.

"What do you do here?" the woman asked. Her eyes were black and her expression vivacious.

"I came with my betrothed to visit the chapel."

The woman flicked a glance across the Green and said, "He hath red hair like my husband. I've a need to speak with my husband about an important matter. Have you seen him?"

"I don't know who he is," Keely answered, "but my betrothed knows many men here. What is his name?"

"Henry," the woman answered with a bemused smile. Then: "Child, beware the treacherous blacksmith."

Keely froze. Her mouth opened in surprise at the woman's warning—almost the same words Megan had spoken on her deathbed.

"*Keely!*"

Keely whirled around. Richard, wearing an amused smile, and the constable advanced on her.

"Were you praying or merely talking to yourself?" Richard teased.

"Neither. I was speaking to this lady," Keely said. She looked at the constable and asked, "Please, sir, can you fetch her husband Henry?"

Both Richard and the constable lost their smiles.

"Dearest, you stand alone," the earl told her.

Keely turned around. "She was here a moment ago. You must know Henry's wife. Didn't you see her talking with me?"

"Was the lady dressed in black and scarlet?" the constable asked, unable to stop himself from making a protective sign of the cross.

Keely nodded, relieved the man knew the lady.

Casting an unhappy glance at the earl, the constable said, "'Tis the ghost of Queen Anne."

Richard burst out laughing and slapped the man's shoulder in easy camaraderie. "Give over, Kingston. Ghosts do not exist."

"My father was constable during those tragic times," Kingston said. "The queen passed her last days in the Lodgings. Many have seen her pacing beneath these windows, but she's never spoken before."

"Her soul is caught between two worlds," Keely said, drawing their attention. "Perhaps if I—" She shut her mouth abruptly when the earl frowned at her.

"I believe we'll save the Menagerie for another day," Richard said, grasping Keely's arm and guiding her toward the door.

When they emerged on the other side of the Lodgings,

Richard led her down the passage toward the Middle Tower. "Never utter a word about what transpired here today," he ordered. "Elizabeth will not thank you for your unsolicited opinions."

"How did the queen die?" Keely asked.

Richard stopped short and looked at her. His emerald gaze mirrored his amazement. "You don't know?"

Keely shook her head.

"Queen Elizabeth's father, King Henry, ordered her mother beheaded on Tower Green."

"Why?"

"For failing to deliver a son."

Keely glanced over her shoulder at the Lieutenant's Lodgings. She worried her bottom lip with her teeth and then turned pleading violet eyes upon the earl. "I can guide her to the Great Adventure."

"Are you mad?" Richard shouted, grasping her upper arms and giving her a shake.

"But she'll never find peace unless——"

"No!"

"Very well," Keely agreed. "I'll ask Megan to do it."

Richard closed his eyes against her incredible stupidity and wondered why he was still bent on marrying her. Yes, Keely needed his protection and guidance, but it appeared the daft *taffy* was hell-bent on seeing both the Devereux and the Talbot families axed on the block.

"Dearest, your mother is dead," he reminded her in a deceptively calm voice.

"Megan promised to return on Samhuinn," Keely told him. "I'll ask her then."

"Good Christ!" Richard exploded, drawing the yeomen's curious stares. He lowered his voice and insisted, "The dead cannot return to visit this world."

Keely opened her mouth to argue the point, but Richard added, "Do not answer me. In fact, keep those lips shut until we reach Talbot House."

During the long ride through London to the Strand, Keely seethed in silence. She had half a mind to end their betrothal. How could she live the remainder of her years beneath the shadow of the earl's disapproval? Her Druid upbringing told her to let things slide, but the English blood flowing through her veins urged her to slap the overbearing arrogance off the earl's handsome face.

Reaching the Talbot courtyard, Richard dismounted and turned to help her, but Keely was too fast for him. She leaped off Merlin and shouted in anger, "I had a wonderful time! Thank you for a lovely day!"

Richard chuckled at the disparity between her words and her emotion, then yanked her into his arms. "You're very welcome, dearest," he said, his voice a soft caress.

Keely sagged against him, his gentleness depleting her of the anger she suffered. After all, the earl's ignorance regarding the afterlife wasn't really his fault. He'd been bred to live in the Here and Now without giving the Beyond any serious consideration.

"Why do you insist on marrying me?" Keely asked. "I'm so different from the other ladies of your acquaintance and unwilling to change my ways."

"You're the only woman who ever inspired jealousy in me," Richard said. "And 'tis most disconcerting to want to challenge a damned tree."

Keely giggled. "Pretend you are a noble oak."

"How do I do that?" he asked.

Keely lifted both of his arms until they stretched out straight in the air on either side of his body. "Behold, your branches."

Richard cocked a copper brow at her. "What do I do now?" he asked.

"Nothing." Keely stepped close and pressed her body against his. She wrapped her arms around his body, then stood on tiptoes and planted a chaste kiss on his lips. Before his arms could trap her against his masculine frame, Keely turned and disappeared inside the house.

Your maidenly days will be ending in less than a month, Richard thought as he watched her retreat. Enjoy your teasing games while you may. . . .

Chapter 10

"Cousins, lift me up."

"Now, little girl. Climbing the earl's tree is a less than sterling idea," Odo said.

"Even now, he could be watching us from yonder window," Hew warned, glancing over his shoulder.

"We need those sprigs for tonight's celebration," Keely insisted. She turned to her brother. "Since my cowardly cousins refuse to help me, will you? The thought of the earl catching us here doesn't frighten you, does it?"

"A marquess outranks a mere earl," Henry boasted. He cupped his hands and crouched down to give her a lift.

"You win, little girl," Odo relented, stepping in front of the boy. "I'll give you the lift."

"I'll do it," Hew insisted, trying to push him aside.

"I'm stronger," Odo said, cuffing the side of his brother's head.

"You are not," Hew disagreed.

"Am—"

"*Not!*"

While the Lloyd brothers argued about who would lift Keely into the tree, Henry locked his hands together and bent down. Keely placed one dainty booted foot in her brother's hands and surged upward, grabbing the lowest of the yew tree's branches. A devilishly wicked grin slashed across the boy's face as he cupped her buttocks through her skirt and gave her a boost.

"Nice arse," Henry said. Then: "I can see up your skirt."

"English swine," Keely called, moving to sit on the tree's thickest branch.

Both Odo and Hew reached out and cuffed the sides of the young Marquess of Ludlow's head.

Keely made herself relatively secure and comfortable on the limb, then reached for the leather pouch hanging with her dragon pendant around her neck. She withdrew the golden sickle and, murmuring the secret prayers her mother had taught her, lovingly began cutting sprigs from the yew. Keely kissed each sprig she severed, then dropped it to the three pairs of waiting hands.

Glancing up at the sky, Keely sighed with contented satisfaction. The Great Mother Goddess smiled upon their holiday venture and promised a perfect evening for their Samhuinn celebration. The morning mists had already evaporated beneath a radiant sun, and the autumn air was mildly crisp. The day was a rarity of clear skies, with only an occasional puffy white cloud marring the perfection of the heavenly blue blanket covering the earth.

"Henry, all the participants around the bonfire tonight will receive a sprig of yew," Keely instructed, giving her complete attention to her task. "Samhuinn is the festival of our ancestors, and the yew tree symbolizes death and rebirth. These sprigs of yew represent our ability to commune with those loved ones who have gone before us into the Great Adventure. Do you understand?"

No reply.

"Henry, do you understand?"

"I understand you have a penchant for trespassing on my property." The voice belonged to the earl.

Keely looked down, and her mouth formed a perfect O. Holy stones, but the earl appeared none too happy. He stood in a challenging stance with his hands resting on his hips. Gazing down at her irritated betrothed, Keely realized the duke had been correct. The earl's pinched expression exactly resembled a man's with a pike stuck up his— Keely decided to *pretend* her actions were perfectly normal.

"Good morning, my lord," she called, masking her unease with cheerfulness. "I'm *visiting* your garden, not trespassing. A world of difference lies between the two, *dearest*."

Richard snorted at the lie, and his emerald gaze dropped from his disobedient betrothed to her cousins. "I believe I heard May and June arguing in the scullery. You have my permission to join them there."

The two Welshmen turned uncertain gazes on their mistress. "Will you be all right?" Odo called to her.

"Do you expect me to beat her for climbing my trees?" Richard snapped at the man.

Wanting to escape the Englishman's anger but reluctant to leave their mistress to his mercy, Odo and Hew looked from the earl to Keely. When she nodded, giving her permission, the two Welsh giants hurried away.

Next, Richard turned his blackest scowl on the marquess who outranked him. Henry suffered no qualms about leaving his sister to the earl's mercy. Without a word, the boy gathered the yew sprigs and started back to Talbot House.

When the earl raised his emerald gaze to his betrothed, Keely had the audacity to give him a disgruntled look. "Why do you intimidate others?" she asked. "Fear is such a negative force."

"Kindly get down here," Richard ordered.

Keely placed the golden sickle back in her pouch and then leaped to the ground in front of him. Instinctively, Richard reached out to steady her. Though she wasn't in any danger of losing her balance, Keely threw her arms around his neck. Peering up at him from beneath the heavy fringe of her ebony lashes, she tried to smile as seductively as she could.

"You promised to refrain from flaunting your heathen beliefs," Richard reminded her, steeling himself against the arousing feel of her body.

"I was preparing for tonight's celebration," Keely replied. She inhaled deeply of his clean masculine scent and murmured, "Mmmm. You smell good enough to eat."

Richard was unable to prevent the corners of his lips twitching into a reluctant smile. His arms encircled her, and his hands cupped her buttocks through the thin material of her skirt and yanked her against the male hardness that her words had provoked.

Nuzzling the side of her neck, Richard whispered against her ear, "I saw your lips moving, dearest. You were worshiping, not preparing."

"I worship gold," Keely said in an accusing voice.

"I worship God," he corrected her. "I do *accumulate* gold."

Keely rested her cheek against his chest and felt the rhythmic beating of his heart. Without looking up, she warned, "As my own mother passed the Golden Thread of Knowledge to me, so shall I pass that Golden Thread to my own children. Knowing this, do you still wish to marry me?"

Placing one finger beneath her chin, Richard gently tilted her face up and gazed into the most incredible violet eyes he'd ever seen. "Are you trying to dissuade me?" he asked.

Keely shook her head. "What I am trying to do is make you understand that I will never forsake the truth. Harmony and beauty exist in my world. The screech of the blue jay, the coo of the mourning dove, and the hoot of the owl are music to my ears. This earthly life is too short to waste arguing with a man who refuses to see what sits in front of his nose." She gestured to the three sacred trees, adding, "Tis the holiest of places. The birch represents birth, the yew symbolizes death and eternity, and the mighty oak opens the gateway to other realms."

"Are you trying to convert me?" Richard asked, cocking a copper brow at her.

"I would never do that," Keely assured him. "You're much too cynical to believe in anything but gold."

"Thank you," he said dryly.

"However, your skepticism does annoy me," she added.

Richard couldn't credit what he was hearing. How had she managed to put him on the defensive? Reasoning with the truly illogical was an exercise in futility. He offered her a truce: "If I can learn to live with your incantations, will you overlook my skepticism?"

Keely gave him an ambiguous smile. "Perhaps."

"Will you do me a favor?"

"If 'tis within my power."

"My mother and Uncle Hal—my stepfather—arrived from Essex last night," Richard began, then hesitated at the thought of offending her.

"And?"

"Could you pretend to be civilized?"

Keely cocked an ebony brow in a perfect imitation of his habit. "I *am* civilized."

Richard gave her an apologetic grin. "You know what I mean."

"I'll consider your request if you join my Samhuinn celebration tonight."

"I wouldn't miss Samhuinn for all the gold in London," he said, playfully tapping the tip of her nose.

Pleased, Keely gazed up at him with a smile on her face and asked abruptly, "May I touch it?"

What the bloody hell did she want? Richard wondered as a flush colored his face and his manhood jerked to attention. In a choked voice, he asked, "To what do you refer, dearest?"

"The fiery crown on the top of your head."

"Be my guest."

Keely reached up and, tentatively at first, ran her fingers through his thick mane of copper. "'Tis cool and silky," she marveled. "I thought 'twould be hot."

"How about a Samhuinn kiss, dearest?" Richard asked.

"When we dance around the bonfire tonight," Keely

promised, stepping back a pace. "Samhuinn begins at sunset. I'll kiss you then." She started to turn away, but his voice stopped her.

"You will be meeting my parents at the noon meal," Richard said. "Think *civilized*."

Keely flashed him a dazzling smile and dropped him a throne room curtsy. "Behold, my lord. You see before you a simpering English maiden." Giving the lie to her words, Keely lifted her skirt and dashed across the lawn toward Talbot House.

Three hours later, Keely stood in front of the pier glass in the ducal bedchamber and eyed herself critically. She wore a forest green, velvet gown that sported a tight-fitting bodice with a square neckline and long flowing sleeves. The gown's skirt divided in the front to reveal her underskirt of ivory silk. On her feet, Keely wore matching satin slippers. Her ebony hair cascaded to her waist in pagan fashion, and around her neck gleamed the jeweled dragon pendant.

Meeting the earl's parents sent Keely's nerves into a tingling riot. What did the dowager countess think of her only son marrying a ducal bastard? And a Welshwoman, to boot.

Because the earl had been kind to her, Keely would try her hardest to make him proud. Yet doubts about her ability to behave like a proper Englishwoman nagged at her. Pretending to be something she wasn't would be difficult. Besides that, how long was she required to keep the pretense up? For a whole lifetime? Or only until they had married?

Worrying her bottom lip with her teeth, Keely studied her betrothal ring. The sight of its precious jewels wink-ing at her from their bed of gold heartened her. The earl believed in her abilities, and failing him was simply out of the question.

Keely crossed the chamber to the window and gazed at the sky's oceanic horizon. Anticipation of the evening's festivities swelled within her breast. With all of its potent and unseen forces, Samhuinn held sway as her favorite moment in the year's cycle and was especially important this year.

The sun rode high in the clear blue sky. Keely knew the Talbots and the Devereux already gathered in the great hall for the noon meal, yet she lingered a moment longer.

Pressing the palm of her hand against the window, Keely whispered, "Soon, Mother. Tonight we will be together again."

Keely turned away from the window and squared her shoulders with proud determination, then quit the chamber. Even if it killed her, Keely vowed to charm her noble in-laws. She prayed the dowager countess would prove as unconcerned with her scandalous birth as the earl had.

Keely stepped into the great hall and hesitated. The two families congregated in front of the hearth, which meant she was late again. And a pox take her malicious sister, Keely thought, if that one started hurling insults at her in the presence of the earl's family.

Duke Robert and a graying middle-aged man relaxed in the chairs in front of the hearth. The Countess of Cheshire and a petite red-haired woman stood with their backs to the hall's entrance and listened to their men's conversation. Young Henry appeared bored by the adult gathering; while standing off to one side, Morgana and Baron Smythe were deep in conversation. The unexpected sight of the baron sent a ripple of unease down Keely's spine. Then her gaze slid to the earl, who'd been staring at the hall's entrance as if willing her to appear.

Richard cast her his most disarming smile, a smoldering expression that heated the entire hall, and sauntered toward her. Like a pretty flower drawn to the sun's radiance, Keely started forward at the same time. They met in the center of the enormous chamber.

"Good day, my lord," Keely greeted him.

Richard kissed her hand. "You look divine, Keely."

"Civilized too?" she asked, giving him a jaunty smile.

The earl laughed, drawing the others' attention. Aware that they had an audience, Richard escorted her the remainder of the distance to the hearth.

"Mother and Uncle Hal, I present Lady Keely," Richard introduced them. "Dearest, I present the Dowager Countess of Basildon and Sir Henry Bagenal."

In spite of her nervousness, Keely dropped them a graceful curtsy and gave them a serene smile. "I am honored to make your acquaintances," she said. Her violet gaze fixed on the countess's hair. "My lady, your fiery crown does resemble your son's," she added.

Richard snapped his head around and frowned at Keely. If the heathen minx started babbling her nonsense now, he would take great pleasure in boxing her ears.

The dowager countess smiled. "Unlike my son's, silver strands of snowflakes do douse my own mane's fire."

In that instant Keely decided she liked the earl's mother. The countess seemed friendly and, more important, unconcerned with social blunders.

"Call me Louise," the dowager countess was saying.

"And call me Uncle Hal," Sir Bagenal added.

"I cannot tell you how pleased I am with Richard's choice for a wife," Louise Devereux said.

"And I cannot tell you how pleased I am with the earl's parents," Keely returned the compliment. *Now what?* she wondered, dropping her gaze to stare at her slippers. What should a bride-to-be discuss with her future mother-in-law? What would be a safe subject? If she said too much, she might appear "uncivilized."

Saving her from making small talk, Duke Robert rose from his chair. "And I'm pleased that everyone else is so pleased," he said with an unmistakably relieved grin. "We'll eat in the other room."

The table inside the family dining chamber, located off the great hall, had been set for nine people. Duke Robert and the Countess of Cheshire sat at the ends of the rectangular oak table. Sir Bagenal, the dowager countess,

Baron Smythe, and Morgana sat on one side while Keely sat between Henry and Richard on the other.

Several servants beneath Meade's supervision entered with dinner's first course of barley soup and Colchester mussels with dijon sauce. One servant poured red wine into their crystal goblets, while another placed freshly baked bread and creamy butter beside their plates.

"Tell us about the wedding," the dowager countess said to her son.

"'Twill be at Hampton Court's chapel," Richard replied, "and Elizabeth has ordered the staff to plan the affair. Beyond that, there's nothing more to tell."

"Keely, show the countess your betrothal ring," Henry piped up, flicking a sardonic smirk across the table at his sister.

Keely glanced sidelong at Richard, who nodded. Then she held her left hand up for the countess to see. "The jewels represent the word *dearest*," she explained, unable to mask the tender emotion in her voice. Embarrassed, Keely glanced at her sister and noted the other girl's unhappy expression, then hid her offending hand on her lap.

"My son has excellent taste in jewels as well as brides," the countess remarked. "Did Richard also gift you with that unusual pendant?"

Keely shook her head and dropped her gaze to her plate. "His Grace gifted my mother with it before I was born. 'Tis her legacy to me."

An awkward silence descended on those seated at the table as they noted the daughter's formality in referring to her father. In spite of her father's august rank, a daughter would call him Papa, not His Grace.

Ashamed both for hurting her father's feelings and for her illegitimate birth, Keely worried her bottom lip with her teeth. Bastard and pissy ingrate—that was what she was. But how could she instantly calm the turbulent emotions she'd harbored for eighteen years?

"'Twill be the wedding of the decade," the Countess

of Cheshire remarked, steering the conversation away from dangerous waters.

"That the Talbots and the Devereux will finally share a bond of blood pleases me immensely," Duke Robert said, then regretted his words.

Another uncomfortable hush fell over the diners as each person recalled that the earl had considered Morgana until he met Keely. Duke Robert redeemed himself by announcing, "Chessy and I plan to wed the day after Richard and Keely. Of course, 'twill be a subdued affair, since we're both long in the tooth and have been married previously."

"Several times for the countess," Morgana chirped.

The Countess of Cheshire cast the blonde a feline smile and bared her claws. "Some women have no trouble catching any number of husbands, while others, poor dears, cannot seem to attract even one."

Ignoring this spiteful byplay, everyone started talking at once. The news of two happy events seemed to cheer all but Morgana. The blond beauty seethed inwardly as she listened to the rounds of congratulations circling the table.

Keely noted her sister's silence and turned the conversation to a less controversial subject than marriage. "Tell me about Essex," she said to the earl's mother. "The earl hasn't shared much about his home county."

"Basildon Castle, our ancestral home, is located there," Louise Devereux told her. "You'll be its lady after you're married, though we do employ an excellent staff."

"Boudicca, the warrior queen, hailed from Essex," Henry said. "She and her tribe of Iceni destroyed the Roman settlement of Camulodunum before marching on London and destroying that too."

"I'm glad to hear you've learned your history lessons," Duke Robert complimented his son.

"Essex possesses rich arable soil, where fields of barley and wheat sway in the breezes off the North Sea," Richard told Keely.

"'Tis bordered in the north by the lush meadows and green trees along the Stour River and in the south by Tilbury Plain," Uncle Hal added. "The Thames estuary and the marshes lie to the east, as well as the islands of Convey, Wallasea, Foulness, and Mersea."

"You'll love Waltham Forest the best," Richard said, casting her a knowing smile. "Herds of roe and fallow deer roam there, and the forest contains every kind of tree imaginable."

"Even oak trees?" Keely asked with a teasing smile.

"Millions," he answered. "And I'm planning to introduce you to each and every one."

Louise Devereux sighed inwardly at the bud of love she saw blossoming between her only son and the lovely girl beside him. Her future daughter-in-law wasn't at all what she'd expected—a fact that pleased her immeasurably. She disliked the shallow misses at the Tudor court.

"Richard made a fortune from Essex's wool trade and Colchester mussels," the dowager countess remarked, watching closely for the girl's reaction to her son's great wealth.

Keely cast the earl an admonishing glance and said, "I do hope you haven't cheated anyone."

"I would never do that," Richard assured her.

"Why should you care if the earl cheats the peasants?" Morgana entered the conversation. "'Twould mean more coins in your pocket if he did."

"Your thoughts mirror mine," Baron Smythe said to the blond beauty. "A man needs to look after his own."

"Farmers and fishermen and merchants are *not* peasants," Richard informed them. "Because I treat them fairly, they fight to do business with me. Thus, I accumulate even more gold than I could otherwise."

"'Tis profitable and honorable," Keely praised the earl, gazing at him with an expression of adoration.

"Why do you even bother?" the baron asked. "Working is so plebeian, and you have more than enough money."

"My lord finds a respectable day's labor most rewarding," Keely shot back, irritated by the baron's criticism.

Richard chuckled and leaned close. "Sweetheart, I am quite capable of defending the way I choose to live," he assured her.

"I would never defend you," Keely said, feigning innocence, making the earl smile. "I merely wished to explain why you work so hard, in case the baron would care to try it sometime."

Several servants entered the chamber from the doorway behind the Countess of Cheshire. One man brought bowls of artichokes dressed in oil and vinegar, while another served them turnips and cabbage. A third carried a tray laden with a variety of Cheshire's best cheeses. Meade walked into the chamber last, and what he carried shocked the watching diners into silence.

Instead of placing the meat platter in front of the duke, as was the custom, Meade set it down before the Countess of Cheshire. It took less than two seconds for Lady Dawn to react to what she saw.

There on the sterling silver tray rested a roasted goose. A gold collar inlaid with diamonds and emeralds adorned what had once been a long neck.

"Anthony!" the Countess of Cheshire cried, and swooned.

Duke Robert leaped out of his chair and raced around the table, while the earl and the baron, seated closer to the unconscious woman, jumped up to assist her and kept her from falling. The duke slapped his beloved's face lightly. When she moaned and her eyes fluttered open, Duke Robert turned a murderous glare on his major-domo.

Richard heard Henry chuckling behind him. He whirled around and caught Keely holding her hand in front of her mouth, while her shoulders shook with suppressed merriment.

Honk! Honk! Honk!

The real Anthony waddled into the room. Behind the goose walked Jasper and Bart.

"My beautiful baby bird," the countess cooed. She roused herself enough to break off a piece of bread and offered it to Anthony. The goose gobbled it up and honked for more.

"Return Anthony to the safety of his chamber," the countess ordered the two boys.

Duke Robert returned to his chair, as did the earl and the baron. Livid, the duke leveled a furious stare at his smiling son and his giggling oldest daughter.

Faced with his anger, Keely struggled against her laughter and won. "I do apologize," she said to the countess. "Pranking you was Henry's idea."

Heedless of his father's fury, the young marquess accepted full credit for the disturbance. "We pranked you good," he told the countess. "'Twas almost too easy to fool you."

"I haven't had this much excitement since my own children were young," the earl's mother said. "I can hardly wait until Devereux House echoes with the sounds of my own grandchildren's laughter." Her remark calmed everyone, including the duke who managed a faint smile.

"I cannot imagine the earl as a boy. Can you tell me what he was like?" Keely said, glancing sidelong at him.

"Richard was even more arrogant a boy than he is a man," his mother told her. "Three older sisters managed to keep him humble."

"Those three witches are the most incorrigible hoydens I ever met," Richard said. He winked at the countess and teased, "Shame on you, Mother, for raising such disreputable females."

"I raised my girls the same as my son," she shot back. "You turned out rather nicely."

Richard grinned. "My brothers-in-law would tell you their wives lack obedience."

"Piss on obedience," the dowager countess said. "Life

is for living, not obeying." She looked at her future daughter-in-law and advised, "Do not believe his lies, child. A smidgeon of challenge keeps a man's interest primed."

Keely smiled and said, "Please tell me about your daughters."

"Kathryn lives with her husband in Ireland and has made me a grandmother six times," the countess replied.

"Three boys and three girls," Richard said.

"Then there's Brigette, who lives in Scotland," the countess went on. "Iain and she have gifted me with four grandchildren."

"Three boys and one exceedingly spoiled girl," Uncle Hal added.

"As the saying goes, 'the leaves do not fall too far from the tree,'" Richard interjected. "I always wished Brigette would be blessed with a daughter who inherited her temperament."

"Heather married Prince Khalid and lives in Istanbul," the countess finished. "I have one grandson, two granddaughters, and a baby on the way from them."

"When Heather sailed to France nine years ago, pirates attacked her ship," Richard said. "Prince Khalid rescued her. They promptly fell in love and married." He glanced across the table at his stepfather and added, "Changing the subject a bit, are you interested in buying a few shares in my Levant Trading Company?"

Uncle Hal nodded and would have spoken, but Louise Devereux said, "Discussing business across the dinner table is terribly ill-mannered, Richard. Leave that dull subject for your study."

"How can you say that?" he asked, surprised by her unaccountable opinion.

"'Tis dull to me," the countess insisted. "I warrant your bride-to-be would much rather speak of other things. Wouldn't you, my dear?"

"Why not tell us about *your* childhood?" Morgana said to Keely, then glanced down the table at the dowager countess. "Your future daughter-in-law was born on the wrong side of the blanket. For the earl's sake, I do hope she hasn't inherited any *bad* habits."

Keely flushed with hot embarrassment. But what could she say? Morgana had spoken with brutal honesty.

"Guard your manners," Duke Robert warned.

"'Tis the truth," the blonde defended herself.

"Morgana, darling," the Countess of Cheshire drawled. "Swallow your tongue."

"My sentiments exactly," Richard said, glaring at the woman he'd briefly considered marrying.

"What a woman carries inside her heart is more valuable than into which household she was born," Louise Devereux told the blonde. "Though we select our spouses and our friends, choosing our family is beyond our ability. We're stuck with whatever fate gives us."

"Isn't that the God-awful truth," the Countess of Cheshire agreed, glancing with distaste at Morgana.

"Well said, my love," Duke Robert added.

Keely felt her brother nudging her thigh. Glancing down, she saw him giving her "the fig." How could she have forgotten that quaint English Samhuinn custom?

"My lady, you defend me so prettily," Keely said to the earl's mother. "I must say—" She held her right hand into the air and poked her thumb through her index and middle fingers.

Everyone but the earl gasped in horrified surprise. Richard bolted out of his chair, grabbed her wrist, and yanked her out of the room.

"What the bloody hell do you think you're doing?" Richard snapped as the door closed behind them. "Is that your idea of civilized behavior?"

"Is telling your mother I like her forbidden?" Keely asked, confused by his anger.

"Telling my mother—?" Richard's emerald eyes widened, and unexpectedly he shouted with laughter. "Dearest, this"—he gave her the fig—"means 'fuck you.'"

''Holy stones! Henry pranked me,'' Keely cried, her hands flying to her breast as she realized the enormity of what she'd done. ''Oh, Richard,'' she moaned. ''I told your mother—what will I do?''

Richard pulled her into the circle of his arms and said in a husky voice, ''I like the sound of my name on your lips.''

''Hang that,'' Keely groaned. ''I can never face your mother again.''

''Consider the bright side, dearest. Queen Elizabeth could have been sitting in my mother's place.''

Keely couldn't quite suppress the horrified giggle that bubbled up in her throat.

''I'll make the necessary explanation,'' Richard said, taking her hand.

Everyone was awkwardly silent when the couple returned to the dining chamber. They'd heard the earl's anger and then his peal of laughter.

Richard cleared his throat and, fighting against a smile, announced, ''Twould appear that Keely has become the butt of a Halloween prank. Henry told her that gesture meant 'I like you.' ''

''I'm sincerely sorry,'' Keely apologized to the earl's mother. Sliding into her seat, she promised her brother, ''I'm going to strangle you.''

''Give over,'' Henry said, wearing the most unrepentant grin. ''Twas a stroke of genius and the best Halloween prank yet, though roasting Anthony was fun.'' He glanced at the earl and threatened, ''Wait until you discover what we've planned for you.''

Richard cast the boy an unamused look. ''Henry, I shall derive the greatest pleasure from holding you down while Keely squeezes the life's breath from your devious body.''

''I'll help,'' Morgana piped up.

''And so will I,'' the Countess of Cheshire said. Keely looked at the dowager countess. ''Would you care to join our Halloween celebration tonight?''

Louise Devereux smiled, delighted with the ebony-haired beauty. "My dear, I cannot think of anything I'd enjoy more."

Beside her, Uncle Hal cleared his throat.

"On the other hand, I can think of one activity that's infinitely more pleasurable," his wife amended, winking at her future daughter-in-law.

"What could that be?" Keely asked in virginal ignorance. "We could include it in tonight's celebration."

Everyone laughed at her expense. Keely blushed, though she couldn't understand what they found so amusing.

"She was referring to what lovers do," Richard explained in a whisper, leaning disturbingly close. "What we shall be doing ten nights from now. . . ."

Chapter 11

"What lovers do . . . "

Remembering the earl's whispered words brought a hot flush to Keely's cheeks and a melting sensation in the pit of her stomach.

Is this desire? Keely wondered as she stared with unseeing eyes out her bedchamber window. Again she felt his warm breath tickling her ear, his sensual lips pressed to hers, his strong hands and his heated gaze caressing her naked breasts.

Pulling herself out of the sensual reverie, Keely gave herself a mental shake. The earl was becoming too important to her. Never would she give her heart or her trust to a man, least of all an English noble.

Becoming aware of her surroundings, Keely gazed with anticipation at the darkening sky and smiled to herself. Samhuinn dusk shrouded the earth.

Her gaze dropped to the section of the duke's garden near the River Thames. Odo and Hew had worked hard all afternoon to build a circle of stone for the Samhuinn fire. They'd filled the stone circle with kindling of yew, the sacred tree of eternity. Now all stood in readiness awaiting the enchanted night.

Dressed completely in black, Keely looked like a stableboy instead of a young woman on the threshold of marriage. She wore tight breeches, baggy shirt, leather jerkin, and scuffed boots. A black woolen cap hid her thick mane of ebony.

"I found a cork," Henry announced, barging into her chamber. "I do hope Papa prefers his wine breathing."

Smiling, Keely turned away from the window and told him, "I've selected your clothing for tonight."

"How can I catch any pretty maids if I'm dressed like a girl?" he grumbled.

"'Tis the ancient Samhuinn custom to disguise yourself as the opposite sex," she explained. "Besides, you'll overhear them discussing your prowess and wondering where you are."

His blue eyes narrowed on her. "Are you pranking me?"

"Would I do that?"

"Yes."

Keely laughed at his suspicion. "I swear 'tis truth. Put these on."

Over his own clothing, Henry donned a threadbare violet wool skirt and linen blouse. Last came a hooded black cloak.

"Keep your head covered," Keely told him, "or no one will believe 'tis me."

"I need a couple of muskmelons."

"Why?" she asked, puzzled.

Henry grinned wickedly. "I cannot be a girl unless I have a pair of titties. I want big ones, too."

Keely blushed.

"On the other hand, two gooseberries will do, since I'm supposed to be you," he teased.

"Very funny," Keely said, slapping his arm playfully.

She stepped back a couple of paces and inspected him. "You do look like a girl."

"Turn around," Henry ordered. Then: "'Tis incredible, sister. You look exactly like a stableboy."

Clutching the wine cork and her brother's dagger, Keely headed for the hearth. She stuck one end of the cork onto the dagger and held the other end to the flame until it charred. Then she blew on the cork to cool it.

"Stand still," Keely said. Using the charred end of the cork, she blackened her brother's face and explained, "Evil spirits cannot recognize us and follow us home if we blacken our faces."

"I wish we had a full moon tonight," Henry said as she streaked his face.

"We always celebrate Samhuinn during the dark moon," Keely informed him. "Never during October's full Hunter's Moon."

"But why?"

"Seeing beyond the horizon into the Other World requires our mortal sight be obscured."

Henry grinned. "At times, sister, you say the strangest things." Lifting the charred cork out of her hand, Henry smudged her face with black and even dotted the tip of her nose.

Grabbing the yew sprigs, brother and sister headed for the door. Henry opened it a crack and peered outside. No one was about. Gesturing to her, Henry led the way down the shadowed corridor to the top of the stairs.

From below drifted the muffled voices of several retainers who were loitering in the foyer. Henry and Keely wanted no one to see their disguises before the celebration began.

"Should we wait until they leave?" Henry whispered.

"Let's make a run for the door," Keely answered. "If we're fast enough, they won't recognize us."

Henry nodded. "One, two, three—*go!*"

Keely and Henry raced down the stairs and darted past the startled retainers in the foyer. Without breaking stride, Henry yanked the door open, and they flew into the courtyard.

Henry kept running down the path that led to the gardens, but Keely paused. With a soft smile touching her lips, she inhaled deeply of dying October's crisp twilight air and felt anticipation surging through her body.

The night had been created for magic. A rising tide of potent energy charged the hushed air with expectancy, while the muted darkening colors of dusk slashed across the sky's oceanic horizon from east to west. No moon would shine from the sky that night, and an eerie splendor permeated the atmosphere.

"Soon, Megan," Keely whispered, "we will be together again."

Keely could hardly wait for the secular celebration to end. When the English skeptics sought their beds, she would commune with her mother.

Keely followed her brother down the path to the section of the gardens near the Thames River. Odo and Hew awaited her there. With her cousins stood May and June, who gaped in surprise at their future Countess of Basildon disguised as a stableboy.

"Please light the Samhuinn fire," Keely bade her cousins.

"I'll do it," Odo said.

"'Tis unfair," Hew protested. "You lit last year's."

"And I'll do it again," Odo insisted, cuffing the side of his brother's head.

"Leave him alone," May defended Hew.

"Do you dare to order Odo?" June cried in outrage.

"Keep out of this," May snapped, reaching to pinch her sister.

The Lloyd brothers hastily stepped between the bickering twins. Odo rolled his eyes heavenward, and Hew answered him with a shrug.

"Together then?" Odo asked.

Hew grinned and nodded.

Too late.

While the two couples were arguing about who would light the Samhuinn fire, Keely and Henry had completed the task. They stepped back a few paces to stare at the crackling blaze. Soon, bright flames in the twilight drew the Talbot and Devereux retainers.

Carrying sprigs of yew, Keely and Henry went their separate ways and circulated through the gathering crowd. Both offered their yew sprigs to one and all.

Keely scanned the growing crowd for the earl, but he hadn't made an appearance yet. She did spy the duke and the countess and hurried in their direction.

"Sprig of yew?" Keely offered, sidling up to him.

Duke Robert accepted the yew and said, "Be certain you wash your face tonight, Henry."

"'Tis Keely," she corrected him, then giggled.

Duke Robert and Lady Dawn stared in surprise at her.

"Henry and I switched identities for the celebration," Keely explained, insinuating herself between them. "Chaos does reign supreme, and the person with whom you speak during the next three days of no-time may not even be mortal."

"Oh, Tally, I have the shivery creeps," Lady Dawn cried. "Is it safe to be outside?"

"Don't worry, lovey. I'll protect you," Duke Robert promised.

"Is everything ready inside?" Keely asked.

"'Tis as you wished, child," Duke Robert answered.

"The fire blazes in the hearth, the apples bob in tubs of water, and the chestnuts await their roasting."

"Even Morgana is cooperating," the countess added.

"She's retired to her chamber for the evening."

"What about the special feast?"

"My best wine and fare sit at the place of honor at the high table," the duke answered.

"'Tis a terrible waste of good food," Lady Dawn remarked.

"Custom requires we offer a meal of honor to those who have gone before us," Keely told her. She gazed at her father's profile and added in a soft voice, "When skeptics sleep, our departed loved ones will return to impart their infinite wisdom and special knowledge."

An eerie dreamy quality in her voice made Duke Robert snap his head around. "What do you mean, child?" he asked.

Keely cast him an ambiguous smile but said nothing. . . .

Drawn by the flames in the night and the sounds of laughter emanating from the duke's garden, Richard walked down the path that led to the Talbot estate.

Emerging from between the rows of shrubbery, he smiled when he saw the revelers and sauntered across the manicured lawn toward them. His sharp gaze scanned the crowd for his betrothed.

And then Richard saw her. Weaving her way through the throng, Keely appeared a fey creature of the mysterious night. Her black cloak swirled around her legs, and its hood shrouded her head.

Surprisingly, no welcoming smile graced the lips of her blackened face as she walked toward and then past him. Richard snaked his hand out and grabbed her upper arm. He whirled her around and yanked her up against his unyielding masculine frame.

"Dearest, I want my Halloween treat," he demanded in a husky voice as his mouth began to move to capture hers.

"Yuch!" The voice belonged to Henry Talbot. "Basildon, you're disgusting!"

Shocked, Richard leaped back as if scorched by fire, and his face reddened with angry embarrassment. What trick was this? His future brother-in-law disguised as his betrothed?

The earl growled, "Where the bloody—?"

"Sprig of yew, m'lord?" asked a laughter-filled voice.

Richard whirled around to see a dirty-faced stableboy. He dropped his gaze to the hand holding the sprig of yew. Gleaming in the light cast by the fire, his betrothal ring winked at him from the urchin's finger.

Pretending he didn't recognize her, Richard smiled lazily and said, "I'll take the sprig, boy." He reached for the yew, but his hand closed around her wrist like a slave's manacle and yanked her against him. With his free hand, Richard pulled the cap off her head and tossed it over his shoulder, then watched as her ebony mane cascaded to her waist.

"About that kiss, dearest?" Richard whispered huskily.

Keely blushed beneath the grime on her face. "With all these people watching us?"

"Come with me." Taking her by the hand, Richard led Keely to a secluded section of the garden where several oak trees offered them privacy. Here, the heavy mist off the Thames crept over the land and swirled around their legs.

Keely leaned against the comforting solidness of one of the oaks and then regretted it. With his hands resting against the trunk on either side of her head, the earl trapped her there.

"Do you like our Samhuinn celebration?" Keely asked, trying to mask her nervousness.

"Samhuinn?" Richard echoed, cocking a copper brow at her. "I thought 'twas Halloween."

Mesmerized by the earl's handsome face coming closer and closer, Keely was unable to reply. She snapped her eyes shut at the last possible moment. His warm insistent lips covered hers, sending a hot shiver down her spine.

Richard flicked his tongue across her lips, which parted willingly for him. He gently ravished her mouth with his tongue, exploring and tasting of its incredible sweetness.

Keely moaned throatily and surrendered to the unfamiliar feelings he was creating in her. Unaware of what she was doing, she entwined her arms around his neck and pressed herself intimately against his masculine frame.

Richard broke the kiss and smiled with tenderness at her dazed expression. Christ, she was as sensual as she was sweet. What joy awaited him in his marriage bed when he initiated her into the ways of carnal flesh!

Keely's violet gaze focused slowly on his smile. "Now you have a dirty face too," she told him.

"Dearest, I'd endure a thousand smudgings for one of your sweet kisses," Richard vowed. "I hope 'tis my kiss that put the sparkle in your eyes."

"'Tis Samhuinn," Keely replied, inadvertently insulting him. "I love when the autumn frosts turn the grass to gray, and the four winds scatter the fallen oak leaves."

Richard's emerald gaze lit with amusement. "You love the harbingers of winter?"

"'Tis natural," Keely said. "How could we revel in the birth of spring without the memory of winter?"

"Am I betrothed to a poet?" he teased.

"No, I'm pagan," she answered in all seriousness. "I can commune with those who have gone before and those yet to come as long as the Samhuinn fire burns."

Richard suppressed the powerful urge to laugh. His betrothed was adorably, delightfully absurd. "How will you keep it ablaze for three days, sweetheart?"

"Odo and Hew promised to tend it during the night," Keely replied. "If the fire dies, the enchantment ends, and the veil between the two worlds closes for another year."

"What if it rains?" Richard asked.

"The Great Mother Goddess never sends rain during Samhuinn."

Her certainty brought a smile to his lips. "You truly believe that?"

"Don't you believe in life after death?" she countered.

"Are there others like you?" Richard asked, ignoring her question. "Druids, I mean."

Keely shrugged her shoulders. "I don't actually know."

"Would you tell me if you knew?"

"No."

That didn't sit well with Richard. "Why not?"

"I can never completely trust any man," she told him honestly. "Do you still wish to marry me?"

"Eventually, you will give me your trust," Richard promised, drawing her into the circle of his embrace. He would have kissed her again, but a voice sounded behind them.

"Keely, is that you?" Henry called. "We're going inside to roast the chestnuts."

"Coming," Keely answered. She looked at the earl and invited, "Will you join us?"

Richard shook his head. "Later, perhaps. I've left an unfinished report on my desk."

"Why do you always work so hard?"

"I enjoy working."

"More than roasted chestnuts?" Keely asked, feigning surprise.

Richard grinned. "Save me one, dearest. Give me an hour to finish the queen's report."

Two hours after midnight, the blackest moments of a moonless night, Keely sat on the edge of her bed and listened to the silence inside the Talbot household. Outwardly, she appeared serene; inwardly, her nerves rioted in a wild heart-pounding anticipation of what was about to happen. The thin veil between the Here and Now and the Beyond would part for her mother and her.

Bred to accept the continuity of life, Keely harbored no fears about the dead. In her philosophy the act of death was akin to the act of birth. The communion between the two worlds filled her with unparalleled excitement, and her life's blood sang with the Song of her Ancestors.

Deciding the hour had arrived to escape from the house, Keely stood and donned her black cloak over the breeches and shirt she still wore. She grabbed the small pouch containing her magic stones and golden sickle, then padded on bare feet across the chamber. She pressed her ear against the door and listened, then opened it and stepped into the dark corridor.

Keeping the palm of her right hand against the wall, Keely glided slowly down the corridor to the head of the stairs. When she reached the foyer, Keely paused and lifted her head to listen for any sign of danger. Nothing seemed out of the ordinary.

Noiselessly, Keely opened the door and stepped into the courtyard. She breathed deeply of the hushed night air.

Suddenly, strong hands grabbed her from behind. She tried to scream, but a massive hand covered her mouth. "Don't struggle, little girl." The voice belonged to Odo. He released her as soon as she relaxed with relief.

"We didn't want you screaming the house awake," Hew said by way of an explanation.

Keely rounded on them and demanded in a whisper, "Holy stones! What are you doing here at this hour?"

"Waiting for you," Odo answered.

"We mean to guard you while you worship," Hew added.

Keely was uncertain if her mother's spirit would appear in the presence of others, and she refused to chance losing the opportunity to commune with her. "Protecting me is unnecessary," she insisted.

"We'll be the judge of that," Odo replied.

"He's right *for once*," Hew added.

Odo cuffed the side of his brother's head. "The choice is yours, little girl," he said, just as determined as she. "Either we stand guard, or you return to your chamber."

Keely took a deep defeated breath. "Very well, but do not interfere. No matter what transpires."

With Keely in the lead, the three of them walked down the path that led through the duke's garden to the earl's. Keely halted when they stepped onto the Devereux property.

"Wait over there near the house," she ordered. "Do not interfere. Do you understand?"

Odo and Hew bobbed their heads in unison like two overgrown children.

Keely watched them retreat to a position close to Devereux House. Then she pulled the hood of her cloak up to cover her head and walked the short distance to where the birch, the yew, and the oak stood together.

"Hello, my friends," she whispered to the three holiest of trees. "Are you enjoying Samhuinn?"

Opening her pouch, Keely withdrew ten stones. She

chose nine black obsidians for positive power and one white agate for spiritual guidance.

Keely used eight of the black obsidians to make a large circle, leaving only the western periphery open. She entered the circle from the west and closed it behind her with the ninth obsidian, saying, "All disturbing thoughts remain outside."

After pulling her golden sickle from her pouch, Keely fused the circle's invisible periphery shut and walked to the center, the soul of the circle. She turned in a clockwise circle three times until she faced the northwest, the sacred direction of the ancestors. Then she set the white agate down beside her.

Keely closed her eyes, focused her breathing, and touched her dragon pendant with its sapphires, emeralds, diamonds, and ruby. A ripple of anticipation danced down her spine and made her shiver.

"The Old Ones are here," watching and waiting," Keely said in a soft voice into the hushed air. "Stars speak through stones, and light shines through the thickest oak." Then in a louder voice, "One realm is heaven and earth."

Keely paused a long moment, gathering the proper emotion much as nature gathers its forces. She fell to her knees, opened her arms to implore, and called in a loud whisper, "Spirit of my journey, guide me to hear what the trees say. Spirit of my ancestors, guide me to hear what the wind whispers. Spirit of my tribe, guide me to understand what the clouds foretell." She dropped her arms and closed her eyes, saying, "Those souls who wish me well may enter this circle. Open my heart that I may see beyond the horizon."

Long moments passed. And then it happened, an image floated across her mind's eye. . . .

A woman's face . . . Warm, gray eyes filled with love . . . A serene smile . . . Megan.

"Mother, I miss you terribly," Keely said in an aching whisper.

"Trust the king who wears a fiery crown," Megan told her.

"Is the earl the one?"

Megan smiled. "See who is here with me." The face of a pretty baby appeared and looked with curiosity at Keely. "'Tis my granddaughter, Blythe."

"Blythe is my daughter?"

Megan nodded. "There are others here who will be born to you, but Blythe is the first."

Keely smiled. "Many others?"

"Beware the blacksmith," Megan warned. "He seeks to murder the king."

"His name, Mother?"

Megan lifted her head and looked away, as if sensing approaching danger. "My time with you is short. On Samhuinn next . . ."

While Keely was communing with her mother's spirit, Richard slipped silently into his garden. He walked up behind her cousins stealthily and stood between them. When they turned surprised gazes on him, Richard nodded first at Odo and then at Hew, but he suppressed the powerful urge to laugh at their dumbfounded expressions.

"I've come to guard her," Richard whispered. "What is she doing?"

"Talking to her mother," Odo answered matter-of-factly.

Richard saw only Keely. He flicked a sidelong glance at Hew. "Do you see anyone?" he asked.

Hew nodded and whispered, "I see Keely. Don't you?"

Richard's lips quirked. "I meant, other than Keely?"

Hew shook his head.

Richard turned to Odo. "Do you see her mother?"

"'Course not," Odo answered. "I'm a disbeliever. Only believers can see beyond the horizon."

"So you believe Keely sees her mother?" Richard asked.

"Yup."

"But why?"

"Have you no faith, m'lord?" Hew asked.

"'Tis the same as the priest changing the wafer and the wine into the body and the blood of Christ," Odo explained.

Richard nodded in understanding and turned to watch his betrothed kneeling in front of three trees and talking with someone who wasn't there. Suddenly, from the corner of his eyes, Richard saw a dark shape crossing the lawn toward Keely. He started forward to intercept whoever it was, but stopped short in surprise when he recognized the person.

"Forgive me, Megan," Duke Robert cried as he raced toward the enchanted circle. "I did love you more than life."

Keely whirled around and screamed, "Breaking the circle is forbidden!"

Too late.

In his frantic attempt to reach his long-lost love, Duke Robert crashed through the invisible periphery of the circle. Keely turned back to her mother, but Megan's image had vanished as if she'd never been there.

"Mother, come back!" Keely cried, and crumpled over on the grass. Her forlorn sobs broke the night's silence.

Richard dashed across the lawn to Keely. He knelt beside her and gathered her into his arms, soothing, "All will be well, sweetheart. I swear I'll set things aright. Don't weep."

"I saw Megan," Duke Robert was saying as if in a daze. "She smiled at me. Keely, she forgives my tragic error."

Keely turned within the circle of the earl's embrace, and her voice was filled with venomous contempt. "My mother may forgive you, Your Grace, but I never will. 'Tis your fault I've lost her again!"

She hid her face against the earl's chest and sobbed, "God forgive me, but I hate him."

In the act of reaching for her when she spoke, Duke Robert flinched and dropped his hand. Tears welled up in his violet eyes, so much like his daughter's, and streamed down his cheeks. For the first time in his life, the duke saw beyond his own needs to those of his daughter. Watching her sob against the earl's chest, Duke Robert realized the enormity of what he'd done. He *had* destroyed the lives of the woman he loved and their only child. *Especially their child.* His oldest daughter, the product of his greatest love, had borne the indignities of false bastardy for eighteen years. A lifetime. While he'd been dancing and feasting and flirting at the Tudor court, his daughter had suffered the vile epithet hurled at her from every direction. Now in his selfishness he'd stolen whatever precious time she had with the mother who'd loved her completely and unconditionally from the moment of her conception. How did he dare ask Keely for her trust and her love?

At a gesture from Richard, the Lloyd brothers helped the duke to his feet. As the three of them walked slowly toward the Talbot House, their voices drifted back.

"Come along, Your Grace," Odo said. "Everyone will feel different in the morning."

" 'Tis natural the girl's upset," Hew added. "She don't know what she's saying."

"Hew's right for once," Odo said. "Keely never hated no one, not even that bastard Madoc. She won't be hating you either, once she sees the sun shining in the morning."

"What if it's raining?" Hew piped up.

"Blinking idiot," Odo said, reaching out to cuff his brother's head.

"Well, it could be a cloudy day. . . ."

Richard lifted Keely into his arms and carried her

across the lawn to his own house. Awakened by the commotion outside, several retainers stood in their night-clothes and watched the earl pass through the foyer. Jennings, clad in his nightshirt, followed his master up the stairs.

When Richard reached the second floor, Jennings rushed forward to open the earl's bedchamber door. "Would you or your lady care for anything?" the man asked.

"Privacy."

"Very good, my lord."

The door clicked shut. Richard gingerly set Keely down on his bed and then lay beside her. He gathered her into his arms and stroked her back soothingly. Her uncontrollable weeping tugged at his heart, but he was at a loss as to what would console her. The only female tears he'd ever seen had been feigned and designed to enhance the woman's beauty as well as manipulate the man.

"I miss my m-mother," Keely was sobbing.

"You said Samhuinn lasts for three days," Richard reminded her. "Can you try again tomorrow night? I swear I'll keep your circle safe from intruders."

His offer startled the weeping out of her. Keely gazed up at him through violet eyes swimming in tears. "You'd do that for me?" she asked.

"My love, I'd do anything for you," he promised.

Keely reached up and placed the palm of her hand against his cheek. Her lips quivered into the ghost of a smile.

"Promise me you'll forgive your father."

Keely lost her smile. "I have no father."

"Oh, but you do," Richard said. "His Grace loves you very much. I saw it in his eyes."

"You ask too much," Keely replied, turning her head away from his piercing gaze. "I can never forgive him. Neither for this night, nor for all the other endless nights of the past eighteen years."

"Listen to me." With one finger, Richard turned her

head to face him and waited until her gaze lifted to his. "Your heart is gentle, dearest. Refusing your father's love will hurt you as much as him."

Richard lowered his head and pressed his lips to hers. His kiss was long, slow, and earth-shattering. *And healing*. Sorrow and loss and the need to feel loved made Keely yield to his advances. His hands caressed her body, while his tongue explored the sweetness of her mouth.

Keely sucked in her breath as a thousand airy butterfly wings fluttered through her belly, little knowing that what she felt was desire. Falling beneath the spell cast by his masculine nearness and gentle touch, Keely gloried in the exquisite feeling of him exposing her naked breasts to his heated admiring gaze and warm caressing hands.

Lowering his head, Richard captured one of her dusky nipples between his lips, drawing and suckling upon it. A bolt of molten desire shot through her body to her secret woman's place between her thighs.

Surrendering herself, Keely melted against him and moaned low in her throat. "Kiss me more," she breathed.

Controlling his own need with difficulty, Richard closed her shirt and planted a chaste kiss on her lips.

Keely opened her eyes and stared in a daze of passion at him.

"I've waited this long, and I refuse to dishonor you before we speak our vows," Richard said, then smiled with tenderness at her disappointed expression. "'Tis a supreme compliment, dearest, for I've never concerned myself with a woman's honor before this. Besides, Elizabeth's courtiers will assuredly inspect our marriage bed for the telltale stains of your virginity. You do want your virginity verified by those gossips, don't you?"

Keely's face flamed with hot embarrassment. Unexpectedly, she lifted her head as if listening. Richard opened his mouth to speak, but she silenced him with a "shh."

Keely pulled away from him, leaped off the bed, and

rushed across the chamber to the window. She fell to her knees and cried, "'Tis raining! The Samhuinn fire has died."

Richard was at her side in an instant. He lifted her off the floor and carried her back to his bed. "You'll speak to your mother next year," he consoled her. "I promise I'll build a damned roof to protect the fire from the rain."

Fully clothed, Richard held Keely in the protective circle of his embrace and whispered words of love and comfort. Her breathing evened, and he knew she slept. Only then did Richard close his eyes and allow himself the luxury of following her into a dreamless sleep.

Chapter 12

Keely stood in a tiny candlelit chamber off Hampton Court's Chapel Royal. With her were Duke Robert and Lady Dawn, but she paid no attention to them. In growing trepidation she stared straight ahead at the unadorned wall and worried about what the next forty years held in store for her.

In a very few minutes Duke Robert would escort her down the aisle and give her in marriage to Richard Devereux. Why the earl insisted upon this union was beyond Keely's ken. A nobody from the misty mountains of Wales, Keely knew she could never fit into this confusing English society. Her husband-to-be savored his reputation as a polished courtier, an insider, and one of the queen's personal favorites. When his wife became an embarrassment, the earl would despise her. How could she survive all the days of her life with a man who despised her? Was she forever doomed to play the outsider, the outcast? Oh, why wasn't there a place for her in God's infinite universe?

In spite of her troubled thoughts, Keely appeared serene and regal as she stared without expression at the wall. She looked like a princess of yore, in a wedding gown that had been created in cream-colored satin and adorned with hundreds of seed pearls. Its form-fitting bodice had a square and daringly low-cut neckline, displaying an ample amount of her alluring cleavage. Narrow tight-fitting sleeves puffed at the shoulders.

Any resemblance to a proper English noblewoman ended there, and the more primitive side of her nature reigned over her appearance. In spite of the countess's protests, Keely let her thick ebony mane cascade to her waist in pagan fashion. She'd left her head uncovered and her face unveiled in defiance of English tradition. The gleaming dragon pendant, her mother's legacy to her, nestled provocatively in the valley between her breasts. The only other splash of color, her jeweled betrothal ring, had been moved to her right hand.

Keely had decided that she was who she was. She would neither hide her origins nor apologize for them.

As was her maiden's privilege, Keely carried a bouquet of orange blossoms. The fragrant white flowers represented her virginity and served as a fertility charm because the blossom and the fruit appear simultaneously on the orange tree.

"I'll see if they're ready," Lady Dawn said, breaking the strained silence in the chamber. The door clicked shut.

Keely sensed the duke's presence beside her, but she refused to acknowledge him. In fact, she hadn't spoken a single word to him since that eventful night in the earl's garden.

"I regret the pain I caused you on Samhuinn and all the other days and nights of your life," Duke Robert said, his voice hoarse with emotion. "I cannot fault you for hating me, child, but know that I love you with all of my heart."

Though harboring a grudge went against her nature, Keely nodded to acknowledge his words but did not respond to them. As she stared straight ahead, she realized the earl had been correct. She felt as emotionally ravaged as her father sounded. How could she forgive him? And yet how could she not?

The door opened. Lady Dawn said, "The groom awaits his bride."

Without a word to each other, Duke Robert and Keely left the chamber and positioned themselves in the rear of the chapel. Duke Robert reached for her hand to escort her down the aisle, but Keely hesitated and hung back. "What's done is past, and 'twas no intentional fault of yours," Keely said, raising her tear-filled gaze to his. "Forgive me for the terrible things I've said. *Papa,* I do love you."

"Child of my heart," Duke Robert murmured, drawing her into his embrace. Father and daughter clung together, reluctant to let go now that they had finally found each other.

The Countess of Cheshire smiled at the heartwarming picture they made and brushed a drop of moisture from beneath her eyes. She heard restless murmurings behind her. The wedding guests were apparently wondering what was preventing the nobody-bride from running down the aisle to marry England's premier earl.

Turning toward the crowd, Lady Dawn spied Richard marching down the aisle to discover what had happened to his bride. The countess smiled inwardly to think that the rogue who'd broken so many hearts feared being jilted at the altar.

In spite of the sacred surroundings, Lady Dawn cupped her hands around her mouth and shouted, "Patience, Devereux! Ludlow and his daughter are bidding each other a final farewell."

For his part, Richard gave no heed to the courtiers, friend and enemy alike, who were now laughing openly at his expense. Seeing his betrothed and her father locked in an embrace, Richard nodded toward the countess and then returned to his place at the altar.

Duke Robert finally set his daughter away from him and gave her an encouraging smile. Taking her hand in his, he guided her toward the head of the aisle.

Keely caught her first sight of the richly decorated Chapel Royal. A thousand candles lit the chapel, casting eerie shadows on its walls. Stars of gold, representing God's heavenly universe, adorned the domed sky-blue ceiling.

Keely dropped her gaze to the assembled crowd. A sea of faces stared curiously at her.

"I cannot do this, Papa," she whispered, her panic rising at the sight of all those potential enemies.

Duke Robert squeezed her hand gently. "You are more worthy and noble than a thousand of them combined," he said. At that, he started down the aisle, forcing her to either step with him or struggle for freedom.

At the end of the aisle stood the altar with its mahogany gates, through which Richard and she would pass to kneel in front of the Archbishop of Canterbury. Bouquets of flowers adorned the sanctuary, each one of them the love-in-a-mist that she had admired at the earl's.

Ignoring the stares of the courtiers, Keely slid her gaze to the incredibly handsome man who awaited her at the altar. Elegantly attired in a forest green doublet with matching pantaloons and hose, Richard again appeared like the pagan god of her dreams sprung to life—and he was smiling at her. His emerald gaze held the promise of love and gave her the courage to place one foot in front of the other until she reached his side.

Keely kissed both of her father's cheeks. Turning to the earl, she smiled and placed her hand in his, then heard the courtiers in the first few pews chuckling. Even the Archbishop of Canterbury smiled.

Richard grinned down at her. "I do believe tradition requires waiting for your father to give you away."

"Oh!" Keely crimsoned with embarrassment. Without thinking, she tried to pull away in order to start over.

"Don't you dare," Richard said, refusing to relinquish her hand. "I've got you now and will never let you go."

Much to Keely's relief, the Christian wedding ceremony lasted less than thirty minutes. The moment that would forever warm her heart happened when Richard slipped the wedding band of gold on her finger and promised in a husky voice, *"Por tous jours.* For always, dearest."

"Are you ready to begin your new life?" Richard whispered, before turning with her to be presented as man and wife to the Tudor court.

Keely nodded solemnly. "Don't say I didn't warn you."

Love lit Richard's eyes with amusement. He planted a chaste kiss on her lips and answered, "I won't."

"Welcome to Our court, Lady Devereux." Queen Elizabeth stepped forward first to congratulate them. "Do you swear to be a loving, faithful, and obedient wife to Our dear Midas?"

Keely curtsied deeply and replied, "My vows of loving and faithfulness are registered in Heaven." She flicked a glance at her husband. "As for obedience, I can only try."

Keely looked at the bouquet of orange blossoms in her hand. Technically, her bridal privilege ended the moment she became a wife. On instinct, Keely offered the bouquet to the queen.

"Thank you, child," Elizabeth said, sincerely touched by her gesture. In a wistful voice heard only by Richard and Keely, she murmured, "Mayhap these bridal blossoms shall be the only ones I ever carry." Without another word, the queen whirled away and led the procession out of the Chapel Royal.

Inside Hampton Court's great hall, Keely sat between her husband and her father. Lady Dawn sat on the duke's left while the queen sat on Richard's right. Beyond Elizabeth were the Archbishop of Canterbury, Louise Devereux, and Uncle Hal. Morgana and Willis Smythe, much to their irritation, sat at a lower table along with Henry, who could not have cared less where he sat.

As tradition demanded, Richard fed Keely the requisite quince, which represented female fertility. She ate the yellow apple to the loud applause and wild cheering of the courtiers who'd begun drinking as soon as they'd entered the hall. Keely couldn't help wondering if the gleam in her husband's eyes meant he was in a hurry for an heir so that he could rush off to Ireland and begin his tour of duty.

The servants entered with course after course of their

wedding feast, the likes of which Keely had never seen. All manner of fish arrived first, including salmon in wine sauce and her husband's Colchester mussels. Next came roasted pheasant, followed by a variety of meat dishes. There were braised sides of beef, broiled venison in pepper sauce, and pork roast with spiced wine. Cheshire cheeses, fruit pies, rose pudding, and pine nut candy arrived last, along with a spectacular wedding cake created in the image of two swans whose necks curved to form a heart shape.

"I do not see Odo and Hew," Keely whispered, leaning close to her husband.

"Your cousins sit in the rear of the hall," Richard replied.

"Who put my family in the back?" Keely glared at him.

"Sitting with May and June was their choice." Richard kissed her lips and warned in a whisper, "Be careful, dearest. That lovely face of yours will freeze into an ugly grimace. Then what will you do?"

"'Tis simple. I'll refrain from looking into mirrors," Keely replied, the hint of a smile touching her lips. "The important question is, what will *you* do?"

"'Tis simple," Richard parried, his courtier's wickedness coming to the fore. "I'll snuff the candles before I futter you."

Keely gasped in offended surprise, and her face flamed with scorching embarrassment. No man had ever spoken so crudely to her.

Richard took pity on her innocence. He drew her into a sideways hug and planted a kiss on her cheek. "I'm teasing. Are my lips burned from touching your face?"

Keely couldn't quite suppress her smile.

While the courtiers consumed everything in sight, musicians circulated throughout the hall and entertained on their pipes and lutes. The dancing began when the feasting ended.

Proud of his bride, Richard escorted Keely around the hall and introduced her to the other courtiers. Keely felt confused by all the unfamiliar faces and names, and utterly conspicuous as the center of everyone's attention. The males swarmed about her, their interested gazes inviting her to seek their company at a later date. The females, especially the younger ones, smiled politely; but their sullen gazes spoke volumes and reflected their unvoiced envy.

"Dearest, would you care to dance?" Richard asked when he managed a minute alone with his bride.

Keely froze in a near panic. She didn't know how to dance, but she'd rather eat pork than admit she lacked that cultured skill.

"The wine made me dizzy," she lied. "Would you mind if I didn't?"

"Of course not, sweetheart. I do owe an obligatory dance to the queen. Let me take you to Lady Dawn."

As Richard and Keely crossed the hall, they passed a group of young females that included the Ladies Morgana, Sarah, and Jane. Keely cringed inwardly as their conversation reached her ears.

"She's my father's penniless bastard," Morgana said in a loud voice.

"Why would Basildon stoop to marry a bastard?" Lady Sarah asked. "He could have had any woman in England."

"Because she's uncommonly beautiful," Lady Jane answered, critically eyeing her rival for the earl's affections.

"Any of us would have better suited him," Morgana remarked. "My bastard sister played the harlot for the earl and contrived for my father to find them. He forced the earl into this unwanted marriage."

Richard stopped short and started to turn around, but Keely touched his forearm and turned a pleading gaze upon him.

"'Tis been a wonderful day," Keely said, her expression stricken. "Do not mar its beauty by calling undue attention to her lies. 'Tis spite that rules her tongue.

Morgana believes I've usurped all that was meant to be hers. Mayhap I'd feel the same in her position."

Richard nodded in understanding but said, "You are a saint who never has a bad word for anyone."

"I did for my father on Samhuinn."

"You were upset," he reminded her.

"And so is Morgana," she replied.

While Richard danced with the queen, Keely stood in the company of his mother and Lady Dawn, but her thoughts centered on her husband instead of the conversation swirling around her. Watching him, Keely wished she possessed the skill to partner him on the dance floor. She'd escaped with her ignorance undetected this time—but what excuse would she use on all the other nights of her life?

Richard returned to Keely's side and led her away on the pretext that he wanted to introduce her to someone across the hall. Nonchalantly, he guided her around the perimeter of the chamber, but when they neared its entrance, he yanked her outside, ordering, "And now, my lady, run."

As they raced through the maze of corridors, Keely asked, "Why are we running?"

"Those bawdy drunks will strip us naked," Richard answered without breaking stride. "I'll share the sight of your beauty with no man."

His words made Keely run even faster, which brought a smile to his lips. He never would have imagined a pagan wench would be so modest.

Reaching the safety of their chamber, Richard slammed the door shut and bolted it. Within seconds, they heard loud banging, men's voices slurred with drink, and female giggles.

"Devereux, you cheated us!" shouted Willis Smythe.

"Disperse," Richard called, "or I'll pauper every last one of you."

As the voices and the laughter drifted back down the corridor and faded away, Richard turned around to stare at his bride. Suddenly shy, Keely dropped her gaze to the floor.

My beautiful bride fears what comes next, Richard realized. His own knowledge extended only to the experienced and willing. How could he best make her relax and enjoy herself? And then it came to him.

Richard unbuckled his belt and dropped it on the floor. His doublet followed that.

Keely refused to look up. She did, however, know what he was doing, as evidenced by the becoming blush that stained her cheeks.

Richard smiled. He removed his shirt and tossed it at her feet.

Staring at it, Keely felt like crawling into a hole. Holy stones! What was she expected to do? She closed her eyes against what she knew was coming next—his pantaloons.

"Look at me, dearest." His voice was a soft caress.

Ever so slowly, Keely lifted her gaze from his boots, to his well-muscled pantalooned thighs, to his magnificently bared chest. She let out a peal of laughter.

There stood the renowned Earl of Basildon with his upper arm muscles dancing to the beat of a silent tune. He grinned and opened his arms, inviting her into his embrace.

And Keely went to him. She walked straight into his embrace and pressed herself against the hard muscular planes of his body. The last thing she saw before his lips captured hers was his devastating smile.

Richard kissed her slowly and lingeringly. He knew he needed to take his time with his bride and coax her into doing his bidding willingly. Only then could he truly find his own satisfaction.

"My beautiful bride," he whispered, drawing back finally, caressing her silken cheek almost reverently.

"What about your tongue touching the tip of your nose?" Keely asked.

"I lied about that," Richard admitted without the slightest trace of remorse.

"Why would you do that?"

Richard cocked a copper brow at her. "To impress you, of course."

Keely gave him a wry smile, and her violet eyes sparkled like amethysts. "I was *very* impressed, but your honesty impresses me even more."

" 'Tis good of you to notice my finer points of character, dearest," Richard said with mock solemnity, keeping their conversation light lest he frighten his nervous bride.

"If you turn around, I'll play the tiringwoman for you."

Exhibiting the practiced skill of a man who has unfastened hundreds of women's gowns, Richard completed his task within mere seconds, but his expertise was lost on his innocent bride. He traced a finger down the delicate column of her spine and then nuzzled the side of her neck with his lips.

Keely shivered at the sensations he created. Holy stones! She felt hot and cold at the same time. But how could that be?

"Cold, dearest?" Richard asked, gently turning her around to face him. "Shall I stoke the fire?"

Self-conscious in her modesty, Keely clutched the bodice of her wedding gown to her breasts and stared at him.

"I'm fine," she managed to say in an embarrassed whisper.

Richard smiled with all the tenderness he felt for her. "You can change behind the screen over there," he said, gesturing with a slight incline of his head.

Keely hurried across the chamber to the refuge of the screen. She stepped out of her wedding gown and placed it neatly across a stool, then removed her undergarments and donned the nightshift that had been made especially for this night of nights.

Holy stones! Keely thought, looking down at herself in the gauzy nightshift. The damned gown was transparent. For all that it covered, she might as well have worn nothing at all! She lingered behind the screen in nervous indecision.

"Perhaps we should send for May and June," Keely called, stalling for time.

"Do you need my help?"

"*No.*" She answered too quickly.

Richard smiled at that.

"I mean, the gown might wrinkle," Keely amended.

"Do you plan to wear it in the morning?" Richard asked, laughter lurking in his voice.

"No, perhaps a daughter of ours . . ." Realizing how absurd she sounded, Keely broke off.

Richard did chuckle then. "Do you possess some minor deformity of which I am unaware?" he teased her.

"No." Still, Keely refused to step from behind the screen.

"Are you a coward?" Richard challenged, hoping she'd respond to that.

Keely stepped from behind the screen. Embarrassment kept her gaze glued to the floor, but a telltale blush stained her cheeks.

Richard stared at his bride through emerald eyes that gleamed with desire. His breath caught raggedly in his throat at the sight of her beauty, and his manhood stirred with anticipation. Petite and curvaceously slim, she was even lovelier than he'd imagined.

Richard admired her shapely legs, the alluring curves of her hips, and the enticing duskiness of her nipples, visible through the gauzy transparent silk. Good Christ, all that he saw now belonged to him. In a few short moments he would bury himself deep within his beautiful bride and possess her body and—*he hoped*—her soul. The high blush coloring her cheeks reminded him that he needed to proceed slowly with her initiation into the joys of marital intimacy.

"Have you lost something on the floor?" Richard asked dryly.

Keely snapped her head up and nearly swooned at the incredible sight that greeted her. The earl wore an emerald silk bedrobe. While she'd been undressing behind the screen, *he'd* been undressing too. She hadn't expected that. Keely knew he wore nothing beneath that bedrobe—and she didn't need her Druid's instinct to tell her so.

Pointedly ignoring her fascinated stare, Richard suppressed his smile and lit the incense inside the brass urn on the bedside table. Almost instantly, the delicate perfumed fragrance of jasmine permeated the air within the chamber. Then he poured a goblet of wine and sat on the edge of the bed.

Finally, Richard looked at her and patted the edge of the bed beside him. "Sit with me," he said. "We'll share the wine."

His invitation moved her into action, but it wasn't the one he'd expected.

"I need something," Keely told him, and hurried across the chamber in the opposite direction.

Keely rummaged through her belongings until she found what she wanted—two dried roots with stems. Turning around, she gulped nervously and walked toward the bed like a felon going to the gallows.

"'Tis dragonwort," Keely explained, holding one root up before she tucked it beneath the pillows. She blushed and added in an embarrassed whisper, "Dragonwort promotes conception."

Richard's gaze softened on her. He nodded solemnly and asked, "And the other?"

"Yarrow," she answered, dropping it inside the brass urn to mingle and burn with the jasmine. "'Tis known for keeping couples happily married."

Richard smiled then, but Keely never saw it. Instead, she whirled around and scanned the chamber in growing desperation. She searched her mind for something—*anything*—that would prevent her from having to sit beside him on the bed.

Knowing she was stalling, Richard watched her with tender amusement lighting his emerald eyes. In a deep husky voice, he ordered, "Dearest, look at me."

Keely turned around slowly. Filled with an emotion she was unable to identify, his emerald gaze mesmerized her.

"Sit with me?"

Keely cast him a nervous wobbly smile and sat on the edge of the bed. She stared straight ahead, as if frozen in stone.

Richard reached over and with one hand gently turned her face toward him, then waited patiently until she summoned the courage to lift her gaze from his throat to his eyes. "Keely, I am the man who sat in a garden and promised never to hurt you," Richard said. "I am also the man who willingly suffered a public humiliation by proposing marriage on bended knee in a hall filled with listening servants. Why are you suddenly afraid of me?"

"I—I'm not afraid," Keely tried to explain. "Not exactly."

Richard put his arm around her shoulder and drew her against the side of his body. "Have you ever been alone with a man?"

"Yes."

Richard snapped his eyebrows together. Her honest answer wasn't the one he'd expected. "Who?" he asked.

"Odo and Hew. And Rhys, of course."

Richard relaxed.

"And—"

"Who?" he demanded.

"Are you angry with me?" Keely asked, her eyes large with fright.

"Never answer my questions with questions of your own," Richard said, his voice stern. "With whom else were you alone?"

"I was alone with you," she reminded him, "at your house."

Richard smiled with immense relief. "Do you understand what we are going to do tonight?"

Keely nodded. She wished with all her heart that she didn't know what her fate would be.

"Tell me, dearest."

Keely stared at him in surprise, then asked, "Don't *you* know?"

Richard struggled against a shout of laughter and won. "Of course, I know," he said with a smile. "I wished to know if what you're thinking is correct."

"You're going to futter me," Keely blurted out baldly, her voice rising with her panic. "Just as you said at dinner."

Richard felt no urge to laugh now. His bride feared him, and he wanted to calm her in order to maximize her pleasure. Whatever happened in their marriage bed that night would color their relations for as long as they lived.

"I should never have said that," Richard told her.

"'Twas my courtier's dim wit coming to the fore. . . . Animals futter, sweetheart. Men and women make love together. 'Tis a sharing of their bodies, their hearts, and their souls." He searched his mind for a solid analogy she could understand. "What are the physical earthly things you love to feel?" he asked.

Keely thought a moment and then cast him a shy, thoroughly enchanting smile. "I love the dewy grass between my toes, warm sunshine on my shoulders, and a gentle summer's breeze tickling my face."

Richard smiled. His bride was the only woman of his acquaintance who would have given such a priceless answer. His heart filled with aching tenderness for this unaffected innocent he'd made his wife.

"Making love feels like all that *and more*," Richard promised.

That perked Keely's interest, and she cocked her head to one side. "Truly?"

Richard nodded knowingly and correctly read the shining interest in her eyes. He stood then and faced her, holding his hand out in invitation, as if he were asking her to dance.

Keely dropped her gaze from his gleaming emerald eyes to his outstretched hand. When she raised her eyes to his again, Richard saw that apprehension had crept into her gaze again. Her small white teeth worried her full bottom lip, an endearing nervous habit of hers that he'd noticed at other stressful moments.

"I'll stop whenever you say," Richard promised. "Trust me?"

In an unconsciously sensual gesture, Keely flicked her tongue out and wet her lips, gone dry from nervousness. She dropped her violet gaze to his hand once more, then reached out and placed her smaller hand in his.

When she stood and faced him, Richard reached out with both hands and slid the straps of her nightshift off her shoulders. The gown fluttered to the floor at her feet. Wearing nothing except for the gleaming dragon pendant, she appeared like a pagan princess.

Keely blushed furiously and bowed her head in maidenly shame.

Instead of reaching for her body as he wished to do, Richard tilted her chin up and said, "Let me admire your *proud* beauty."

Keely knew what he meant. She raised her head high like a beautiful pagan queen and squared her shoulders, which thrust her perfectly formed breasts forward.

Richard worshipped her with his eyes. His gaze dropped from her hauntingly lovely face to her dusky-nippled breasts and then traveled down to her tiny waist, her slim yet curvaceous hips, and finally her dainty feet.

When his scorching gaze returned to hers, he asked, "Do you feel the sun's warmth yet?"

Keely smiled at his words.

Without taking his gaze from hers, Richard began to unfasten his bedrobe's belt.

"Stop," Keely said, panicking.

The instant she said the word, Richard stilled his hands. "As you stand naked before me, dearest, I would stand naked before you," he coaxed. "I need to feel your admiring gaze on my body."

A long silent moment passed between them. Finally, Keely nodded.

Richard shrugged his bedrobe off and stood proudly before her in all of his masculine glory. Unfortunately, Keely refused to drop her gaze below his neck.

Richard's lips twitched with the urge to laugh, but he controlled himself. Instead, he affected a slightly pleading tone in his voice when he said, "Look at my body, Keely. *Please?*"

Slowly, Keely dropped her gaze from his broad shoulders to his magnificent chest covered with a mat of copper hair. Her gaze dipped lower to his tapered waist, but her eyes widened when she saw the apex of his manhood, which stiffened beneath her curious stare.

"May I touch you, sweetheart?" he asked, his voice a soft caress.

Keely lifted her gaze to his. For one awful moment Richard thought her maidenly fears would overrule her apparent curiosity. Then she nodded.

Richard stepped a hairbreadth closer. He reached out with one hand and caressed her silken cheek, then glided his fingertips down the column of her slender neck to her shoulders.

Everywhere he touched her burned. Keely closed her eyes and whispered, "I can feel the sun's warmth."

Richard smiled at that. Reluctant to frighten her by reaching for her breasts, Richard glided the tips of his fingers along their gentle swell and continued down her side to the alluring curve of her hips.

Keely sighed. "I do feel the summer's breeze," she murmured.

"If you wish to feel the dew," he whispered hoarsely, "then I must kiss you."

Keely opened her eyes. She smiled and nodded at him.

Ever so gently, Richard drew her into his embrace. Allowing her no time to think, he captured her mouth in a lingering kiss that stole her breath away.

Keely reached up, entwined her arms around his neck,

and pressed her nakedness against his. For the first time in her young life, she experienced the incredible sensation of masculine hardness touching her female softness. *And she liked it.*

Without warning, Richard scooped her into his arms and placed her on the bed. Then he lay down beside her and gathered her into his embrace.

As his lips hovered above hers, he asked in a seductive whisper, "Shall I stop?"

"Not yet," she answered without opening her eyes.

Richard smiled with tenderness. His mouth claimed hers in a slow soul-stealing kiss that seemed to last forever. Swept away by his passion, Keely returned his kiss in kind. And then some.

Richard flicked his tongue along the crease of her mouth, and Keely willingly parted her lips for him. He explored the sweetness beyond them, and she surprised him by following his lead. Their tongues touched tentatively and then grew bold, swirling wildly together in a primitive mating dance as old as time itself.

"Can you feel the sun's warmth?" Richard breathed against her lips.

"Yes."

"Me too."

Keely moaned. His words tugged at her heartstrings and inflamed her blossoming desire.

Richard sprinkled dozens of feathery-light kisses on her temples, eyelids, nose, and throat. He held her tightly as if he wished never to let her go. His mouth returned to hers, and they kissed for an eternity. Richard caressed her silken body from the delicate column of her throat to her thrusting breasts to the juncture of her thighs.

Feeling her shiver, he whispered, "'Tis the summer's breeze, sweetheart."

Again, his lips claimed hers in an earthmoving kiss. His hands caressed her as lightly and gently as the summer's breeze, while his lips moved down her throat and then beyond.

Capturing one of her dusky nipples between his lips, Richard suckled upon it and ignited a heat between her thighs that banished all coherent thought from her mind. Keely burned to be possessed by her husband.

"I need—*something*," she panted, her innocence making her ignorant of what she yearned for. But her husband knew.

"Spread your legs for me," Richard said, his voice thick with desire.

Without hesitation, Keely did as she was told. Richard kissed her thoroughly, and then, watching her face, he slowly inserted one long finger inside her.

Panicking, Keely opened her mouth to cry stop, but Richard was too fast for her. He covered her mouth with his own, drugging her senses with the urgency of his kiss.

When he judged her shock had passed, Richard inserted a second finger inside her. "Be easy, my love," he cooed to her. "Accustom yourself to the feel of it. You're so wonderfully tight. I want to make you ready to receive me. . . . Can't you feel the sun's burning warmth between your thighs?"

Without waiting for an answer, Richard dipped his head to her breasts and suckled upon each of her aroused nipples. His talented fingers began to move rhythmically and seductively inside her.

Keely relaxed, and catching his rhythm, she began to move her hips. She enticed his fingers deeper inside her writhing body and moaned her need. Her hips moved faster and faster. And then his fingers were gone.

"No," she whimpered, protesting their desertion, as her eyes flew open.

Richard knelt between her thighs. His engorged manhood teased the dewy pearl of her womanhood. Keely moaned at this incredibly sensuous torture and closed her eyes.

"Look at me, my love," Richard ordered, his manhood poised to pierce.

Keely opened her eyes and stared in a daze of desire at him.

"One moment of pain, my love," Richard promised.

"Like a passing cloud blocking the sun's warming rays."

Richard pushed himself inside her with one powerful thrust and buried himself deep within her trembling body. Clutching him, Keely cried out in surprised pain as he broke through her virgin's barrier.

But she never said stop.

Richard lay perfectly still for several long moments, letting her become accustomed to the feel of him inside her. He began moving seductively, enticing her to move with him.

Keely wrapped her legs around his waist as innocence vanished and primal instinct surfaced. She moved with him and met each of his powerful thrusts with her own.

Suddenly, unexpectedly, a thousand suns exploded inside Keely. Wave after wave of volcanic sensation carried her to paradise and beyond.

Only then did Richard unleash his own powerful need. Clutching her tightly, he groaned and shuddered and poured his potent seed deep within her womb.

They lay still for long moments, their labored breathing the only sound in the chamber. Richard finally rolled to one side, pulling her with him, and planted a kiss on her forehead. He gazed with budding love at her wondrous expression.

With her heart shining in her eyes, Keely looked at her husband and said, *"Stop."*

"Stop?" Richard cocked a copper brow at her as his emerald eyes lit with amused surprise.

He was unable to suppress the chuckle bubbling up. Within three seconds, his chuckle gave birth to a howl of hearty laughter, and his shoulders shook with uncontrollable mirth.

"You're shaking the bed," Keely said, and then dissolved into giggles.

Richard pulled her across his chest. One of his hands

massaged the fragile nape of her neck while his lips claimed hers in what he intended to be a passionate kiss; but for the first time in his life, the worldly wise earl laughed into the mouth of the woman he was kissing. Surrendering to the inevitable, he pulled his wife down on top of him and stroked her back while he tried to tame his mirth.

Keely rested her head against the mat of dark copper curls that covered his chest. She heard the rhythmic beating of his heart and sighed with contentment.

Lifting the gleaming pendant from between her breasts, Richard asked, "Do you always wear the dragon?"

"I shall never willingly remove my mother's legacy," Keely answered.

"You loved her very much."

"I still do. Love lives for all of eternity. It cannot die with the loved one's passing."

Richard felt strangely comforted by that thought.

"'Tis time for sleeping," he said.

"I'm not tired." In fact, every nerve in Keely's body tingled in a wild riot, the natural by-product of her husband's lovemaking.

"I have a gift for you," he said.

"And I for you," she replied in a soft voice.

With no regard for modesty, Richard rose from the bed and walked across the chamber. Keely lingered there a moment longer and admired her husband's magnificent body with its broad shoulders, strong back, tapered waist, and firm buttocks.

Feeling her eyes upon him, Richard glanced over his shoulder and winked suggestively at her.

Keely blushed and leaped off the bed, then remembered her own nakedness. Grabbing her husband's discarded bedrobe, she quickly covered herself. Keely heard his husky chuckle and cast him a quelling look before heading across the chamber to her own belongings.

They rendezvoused at the bed. Refusing to relinquish her husband's bedrobe, Keely sat on top of the coverlet and tucked her legs beneath her. Richard sat with his back resting against the headboard and covered his more interesting features with the coverlet.

"Happy wedding day, dearest," Richard said, handing her the smaller of the two packages in front of him.

Keely opened the lid of the lacquered box and stared at its contents. On a bed of blue velvet lay the most beautiful brooch she'd ever seen. A gold flower basket filled with love-in-a-mist, the brooch's blossoms had been created in sapphires, amethysts, and diamonds.

Looking up at his expectant expression, Keely said in a voice no louder than a whisper, " 'Tis worthy of a queen."

Richard leaned forward and planted a sweet kiss on her lips, saying, "You are *my* queen."

Keely stared at the brooch and valiantly blinked back the sudden tears that filled her eyes, but her bottom lip trembled with the effort. Once again she wondered what the earl would do when he realized he'd married the wrong woman. She could never fit into his world, nor would his world accept her for what she was. By God's holy stones, she didn't even know how to dance.

"Open the other," Richard said.

Keely shook her head. She pasted a bright smile onto her face and insisted, " 'Tis your turn, my lord." She offered him one of two packages and added apologetically, "I fear 'tis not so fine as what you've given me."

"I'll be the judge of that," Richard said, opening the box. A heavy band of gold with an immense red carnelian stone stared up at him.

"As you already know, the carnelian protects its owner," Keely told him.

Richard handed her the ring and then gestured for her to slip it onto the third finger of his left hand, saying, "Thank you, Keely. I will cherish it . . . *por tous jours.*"

"For always," Keely whispered, slipping the ring onto his finger. With irrepressible mischief shining in her eyes, she added, "I couldn't ask His Grace for money because

I wasn't speaking to him at the time. So Odo and Hew robbed a fancy lord along the Strand. I do hope the fact that the ring is stolen doesn't bother you."

"Your cousins stole—?"

Keely burst out laughing. "I'm teasing."

"'Tis a magnificent gift, but not quite as magnificent as your amethyst eyes," Richard told her. "Did you know that the amethyst represents virtue?"

Keely shook her head. "What about emeralds?" *Like your eyes,* she thought.

"Emeralds signify constancy."

I hope so, she thought but said nothing.

Richard offered her his second gift. "In view of your unusual beliefs, I thought you could use a bit of redemption," he teased.

Wearing a puzzled smile, Keely unwrapped the package. "A book?"

"'Tis *Lives of the Saints.*"

Instead of laughing as he'd expected, Keely frowned at the book without really seeing it. She recalled the gibberish she'd seen that day in the study and worried her bottom lip with her teeth. Her husband knew she was a penniless bastard. What would he now think upon discovering she was also ill-educated?

"Is there a problem, dearest?"

Keely heard the concern in his voice. Too embarrassed to meet his gaze, she stared at his chest and confessed, "My lord, I am unable to read any language but English."

"I know," Richard said, his expression tender. "If you look closely at the book, sweetheart, you'll see that I've translated *Lives of the Saints* into English."

Keely smiled with relief and held the book in her arms almost reverently. "What a wonderful gift. I've never owned a book before."

"Will you read it?"

"Someday."

"Soon, I hope."

"In view of *your* lack of faith," Keely said, handing him her second gift, "I decided you could use a smidgeon of salvation."

Richard unwrapped the package. Puzzled, he stared at it for a long moment and then, realizing what it was, shouted with laughter. Richard unfolded the hooded white ceremonial robe and caressed his bride's handiwork, his initials *R* and *D* embroidered with golden threads.

"Will you wear it?" she asked.

His lips twitched. "Some night," he promised.

"Soon, I hope."

Richard pulled her down on the bed and stroked her back, saying, "You must be exhausted, sweetheart."

Keely shook her head but rested her cheek against his chest. "Your advice about forgiving my father was correct," she said. "I feel as if a tremendous weight has been lifted off my spirit."

"And so does he, my love."

He'd called her "my love," Keely thought. Did her husband harbor tender feelings for her? Or were his words a figure of speech, another English custom of which she was unaware?

"What are you thinking?" Richard asked, noting her troubled expression.

Keely reared up and faced the object of her thoughts. Nose to nose with him, she asked, "Would you have stopped if I'd asked you?"

His hand paused in its stroking. Richard gazed into her eyes and lied, "Yes, dearest. Your merest wish is my command."

Keely arched an ebony brow at him and then gifted him with a sweetly flirtatious smile. "What if I say *start?*"

A devastatingly lazy smile spread across his handsome features. Richard gently flipped her onto her back and, with his sensuous lips, wiped the smile off her face. An hour later they dropped into a sated sleep.

Richard awakened during those hushed magical moments before dawn when the world still slept. Without bothering to open his eyes, he moved toward the middle of the bed in search of his wife's hot little body. It wasn't there. One emerald eye opened first, and then the other. Where the bloody hell had she gone? Richard rolled over and saw her.

Naked, with her ebony mane cascading to her waist, Keely stood in front of the window and gazed outside at the dawn. The palm of her hand rested against the window glass, and her lips moved in a silent chant.

The hint of a smile touched Richard's lips. His wife was greeting the sunrise, as she'd said she did each morning of her life.

Richard arose and padded on bare feet across the chamber. Holding the veil of her ebony mane aside, he brushed his lips along the nape of her neck and sensed every fiber of her being smile a good morning greeting to him.

Without shame or modesty, Keely leaned back against the hard muscular planes of his body. His strong arms encircled her and cupped the perfect globes of her breasts, his thumbs flicking seductively across her sensitive nipples.

Feeling her sharp intake of breath, Richard smiled inwardly and asked, "What do you see?"

"Beyond the horizon." Her voice sounded soft and dreamy.

"What lies beyond the horizon, my love?"

Keely turned within the circle of his embrace. She entwined her arms around his neck and planted a kiss on his lips, then answered, "Our daughter Blythe has begun her long journey to us."

Richard gave her a puzzled smile. What she said made no sense at all, but by now he'd known her long enough to realize that any explanation she offered would only confuse him more. So he nodded once, accepting her words without question.

"What would you like to do on this first full day of our married life?" he asked.

"Our marriage needs a propitious beginning," she answered gravely. "Duty requires that we return to Devereux House. Oh, and we'll need a barge large enough to carry Merlin. She must accompany us."

"Why?" Richard asked, already regretting the need for an explanation.

"'Tis an ancient Welsh custom," Keely explained. "When a bride walks her horse through her husband's home, good luck follows."

Laughter lurked in his voice when he asked, "You think to march Merlin through Devereux House?"

Keely nodded.

"She'll conduct her business on my floor," Richard argued.

"Merlin is a well-mannered lady and would never even consider so foul an action," Keely assured him. "Besides, 'tis important for the well-being of our marriage."

Richard absolutely refused to allow a damned horse into his house. Nor did he intend to pass the day arguing with his wife about it.

"Cheshire and your father will be wed this afternoon," he reminded her. "We haven't the time to journey to Devereux House. Will this venerable custom await our homecoming at a later date?"

"I suppose so," she answered with an uncertain frown.

Richard stepped back a pace and held his hand out in invitation, saying, "Come to bed."

Keely dropped her gaze from his emerald eyes to his hand and then his manroot, lying flaccid at his groin. She reached out slowly and said, "My lord, you carry a beauty mark on the top of—oh!" Beneath the light touch of her fingertip, his manhood stiffened, surprising her. "Why, it has a life of its own."

"This randy fellow makes no move without my knowledge and approval," Richard said. "What you see is a freckle, dearest. Ladies have beauty marks, and gentlemen have handsome freckles."

Richard scooped her into his arms and carried her across the chamber. He tossed her unceremoniously onto the bed and, with an exaggerated growl of lust, fell on top of her.

Keely and Richard passed the whole of the morning and part of the afternoon basking in the sun's warmth and sighing at the gentle summer's breeze. *All within the kingdom of their bed.*

Chapter 13

"Are you ready?" Richard asked, entering their bedchamber. "'Tis late."

At the sound of her husband's voice, Keely turned away from the window and stood motionless while he stared at her. His awed expression pleased her immensely.

With a smile playing upon his handsome face, her husband stood five feet inside the room and looked her up and down appreciatively. His emerald gaze drifted downward from her lovely face, lingered on the exposed cleavage of her creamy breasts, and then traveled the remaining distance to the tips of her dainty slippered feet.

His smoldering gaze made Keely feel like a princess in a gown of violet velvet that exactly matched her eyes. Her only adornments were the dragon pendant that hung on the gold chain around her neck, the love-in-a-mist brooch, and the rings he'd given her.

"What do you think?" Keely asked, twirling in a circle for his perusal, her eyes sparkling as brightly as the amethysts in her love-in-a-mist brooch.

Richard closed the distance between them and, in courtly manner, bowed low over her hand. "I think you are the most beautiful woman in all of Christendom," he said.

As they left the chamber, Keely flicked a glance at his somber apparel. "Why do you always wear black, my lord?" she asked. "'Tis the color of mourning."

"Never reveal this to another soul," Richard confided as if confessing a dark secret. "Black is the only color that I'm certain matches both my red hair and my green eyes."

Keely smiled at his admission. She never would have

guessed that her arrogant husband harbored an insecurity about anything, much less the clashing of colors.

"Will Louise and Uncle Hal attend my father's wedding?" she asked.

"No, they returned to the Strand this morning," Richard answered. "My mother feels uncomfortable at court."

So do I, Keely thought. "What about Henry?"

Richard shook his head. "Your father sent him back to Talbot House this morning with Uncle Hal and my mother."

"I don't suppose Morgana approves of the match enough to attend?"

"Probably not."

Richard escorted Keely through a confusing maze of dimly lit corridors to the Long Gallery. Beyond the gallery was the Chapel Royal where her father and the countess would be wed.

Stepping into the deserted Long Gallery, Keely felt a prickly sensation tickle the nape of her neck. "'Tis drafty in here," she remarked.

Richard glanced at the rows of long, tapered candles on either side of the gallery. Their flames flickered not one whit.

Keely's gaze followed his, and her eyes widened in surprise. No draft in the world could tease a person's neck without playing havoc with a candle's flame.

Walking deeper into the gallery, Keely felt an oppressiveness settle heavily upon her. She cast a nervous sidelong glance at her husband, who acted as though nothing were wrong.

Uneasiness made Keely slow her pace, and rising panic made her heart beat faster. Nothing was amiss here, she told herself. Hadn't she passed through this same gallery the previous day on her way to her own wedding? True, she'd been immersed in misery because of the rift with her father, but could that misery have prevented her from sensing the sad bleakness inside this chamber? The only other time in her life when she'd felt this hopelessness had been that horrifying day at the Tower of London.

Keely halted twenty paces inside the seemingly endless chamber. Suddenly, unexpectedly, she whirled away from Richard and bolted out of the chamber the way they'd come. Keely heard her husband call her name but ignored him. Closing her eyes, she leaned against the corridor wall outside the gallery and welcomed its coolness seeping into her body.

"What is it?" Richard asked. "Are you ill?"

Keely heard the worry in his voice and opened her eyes. She shook her head, saying, "I felt something."

"What did you feel?"

"Is there another way to the chapel?" she asked, ignoring his question. "I cannot walk through that chamber."

Richard narrowed his gaze on her. "But why not?"

"Troubled spirits haunt that place," Keely answered.

"Ghosts exist only in idle minds like yours," Richard snapped, becoming irritated. "You promised you would refrain from flaunting those silly beliefs of yours."

Keely straightened away from the wall. "Saying my beliefs are silly does not make them so. I know what I felt, you—*skeptic*!" She started to turn away, but he grabbed her forearm.

"Where do you think you're going?" Richard demanded. "Even as we speak, Cheshire and your father are exchanging vows. How will I explain your absence?"

"Tell them anything you like," Keely snapped, yanking out of his grasp. "My father accepts me for what I am. *Even if you do not.*" At that, she whirled away in anger and left him standing alone in the corridor.

"Shit," Richard swore as he watched her retreat. He stood in indecision for a long moment. Should he go after her? Familial duty demanded one of them attend the wedding ceremony. Turning on his heel, Richard marched through the Long Gallery toward the Chapel Royal.

Meanwhile, Keely walked briskly through the maze of

corridors but couldn't quite recall which one led to her chamber. Nothing seemed familiar, and she saw no one whom she could ask. Rising panic made her feet move faster until, rounding a corner, she collided full-force into another person.

Strong hands grabbed her upper arms and kept her from falling. Startled, Keely looked up and saw a familiar face.

"Good afternoon, countess," Baron Willis Smythe greeted her.

"Countess?" Keely echoed, confused.

Smythe grinned and reminded her, "By marriage you are now a countess."

Keely's expression cleared, but her cheeks pinkened into a becoming blush. "I forgot," she murmured.

A deep rumble of laughter welled up in his chest. The baron's interested gaze dipped to the alluring swell of silken flesh above her low-cut bodice. Lust lurked in his eyes, but innocence blinded Keely to it.

"Have you forgotten your vows so soon, my lady?" Smythe asked in a husky voice.

"I'm hopelessly lost," Keely confessed, ignoring what she considered an impertinent question. "Could you direct me to my husband's chamber?"

"Where's Richard?"

"I sent him along to my father's wedding," she explained, "but I became ill and need to retire for a while."

"Damsels in distress are my specialty," Smythe said, taking her arm in his. "Allow me to escort you there."

When they reached her chamber, Keely turned to thank him. The baron stepped perilously close and kissed her hand.

"Shall I come inside and keep you company until the earl returns?" Willis suggested, his voice low and seductively husky.

"No!" Keely dashed into her chamber and slammed the door, then threw the bolt to lock herself in. She heard the baron's chuckle as he walked away.

Relieved to have escaped Smythe's company, Keely leaned back against the door and breathed deeply. She didn't like Willis Smythe. An aura of untimely death surrounded him like a shroud, and the unholy gleam in his eyes reflected something more sinister than a wicked sense of humor.

Angry with her husband, Keely began pacing back and forth across the chamber. The earl had known what she was before he married her. Did he now think to change her? Attempting to do so would be an exercise in futility. What she believed and felt was beyond his control. He would enjoy greater success if he ordered the birds to stop singing. Why hadn't he heeded her warning when she'd told him that she could never adapt to his courtier's way of life? Married less than one day, the earl and she had already started down that road called Failure. Was she forever doomed to be the outcast, the unhappy outsider? Where in God's great universe was her own safe haven?

Keely forced her mind away from her doomed marriage, but her thoughts next drifted down the maze of Hampton Court's corridors to the unseen presence in the Long Gallery. Some unknown, tragic event held a tormented soul captive there, as at the Tower of London. What manner of men were these English to create such utter hopelessness?

Keely froze when she heard a knock on the door and wondered if Baron Smythe had returned. "Who is it?" she called.

"A page, my lady."

Keely opened the door and saw the boy dressed in the queen's livery. "Yes?"

"Lord Basildon bade me escort you to the hall," the boy told her. "Will you come?"

Keely nodded and followed him down the corridor, but troubled thoughts filled her mind. She'd angered her husband, and so he'd sent a page to fetch her. If the earl were anything like Madoc, he would entertain his anger for days. How would she ever win his affections back?

The page disappeared at the hall's entrance. Keely took a hesitant step inside the chamber and halted. Hundreds of colorfully garbed courtiers crowded into the queen's Presence Chamber. Fear of stepping into that milling throng of strangers kept Keely rooted where she stood.

The chamber was enormous. England's finest musicians stood on the left side of the room and played their various instruments. On the long wall of the chamber, directly opposite the entrance where Keely stood, Queen Elizabeth sat in a chair upon a raised dais surrounded by imported carpets. The middle of the chamber had been saved for dancing.

Appearances meant everything at the Tudor court, and the males outshone the females in that regard. Doublets, hose, and accessories created in golden brocade, crane-colored silk, or murrey velvet harmonized on each nobleman. Earrings fashioned with gold and precious gems dangled from their ears, and rouge colored many a masculine cheek.

The noblewomen wore gowns so scandalously low-cut, they made Keely's plunging neckline appear virginal, and they bedecked themselves in every priceless jewel they owned. How these ladies managed to walk upright beneath the weight of all those gleaming golden chains was beyond her ken.

Staring at these parading peacocks, Keely's courage eluded her. Never would she be accepted into this world, nor could she accept this decadent style of living.

Keely decided to return to her chamber. As she started to turn away, a familiar voice stopped her.

"Feeling better, dearest?"

Keely whirled around to face the only black-clad bird of prey in this aviary of canaries, her husband. She nodded and asked, "Where's my father?"

"I'll take you to him," he said with a smile. Richard held her hand and forced her to plunge with him into the crowd of courtiers. As they made their way through that throng, the noblemen and their ladies nodded or bowed or smiled at them. Keely felt proud that others held her husband in such obvious esteem. Nearing the dais, Keely saw Lady Dawn and her father, who turned to greet her.

"Richard told us you'd taken ill," Duke Robert said, planting a kiss on her cheek.

"I feel much better now," Keely assured him, "but terrible about missing your wedding. Please forgive me."

"There's naught to forgive, child." Duke Robert winked at the earl and joked, "Perhaps my grandchild is rising in the oven."

Keely blushed furiously. Richard chuckled, more at his wife's offended modesty than at his father-in-law's teasing.

"I'm very happy for you, *Your Grace*," Keely said, giving her new stepmother an affectionate hug.

"What a sweet child you are," Lady Dawn gushed. "Why, I'd nearly forgotten that I am now a duchess. Marrying Tally is reward enough."

"I find that hard to believe," a woman near them said loudly to her friends.

In an equally loud voice that carried back to the woman, Lady Dawn said, "Margaret Lennox has a personality that exactly matches her ugly face. Beware of her, Keely."

"Sweetheart," Richard whispered close to his wife's ear, "do you mind if I dance with the queen before I dance with you?"

Keely shook her head and smiled at him. She watched her husband, a gallant figure of a man, walk toward the dais and then bow deeply in front of Elizabeth. Keely could almost feel the warmth of the devastating smile that he gave the queen.

"Would you care to dance with your father?" Duke Robert asked, drawing her attention.

Keely froze. Admitting she didn't know how to dance

was out of the question. Embarrassed, she searched her mind for a plausible reason to refuse.

"The exertion might make me ill again," Keely said.

"Please, Papa, dance with your bride."

"You don't mind?" Lady Dawn asked.

Keely pasted a bright smile onto her face and shook her head. She watched as the Duke and Duchess of Ludlow stepped onto the dance floor together.

Alone in the midst of strangers, Keely felt like an outsider again and horribly conspicuous. Several lords and their ladies looked at her as they passed by, but no one deemed her worthy of conversation or acknowledgment. What little confidence Keely possessed dwindled with each passing moment.

Much to her relief, the music ended, and Keely watched her husband escort the queen to the dais. She would have started toward him then, but as he turned away from the dais, a young noblewoman cornered him. Keely's spirits plummeted when her husband stepped onto the dance floor with Lady Jane, the sultry brunette who, as the countess had told her, desired bedsport with Richard.

Morgana happened by with a handsome young courtier. Keely heard the word *bastard* and cringed inwardly. She flicked a self-conscious glance around her. Now the men's interested stares seemed more like lascivious leers, while the women's smiles appeared vicious instead of coolly polite.

Keely knew she couldn't bear to stand there alone very much longer. But where could she go? She didn't know anyone with whom she could converse. And even if she did, Keely feared she would appear "uncivilized," as her husband had once pointed out.

Duke Robert and Lady Dawn arrived just in time to save her the humiliation of leaving the Presence Chamber alone while her husband danced with another woman. In spite of her badly frayed nerves and wounded pride,

Keely held her head high but breathed an inward sigh of relief when her father returned.

The musicians ended their composition and began another. Excusing themselves, Duke Robert led Lady Dawn onto the dance floor again. Still Richard did not reappear.

In growing misery, Keely scanned the chamber and found him. This time the earl danced with Lady Sarah, the blonde who'd been angling after him for marriage. Keely stared glumly at the carpet beneath her slippered feet, but her abject misery slowly gave birth to anger. The earl knew she was unacquainted with these people, yet he had abandoned her to fend for herself. How could she compete for his attention against such sophisticated ladies as Jane and Sarah? Even Morgana suited him better than she did. Why had he sent for her if he planned to ignore her?

"Where did your smile go?" a voice beside her asked.

Keely snapped her head up and turned a frigid violet gaze upon her husband. "I left it at the altar, my Lord Waverer."

"Give over, sweetheart," Richard said with a smile meant to melt her heart as well as the icy look in her eyes.

"'Tis a party. Dancing and mingling are expected."

"Mingling?" Keely echoed, her voice tinged with sarcasm. "Is that what adultery is called here at court? You English have such pretty terms for every vile action under the sun."

"*Adultery?*" His emerald gaze narrowed on her, but when he spoke, amusement lurked in his voice. "Are you jealous of my partnering others on the dance floor?"

"No." Keely lifted her nose into the air and turned away.

Richard leaned dangerously close, so close, she felt the warmth of his breath tickling her cheek. "I do apologize for neglecting you," he whispered against her ear. "Forgive me, my love."

Keely glanced sidelong at him. His use of the phrase

my love softened her heart and brought a reluctant smile to her lips. She nodded, accepting his apology.

"Shall we tickle the carpet, dearest?" he asked.

His invitation surprised Keely. "'Tis expected like the mingling?"

Richard nodded.

Before he could take her hand in his and lead her onto the dance floor, Keely dropped gracefully to her knees. She reached out and rubbed her fingertips across the carpet in front of her.

Richard gaped at her in surprise. What the bloody hell was she doing?

All around them people laughed, but no one laughed harder than Ladies Morgana, Jane, and Sarah. Those courtiers who managed to suppress their mirth for the earl's bride's sake stared in horrified fascination at his bizarre behavior. Even Queen Elizabeth riveted her sharp gaze on them, while Robert Dudley stood beside her and hooted with derisive laughter.

Richard crouched down to be eye level with his wife and asked mildly, "Dearest, what are you doing?"

"I'm tickling the—" Keely broke off at the sudden realization that he hadn't been asking her actually to tickle the carpet. She heard the howls of laughter directed at them and turned a stricken expression upon her husband.

"Darling, I was asking you to dance," Richard said gently, but his lips twitched with a powerful urge to laugh.

And that was Keely's undoing.

Mortified beyond endurance, Keely leaped to her feet and raced through the shocked crowd out of the hall. She heard her husband calling her name, but she never looked back or stopped. The sound of the courtiers' laughter chased her through the maze of corridors to her own chamber.

Keely slammed the door shut and leaned back against it. Hot tears of humiliation streamed down her cheeks.

She could never face those people again. Her husband's world would never be hers; she didn't belong there. Cut from a different mold, Keely knew she would never successfully fit into the life of a courtier. A descendant of Welsh princes and a Druid priestess she may be, but to these Englishmen she was merely an ignorant Welsh bastard who'd forced her presence on her unsuspecting noble sire and tricked England's favorite son into an unwanted marriage. She was truly the Princess of Nowhere.

Slowly, wearily, Keely walked across the chamber and sat on the edge of the bed. She needed desperately to escape this world of unhappiness.

Home. Like a siren's song, the misty mountains of Wales called to Keely.

Oh, what a coil she'd wrapped herself in! Leaving the earl would shatter her heart; but staying in his world with him would destroy her.

Surrendering to hopelessness and sorrow, Keely covered her face with her hands and wept for what was. *And for what could never be.*

The door opened and closed quietly. Richard crossed the chamber to the bed and sat down beside his wife. He put his arm around her and drew her close against his comforting strength. His heart ached at the sight and the sound of her weeping.

With his handkerchief, Richard wiped the tears from her face and told her, "Elizabeth requires her courtiers to remain in the Presence Chamber until she leaves. 'Tis a sign of respect for the Crown."

"I am no courtier," Keely said in an aching whisper.

"The Countess of Basildon is most assuredly a courtier," Richard said with an encouraging smile, trying to put a brave face on the embarrassing situation.

Keely gazed at him through violet eyes swimming with tears. "I must return to Wales, my lord. Our marriage can be annulled."

"'Tis impossible once a marriage is consummated, sweetheart," Richard said, sounding more reasonable then he actually felt. No matter what happened, he'd never let her go.

"Then a divorce will do."

Richard tipped her chin up, gazed into her eyes, and felt her pain. In a voice that brooked no argument, he said, "For better or for worse, we are husband and wife until death do us part."

"As every noble in England saw, 'tis apparently for the worse."

"Not so." Drawing her into his embrace, Richard stroked the delicate column of her back in a soothing motion. "The fault lies with me. Am I forgiven?"

" 'Twas *my* ignorance that caused such hilarity," she said, absolving him of any guilt.

" 'Twas *my* ignorance that caused the hilarity, sweetheart. I used a courtier's figure of speech with a lady who'd never before attended the court." Richard gazed into her disarming violet eyes and said, "Return with me now, and we'll dance together. Within the hour, those shallow minds will fix upon a different piece of gossip. Trust me, beauty."

Keely lowered her gaze and whispered, "I—I cannot."

"The longer you hide yourself away, the longer those blockheads will smile behind their hands."

"You misunderstand," Keely said in a small voice. Then, as if confessing a monstrous crime, she blurted out, "I never learned to dance."

" 'Tis a problem easily solved," Richard replied. He stood and gently forced her to rise with him. When she faced him, he smiled and bowed to her in courtly manner.

Taking her cue from him, Keely managed a wobbly smile and curtsied. "Now what do I do?" she asked.

"Keep this part of your arm pressed against your body," Richard instructed, demonstrating as he spoke. "Hold your open palms up toward me. Excellent! Sway your right side toward my right side, and touch your palm to mine." When she'd done as he'd instructed, Richard said, "We'll do the same with our left palms."

"'Tis simple," Keely said, her easy smile enchanting him.

His wife was entirely too beautiful for Richard to resist. He pulled her into his arms and kissed her thoroughly, healing the emotional pain she'd endured that evening. When she entwined her arms around his neck and pressed herself provocatively against him, Richard muttered, "The queen be damned."

He lifted her into his arms and placed her across the bed, then lay down beside her. He yanked the bodice of her gown down, freeing her breasts, and suckled upon her dusky nipples.

"Ahem." Another voice sounded within their chamber.

Dazed with desire, Richard turned his head slowly and looked toward the doorway. Willis Smythe stood there, his lust-filled gaze fixed on the sight of Keely's bared breasts with their aroused dusky peaks.

Keely gasped in embarrassment and tried to cover herself. Unfortunately, her husband's body pressing her down prevented movement.

"The queen demands your presence," Willis informed them, his gaze still riveted on Keely's bared breasts.

"Get out," Richard ordered, his voice soft but deadly.

"But Elizabeth—"

"I said, get out!"

Willis Smythe didn't need to be told a third time. He grinned unrepentantly, inclined his head, and left the chamber.

Richard looked at his wife's crimson face and regretted his decision to remain at court until after the Christmas holidays, but it was too late to change his mind. He'd already promised Elizabeth they would stay through Twelfth Night, when the court was scheduled to move to Richmond Palace, her winter's warm box. Leaving early would be insulting at best and suspect at worst.

Richard rose from the bed and adjusted his codpiece while his wife covered her breasts. "'Twill never happen again," he promised.

Keely nodded. Their lack of privacy was no fault of his.

"I'll make our excuses to the queen," Richard said, giving her a quick kiss. "Lock the door, and do not open it for anyone but me." He left the room but waited outside until he heard the bolt thrown. With anger etched across his face, he marched down the corridor.

Gaining the Presence Chamber, Richard made his way through the crowd. He reached the dais and waited in silence until Elizabeth deigned to acknowledge his arrival, then bowed low in front of her.

"We have noted your rudeness in leaving Our presence without permission," Elizabeth said, irritated.

Richard flicked a glance at the smirking Earl of Leicester, who stood close beside the seated queen. "Majesty, I do beg your generous pardon," Richard apologized. "My wife took ill suddenly."

"'Tis serious?" Elizabeth asked, playing the courtiers' game, a dissembling pastime consisting of two players—monarch and courtier—and any number of spectators. Everyone in the hall knew that she had witnessed the entire embarrassing fiasco of his wife tickling the carpet.

"I believe 'tis the excitement of being in your august presence," Richard lied with a sincere smile. "I'm positive my wife will feel much better in the morning."

Elizabeth nodded. His polished excuse brought the hint of a smile to her lips. She always enjoyed playing the courtiers' game with her dear Midas, who was an exceedingly worthy opponent.

"May I have leave to return to my chamber and offer my wife whatever comfort is possible?"

"Carry your lovely bride Our heartfelt tidings for her quick recovery, my lord."

"Thank you, Majesty."

Richard bowed deeply and backed away. Turning toward the assembly, he scanned the chamber until his sharp gaze fell on Willis Smythe dancing with Lady Jane. With grim determination stamped across his features, he marched onto the dance floor and pushed his way through the myriad couples who stopped dancing and watched his unprecedented behavior.

Lady Jane saw him first but missed the murderous gleam in his eyes. "Have you come to your senses and dumped the little *taffy*?" she purred.

Richard ignored her. He fixed his gaze on his friend, who inclined his head and waited for whatever was coming.

"We've shared many things, but never make the mistake of counting my wife among them," Richard warned in a deadly voice. "Look at her again, and that hour will be your last on this earth." Without waiting for a reply, he turned on his heel and shoved his way through the titillated audience of courtiers.

"Basildon!"

Richard halted at the hall's entrance and turned in the direction of that voice. He saw the only other man there who was dressed completely in black, Lord Burghley.

"Is there a problem?" Burghley asked.

Richard flicked a glance over his shoulder in the direction of his former friend and then answered, "No longer." Without another word, Richard quit the chamber. He never saw the pleased smile that appeared on his mentor's face.

Chapter 14

Life at the Tudor court was hell.

Keely endured the longest six weeks of her life. She learned to smile at people she disliked; she learned to find her way through Hampton Court's labyrinth of corridors; and she learned the pavane, the slowest and most stately dance for couples.

The thought of learning the sprightly five-step galliard was enough to give Keely the hives, but she needn't worry about that formidable dance until the following year. Keely carried the earl's child and pleaded her condition on the grounds that the lively galliard could dislodge their baby.

Suffering with morning sickness gave her a good reason to miss the ridiculously long Sunday service in the Chapel Royal. She'd used that particular excuse this very morning.

"How do I look?" Keely asked, turning in a circle for her tiringwomen.

Her high-necked gown had been created in sapphire blue cashmere with a matching shawl and slippers. Around her neck Keely wore the gleaming dragon pendant.

"How lovely you are!" May gushed, clapping her hands together.

"The most beautiful woman at court," June agreed, bobbing her head.

"I owe my appearance to my talented tiringwoman," Keely said, returning their compliments.

"Women," June corrected her.

May reached out and pinched her sister's arm, scolding, "Tiringwomen do not correct their ladies."

"So sorry, Lady Keely," June apologized, rubbing her arm. "Your beauty will shame all those other ladies."

"I doubt that," Keely replied, walking toward the door. "Wish me luck."

"Good luck," May and June chorused together.

Keely started down the corridor that led to another corridor, which in turn brought her to the wing of the palace that housed the queen's privy chambers. She carried a large tapestry bag containing her husband's linen handkerchiefs, which she intended to embroider.

This invitation was the first she'd received to visit the queen's privy sitting room for an afternoon of sewing with the other ladies. Keely worried which topics would be suitable for conversation. She'd never enjoyed a close female companion except her mother. About what did these Englishwomen think and talk?

Keely recalled her husband's parting words to her that morning. *"Keep your lips closed and your ears open. Above all else, be discreet."* Apparently, the earl was also worried about what would transpire in the queen's privy chamber.

Reaching the end of the last corridor, Keely faced the entrance to the Long Gallery and hesitated in indecision. Dared she enter or not? The Long Gallery was the only path she knew to the royal apartments. Keely was no coward; nor did she fear the dead. But the torment of the soul trapped within the gallery had literally sickened her the last time she'd entered that chamber.

Summoning her reserves of inner strength, Keely opened the door and stepped inside. The door clicked shut behind her.

Keely stood perfectly still, and her sharp gaze scanned the chamber. Nothing appeared out of the ordinary. She moved forward several paces, felt a prickly draft teasing the nape of her neck, and stopped short.

Keely looked at the rows of long tapered candles on either side of the gallery. Once again their flames burned steadily.

Still, Keely refused to retreat. Steeling herself against the unseen, she walked deeper into the gallery. An oppressive heaviness settled upon her, and bleak hopelessness weighed her spirit down. Suddenly, an unfamiliar name surfaced into her consciousness: Cat Howard.

Keely halted. Something unspeakably evil had happened in this chamber to a woman named Cat Howard.

Losing her nerve, Keely whirled around and dashed out of the Long Gallery. Alone in the corridor, she tried to compose herself. When reality finally seeped into her senses, Keely worried her bottom lip with her teeth and considered a logical way out of this untenable predicament. She was unable to pass through the Long Gallery, but only a complete fool would refuse the queen's invitation. One did not snub Elizabeth and live to tell the story.

And then there was the minor matter of her husband. Richard would be furious if she failed to attend the queen.

Keely needed to get to that royal sitting room. There just had to be another route.

Keely squared her shoulders and walked back down the corridor. Rounding a corner, she spied a page dressed in the queen's livery and called, "Please wait, boy."

The boy stopped and turned around.

"Can you tell me how to get to the royal apartments?" Keely asked.

The freckle-faced boy gave her a grin. "Walk through the Long Gallery, my lady."

"I mean, other than through the gallery," she amended.

"Through the privy garden."

Keely dazzled the twelve-year-old with a relieved smile, thanked him, and asked, "What's your name?"

"Roger Debrett."

"Lead the way to the privy garden, Roger."

"With pleasure, Lady Devereux."

Roger led her outside the palace to the wide expanse of

lawns that teemed with courtiers. The two of them passed dozens of nobles and servants who were coming or going to the courtyard and the stables.

At one point, Keely saw her father speaking with the Earl of Leicester and waved to them. Finally, Roger halted in a deserted section of the landscaped garden.

"Here we are," he said.

" 'Tis a stone wall," Keely replied.

"The privy garden lies on the other side of the wall."

Keely looked from Roger to the wall. Her gaze slid past and then returned to the majestic leaf-barren oak that stood like a sentinel beside the wall.

Keely smiled to herself and advanced on the oak, calling over her shoulder, "Give me a boost."

"Sneaking into the queen's garden is unwise," Roger advised her, beginning to regret escorting Basildon's beautiful countess here. Borrowing trouble was folly in the extreme. He wanted to live long enough to futter a few pretty maids.

"The queen invited me to sit with her this afternoon," Keely told him.

"Why don't you walk through the Long Gallery like everyone else?" Roger asked.

" 'Tis haunted."

The boy gaped at her in surprise. "A ghost haunts the Long Gallery?"

Keely nodded in all seriousness. "Will you give me a boost?"

Roger waged an inner battle. On the one hand, he feared catching trouble. At the same time, he itched to be away and spread the gossip that Lady Devereux believed the Long Gallery haunted.

Giving her a mischievous grin, Roger crouched down and cupped his hands together. Keely placed a slippered foot in his hands, and up she went.

Keely inched her way carefully along the oak's thickest branch and leaped the short distance to the top of the stone wall. She sat down and caught the tapestry bag that

Roger tossed her. "My thanks for all your help," she called.

"At your service, Lady Devereux." Roger grinned and bowed from the waist, but he lingered where he was to be certain she didn't injure herself leaping into the garden.

Keely threw her bag down. From her sitting position, she dropped into the garden but turned toward the wall when she heard the page calling.

"Lady Devereux, are you well?"

"Fine, Roger. Thank you."

Keely spared a moment to brush the dust from her skirt and then turned in the direction of the palace. What she saw formed her lips into a perfect O of surprise.

Standing less than ten feet away, three people stared at her. Queen Elizabeth and Lord Burghley appeared shocked. Richard looked furious.

Keely silently cursed her stupidity for failing to cast an invisibility shield around herself. There was nothing to be done for it now. She dropped a throne room curtsy as the three of them advanced on her.

"What do you think you're doing?" Richard demanded.

Keely looked from her angry husband to the queen and Burghley. She couldn't seem to find her voice.

"Answer your husband," Burghley ordered. "What are you doing in the queen's garden?"

"Her Majesty invited me to sit with her this afternoon," Keely explained.

"Yes, but why are you vaulting over the wall to get here?" Elizabeth asked in a mildly amused voice. Nothing could mar the excellent news that her dear Midas had just delivered.

Keely wet her lips, gone dry from nervousness. Before answering, she glanced at her husband. His gaze warned her to caution, but as she saw it, only the truth would suffice in this matter. Nothing else made sense.

"A fear comes upon me whenever I step into the Long

Gallery," Keely told the queen in a voice barely louder than a whisper.

"What do you mean by a *fear?*" Lord Burghley asked. "Explain yourself."

Keely looked at Richard. Her husband had suddenly developed a twitch in his right cheek.

Dropping her gaze to the ground, Keely answered, "I believe a ghost haunts the Long Gallery."

Keely peeked at her husband. The twitch had spread to his left cheek.

"You've seen a ghost in my gallery?" Elizabeth asked, astounded.

"I never saw it," Keely qualified, shaking her head. "I sensed its presence."

Heedless of protocol, Keely looked at her husband and pleaded for understanding, "I started to walk through the gallery, but its aura of hopelessness frightened me. I swear, my lord, I tried to do as you bade me."

Her pathetically remorseful expression softened Lord Burghley. He glanced at his furious protégé. and remarked, "If Lady Devereux climbed undetected into the privy garden, others could do the same. We must tighten Her Majesty's security." He looked at Keely and added, "You have drawn our attention to a most important matter, Lady Devereux. We owe you a debt of gratitude."

Richard snapped his head around to stare at his mentor. He couldn't credit what he'd just heard.

"Her Majesty's safety is of paramount importance," Burghley went on. "Don't you agree, Richard?"

"Yes, of course."

Keely gave the somber Burghley a grateful look.

"Why were you absent from mass today?" the queen asked, unwilling to let the girl off the hook. She wondered idly when Devereux would leap to his wife's defense.

"I suffered from the morning sickness," Keely answered.

"Feeling better, dearest?" Richard asked, his emerald gaze softening on her.

Keely nodded and managed a nervous smile.

"Congratulations," Elizabeth said, and then flicked a meaningful glance at Burghley. She looked at the young woman standing in front of her. "So will you give my dear Midas his heir and send him off to Ireland?" she asked.

Keely shook her head. "I carry a girl."

Elizabeth chuckled at the ridiculous notion that Keely could possibly know what her husband had planted inside her. Burghley smiled. Except for the twitch that returned to his cheek, Richard kept his face expressionless. Uncomfortably, he wondered if his wife did possess unnatural abilities. The chit had sneaked into the Queen of England's privy garden and was about to walk away unscathed.

"Follow this path to the end," Elizabeth instructed Keely. "'Twill bring you to my apartments, where several of the ladies already gather."

Keely curtsied, lifted her tapestry bag off the ground, and started down the garden path. Though she felt three pairs of eyes watching her, she never looked back.

The queen's female entourage consisted of sixteen women: four chamberers who slept at the foot of her bed and performed the duties of tiringwomen, six married ladies who acted as official companions, and six unmarried maids of honor. Because the official companions and maids of honor had very few duties, they passed an inordinate amount of time in gossiping, flirting, and spreading rumors.

Dim and stuffy, the queen's privy chamber sported only one small window. Adornment smothered the tiny, richly appointed room.

Keely's spirits sagged when she walked into the room. The only ladies present were Morgana, Sarah, and Jane. Their reactions to her unexpected arrival varied. Morgana lifted her nose into the air and made an exaggerated show of turning away, which made Sarah giggle. Jane inspected her rival for the earl's affection, starting at the top of her uncovered ebony mane and ending at the tips of her slippered feet.

"Sit down," Lady Jane invited her.

"Thank you," Keely said, managing a polite smile. Holy stones, but she felt conspicuous. Keely opened her tapestry bag, removed one of her husband's handkerchiefs as well as a needle and thread, and began embroidering his initials on one of its corners.

"I cannot believe I am forced to sit with this Welsh bastard," Morgana grumbled, loud enough for all to hear.

Keely pretended deafness. How could she defend herself against the truth? At least, neither her husband nor the queen was present to witness her humiliation.

"I wonder how England's premier earl could have been tricked into marrying an ignorant *taffy*," Sarah remarked, taking her cue from the other girl's attitude.

Keely said nothing but lifted her gaze to look at the other girl. Jealousy rules her tongue, Keely told herself. All the slurs in the world could never change the fact that the earl had desired her above these three women. That thought gave her the patient courage to endure whatever they would fling at her.

Keely felt somewhat encouraged when Jane deigned to smile at her. "What a beautiful necklace," Keely complimented the sultry brunette in return.

"Thank you," Jane purred, fingering the double strand of pearls.

"'Twas Devereux's last New Year's gift to her," Sarah piped up.

Keely felt her heart sink to her stomach. Apparently, the earl and the brunette had been on very friendly terms.

"My husband is a generous man," Keely said in a choked whisper.

It was then the brunette went in for the kill. "Basildon

is generous in more ways than you know," Jane told her.

"What do you think of his freckle? Is it not the cutest thing you've ever seen?"

Keely's composure crashed. The English blood that surged through her body screamed at her to throttle the slut; but before she could act upon that impulse, the voice of reason sounded from the doorway.

"Everyone at court knows where Devereux carries a freckle," Lady Dawn announced, walking with two companions into the chamber. "Even those who never bedded the man speak about that distinguishing mark."

Keely relaxed. The three vampires sitting across from her wouldn't dare draw blood while Cheshire remained within their midst.

"Keely, darling. I present Lady Blair and Lady Tessie," Cheshire drawled.

Keely smiled at them. Lady Blair was short, dark-haired, and moderately pregnant. Lady Tessie was short, blond, and exceedingly pregnant.

"You cannot believe how aggravated I am with Pines," Tessie complained.

Lady Dawn leaned close to Keely and whispered, "Lord Pines is her husband."

"I asked Pines if he would watch me model my two new gowns because I wasn't certain which I should wear today," Tessie went on. "Both looked absolutely horrible, but I desperately needed to know which gown looked less horrible. Pines said, 'I have no wish to commit matrimonial suicide,' and bolted out of our chamber."

"Husbands can be so unhelpful," Lady Dawn commiserated with her friend. She flicked a glance at the two unmarrieds and added, "Poor Morgana and Sarah wouldn't know about that, though."

Sarah blushed with embarrassment. Morgana curled her lip at her new stepmother and muttered something unintelligible.

Lady Dawn turned to Lady Blair and Lady Tessie and asked, "How is dear Horatio?"

"Vastly improved," the other woman replied. "He's even gained some weight."

Keely smiled politely and inquired, "Horatio is your husband, my lady?"

Morgana, Sarah, and Jane burst out laughing. Keely blushed, though she didn't actually understand why they were laughing at her.

"Horatio is a pig," Blair told her. "Though I do love him like a son."

"I see." Keely decided the whole damned English race was insane. The vile lot of them were vicious or eccentric or seducers.

"When is your baby due?" Keely asked Lady Blair.

"April."

"Mine arrives in February," Tessie spoke up.

Keely flicked a glance at Lady Dawn and announced, "I am due in August."

Six ladies gaped at her in surprise; Lady Dawn recovered first. She bolted out of her chair and hugged her stepdaughter.

"I'm much too young to become a grandmother," Lady Dawn moaned suddenly. "What will Ludlow do when he realizes he's married someone's grandmother?"

Everyone laughed. Even Morgana managed a smile.

"I'm quite certain I carry a boy," Lady Blair joked. "I was on the top when *it* happened."

"I carry a girl," Keely said, falling in with the woman's merriment. "I was on the bottom."

"Oh, God! I do believe I'm carrying a *puppy*," Tessie cried.

Dawn, Blair, and Jane burst out laughing. Keely, Morgana, and Sarah looked confused.

"I don't understand," Keely admitted.

Lady Dawn leaned close and whispered in her ear. Blushing furiously, Keely dissolved into giggles.

"Tell Sarah and me what the joke is," Morgana said. "We want to know too."

Forgetting the enmity that existed between them,

Keely quipped, "Tis unseemly for a maiden to listen to such vulgar talk."

"How dare a common bastard speak to me in that haughty tone," Morgana snapped. "Why, you're no *real* lady at all! Do you even know if Devereux sired your brat?"

Keely paled. Lady Dawn opened her mouth to defend her, but another voice spoke.

"Morgana Talbot, control that ugly spite," Queen Elizabeth ordered, marching into the room.

All seven ladies leaped out of their chairs and curtsied deeply to the queen. They stood in uncomfortable silence, awaiting her signal to sit.

"Cast no aspersions on Devereux's heir," Queen Elizabeth said, fixing her gaze on Morgana. "Apologize at once."

"'Tis unnecessary," Keely said in a small voice.

That sharp gray-eyed gaze slid to Keely. "'Tis, We say."

Reluctantly, Morgana turned to Keely and said, "I beg your pardon."

Uncertain of how to respond without making her sister even angrier, Keely nodded her acceptance of the girl's frigid apology. Everyone in the chamber, including the queen, knew the blonde's apology was insincere.

"I refuse to be bothered by bickering bitches," Elizabeth said. "All of you get out."

The seven of them started to leave, but the queen changed her mind. "Lady Devereux, remain with me."

Six surprised expressions turned to Keely. No one felt more surprised than she.

"Sit here," Elizabeth ordered when the others had gone. "I would become acquainted with my dear Midas's wife."

Keely sat down, folded her hands in her lap, and worried her bottom lip with her teeth. Never in her wildest imaginings had she ever thought she'd be sitting across from the Queen of England. Holy stones, what did one say to a queen?

"Lady Devereux, tell me about the spirit in my gallery," Elizabeth bade her.

"You may call me Keely, Your Majesty."

"Thank you, *Keely*," the queen said dryly. "Now, about that spirit?"

"You believe me, Your Majesty?" Keely asked.

"Are you lying?" Elizabeth asked.

Frightened, Keely shook her head vigorously. "No, but my husband—"

"Piss on Devereux," Elizabeth interrupted. "Men are fools who think only with their pricks."

Keely crimsoned in embarrassment. This wasn't the way she'd imagined a queen would speak. However, she'd never actually spoken with a queen before now.

"The ghost in my gallery?" Elizabeth prodded.

"Did a Cat Howard once live here?" Keely asked.

"*Cat Howard?*"

Keely nodded. "You knew her?"

"My father's fifth wife," Elizabeth replied absently, staring off into space. She recalled the stories of her childhood. Cat Howard had been arrested in the Long Gallery and, screaming like a madwoman, had tried desperately to reach the king in the Chapel Royal. Poor beautiful Cat Howard, cut down in her youth. *Like my own mother.*

"'Tis an unpleasant memory?" Keely whispered.

Elizabeth looked at her and changed the subject. "So, Keely. Will you give Devereux his heir and send him to die in Ireland?"

"No, I carry a daughter," Keely answered.

"How do you know?"

"My mother told me."

"*Cheshire?*" Elizabeth asked in disbelief. "Cheshire knows less than nothing about babies."

Keely smiled. "I meant, my *real* mother."

The queen's gray gaze narrowed on her. "I understood that your mother was deceased."

Keely bit her bottom lip in nervousness, then lied, "Megan spoke to me in a dream."

"You believe in such premonitions?" Elizabeth asked.

"Well," Keely hedged. "I do if you do."

Queen Elizabeth burst out laughing. "You have inherited your father's courtier's wit."

Keely breathed a sigh of relief and smiled nervously. She wondered how long she'd be required to sit with the queen. Each minute seemed like an hour, and she longed to be safely away.

"Tell me why you are unhappy here," Elizabeth said.

"But how did you know?" Keely asked, surprised.

"I know everything about everyone at my court."

"I miss my brother," Keely told her. "I did write Rhys a letter but have received no reply yet."

"And?"

Keely fixed her gaze on the floor. "I feel conspicuously out of place whenever I am in the company of your courtiers. I can never be as the other ladies."

"Many a courtier has come and gone," the queen told her. "The ones who are the most successful develop an attitude and accentuate what makes them different in order to gain attention."

"I—I don't think my husband wants me to be different," Keely said, "but I cannot change what I am. Everyone at court knows my base origins, and I am too shy to mingle effectively."

"You are noble enough to have attracted Devereux," Elizabeth countered.

"I do not believe 'twas my nobility that attracted the earl," Keely replied. "However, 'tis kind of you to say so."

"I am never kind," Elizabeth said seriously. "If Devereux constantly worries about you, his mind will wander from my personal finances, and that inattention could cost me a great deal of gold."

"I would never want that to happen," Keely assured her.

"We are in accord," Elizabeth replied. "You shall make my dear Midas happy, and in turn, he shall make me happy by fattening my purse with gold. Take this sage advice: Whenever you feel especially vulnerable, imagine all those haughty nobles without any clothing."

"You mean, picture them naked in my mind?"

"Precisely."

Unconsciously, Keely dropped her gaze to the queen's body.

"Except me," Elizabeth qualified.

Keely snapped her gaze back to the queen's.

"Picturing them naked will give you the confidence you need to mingle successfully," Elizabeth said. "Many years ago, I gave your husband the same advice."

That surprised Keely. "My lord had trouble mingling?"

"Devereux was only a boy at the time," Elizabeth admitted. "He'd come to court one season to act as a page."

"Your advice helped him?"

Queen Elizabeth smiled with the remembrance. "More than a few ladies slapped his face. You see, Richard insisted on picturing only the females naked. To make matters worse, he told them what he was doing and even insisted that I'd ordered him to do so. Of course, when he grew up, the ladies dropped like ripened apples into his arms." Abruptly, the queen said, "I have work to do. 'Tis time for your departure."

Keely stood and curtsied, saying, "I am honored to have been invited to sit with you, Your Majesty."

"Run along, child."

Keely backed out of the chamber and closed the door behind her. Turning around, she realized she stood at the entrance to the Long Gallery. Holy stones, she'd forgotten about returning through it. She couldn't very well knock on the queen's door and ask permission to leap over that wall again.

Mustering her courage, Keely stepped into the gallery and stopped short. Her husband stood there.

"What are you doing here?" she asked.

"Waiting for you," he answered, sauntering toward her.

"But why?"

"Cheshire told me you were alone with Elizabeth," he replied. "I knew walking through the Long Gallery would frighten you."

Richard held his hand out, and Keely accepted it. Without warning, he scooped her into his arms. "I run faster than you," he said.

Keely smiled and entwined her arms around his neck. She closed her eyes and hid her face against his chest as he sprinted through the chamber.

Two minutes later, Richard told her, "You can open your eyes, dearest. We've left the gallery."

Keely opened her eyes and looked at him, saying, "I can walk back to our chamber."

"Carrying you gives me pleasure." With his wife in his arms, Richard marched past dozens of amused courtiers and servants. He nodded at each one and ordered his giggling wife to give them the royal wave.

Reaching their chamber, Richard set Keely on her feet. Before she could turn away, he yanked her into his arms, and his lips captured hers in a lingering kiss.

Finally, Richard stepped back and said with a smile, "Now that we have the kiss out of the way"—his smile vanished—"what the bloody hell possessed you to climb the wall into the privy garden?"

"'Tis as I said—"

"I don't give a blasted damn what your reason was," Richard snapped. "Do you realize you might have injured our babe? *Do you?* I'd just delivered good news to the queen—but what if Elizabeth had been suffering a foul mood? What would have happened then?"

"She did invite—"

"Elizabeth invited you to *walk* through the door!" Richard bellowed, his voice rising with his anger. His wife's foolishness frightened him, and that made him even angrier.

"There's no need to *shout!*" Keely shouted.

"Lower your voice to a respectful tone when you speak to me," Richard ordered. Then: "You promised you'd refrain from flaunting those stupid beliefs of yours."

"The queen believes me."

Suspicious, Richard cocked a copper brow at her. "What exactly did Elizabeth and you discuss?"

"The queen believes the ghost is Cat Howard."

"Elizabeth actually believes Cat Howard haunts the Long Gallery?" Richard echoed, shocked.

Keely nodded. She lifted her nose into the air and turned her back on him.

"Good Christ! You silly women are all alike," Richard exploded. He marched across the chamber but paused at the door. "I'm warning you, Keely," he threatened. "Keep quiet about what you believe. Or I promise, you will regret it." Richard stormed out of the chamber and slammed the door behind him.

Keely whirled around, lifted her tapestry bag, and threw it at the door. "Embroider your own handker-chiefs!" she shouted.

Marching across the chamber, Keely dropped into the chair in front of the hearth. Angry tears welled up in her eyes, but she brushed them away. She absolutely refused to shed tears for the insensitive lout she'd married.

Anger made her stomach churn. She took several deep calming breaths.

Extreme agitation could mark the babe, Keely told herself. Remaining placid was of utmost importance. She refused to chance injuring her daughter.

Keely leaned back, closed her eyes, and thought of her angry husband. Richard was a heretic who believed in the Here and Now and worshipped gold. Yet arrogance and ignorance had been bred in him—his attitude was not completely his fault.

And he feared for their daughter's safety. That thought warmed her heart and made her more determined to hold her patience with him.

Slowly, Keely rose from the chair and retrieved her tapestry bag from the floor. She sat down again and began to embroider his handkerchiefs.

Dealing with simpletons or loved ones required patience, Keely concluded. The earl filled the bill on both accounts. A simpleminded heretic, Richard refused to see beyond the horizon, but she loved him in spite of that gigantic flaw.

She loved him. An aching emotion welled up in Keely's breast. Holy stones, she'd fallen in love with her exasperating English husband.

Keely sighed, fighting back the raw regret that threatened to break her heart. *Too bad her husband didn't love her.*

Chapter 15

Slipping out of her husband's embrace, Keely rose from the bed and stared down at him. Sleep softened his features and gave him a boyish appearance. That he hadn't harbored his anger surprised Keely and filled her with hope. She'd always assumed that all men cherished their grudges as her stepfather had, but Richard had returned to their chamber the previous evening and behaved as though they hadn't exchanged angry words.

Keely pulled the coverlet up to his shoulders and then padded on bare feet across the chamber to the window. The day had dawned dark and cheerless; a forbidding overcast threatened snow—usual fare for the twenty-first day of December.

Keely's heart hummed with the song of her Druid ancestors. Today marked the winter solstice, Alban Arthuan, the festival of light, when the sun vanquished the world's darkness and the days grew steadily longer.

Keely wished she could celebrate the holiday outside and search for the sacred mistletoe, but the earl had spoken wisely. If they caught her, the ignorant English would burn her at the stake for being a witch.

Glancing toward the bed, Keely considered awakening Richard but then thought better of it. Participating in a pagan ceremony would certainly never make her husband's daily list of things to do.

Keely pulled her white ceremonial robe over her nightshift. Then she collected the requisite holy items: magic stones, golden sickle, and Yule candle.

Keely chose eight white agates for spiritual guidance and one black obsidian for repelling dark magic. Using the agates, she made a circle in the middle area of the chamber and left only the western periphery open.

Entering from the west, Keely closed the circle with the last white agate and whispered, "All disturbing thoughts remain outside."

She set the black obsidian and the candle down in the soul of the circle, then fused its invisible periphery shut with her golden sickle. Returning to the circle's center, she turned clockwise three times until she faced the east.

Dropping to her knees, Keely closed her eyes and chanted into the silence, "The Old Ones are here, watching and waiting. Stars speak through stones, and light shines through the thickest oak. One realm is heaven and earth."

Keely reached for the candle and lifted it toward the east. "Hail, Great Mother Goddess, bringer of light out of darkness and rebirth out of death," she prayed. "I beg a favor: Guard my unborn child and keep her safe. And though he is a heretic, deliver my husband from the unseen evil I sense lurking near."

After snuffing the candle, Keely stood and walked to the circle's western periphery, then lifted the agate and broke the enchantment. She spared a glance toward the bed and froze.

Richard lay on his side and watched her. "How do you feel?" he asked in a voice husky with sleep.

"Fine." Keely could already hear the blistering lecture coming her way.

"'Tis exceedingly strange how the queasiness strikes you only on Sunday morn as we dress for chapel," Richard remarked, the hint of a smile flirting with his lips.

Keely ignored his astute observation. She finished collecting her magic stones and put them away, then tossed her ceremonial robe aside and returned to the bed.

Richard lifted the coverlet in invitation, and Keely slid in beside him. He pulled her into his arms, and she rested her head against his chest.

"You were worshipping, dearest," Richard said, his

thumb caressing her silken cheek. "Thank you for remembering me in your prayers."

"You are very welcome." Then Keely complained in a rueful voice, "Worshipping inside does hinder my style."

Richard chuckled and then yawned. "'Tis early," he said. "Let us return to sleep."

Keely closed her eyes and snuggled against her husband's body. She felt safe within the circle of his arms. Contented silence reigned for several moments.

"Richard?"

"Yes, dearest?"

"When are you going to use the ceremonial robe I made?"

"Perhaps when you finish reading *Lives of the Saints*."

"But I haven't even started it yet."

"I know. . . ."

Card-playing, gambling, fortune-telling, and tennis amused the courtiers during times of inclement weather. Before dinner, Richard left the bedchamber to search for Duke Robert, who'd invited him to a high-stakes game of chance.

Keely wanted none of the usual pastimes that day. Instead, she sat alone in front of the hearth in her chamber and sewed baby clothes. Occasionally, she leaned back in her chair, stared into the hearth's hypnotic flames, and tried to conjure her daughter's image in her mind's eye. Would she be red-haired and green-eyed like her father? Or would she possess her mother's ebony tresses and violet eyes? Red-haired and violet-eyed? Perhaps, ebony-haired and green-eyed?

"Are you there, little girl?" A knock on the door, and Odo's voice yanked Keely out of her pleasant musings.

"Come in, cousin," Keely called.

The door opened. Odo, Hew, May, and June filed inside but stood near the doorway. All four of them wore broad grins.

"'Tis the Yuletide," Odo said.

"And we've brought you a gift," Hew added. Keely dropped her gaze to their empty hands and then cast them a puzzled smile.

"Close your eyes," Odo ordered.

"And I'll get it," Hew said.

Odo cuffed the side of his brother's head. "I'm older, so I'll fetch it."

May rounded on Odo and ordered, "Don't you dare strike him."

"Show respect when you address Odo," June scolded her.

"Mind your own business," May snapped, pinching her sister's arm.

"Leave her alone," Odo barked.

"Lower your voice when you speak to May," Hew entered the verbal fray. "She isn't your servant."

Without waiting to be announced, Keely's gift walked into the chamber. He smiled at her and held his arms open in invitation.

"*Rhys!*" Keely leaped out of the chair, dashed across the chamber, and threw herself into her brother's arms.

Rhys held her protectively tight and allowed her a few minutes of weeping against his chest. "Why aren't you outside searching for the elusive mistletoe?" he teased.

"The damned English heretics would clutch their chests and die," she answered with a watery chuckle.

"'Tis one way to rid ourselves of the vermin." Rhys set her back and brushed the tears from her cheeks with his fingertips, saying, "Ah, sister. The sweetest wild flower in the fields fades beside your beauty."

"And you are one of the most handsome men I've ever seen," Keely returned the compliment. "I missed you terribly."

Tall and well built, Rhys Lloyd had midnight black hair and warm gray eyes. Those eyes of gray narrowed on her. "One?" he echoed. "You always said I *was* the handsomest man. Has that new husband of yours replaced me in your esteem?"

Ignoring his question, Keely held his hand and led him across the chamber. "Come, brother. Warm yourself in front of the hearth."

"Everyone out," May ordered, herding the others toward the door. "Let them have some privacy." No one argued with her.

"Cousins, 'tis the most excellent gift I've ever received," Keely called. "I love both of you very much."

Odo and Hew blushed and then followed the twins out.

Rhys sat down in the chair before the hearth. Keely dragged a stool across the chamber, sat, and reached for his hand.

"Tell me, brother. How did you find me?" she asked.

"Ludlow's servants directed me here," Rhys answered. "Madoc is dead and buried."

"Dead?" Keely echoed, shocked. "But how?"

An uncharacteristic blush colored Rhys's ruddy complexion. "Madoc died pleasurably, if you ken my meaning."

Keely shook her head.

"The maid's lusty energy killed him," Rhys explained.

"Oh." Keely recalled her mother's prophecy: *"What Madoc desires most will kill him in the end. . . ."*

"You can return to Wales if you wish," Rhys said.

" 'Tis six weeks too late for going home!" Keely cried, tears welling up in her eyes. She held up the garment that she'd been sewing. "I carry my husband's child."

"I'm going to be an uncle?" Rhys smiled and yanked her into a sideways hug. "I would have come for you sooner, but Madoc refused to tell me where you'd gone. I'd just received your letter when Madoc died suddenly."

Keely nodded with understanding.

"If your husband displeases you, leave him," Rhys said. "The babe and you will always have a home with me in Wales."

Keely rested her head against his shoulder, saying,

"Thank you for that. Richard pleases me, but I want him to love me too."

"Love appears in many forms, sweetheart," Rhys told her. "Perhaps—"

"And what form are you?" demanded a voice from the doorway.

Keely snapped her head up and saw Richard standing there with her father. Her husband didn't look especially happy. In fact, he appeared unaccountably hostile. What had she done wrong now?

Rhys rose from the chair and faced the two men. Though his sister's inexperience blinded her to it, he recognized the jealousy in her husband's expression and tone. Christ, the Englishman's feelings were as easy to read as an open book. Obviously, the English earl loved his sister, and that was enough for Rhys to like him.

"I'm waiting for an answer," Richard snapped.

"*Brotherly* love," Rhys said dryly.

"'Tis Rhys," Keely explained, rising from the stool, ready to defend her brother against her angry husband. "He's ridden all the way from Wales."

Richard relaxed visibly. His expression cleared, and a welcoming smile spread across his features. He marched across the chamber and offered his brother-in-law his hand.

Duke Robert grinned. "I owe you a debt of gratitude for protecting my daughter all those long years."

"Both His Grace and I are indebted to you," Richard said.

"Keely was my baby sister long before she journeyed to England," Rhys replied. "Protecting her was a pleasure as well as a duty."

"'Tis the Yuletide," Keely interjected, holding her brother's hand, reluctant to let him go after so many long months. "Promise you'll stay with us through the New Year."

"I left Corgy in charge in my absence, and you know

he's only a mite smarter than Odo and Hew," Rhys told her. "Will you settle for Christmas?"

"Yes, happily." Keely turned to her father. "Rhys has brought news, Papa. Madoc is dead."

Duke Robert would have offered his condolences, but he wasn't the least bit sorry. Instead, he nodded at his daughter and said to Rhys, "Come along, Baron Lloyd. We'll commandeer a chamber and anything else you require."

Before quitting the chamber with the duke, Rhys hugged Keely and kissed her cheek. "I'll see you later," he told her. "Remember what I said."

Richard sat in the chair in front of the hearth and pulled his wife down onto his lap. "What does Rhys want you to remember?" he asked.

"That I always have a home with him in Wales," Keely answered, staring at his chest.

"Your home is with me."

Keely slowly looked up and stared him straight in the eye. "I can never feel at home in England, my lord."

"You'll settle in."

"But I'll never *fit* in."

"Don't be ridiculous," Richard scoffed. "The Countess of Basildon belongs in England."

"Those courtiers harbor nothing but contempt for me," Keely insisted. "I am the *taffy* bastard who tricked England's favorite son into marriage."

" 'Tis playacting at its finest," Richard tried to explain. "Their own insecurities consume them. If the Countess of Basildon deigns to mingle, those arrogant idiots will feel honored and reciprocate."

"Perhaps I find them unworthy of my company."

"Damn it, Keely. You stand in that hall with your head hung low and your eyes downcast. Why are you ashamed of yourself?"

"I am *not* ashamed!" Keely cried, leaping off his lap. "I am a true princess of Wales, descended from Llewelyn the Great and Owen Glendower. Why, my bloodline is purer and nobler than the queen's!"

"Prove it," Richard challenged, rising from the chair to tower over her. "Escort Rhys around the hall tonight. Introduce him to the other courtiers."

Insecurity made Keely worry her bottom lip with her teeth. Though she'd never admit it, Keely didn't think she had the courage. "I'll consider it," Keely said finally.

Richard read the fret mirrored in her gaze and gentled his voice. "I'll remain by your side while you do, dearest."

"I'll remain by your side while you do, dearest. . . ."

Another broken promise from an English lord, Keely thought, hurt and irritated. She should have known better. Her charming husband had nearly lulled her into forgetting the harsh lessons of her own mother's life. Such a lapse in distrust could prove dangerous to her peace of mind and would never happen again.

As soon as Lord Burghley's summons arrived, Richard had deposited Keely with Duke Robert and Lady Dawn and left the hall. An hour had passed since his departure.

Keely kept her attention fixed on the hall's entrance and let the courtiers' conversations swirl around her while she anxiously awaited Rhys's arrival. Could Richard's assessment of her situation be correct? If she mingled with these English nobles, would they acknowledge her? Or would they snub her for being a bastard?

That Rhys should learn that she played the outcast was simply out of the question. Fiercely protective of her, Rhys would probably challenge those courtiers who slighted her. Her brother enjoyed a reputation for being a ferocious warrior, but he was undoubtedly incapable of dueling with every man in England.

Keely scanned the hall and sensed a change in its atmosphere. The courtiers seemed wilder and freer that evening because the queen had absented herself from the festivities.

Keely's violet gaze touched the hall's entrance at the precise moment Rhys appeared. She started moving through the crowd toward him.

Her brother had never looked more handsome or virile than he did at that moment—every inch as spectacular as her husband. In fact, Rhys wore formal court garb borrowed from Richard and appeared like a black bird of prey ready to swoop down on unsuspecting canaries.

"How now, brother?" Keely greeted him with a smile.

"Sister, your vibrant beauty shames these pallid Englishwomen," Rhys said, returning her smile. "Turn around, and let me admire you."

Keely giggled and twirled in a circle. The young girl who wandered the Welsh forests had disappeared, though her essence remained. In her place stood a very desirable woman wearing a daringly low-cut gown that enhanced her alluring beauty.

Rhys thought the gown was much too revealing but kept his peace. Keely belonged to the English earl now, and he would never gainsay his sister's husband.

"You must meet my father's new wife," Keely said, grasping his hand. "She's been exceedingly kind to me."

Together, Keely and Rhys plunged into the crowd. With her brother's hand in hers, Keely felt unusually confident. The whispered murmurings of who the handsome stranger could be filled her with pride.

"Lady Dawn, I present my stepbrother Baron Rhys Lloyd," Keely introduced them.

Rhys bowed over the duchess's hand and said, "My thanks for your many kindnesses to my sister."

"If I weren't madly in love with my Tally," Lady Dawn purred, giving him a feline smile, "I'd make a complete fool of myself over you, baron, as these young ladies casting surreptitious looks in this direction are about to do."

"Come, Rhys," Keely said, accepting the challenge her husband had issued. "I want to introduce you to a few of the courtiers."

Linking her arm through his, Keely led her brother

around the hall. She spied her stepmother's pregnant companions from the previous day and advanced on them.

"Lady Tessie and Lady Blair," Keely said with a winsome smile, "I wish to make my brother, Baron Lloyd, known to you."

Rhys bowed over Tessie's hand and complimented her: "You look divine in that heavenly blue gown."

Tessie sighed. "I wished Pines was as pretty with a compliment as you."

Rhys turned next to Lady Blair and bowed in courtly manner. He opened his mouth to compliment her as well, but his sister spoke first.

"How is dear Horatio today?" Keely asked, suppressing the powerful urge to laugh.

"My heavens, Horatio is eating like the proverbial pig."

Keely giggled and led her brother away, whispering, "Horatio *is* her pet pig."

Rhys glanced sidelong at her. "You're kidding?"

Keely shook her head. "Lady Dawn owns a pet goose named Anthony."

"Introduce me to a few unmarried women," Rhys said, "like those three beauties watching us over there."

Keely glanced in the direction he gestured. Ladies Morgana, Sarah, and Jane stood on one side of the hall and stared at them. No doubt they wondered about the handsome gentleman's identity.

Keely had no intention of going anywhere near them. Let them drool from a distance. If they insulted her in her brother's presence, their lives could be endangered.

"You really should meet Lady Mary," Keely said, trying to lead him in the opposite direction from the three well-known witches. "She's the buxom blonde standing with the Italian, Signor Fagioli. See the long-haired giant peeking down the blond woman's bodice."

Keely started to lead him toward the couple, but Rhys

hung back. His hand on her arm prevented forward movement, and she turned a questioning gaze on him.

"I much prefer to meet those beauties over there," Rhys insisted.

"Trust me, brother. You don't want to know them."

Rhys grinned. "Pray tell me why."

"Because they heartily despise us Welsh," Keely informed him. "Especially me."

"Why?"

Keely dropped her gaze to his chest and shrugged.

"Jealousy rules their actions," Rhys said, tilting her chin up. "Come, sister. I'll gladly meet this Italian signor."

"Keely!" called a familiar feminine voice.

Keely turned around reluctantly. The voice belonged to her sister.

"Bring your handsome friend to join our group," Morgana invited her, flicking a glance at Rhys. "Are you avoiding me, dear sister?"

Keely gaped in surprise at her "dear" sister. A fluttering oak leaf could have knocked her over.

"I am Keely's half-sister, Lady Morgana Talbot," the blonde introduced herself.

Rhys grinned wolfishly at Morgana. His interested gaze perused her from the top of her blond head to the tips of her dainty slippered feet, but it lingered a moment longer than was proper on the alluring display of silken flesh above the bodice of her low-cut gown.

"We share a common interest," Rhys remarked. "I am Keely's stepbrother."

The fierce Welsh baron and the pampered English beauty ignored their common interest, namely Keely. His warm gray eyes locked on her sultry blue eyes, and for several long moments the world faded and only the two of them existed.

"For our sister's sake, we should become better acquainted," Morgana said, lowering her gaze in simulated shyness. "Would you care to dance?"

"Unfortunately, my education lacked that refined skill," Rhys admitted with no trace of embarrassment, giving her an easy smile. "Perhaps a deserted alcove would better suit our becoming acquainted?"

Morgana's smile was angelic yet seductively inviting.

"I do believe I know of such a place."

"I'm sure you do," Rhys replied in a husky voice. Turning to his shocked sister, he said, "Will you excuse us?"

Before Keely could even acknowledge what he'd said, the unlikely couple walked away. Flabbergasted, Keely could only stare after them.

How did Rhys have the courage to admit to his ignorance about dancing? Keely wondered. She'd been mortified beyond endurance. The answer came to her then; Rhys was legitimate issue and a baron. While she was merely a—

"Good evening, countess."

Keely turned toward the voice. Willis Smythe stood beside her. His gaze, fixed on her cleavage, made her feel positively naked.

"Good evening, my lord," Keely said, pasting an insincere smile onto her face. Holy stones, she felt as shallow as the other courtiers in the chamber. But if she forced herself to mingle with a man she despised, mingling with the others would be easy.

"Has your husband deserted you again?" Smythe asked.

Keely cast him a flirtatious smile. "I'm afraid so."

"I believe the pavane is your favorite dance," Willis remarked. "Shall we?"

"The pavane is my *only* dance," Keely quipped, placing her hand in his.

Keely suppressed the urge to shudder as he led her onto the dance floor. Willis bowed to her in courtly manner, and she curtsied in return.

"You look especially lovely tonight," Smythe complimented her, his gaze on the enticing swell of her breasts as the pavane began.

"I'm flattered that you appreciate the cut of my gown," Keely said dryly.

Smythe gave her a smile meant to melt the frigid look in her eyes. "I understand that congratulations are in order. And how is the mother-to-be feeling?"

"Wonderful, at the moment. 'Tis the morning sickness that prevents me from eating breakfast."

"Isn't skipping breakfast unhealthy for the babe?" Smythe asked conversationally. "I would have thought an expectant mother would fill herself with eggs, cheese, milk, and ham."

"Eat ham?" Keely echoed, crinkling her nose to emphasize her revulsion. "I heartily despise pork in any form. Though 'tis one of Richard's favorites."

Keely swayed to the right to touch her left palm to his and stopped short. Beside the baron stood her husband. *Her angry husband.*

"I warned you, Smythe," Richard said, his voice low, his emerald eyes glinting with murderous intent.

"Give over, Devereux," Willis replied. "'Tis merely a dance."

"You did leave me to fend for myself," Keely reminded her husband, as the dancers around the three of them inched closer to eavesdrop on this confrontation.

"I forbid you to dance with this man," Richard said. "Choose another partner."

Of all the unbridled gall, Keely thought. Her husband could dance and flirt with whomever he pleased, but she must stand alone until he attended her.

"My lord, you do make a spectacle of us," Keely said, forcing a calmness into her voice that she didn't actually feel.

"Do not provoke me," Richard growled, reaching out to grab her wrist, insidious jealousy ruling his actions and words.

Keely stepped back a pace, lifted her right hand in the

air, and gave her husband the fig. Whirling away, she marched proudly out of the hall. When she reached the corridor, Keely lifted her skirts and sprinted the rest of the way to their chamber.

How dare her husband order her to mingle and then publicly reprimand her for doing so! Keely fumed as she paced back and forth in front of the hearth. How dare he—the door crashed open.

"Stay away from Smythe," Richard ordered, advancing on her. "Cease encouraging the attentions of other men."

Keely opened her mouth to reply, but Richard was faster.

"Do not deny it," he warned. "I have eyes in my head to see how those men look at you."

"*I* am not the Devereux whose private beauty mark is intimately known and universally admired by every female at court," Keely shot back.

That stopped the earl's intended tirade.

"I have heard enough. You will pass the remainder of the evening in this chamber, where you will reflect upon the error of your ways," Richard said, his voice stern. At that, he stormed out of the chamber and slammed the door behind.

Keely glared at the offending portal. "I hope you break your big toe," she cursed.

Suddenly, Keely heard a masculine shout and a loud crash in the corridor. She yanked the door open and stared in surprise at the sight that greeted her: the earl sprawled among the rushes on the stone floor of the corridor.

Slowly, Richard raised his emerald gaze to hers and said a bit sheepishly, "My haste tripped me."

Keely slammed the door shut. She covered her mouth with her hands and dissolved into muffled giggles, but the disturbing thought that her marriage was a failure sobered her almost instantly.

Keely sat down in the chair in front of the hearth and

sighed. She had always yearned for two things: a father and a home. Winning her father's acknowledgment and love had happened so unexpectedly, she couldn't believe she would be lucky enough for both dreams to come true. Without a doubt, Keely knew that that special place called home would forever elude her.

Born and bred a Welshwoman, she could never fit into this strange English society, but she would remain in England for the sake of her child. Keely could accept life without her husband's love if he proved a loving father to their children. An imperfect world sometimes forced the heart and the soul to compromise and make do with what was offered.

Living at the Tudor court, however, was an entirely different matter. Remaining amidst its superficiality even for one more day seemed like an impossible task.

Keely needed the sun warming her shoulders. She needed the wind caressing her face. What she needed most of all was to worship at the sacred site in the earl's garden where the yew, the birch, and the oak conversed. Keely decided she would return to Devereux House in the morning, with or without the earl.

The power of her positive thinking lifted Keely's spirits. She packed a few belongings in her leather satchel and went to sleep in a much better frame of mind than when she had awakened.

Hoping to avoid another argument with his wife, Richard returned to their chamber later than usual. He undressed in the darkened chamber, tossed his clothing onto the floor, and climbed into bed. Snuggling against his wife, he promptly joined her in sleep.

Only a few moments seemed to have passed before Richard swam up slowly from the depths of unconsciousness. A hammer—no, a battering ram—pounded inside his head, and his eyelids felt too heavy to open. Good Christ, why had he drunk so much wine?

Seeking the comfort of his wife's body, Richard inched

closer to the middle of the bed. Keely wasn't there. Then he heard her humming softly as she moved about the chamber.

"What time is it?" he moaned without opening his eyes.

" 'Tis early."

Sensing her presence beside him, Richard opened his eyes just as she set a sheet of parchment down on the pillow. Blinding sunshine streamed through the window behind her. He squinted against the painful brightness.

"What is this?" Richard asked, his gaze sliding to the parchment.

"A note for you," Keely answered.

"A note from whom?"

"From me."

Richard cocked a copper brow at her. "Well, what does it say?"

Keely lifted her leather satchel off the floor and turned away, saying, "I'm going home."

Richard groaned. The last thing he needed this morning was a runaway wife. Why couldn't the witch wait until his head cleared before she started creating new problems?

"I forbid you to leave this chamber," Richard ordered in his most authoritarian voice.

"Dearest, mix feverfew herbs in a mug of warmed cider for your headache," Keely told him. She gave him a sunny smile and then quit the chamber.

Richard leaped out of the bed and marched across the chamber. He yanked the door open but stopped short.

A passing serving wench winked at him and giggled.

" 'Tis true!" she exclaimed. "You do sport a freckle on the tip of—"

Richard slammed the door shut and hurried across the chamber to fetch his discarded clothing from the previous night. Because his industrious wife had already folded and put them away, Richard wasted five minutes searching for breeches, shirt, and boots.

When he opened the door again, Richard nearly tripped over the breakfast tray, which had been delivered while he was dressing. He paused for a moment and then picked it up. The tray was laden with hard-cooked eggs, cheese, bread, and a small mountain of ham slices. Richard looked at the tempting slices of ham, but the thought of eating sickened him. Too much wine the previous night had stolen his usually robust appetite.

His impetuous wife had no concern for the babe she carried. Determined to return to Wales, she would endanger their child by starving herself. First, Richard intended to cram her breakfast down her throat, starting with the ham she despised. Then he'd lock her in their chamber.

Reaching the lawns outside the palace, Richard spied his wife up ahead. Keely walked along almost leisurely—an unusually slow gait for a runaway. A smile flirted with the corners of Richard's lips as he admired the gentle sway of her hips. His headache dulled to a minor throb, the sight of his sweet wife a balm to his health and well-being.

Lecturing and ordering hadn't once bent the independent witch to his will, Richard thought. Would his fabled Devereux charm be more persuasive?

Richard walked into the dimly lit stable and saw his wife standing in front of Merlin's open stall. At least she'd had enough sense to refrain from lifting the heavy saddle.

Inside the stall Hew was readying Merlin for travel while Odo was trying to persuade Keely not to leave. All three looked at the earl when he approached.

"Breakfast is served," Richard announced, gifting her with his devastating smile.

"I never eat breakfast," Keely replied, seemingly immune to his masculine wiles.

"Don't forget the babe needs the nourishment."

"I'll dine later." Dismissing him, Keely turned toward the stall and stroked Merlin's forehead.

Richard set the tray down. Trying to hold his patience, he silently counted to ten and then added another twenty for good measure. Though he'd never before suffered from a quick temper, his frustrating wife brought out the worst in him. *And the best.*

"You're riding to Wales alone?" Richard asked, keeping his voice mildly curious.

Surprised, Keely snapped her head up and looked at him. "Wales is not my destination."

"Tell me, what exactly is your destination?" Richard asked, successfully suppressing the urge to shout at her.

"Devereux House."

Richard relaxed and stepped closer. "Could we speak before you leave?" he asked, drawing her away from the stall.

Keely nodded. "What would you like to discuss?"

Richard opened his mouth to speak, but heard Odo shout, "No, Merlin! Bad horse!"

Keely looked over her shoulder at the horse devouring their breakfast. "Never mind," she called. "Let her enjoy it."

"Keely, why are you leaving?" Richard asked.

"I told you. Living at court doesn't agree with me."

"Why?"

Keely dropped her gaze to his chest as if embarrassed to divulge her inner thoughts. "'Tis destroying our marriage. You either ignore me or fault me for whatever I do. Perhaps I will not displease you so much if we live at Devereux House."

"You do *not* displease me," Richard said, tilting her chin up, his emerald gaze locking on hers. "In truth, the court holds no appeal for me, but I promised Elizabeth we would remain through Twelfth Night. We'll return to Devereux House when the court moves to Richmond for the winter."

"Another two weeks in this place will surely kill me," Keely replied.

"Do not exaggerate," Richard teased, tracing a finger

down her silken cheek. Then he coaxed, "If you stay, I promise to wear my ceremonial robe when we go home."

Keely stared into his emerald eyes for several long moments and considered the sincerity of his offer. That her husband was bribing her to stay was obvious. If he cared enough to do that, perhaps their marriage could succeed after all.

"Come, love," Richard said with a lazy smile. "I'll let you watch me eat breakfast."

An agonized screeching rent the air behind them. Whirling around, Richard and Keely saw Merlin stagger against the side of the stall, fall to her knees, and then flop onto her side. Horrific shrieks of pain burst from the shuddering mare.

Concerned for his wife's safety, Richard grasped her upper arms and held her captive, but desperation gave her strength. Keely pulled out of his grasp and dropped to her knees beside her downed mare's head.

"Richard, help her!" Keely cried.

Richard glanced at the empty breakfast tray and then at Odo and Hew, who nodded in unspoken agreement. "Easing her death is all I can do," he told his wife, already reaching for the dagger Odo held out. "Please wait outside the stable."

"I'm staying," Keely refused. "Do it quickly."

Richard knelt beside her and neatly slashed both sides of the mare's neck, severing the main arteries. Heedless of the sea of blood, Keely held the dying mare's head in her lap and whispered words of comfort to ease Merlin's passing. Within mere minutes, the shuddering horse stilled and heartbreaking silence reigned inside the stable.

Only when the horse lay in peace did Keely succumb to her tears. "I—I d-don't understand," she sobbed. "W-hat h-happened to her?"

Richard drew her against the comforting solidness of his body and answered honestly, "Someone poisoned the food."

"Who would poison my horse?" Keely cried, incredulous.

"Dearest, whoever did this harbored no intent to poison Merlin . . . Let me take you to our chamber now."

"Rhys gifted me with Merlin for my twelfth birthday," Keely said, gazing sadly at the mare. She caressed her beloved horse, then nodded at her husband and stood with his assistance.

Richard lifted her into his arms and carried her out of the stables. Keely wrapped her arms around his neck, hid her face against his shoulder, and wept softly.

Crossing the lawns toward the palace, Richard halted when he saw two people hurrying toward him. Dressed for riding, Rhys Lloyd and Morgana Talbot advanced on him. This was all he needed to make the worst morning of his life complete.

"What have you done to my sister?" Rhys demanded, staring at the blood that covered them.

"Someone poisoned Merlin. I had to—" Richard broke off when his brother-in-law nodded in understanding.

Morgana opened her mouth and shrieked in a panic.

"There's a poisoner at—?"

Rhys covered her mouth with his hand and yanked her roughly against his unyielding body. The blonde struggled in his arms, but only muffled squawks of protest escaped her mouth.

"Congratulations, baron," Richard said dryly. "I've wanted to do that for a long, long time." Without another word, he headed toward the palace.

You son of a Welsh bitch!

Richard paused and looked back in time to see Morgana slap the Welshman's face. Rhys crushed Morgana against his body and kissed her until she went limp within the circle of his embrace.

Richard turned toward the palace. Willis Smythe, his gaze fixed on the kissing couple, stood there.

"What's happened?" Willis asked, his gaze sliding to the Devereux' bloodsoaked clothing.

"Someone poisoned my wife's horse," Richard answered.

Willis paled and echoed in a whisper, "A poisoner loose at court?"

Richard nodded.

Concern etched itself across the baron's features, and worry shone from his eyes. "Are you well? Is there aught I can do to help?"

Remorse and guilt for distrusting his friend swelled in Richard's chest. "Please send a page to find my wife's women."

"I'll fetch them myself," Willis replied, then hurried away.

Gaining his chamber, Richard set Keely down on the bed and then sat beside her. He brushed the tears from her pale cheeks and tried to reassure her with a smile.

Keely turned her head to the side and kissed the palm of his hand. "Richard, someone poisoned *our* breakfast."

"I know."

"What will you do?"

"There's naught to fear, dearest," Richard soothed her. "I intend to speak with Burghley and Elizabeth as soon as May and June arrive to keep you company." He leaned close and planted a kiss on her forehead.

"I hope you're going to change before you see the queen," Keely said. "She'll faint at the sight of all that blood."

Richard gave her a quick kiss and then collected a clean shirt, breeches, and doublet. He buckled his leather belt, asking, "Where's my dagger—the one with my insignia?"

"I haven't seen it," Keely answered. "You've lost a button on that doublet."

"So I have." Richard hurriedly changed his doublet and then returned to the bed.

"What do you think the queen will do?" Keely asked.

"Well, Burghley will advise her to keep this incident as

quiet as possible while his agents investigate," Richard answered. "Panicking everyone at court would serve no good purpose. Though I'm almost positive Elizabeth will banish the Italians."

"The Italians?" she echoed. "But why?"

"Because, sweetheart, the Italians are known for their expertise with poisons," he explained. "'Tis one of their preferred methods of assassination."

"But why would any Italian wish to assassinate us?"

"I don't know and probably never will," Richard admitted with a shrug. He smiled, and in an attempt to calm her, he added, "Trust me, darling. The danger has passed. Whoever poisoned our breakfast will not dare a second attempt, because now our guard is up. And those few courtiers who do discover what has transpired will only eat food that their own servants have brought from the kitchens."

The door swung open. May and June entered on the run.

"I shan't be long," Richard said, rising from the bed. Keely grabbed his hand. "You will be careful?"

Richard nodded. He turned to his cousins and ordered, "Do not leave your mistress alone. Accept no food unless you personally fetch it from the kitchens."

With that, Richard left the chamber. Once outside in the privacy of the corridor, he paused for a moment and leaned against the wall, the frightening enormity of what had almost happened hitting him with the impact of an avalanche.

What if he'd crammed that food down his wife's throat as he'd intended? Keely would be lying dead in the stable instead of Merlin. Whom had the poisoner meant to dispatch? Keely or himself? *Or both?*

Chapter 16

"Happy Christmas, my lord," Keely whispered, her lips hovering above her sleeping husband's.

"Good morning, dearest." Richard kept his eyes closed and savored the comfortable feeling of his wife's weight on top of him. "How about my Christmas kiss?"

The man was insatiable, but Keely didn't mind. She pressed her lips against his and poured all of her love into that single stirring kiss.

Richard wrapped his arms around her, imprisoning her against the muscular planes of his body, and returned her kiss in kind. "I love Christmas," he murmured, "especially its kisses."

The reality of the cloak she wore seeped into his drowsy senses, and he opened his eyes. Predawn light kept the chamber eerily shadowed.

"What time is it?" he asked.

"'Tis six o'clock," she answered.

"Nobody rises at six o'clock."

"I do."

"If you're planning to run away," Richard said, eyeing her with feigned suspicion, "please wait for a later hour. Chasing you to the stables in the middle of the night tires me."

Keely smiled and planted a kiss on his lips. "Rhys leaves for Wales at dawn. I want to bid him a safe journey."

Richard yawned and stretched. "Very well, I'll accompany you. I do hope you appreciate my sacrifice in rising at this ungodly hour."

"If you refrained from drinking and gambling half the

night with my father," Keely said, cocking an ebony eyebrow at him, "you might appreciate the serenity of the morning."

"Only those with no prospects appreciate morning's serenity," Richard replied, moving as if to rise. "The truly shrewd like me use the court's nightly entertainments to conduct business."

"Modesty becomes you," Keely teased, pressing him back on the bed with the palm of her hand.

"Let me up, dearest. Walking alone to the stables at this hour can be dangerous."

"Stay where you are, my lord. Roger has already agreed to escort me."

"Who has?"

"Roger, my favorite page."

"Isn't he the brat who boosted you over the wall?"

Keely nodded.

"Hurry back," Richard said in a husky voice. "I have a magnificent Christmas gift for you."

"What is it?"

"The same thing I have for your New Year's gift."

"Which is?"

Guiding her hand to his groin, Richard smiled and answered, "Morning cock."

"*Lecher.*" Keely planted a quick kiss on his lips and then left the chamber.

Waiting for her in the corridor, Roger gave Keely a sleepy smile of greeting when she appeared. Together, the countess and the page made their way through the maze of Hampton Court's dimly lit corridors. The closer Keely got to the world outside the palace walls, the faster she walked. Anticipation surged through her body. She hadn't felt the rising sun on her face in months—except through a window.

Bursting through the door to the grounds outside, Keely felt she had entered a whole new world. In spite of the earliness of the hour, myriad people bustled about. Arriving and departing noblemen with their families hurried back and forth across the winter-gray lawns, servants prepared for their masters' awakening, and purveyors of every bauble imaginable readied themselves for another profitable day.

Brightening the eastern horizon, fingers of orange light reached for the world of men. This Christmas promised to be a day of incomparable beauty—spectacular sunshine, heavenly blue skies, crisp air.

Keely breathed deeply of the winter's pristine air. Mornings like this made her yearn to worship in her own special way. Alas, life at the Tudor court was long on luxury but short on privacy.

"What's the latest gossip?" Keely asked as they walked across the lawns in the direction of the stables.

"I heard that Lady Jane slept with someone other than her husband last night," Roger answered.

Keely cast the boy a quelling sidelong glance. She had no wish to hear about Lady Jane's latest conquest.

Unused to reading subtle nuances of expression, Roger missed the meaning of her look and continued, "That particular killer lamb becomes bolder by the day. Or should I say 'bolder by the night'?"

" 'Tis unkind of you to bandy such tales about," Keely told him, suppressing a smile. Though she harbored no special regard for her husband's former mistress, Keely felt obligated to guide a boy of Roger's tender years onto a more virtuous path. That a twelve-year-old should speak so casually of adultery was unseemly.

"Jane's penchant for bending the marriage vows is common knowledge," Roger replied. Glancing sidelong at her, he added, "I also heard your cousins and the earl's have become quite close."

Keely nodded. "Yes, they've become remarkable friends."

"I'd say *intimate* best describes their relationships."

Surprised, Keely snapped her head around to look at him. "Do you mean—?"

"Exactly."

In the stableyard, Odo and Hew stood on either side of Rhys's stallion and verified that all was in readiness for traveling. Rhys smiled with relief when he spied his sister.

"I knew you'd come." Rhys gathered her into his arms and gave her a hug.

"I miss you already," Keely said, looking at him through violet eyes beginning to brim with tears. "You will be careful?"

Rhys nodded. "Remember, sister. You always have a home with me in Wales."

"Thank you, brother." Keely cast her cousins a side-long glance. "Too bad you cannot stay to see Odo and Hew married."

"What?" Odo exclaimed.

"Wedding?" Hew cried.

Keely ignored their outbursts. "They've enjoyed their wedding nights with my tiringwomen," she told her brother. "Now the married life awaits them."

"I'm certain they'll be happy husbands before I reach Wales," Rhys said with a smile. "You will send word as soon as the babe is delivered?"

"Of course." Reluctant to let him go, Keely rested her head against his chest.

"Bid Morgana farewell for me," Rhys bade her. "Tell the duke I have an interest in his daughter and will write to him at first opportunity."

"'Twould be matrimonial suicide to marry her," Keely told him. "Besides, my sister loves the courtier's life too much to marry you and live in Wales."

"Morgana is merely high-spirited," Rhys said. "She needs a strong man to tame her."

"I suppose you know what's best for you," Keely replied. "You always did love a challenge."

Brother and sister embraced a final time. Rhys planted a kiss on her forehead, set her away from him, and mounted his horse.

"Godspeed!" Keely called as he rode away. She stood in the stableyard and watched her brother until he disappeared from sight. Fat teardrops streamed down her cheeks, but she wiped them away with the back of her hand.

Loss is the only sure thing in life, Keely thought. Megan, Rhys, and Merlin had vanished from her life; but in their places she'd gained Richard, Duke Robert, Henry, and Lady Dawn.

Keely gave herself a mental shake and rounded on Odo and Hew. "I refuse to let you dishonor my husband's cousins," she said. "Prepare yourselves for your wedding day. . . . Come, Roger."

Instead of returning directly to the palace, Keely and Roger strolled across the lawns. The boy's downcast expression told Keely that something was troubling him. The two of them sat on a stone bench in a deserted section of the grounds.

"My lady, I need your help," Roger blurted out suddenly.

"In what way?" Keely asked.

"The other pages do clamor for my skin."

"I don't understand."

"I charged each page a gold coin to accompany me on a tour of the haunted Long Gallery," Roger explained. "Your ghost never appeared, and the boys are demanding the return of their money."

Keely bit her bottom lip to keep from laughing.

"What am I to do? The gold is gone," Roger moaned.

"I—I wondered, would you accompany us to the Long Gallery and conjure that spirit? My father would be eternally grateful to you for saving his heir's life."

"On what did you waste the gold?" Keely asked, hoping she sounded suitably stern.

"I never wasted it," Roger answered. "I invested all but one gold piece in your husband's Levant Trading Company. When I'm older, I want to be just like the earl."

Keely did smile then. Through Roger and his money-making scheme, she saw the image of what her husband must have been like as a boy. Keely supposed she really ought to help him out of his predicament.

"How did you spend the uninvested gold piece?" she asked.

"I bought an aphrodisiac."

"What's that?"

Roger blushed but answered, "'Tis a love potion to make a woman *desire* me."

Now it was Keely's turn to blush. Holy stones, was that the only thing the males of the species ever sought? Apparently, the queen had been correct. Men *did* think with their pricks.

"Blushing is unnecessary," Roger told her, sounding like an experienced man of the world. "After all, love-making is a natural part of life."

Keely rolled her eyes. "From what is this love potion made?" she asked.

"The apothecary said there are many different kinds," Roger answered. "I purchased brains of partridge calcinated into powder and swallowed with red wine."

Keely gulped back the nausea rising in her throat. "Did it work?"

Richard flicked her a wicked grin. And *that* effectively answered her question.

"Who was the lucky lady?"

"A gentleman never kisses and tells."

Trying to discourage the boy's immoral endeavors, Keely hid a smile and turned her head. Not ten yards away stood double rows of hedges. Her gaze drifted past them and then returned to a gleaming object that lay beneath one of them. It appeared to be a blade reflecting the newly risen sun.

"What is that over there?" she said, standing.

Keely crossed the short distance between the bench and the hedges. Roger followed two steps behind her.

Keely screamed and fell to her knees. Hidden between the rows of hedges lay the lifeless body of a woman.

While Keely covered her mouth and gagged dryly, Roger shouted, "Help! Guards! *Murder!*"

Within mere seconds, pandemonium ensued. The palace guards arrived on the run. Close behind them followed curious nobles and servants.

At their captain's order, several guards held the gathering crowd at bay. Two others dragged the woman's body from between the hedges.

Keely nearly swooned at the sight of Lady Jane's battered face. Standing beside her, Roger put his arm around her shoulders and held her steady against his legs.

The captain of the guard stepped forward to inspect the body. A hushed silence fell over the crowd, the only sound being whispered words relaying the dead woman's identity.

"Lady Devereux?"

Keely looked up at the captain.

"Do you recognize these?" he asked, holding his hands out.

Keely stared in surprise at what he held. Both the jewel-hilted dagger and the gold button bore her husband's insignia. Keely tried to speak, to refute what she was seeing, but no words came out of her mouth.

"Lady Jane was Basildon's mistress, wasn't she?" the captain asked baldly.

"My husband keeps no mistress!" Keely cried. "Hurting a woman is beyond the earl's capabilities. Besides, he passed the night in our bed."

"Queen Elizabeth will decide where and how Basildon entertained himself last night," the captain said coldly. He turned his back and walked away.

Stunned, Keely dropped her gaze to the woman's battered face. She knew without a doubt that Richard was incapable of so vile an act. Whoever poisoned Merlin had murdered Lady Jane and left Richard's belongings beside the body.

"Beware the blacksmith . . ." Megan's dark prophecy

The angry murmurings of the crowd echoed in Keely's ears until she slumped against Roger in a dead faint.

Keely sat on her husband's lap in the chair in front of the fireplace in their chamber. Resting her head against his shoulder, she stared into the hearth's hypnotic flames and pondered her marital dilemma. Though she would never be accepted into this English society, Keely now knew she could never return to Wales and leave her husband behind. Not in this hour of his need. *Not ever.*

"'Twas a gruesome sight," Keely told him, her voice no louder than a horrified whisper. "Her face was battered, and a huge welt circled her neck."

"Hadn't her throat been slashed?" Richard asked.

"No, she'd been strangled with that necklace you gave her," Keely answered, her voice cracking with raw emotion on the word *strangled.*

"Dearest, clear your mind," Richard soothed, planting a kiss on the crown of her head. "Reliving the murder scene can hardly be healthy for the babe."

"Whoever poisoned Merlin meant to dispatch you," Keely said. "I'm afraid he found another way to get rid of you."

"So you've figured that out too?" The ghost of a smile touched Richard's lips. "You're too smart by half, dearest."

"'Tis good of you to notice," Keely replied. "Do you have any idea who'd want you dead?"

Richard sighed. "Any number of courtiers would like to see me vanish permanently."

"If we'd walked Merlin through Devereux House the day after our wedding, this would never have happened," Keely said.

"Probably not, but we'd be knee-deep in horse shit."

Keely gave him an unamused look. "Perhaps if we cast the sacred circle, the Goddess will share her wisdom."

"Why don't you kiss me instead?" he teased.

"Be serious," Keely snapped, irritated by his lack of concern.

"Easy, dearest. A dagger and a button prove nothing," Richard said. "Besides, Elizabeth knows her personal finances will suffer if she executes me."

"The blacksmith murdered Jane," Keely said abruptly.

"Do you know who he is?"

Richard looked confused.

"Whatever Megan saw came to pass," Keely explained. "On her deathbed, she told me: 'Walk among the powerful, but find happiness where the birch, the yew, and the oak converse. Trust the king who wears a flaming crown and possesses the golden touch. Beware the blacksmith.'

"Queen Elizabeth is the powerful one," she continued. "The birch, the yew, and the oak converse together in your garden. And you are the king who wears the flaming crown."

Richard grinned. "I'm an earl, sweetheart, not a king."

"All of England calls you Midas."

Richard lost his smile. A grain of truth lay in what she said. Perhaps her mother had possessed a special talent to foresee future events. A few rare people did enjoy such a gift. But if that were true, who could the blacksmith be?

"When we visited the Tower, Queen Anne's spirit also warned, 'Beware the blacksmith,'" Keely went on. "My mother warned me again on Samhuinn. If only—"

A knock on the door interrupted her words.

"They've come for you!" Keely cried, her voice rising in panic as she clutched her husband.

Richard wrapped his arms around her and called out, "Who's there?"

The door opened slowly. Willis Smythe peered into the room and asked, "May I come in?"

Richard stared at his former friend for a long moment. Then he nodded permission to enter.

Secure in her husband's embrace, Keely flicked a troubled glance at the baron. Looking at him disturbed her peace of mind. With his blue eyes and his black hair, Smythe was handsome enough, but that aura of untimely death still surrounded him like a shroud. Keely felt in her Druid bones that the baron's demise was fast approaching. What appeared to be a misty black cloud hovered over his head.

"How can I help?" Willis asked, standing near the hearth and facing them. Concern etched itself across his darkly handsome features. "Is there anyone you'd like me to question?"

"I have no idea with whom Jane was involved," Richard replied.

Willis nodded. "Is there aught I can do to ease matters?"

Richard shook his head. Smythe had been his closest friend since they'd fostered together at Burghley's. Remorse for distrusting Willis coiled around Richard's heart.

"I heard that Jane was strangled with her own necklace," Willis told them, his voice low.

"Keely told me," Richard replied. "I believe whoever poisoned my wife's horse also murdered—"

A knock on the door interrupted his words. Keely gasped. Richard and Willis snapped their heads around to stare at the door.

Duke Robert and Lady Dawn burst into the chamber. Both Richard and Willis relaxed. Keely released the breath she hadn't realized she'd been holding.

Keely rose from her husband's lap and flew into her father's arms. Richard stood and shook his father-in-law's hand.

"Oh, my poor dears," Lady Dawn gushed. "What an unfortunate misunderstanding!"

"Elizabeth is meeting with her advisers," Duke Robert told them. "Dudley is bent on convincing her to lock you in the Tower."

"No! They can't!" Keely cried.

"Now, dear. Becoming upset won't help," Lady Dawn said, giving her a comforting hug.

"I have faith in Elizabeth's judgment," Richard said.

"Dudley paints you to be a demented monster. He's insisting you tried to poison Keely and then strangled Jane," Duke Robert informed them. "Burghley is arguing that anyone could have murdered Jane, especially a jealous husband who wearied of his young wife's infidelities."

"One of her lovers could have done it," Willis added.

"Whoever killed Jane stole my dagger and insignia button," Richard said. "Cold-blooded design spawned the deed, not passionate outrage."

Bang! Bang! Bang!

Everyone turned to stare in horror at the door as if the wooden structure had suddenly become a deadly dragon. Keely threw herself into her husband's arms in an effort to protect him from whatever lay beyond the door.

"Basildon!" the Earl of Leicester called from the corridor. "By the authority of Her Majesty, I charge you to surrender yourself to the Crown's justice."

Richard nodded at his father-in-law. Duke Robert stepped forward and opened the door.

Robert Dudley, the Earl of Leicester, swaggered into the room. Behind him walked Lord Burghley, who appeared distinctly unhappy.

"Remain in the corridor," Duke Robert ordered the queen's men.

The soldiers looked at Dudley, who glanced over his shoulder and nodded at them. Duke Robert closed the door.

"Quite a little gathering," Dudley remarked with a smile of immense satisfaction.

"I assume I'm to accompany you to the Tower," Richard said blandly. "Give me five minutes to pack a few necessities."

Dudley nodded his permission.

"Papa, do something!" Keely cried. People died in the Tower, and she refused to let its gray stone walls swallow her husband and trap him there with those tormented souls for all of eternity.

"Dearest, help me pack," Richard said, putting his arm around her shoulders and drawing her across the chamber.

"Tis an outrage!" Duke Robert insisted. "Richard never killed anyone."

"For safety's sake, Elizabeth has decided to detain him," Dudley replied. "If he's found innocent, Basildon will be released."

"Never fear, Ludlow. Richard will receive fair treatment," Burghley said. "Walsingham and I intend to investigate this case personally. Richard's dagger appearing at the crime scene is too neat for belief. Why, even Leicester could have done the deed and planted false evidence there."

"I find that theory unamusing," Dudley drawled. With his satchel packed, Richard turned to his wife. He pulled her into his arms, and his mouth swooped down to capture hers in a lingering, heartbreakingly desperate kiss.

"Have a care for the babe," Richard whispered. *"Por tous jours."*

"For always," Keely promised, reaching for her dragon pendant. "Wear this, and the power of my mother's love will protect you."

Richard stayed her hands. "You wear it, dearest. My mind will rest easy knowing you're safe."

"Make haste," Dudley snapped.

"I will accompany you to the Tower to verify my son-in-law's safe arrival," Duke Robert said.

"I'll go along too," Willis piped up.

Richard gave Keely a last quick kiss and then turned to leave. Flanked by Dudley and Duke Robert, he quit the chamber.

"Tis a terrible mistake!" Keely cried, starting for the

door. "I must speak with the queen." At that moment, she would have braved a thousand haunted Long Galleries in order to free her husband.

Gently but firmly, Lord Burghley grasped her forearm and prevented her from leaving. Keely tried in vain to break free of his hold.

"Rash action is always unwise," Burghley scolded her, though not unkindly. When she stilled, he said, "Elizabeth will refuse you an audience. In fact, she has commanded me to charge you to return to Devereux House immediately."

"How will I discover the villain's identity?" Keely asked.

"Never fear, child. I shall take care of it," Burghley answered. "The truth will out."

Keely cast him a doubtful look and announced, "I know who murdered Jane."

Burghley stared at her in surprise. "I beg your pardon?"

"The blacksmith did it, but I cannot figure out who he is."

"Explain yourself."

"On her deathbed, my mother prophesied that I should beware of the blacksmith," Keely told him.

"My daughter-in-law is very spiritual," Lady Dawn interjected. "Her mother had the second sight."

"*The sight?*" Burghley echoed, shaking his head in disapproval. Their incredible silliness boggled his logical mind.

"I believe *blacksmith* is a nickname or a description of the person," Keely added.

"Thank you for your help, Lady Devereux," Burghley said, patting her arm. "I will certainly ponder your words."

He turned to leave, but Keely's voice stopped him at the door. "My lord, when may I visit my husband?"

"By the queen's order, there will be no visitors" came his reply.

Keely burst into tears. Lady Dawn led her to the chair in front of the hearth and forced her to sit down, just as May and June raced into the chamber.

"I'll get you something to eat while your women pack," Lady Dawn said.

Keely shook her head. "Hunger eludes me. I'll eat when I reach Devereux House," she said.

A knocking sounded on the door, but Keely paid it no heed. Richard had gone to the Tower, and that was the only thing that mattered now.

Lady Dawn opened the door and saw an adolescent boy standing there. "Yes?" she asked.

"May I speak with Lady Devereux?"

Lady Dawn flicked a glance at her daughter-in-law. "She's busy at the—"

"Who is it?" Keely asked.

"'Tis I, Roger."

"Come in, Roger."

Lady Dawn stepped aside and allowed the boy entrance.

"I've come to say farewell," Roger said, standing in front of her.

"I shall miss you," Keely replied, making him blush. She rose from the chair and searched through her belongings for the coin pouches her husband had given her. Turning to Roger, she asked, "How many boys did you swindle?"

"I never—"

"How many?"

"Ten, but—"

Keely counted ten gold coins and offered them to him.

"I cannot accept your money, my lady."

"Consider it a loan," Keely said with a smile. "I'll be your silent partner in my husband's company."

Roger grinned and took the coins. "I'll keep my ears open and tell Burghley whatever I overhear."

"Thank you, Roger." Keely kissed the boy's cheek.

"Godspeed, my lady." Roger bowed formally and quit the chamber.

Christmas Day aged into night. Muted shades of lavender and deep indigo slashed across the horizon from east to west, until the Yule's full Oak Moon shone from the perfect setting of a black velvet sky. Woodsmoke from the Strand's great houses scented winter's crystalline air, and delicately fine mist rode the river and swirled up its banks onto the shore.

Ghostlike, two barges glided in silence down the Thames toward the Strand. Wrapped in a fur-lined cloak, Keely sat on the canopied barge. With her were May and June. The second barge carried Odo, Hew, and the earl's stallion. Even Black Pepper stood statue-still as if he sensed the tragedy unfolding around his master.

Earlier in the day, Lady Dawn had sent one of the Talbot couriers to inform the earl's parents of what had befallen their son and to advise his household staff to prepare for their lady's homecoming. Nearing Devereux House, Keely saw her brother Henry and Jennings, the earl's majordomo, waiting on the quay. Behind them on the lawns stood several servants.

When the two barges had docked, Jennings stepped forward and said, "Welcome home, my lady." The majordomo turned to her tiringwomen and ordered, "Make haste, girls. Prepare your mistress's chamber."

May and June lifted their skirts and sprinted toward the mansion.

Jennings glanced over his shoulder and nodded at the earl's footman, who rushed forward to retrieve the countess's baggage from the barge. "Cook prepared a light supper for you," Jennings told Keely. "Shall I bring you a tray in your chamber?"

"No, serve me in the earl's study," she answered, then turned to her brother.

Henry kissed her cheek and escorted her off the quay so that Odo and Hew could safely disembark Black Pepper. "Hal and Louise sailed downriver to the Tower to bring Richard a few necessities," her brother informed her. "From there, they'll travel to Hampton Court to plead his case and help with the investigation."

Keely nodded in relief.

"Little girl!" Odo called, drawing her attention as he led the horse away. "We'll put Black Pepper down for the night."

"And then ourselves," Hew added. "Send word if you need anything."

"Thank you, cousins. I'll see you in the morning."

Henry guided her toward the mansion, saying, "I will be staying with you at Devereux House while everyone is away."

"'Tisn't necessary," Keely replied, "though I do appreciate your offer."

"'Tis necessary," Henry insisted in a disgusted tone of voice. "In Morgana's absence, Ashemole has fixed her attention on me. The hag is a pain in the arse."

Keely stifled a giggle and asked, "How so, brother?"

"The crone's been nagging me about my immoral behavior," Henry answered. "I do believe she's been spying on me."

"Very well, brother. I shall be glad for your company," Keely said. "Care to sup with me?"

"I've already eaten," Henry replied, giving her a sheepish smile. "Besides, I have an important—"

"Tell me no more," Keely interrupted, wondering who the lucky maid was. "I'll see you on the morrow."

The earl's study was exactly as Keely remembered. Near the windows on one side of the room stood a desk made from sturdy English oak. Rows of books lined two walls from floor to ceiling, and the fourth wall sported the hearth where an inviting fire crackled. The two chairs where the earl and she had once sat together still perched before the hearth.

Keely sighed deeply, sadly. How empty the study seemed without her husband's commanding presence.

How would she get along without having him near? More important, how could she win his freedom? She'd been banished to Devereux House, while the murderer hid within the crowded halls of Hampton Court.

Wandering across the chamber, Keely sat down at the desk. She placed the palms of her hands on its smooth flat surface and felt her husband's presence.

Sweet memories of Richard crowded around Keely. She recalled the day he massaged her feet and then stole a kiss—her very first. Again, she saw him kneeling in her father's hall and proposing marriage before an audience of a hundred ducal retainers.

Two fat teardrops rolled down her cheeks, but Keely brushed them away with her fingertips. Weeping would not help her husband, she told herself. What Richard needed was the Goddess's protection, and she would ask for that at dawn.

Keely rose from the desk and made herself comfortable in the chair in front of the hearth. The babe wearied her. Closing her eyes, Keely listened to the servants moving around quietly as they readied the table for her supper.

"My lady?" Jennings whispered, standing beside the chair. "Supper is served."

Keely opened her eyes and nodded, then let him escort her to the table. "Thank you, Mr. Jennings," she said, dismissing him, but the majordomo hovered near in the event she required anything else.

Fine linen covered the table. On top of the linen sat a bowl of split pea soup with beans and onions, a platter of roasted chicken with pine nuts, and a small dish of puréed quinces.

"There's only one place setting," Keely said, glancing at the majordomo.

"Yes, my lady. You sup alone."

"The earl may return to us at any moment," Keely said with a wobbly smile. "We must always set a place for him."

"Of course, my lady. Forgive me." Jennings hurried

away to fetch a plate that he knew might remain unused for many months.

Keely dropped her gaze to the bouquet of flowers the majordomo had set on the table in an effort to cheer her. A sob of emotion caught in her throat as she stared at the blue love-in-a-mist blossoms. Losing control of herself, Keely surrendered to the tears she'd been fighting all day.

"Do not weep, my lady," Jennings said when he returned with the earl's place setting. "The queen depends on his lordship. I'm positive he will soon be returned to us."

" 'Tis winter," Keely said, accepting his offered handkerchief. "From where did these love-in-a-mist come?"

"The earl commissioned London's most talented seamstress to fashion them out of silk," Jennings smiled.

" 'Tis uncanny how real they appear."

"Yes," Keely agreed, her husband's thoughtfulness touching her heart.

After she'd eaten, Keely dismissed Jennings and wandered across the study to the windows. She stared up at the full Oak Moon and conjured her husband's image in her mind's eye.

Oh, what must Richard be suffering, locked away in the saddest place on earth! Was his cell warm enough to prevent illness? Would his jailers feed him well? And what about candles? Could they be so cruel as to shut him away without light?

The full Oak Moon that looked down upon Keely's anxious expression also shone several miles downriver. East of London proper rose the Tower's pepper-pot turrets and forbidding gray walls.

With worry etched across his handsome features, Richard stood at a second-floor window inside Beauchamp Tower and gazed up at the full moon. His wife should be safely ensconced at Devereux House by now, he told himself. She would be well protected there, no matter how long the queen detained him.

A noise sounded behind him. Richard glanced over his shoulder at the three men descending the spiral stairs that led to the third story.

"Your bed is ready, my lord," the first yeoman said. "Complete with fur coverlet and all."

"A fire's blazing in the hearth," the second man added. "I've left an ample supply of kindling, but I'll deliver more in the morning."

"Thank you, good fellows." Richard handed both men a coin as they left. His gaze slid to the Tower constable. "And you, Kingston, must earn your coins," Richard said with a lazy smile.

"I eagerly await the opportunity," Kingston replied, rubbing his hands together in anticipation.

The door swung open, admitting the chaplain royal. The minister carried a silver tray laden with roasted chicken, bread, cheese, and a jug of Scots whisky.

Setting the small feast on the table, the chaplain said over his shoulder, "Your mother is a saint, Basildon. She's loaned us her favorite cook to serve you in your confinement."

Richard sat down at the table with the constable and the minister. He reached for a drumstick, arched a copper brow at them, and asked, "Are we ready?"

The two men nodded eagerly.

Richard filled three mugs with whisky, then produced a deck of cards and a pair of dice. "Gentlemen, let the gambling begin."

Chapter 17

Once in a blue moon. Forever when lovers leap over the fire.

The Great Mother Goddess whispered those prophetic words to Keely. She would see her husband once when the blue moon rode high in the sky and forever when young lovers leaped together over the Beltane fire. According to Keely's calculations, the full Blue Moon would appear on the last day of March that year; and of course, the Beltane fires always blazed on the first day of May.

Once on the last day of March, Keely thought, hope filling her beleaguered heart. *Forever* on the first day of May.

Those three months passed excruciatingly slowly.

Bitter January arrived with its frosted trees and sparkling icicles. Angry flocks of starlings gathered in the hagberry elm and complained about the tree's dearth of berries. Each afternoon, Keely strolled about her husband's garden. She sensed the unseen signs of life in the frozen world around her, the buds of her beloved oaks swelling even as she did. In the evenings, Keely wove Beltane baskets from splints of oak as January's full Wolf Moon waxed and waned.

Gradually, the hauntingly melancholy sunsets of January lengthened into February, with its receding blanket of snow. Candlemas came and went, as did the full Storm Moon. Dormant seeds, hidden within the earth, stirred anew with unseen life.

Nature delivered the clear blue skies of March, month of rebirth, hope, and the full Blue Moon. The full Seed Moon shone during March's first week. Migrating robins appeared during the month's third week and grazed in the still-brown grass while an amorous starling serenaded his lady with a courting song. Courageous crocus broke free of the thawing earth and opened their petals to the warmth of the waxing sun.

The last day of March dawned with radiant promise. Since the days of her morning sickness had passed, Keely rose from her bed as the sun streaked the eastern horizon with orange fingers of light. Excitement coursed through her body, and her life's blood sang the song of her beloved.

Keely knew with her Druid's instinct that the Goddess had spoken wisely. This was the day she would again see her husband: *once in a blue moon.*

Keely pulled her boots on over her stockinged feet and wrapped herself in her fur-lined cloak. She collected her pouch of holy stones and golden sickle, then left her chamber.

The earl's household staff was just beginning to stir as Keely escaped into the garden. Here the welcome harbingers of spring surrounded her, but Keely felt the watching eyes of well-intentioned spies—Odo and Hew.

Keely smiled inwardly. Odo, Hew, or Henry guarded her whenever she left the shelter of the house. At this early hour, Henry was probably sleeping beside his lady-of-the-moment. That left her cousins to guard her while she worshipped.

Keely crossed the garden to the sacred place where the birch, the yew, and the oak stood together like old friends. From her pouch, she chose nine stones: three black obsidians for defense against dark magic, three purple amethysts for breaking bad luck, and three red carnelians for general protection. With these holy stones, Keely created the sacred circle, leaving only the western periphery open. She entered from the west and closed it behind, saying, "All disturbing thoughts remain outside."

After removing the golden sickle from her pouch, Keely fused the invisible periphery shut and then walked to the center, the soul of the circle. She turned clockwise three times until she faced the east and the rising sun.

"The Old Ones are here, watching and waiting," Keely chanted into the morning's hushed air. "Stars speak through stones, and light shines through the thickest oak. One realm is heaven and earth."

Keely paused a long moment and touched the dragon pendant, lying hidden beneath her cloak. "By the power of Father Sun, the evil in my husband's life is done." She turned in a clockwise circle three times, chanting, "Spinning around, spinning around, spinning around. As I do, these words of magic be bound." Then, in a voice that carried throughout the garden, "May the Goddess bless Odo and Hew for rising so early each morn to protect me while I pray."

With that, Keely walked to the western periphery of the circle and broke the enchantment. After collecting her magic stones, she retraced her steps toward the mansion but called over her shoulder, "Thank you, cousins."

Odo and Hew stepped from their hiding place behind the hedgerow and followed her to the house. "How do you think she knew we were there?" Hew asked, scratching his head in puzzlement.

"I honestly don't know," Odo answered with a shrug.

"Do you think the wind whispered in her ear?" Hew asked.

"The only wind in this garden was your stinking fart," Odo answered, reaching out to cuff the side of his brother's head.

Hew ducked the blow, saying, "'Twas a silent one."

"Maybe she *smelled* it," Odo said, "like I did."

Following her usual morning routine, Keely went directly to the study for an early breakfast. She took all of her meals in the study, where she felt the closest to her husband.

The table had already been set with plates for her and the earl. Between the two plates sat the ever-present bouquet of silk love-in-a-mist flowers. Breakfast consisted of eggs in a pastry case, bread, butter, cheese, and a mug of almond milk.

Jennings walked into the study and announced in a formal tone of voice, "His Grace, the Duke of Ludlow, wishes an interview."

As her father brushed past the majordomo, Keely gave a little squeal of joy and flew into his open arms. "Oh, Papa!" she cried. "I've missed you these past months."

Duke Robert planted a kiss on her forehead, then led her back to the table and sat down opposite her. Smiling, he pulled an orange from his pocket and said, "For my grandchild."

Keely smiled and accepted the orange.

"How did you know I would visit this morning?" Duke Robert asked, noting the unused plate in front of him. "Or is this for Henry?"

"Henry never rises this early," Keely answered, giving him an ambiguous smile. "We set a place for Richard at every meal in case—is he well? Do you have news?"

"You have the queen's permission to visit your husband this afternoon," the duke told her.

Keely reached across the table and covered his hand with her own. Unshed tears glistened in her violet eyes. "Thank you, Papa. What made the queen change her mind?"

Duke Robert chuckled. "Richard made several costly blunders with her personal finances. His letters of apology do fault his long separation from you as the reason for his unintentional carelessness."

Keely smiled, dazzling her father with her joy. There existed no more beautiful sight in all the world than a happy pregnant woman.

"Burghley and I have been arguing in favor of house arrest," the duke went on. "I'm positive your husband's unintentional blunders will continue until he's ensconced at Devereux House. At eleven o'clock, I will escort you downriver."

Keely would have spoken then, but Henry barged into

the study and drew their attention. With his head hung low, he looked like a bedraggled tomcat after fighting with rivals and carousing with an army of females.

"She was the best piece of arse I ever—," Henry broke off when he saw his father—his furious father.

"Daughter, excuse my crude words," Duke Robert turned on his son and shouted, "Do you want that pecker of yours to fall off?"

"Do you want it to atrophy from disuse?" Henry shouted back, his three months of freedom inciting him to rebellion.

Keely burst out laughing.

"Do not encourage him," Duke Robert said, his right cheek twitching. Slowly, he rose from the table and advanced on his son.

Henry took an instinctive step back.

"Papa!" Keely called, fearing her father would strike him.

"Clean yourself up," Duke Robert ordered, towering threateningly over his son. "Report to my study at Talbot House in one hour. 'Tis past time we discussed several important issues."

Henry nodded and left the room.

"'Tis my fault for failing to chaperone him," Keely said, drawing her father's attention. "I've been so caught up in my own misery—"

"Do *not* shoulder the blame for your brother's outrageous behavior," Duke Robert interrupted. "His task was to guard you, not the other way around. I'll return for you at eleven."

"Papa?"

Duke Robert paused at the door and turned around.

"Go easy on him," Keely said. "Please?"

"I have no intention of murdering my only son," Duke Robert assured her, a hint of a smile flirting with the corners of his lips. "You may find this difficult to believe, but I was young once too."

* * *

Keely stepped outside at the appointed hour and hurried across the lawns to the quay, where her father waited. Anticipation flushed her cheeks, and the life's blood that surged through her body sang the song of her beloved. She had opened her heart and listened to the Goddess, who was now rewarding her for her unwavering faith.

Almost five months pregnant, Keely was beginning to outgrow her gowns. She wore her finest and loosest day dress, fashioned in violet velvet with a modestly high neckline. Over that she wore a lightweight black woolen cloak, and in her hands she carried an enormous tapestry bag filled with the holy objects she needed to protect her husband.

Early spring teased the world with clear blue skies, radiant sunshine, and gentle breezes. The sun's rays warming her shoulders and the gentle breeze tickling her face brought with them the most pleasant of memories—her husband's lovemaking. Keely suffered the urge to kick her boots off and feel the grass between her toes.

At the quay, Duke Robert hopped onto the barge and then helped her to board. Father and daughter sat together as the ducal barge glided downriver.

"What do you carry in the bag?" he asked.

"A few necessities for Richard," she answered, an ambiguous smile turning the corners of her lips up. "How fares Henry?"

"Repenting his sins." The duke cast her a sidelong glance. "Shall I produce his warm breathing body?"

Keely touched his forearm, and when he turned to her, she looked him straight in the eye. "I trust you, Papa," she said.

Sudden tears welled in the duke's violet eyes, so much like his daughter's. Duke Robert put his arm around her and planted a paternal kiss on her forehead. "Thank you, child," he said, his voice hoarse with emotion. "I've been waiting to hear those words."

"On my wedding day, I told you I loved you," Keely reminded him.

"True, but a world of difference lies between loving and trusting," Duke Robert replied. "Sometimes the one we love proves untrustworthy. Now, before you remark upon how sage I am, remember that advanced age brings a bittersweet wisdom."

"You're still young," Keely insisted. Then: "Papa, tell me about Megan and you."

The duke's eyes clouded with remembered pain. "Once the danger to your husband is past, I will answer all of your questions," he promised. "Can you be content until then?"

Keely smiled and nodded. Duke Robert was all that she had ever wanted in a father, everything she'd thought would make her happy, and now the world had spun upside down. Her happiness hinged on her husband. If only Richard were freed . . . If only she belonged in his world. . . . *If only he loved her.*

Their journey downriver took longer than usual. The world of men had recently awakened from its long winter's slumber, and the traffic upon that great street of water called the Thames proved horrendously congested. Though inconvenienced by the crush of barges, the boatmen seemed carefree and called greetings to friend and stranger alike. The ducal barge slipped beneath London Bridge and passed enclosed ship basins, from which the mingling scents of spices, grain, and lumber wafted through the air.

Soon Keely saw the pepper-pot turrets and forbidding gray walls of the Tower of London. She worried her bottom lip with her teeth and wondered in what condition she would find her husband. How would Richard greet her after all these months? Had he missed her? Had she even fleetingly crossed his mind?

Their barge docked at the watergate of St. Thomas Tower, also known as Traitor's Gate. Built in the 1290s by Edward I, the watergate had become the most dreaded portal in all of England. Such notoriously dangerous criminals as Anne Boleyn and her daughter, Queen Elizabeth, had passed through it. Some had returned to the world of men; some were never seen again.

Keely stared up at St. Thomas Tower but saw a hideous glaring monster, its gate the mouth that had swallowed her husband. "Tormented souls have passed through this gate," she said as her father helped her disembark.

"Aye," Duke Robert agreed, guiding her toward the Lieutenant's Lodgings. "Thinking about them will mar the babe, though."

"Did they bring Richard—?"

"Lingering upon past sorrows is futile," Duke Robert interrupted. "Your husband enjoys the best of health. He's a bit bored with his confinement and a trifle irritated about losing so much gold."

"You mean, the blunders on the queen's accounts?"

"No, child," Duke Robert chuckled. "Losing games of chance to one's jailers is expected of a man of your husband's august rank and reputation. 'Tis expedient to do so. A bribe of sorts. He loses at cards and dice, and the constable sees that he enjoys the best of everything. Why, 'tis one of England's oldest traditions."

Keely stopped walking and looked in surprise at him. "You mean, I've been losing sleep over a man who's been gambling for three months?"

"A man can only read so much," her father replied.

Duke Robert led Keely through the Lieutenant's Lodgings to the grassy inner courtyard on the other side of the building. Keely recognized the Chapel of St. Peter ad Vincula on the far side of the green, where Richard and she had once attended services.

The atmosphere inside the Tower Green was eerily hushed as if the Tower's stone walls trapped unearthly silence within. A cool stillness pervaded the air.

Advancing on Beauchamp Tower, which perched above the Green and the menacing scaffold, Keely peered over her shoulder at the Lodgings. She scanned the area beneath its windows but saw no sign of the queen's restless spirit.

The chaplain royal awaited them at the entrance to Beauchamp Tower. "Are you ready, Your Grace?" the minister asked, unmistakable glee sparkling in his eyes.

"Aye, but I feel unlucky today," Duke Robert replied, shaking the other man's hand.

The chaplain nodded at Keely and then led the way up the stairs to the second floor. Keely walked behind him, and her father followed her.

Keely wet her lips, gone dry from nervous apprehension. For three long months, she'd yearned for this moment, but a sharp feeling of insecurity now swept through her and her step slowed. What if her husband wasn't glad to see her? How could she endure the pain?

And then, Keely reached the top of the stairs. Almost reluctantly, she walked into the chamber.

Richard stood there. When he saw her, he smiled and opened his arms. With a cry of relieved joy, Keely threw herself into his embrace and burst into tears.

Richard crushed her against the comforting planes of his muscular body and planted a kiss on the crown of her head. "Don't cry, dearest," he soothed, stroking her back. "I thought seeing me again would make you happy."

Keely gave a watery chuckle. She gazed up at him through fathomless pools of violet. Placing the palms of her hands against his cheeks, she said, "'Tis the babe. She makes me emotional."

"Does *he*?" Richard countered with a soft, teasing smile.

Keely recognized the gleam of desire glowing in her husband's emerald eyes. She stood on her tiptoes, hooked one arm around his neck, and gently drew his smiling face closer.

Mesmerized by the siren's call in her expression, Richard lost his smile. His mouth hovered above hers for the merest fraction of a second, and then his warm insistent lips claimed hers in an earth-shattering kiss.

An urgent and demanding desperation to join their young bodies and to become one overpowered them. That single devastating kiss melted into another. And then another.

Duke Robert cleared his throat loudly, and the other two men in the room chuckled. With herculean effort, Richard broke the kiss and grinned at his father-in-law.

"Come, dearest," Richard said, removing her cloak and handing it to the duke.

Refusing to relinquish her hold on her husband, Keely looped her arm through his and caught her first glimpse of his prison. Though far from luxurious, the chamber was well-lit, airy, and clean. Built into one wall was the hearth, and in the center of the room stood a table with three chairs.

"Good day to you, sir," Keely greeted the constable.

"You're looking well, my lady," Kingston replied.

"I do appreciate your taking good care of my husband," she said.

"The pleasure belongs to me, my lady."

"I'll show you my chamber upstairs," Richard said, taking her hand in his.

Clutching her tapestry bag, Keely blushed and smiled at their audience of three, then accompanied her husband to the spiral staircase in one corner of the chamber. At the top Richard opened a door and led the way into his third-floor bedchamber.

Keely stopped short at the surprising sight that greeted her. His prison in the Tower appeared more comfortable than her old bedchamber in Wales.

Against one wall stood a four-poster bed, complete with draperies and fur coverlet. Beside the bed was a small table that bore a silver tray, containing a wine decanter, two crystal goblets, a hunk of bread, and an array of cheeses. A cheerful fire glowed within the hearth, before which sat a comfortable-looking chair. Two windows allowed the afternoon sunlight to filter into the room.

With a smile of amused confusion lighting her expression, Keely turned to him. "Why, you haven't been suffering at all," she said.

"Living without you is the worst torture imaginable," Richard replied, drawing her into the circle of his embrace. "Come to bed, dearest."

"Patience, my lord," Keely said. "We must do this correctly if we want the Goddess to protect you from harm."

Richard cocked a copper brow at her. He'd waited three long months to see her. Was she now going to play the coy maiden?

"Please, place the coverlet on the floor in the center of the chamber," she said.

While he hurried to do her bidding, Keely opened her tapestry bag. She pulled two ceremonial robes out as well as her pouch of magic stones.

"Disrobe and put this on," she ordered, handing him one of the robes.

Richard gave her a skeptical look.

"I'm heavy with your child," Keely said with a puckish grin. "Humor me."

Both Richard and Keely disrobed and covered their nakedness with the ceremonial robes. Keely reached for her pouch of stones but then paused to adjust the hood of her husband's robe over his head.

"Don't bother," he said, touching her hand. "I won't be wearing it long."

Keely chose eight dark carnelians for protection and courage. With these, she formed a makeshift circle around the fur coverlet and left only the western periphery open. Without saying a word, Keely offered her hand to her husband.

Richard dropped his amused gaze from her amethyst eyes to her hand. His smile was pure love as he placed his hand in hers.

She led him into the safety of the circle and closed it behind them, saying, "All disturbing thoughts remain outside."

Removing her golden sickle from the pouch, Keely walked around the inside of the circle and fused its invisible periphery shut. She turned to her husband and closed her eyes, praying, "Great Mother Goddess, fierce guardian of all your children, accept this humble offering of our bodies. Shield my wonderful husband from his enemies, the evil-doers."

"Thank you, dearest," Richard whispered. Then: "Now what?"

Keely smiled seductively and pushed the white ceremonial robe off his shoulders. Beginning at the top of his head, she worshipped him with her eyes. His crown of burnished copper hair was a fiery sunset, and his eyes were the green of her beloved forests in springtime. His body was as solid and perfectly formed as a majestic oak. Richard was indeed her pagan god sprung to life.

Dropping her gaze, Keely admired his broad shoulders and well-muscled chest, with its mat of copper hair. Lower, her heated gaze dipped to his tapered waist and then his aroused manhood.

Keely forced herself to lift her gaze to his. She shrugged the robe off her shoulders and stood before him proudly. Wearing only her gleaming dragon pendant and the curtain of ebony hair that fell to her waist, Keely was his pagan princess.

The powerful primitive urge to cover her body with his own and mate surged through Richard. For her sake, he held himself in check and followed her lead.

Richard dropped his gaze from her hauntingly lovely face to her breasts with their enlarged dusky nipples, the exquisite proof that his child grew within her womb. Lower his gaze drifted to her curving hips and gently rounded belly.

With a groan of mingling emotion and need, Richard dropped to his knees in front of her. He wrapped his arms around her hips and kissed the mound of her swollen belly.

"My seed has grown," he whispered, his voice hoarse with tender awe.

"Aye," she murmured, stroking the crown of his head.

Richard slashed his tongue across her moist female's place and heard her sharp intake of breath at the unexpected pleasure. He cupped her buttocks and held her steady while his exploring tongue made her squirm with hot desire.

Up and down, Richard flicked his tongue in a gentle assault on her womanhood. He licked and kissed her dewy jewel, while his talented fingers teased and taunted her sensitive nipples.

Surrendering to the exquisite feeling, Keely melted against his tongue. She cried out and clung to him as wave after wave of throbbing pleasure surged through her.

Richard pulled her down in front of him and kissed her passionately, pouring all of his love into that stirring kiss. Gently, he pushed her down on the fur coverlet and positioned himself between her thighs.

"The babe?" he asked.

"She will be fine."

With that, Richard plunged deep inside her and sheathed himself to the hilt. He withdrew slowly and then slid forward, piercing her softness, teasing her over and over again, until she trembled with rekindled frantic need. Holding her hips steady, Richard thrust deep and rode her hard. Again and again, he ground himself into her tight throbbing softness.

With mingling cries, Richard and Keely exploded together and then lay still as they floated back to earth from their shared paradise. He moved to one side, pulled her with him, and cradled her in his arms. Long moments passed in silence.

"Were we very loud?" Keely whispered, breaking the

silence. "Do you think my father knows what we're doing?"

"'Twould be highly insulting if he believed we were talking," Richard answered.

The thought that her father knew what they were doing—*at the very moment they were doing it*—made Keely blush. And then she remembered her father wasn't alone belowstairs.

"Holy stones!" Keely moaned, hiding her face against his chest. "I futtered my husband above the minister's head."

Richard burst out laughing. "Dearest, you are so incredibly sweet."

She peered up at him. "Good enough to eat, I hope."

Richard rolled her onto her back and kissed her while one of his hands caressed her silken length as lightly as a summer's breeze. He heard her ragged sigh of desire and dipped his head to suckle upon her sensitive nipples.

Their loveplay was tormentingly slow this time, and Richard savored each of his wife's delicate shivers and arousing moans. Temporarily depleted of energy, both felt reluctant to waste precious moments in sleep.

"I'll fetch us a goblet of wine," Richard said, starting to rise.

Keely touched his forearm to stop him. "Breaking the circle without giving thanks is forbidden."

Richard nodded and then helped her stand.

Keely wrapped her arms around him, rested her head against his chest, and prayed, "We thank the Goddess for accepting this humble offering of our bodies joined as one."

She walked to the western periphery of the circle and picked the carnelian up. "This way," she said.

Richard followed her out of the circle and then led her across the chamber. He filled a goblet with wine and sat beside her on the bed. Leaning against its headboard, they shared the wine and the cheese.

Muffled laughter drifted up from the second floor, and Keely whispered, "What are they doing?"

"Drinking and gambling." Leaning closer, Richard flicked his tongue along the fragile column of her neck, sending delicious shivers down her spine. "Mmmm. Good enough to eat."

"Is *that* what you meant the night of our betrothal?" Keely asked, surprised.

Her shocked expression of innocence tickled him. Richard gave her a wolfish grin and admired the pretty blush staining her cheeks. "Share the news from Devereux House, dearest."

"Odo and Hew stole your cousins' virginity," Keely told him. "Of course, we'll see them wed as soon as you come home. My young brother is determined to snatch everyone else's virtue. If the queen keeps you here much longer, there will be nary a maiden left in your household."

"Henry is a man after my own heart," Richard teased her. "Oh, the glory of my roving days—gone forever and nevermore to return."

When Keely cast him an unamused look, Richard kissed her for her trouble. He slipped one hand beneath the coverlet and caressed the mound of her belly, saying, "I pray I'm home in time for the babe's birth."

"Elizabeth will free you in no more than a month," Keely replied.

"I beg your pardon?"

"The Goddess passed her wisdom through me," she explained. "She revealed that we would be together when the Beltane fires blaze. 'Tis the first day of May."

A skeptic to the end, Richard decided to humor her. He kissed her hand in courtier's fashion and said, "I feel so much better knowing that. Come, dearest. I want to show you something."

Richard rose from the bed and offered her his hand. He led her across the chamber to the wall beside the hearth.

"See what I did." Richard pointed to words carved into the stone. "I've immortalized us."

Keely stepped closer and peered at the words *Richard and Keely*. She looked up at him and smiled. Their names would be linked together for all of eternity, even if they were not.

"And we're in excellent company," he added. "See here."

Keely read the words *Jane* and *Guildford*. "Who are they?" she asked.

"Jane Grey, England's ten-day queen," Richard answered. "Guildford Dudley, the present Earl of Leicester's brother, married her. Together, they ruled England for ten days, until Mary Tudor and her army put an end to it. This chamber housed him while he awaited the executioner's ax."

"What happened to Jane?"

"She met the executioner after her husband."

Tears welled up in Keely's eyes. Richard pulled her into his embrace and stroked the delicate column of her back. "'Twas foolish to upset you with so sad a tale," he apologized. "I swear I'm in no danger."

A knock on the door drew their attention. "I'm sorry, child," the Duke of Ludlow called. "You must prepare to leave."

"Give us five minutes," Richard answered.

Keely hid her face against her husband's chest and wept quietly.

Richard planted a kiss on the ebony crown of her head. "Shall I help you dress?" he asked.

Keely shook her head and struggled against her tears. Refusing to allow his parting memory of her to be anything but cheerful, she pasted a sunny smile onto her face and teased, "We'd be here another five years if you dressed me."

Richard smiled, relieved that her mood had passed. Everyone knew extreme sadness in a pregnant woman could mar the child.

When they descended to the second floor, Richard flicked a glance at the constable. "Is it permissible to walk them downstairs?" he asked.

Kingston noted the lady's tear-bright eyes and took pity on the lovers' plight. "I'll accompany you."

Reaching the courtyard below, Richard enfolded Keely within the circle of his embrace and kissed her passionately, stealing her breath away. He gently brushed the teardrops off her face and said with a smile meant to encourage, "Remember, dearest. Your Beltane fire will see us together again. 'Tis a matter of a few weeks only."

Through twilight's fading light, Richard watched his wife and her father cross the Tower Green. Keely looked back once and waved, then disappeared inside the Lodgings.

Richard turned away, but a movement near the Lodgings caught his eye. He whirled around and saw a woman pacing back and forth in front of the Lodgings' windows. Unexpectedly, she turned in his direction and stared at him.

A ripple of unease danced down his spine, yet Richard was unable to tear his gaze from hers. He recognized the woman whose portrait he'd passed hundreds of times in the Long Gallery at Richmond Palace—Anne Boleyn, the queen's long-dead mother.

And then Richard heard her words of warning as clearly as if she'd been standing beside him: *"Beware the blacksmith."*

Chapter 18

"Greedy Tudor bitch!"

Morgana Talbot heard the bitter grumbling from within the chamber and paused, staring at the door instead of knocking on it. The angry voice certainly belonged to the baron, but cursing was so unlike him. At least, she'd never heard Willis utter crude words.

Had coming here been a mistake? Morgana wondered. She had planned to give the handsome baron a tongue-lashing for failing to meet her at the appointed hour. After all, Willis had invited her on a romantic outing upriver to see how April's warmth had transformed the surrounding countryside. But now . . . .

Willis sounded out of humor. On the other hand, she *was* the Duke of Ludlow's daughter, while he was merely a near-penniless baron. Any decent man would have sent his regrets instead of making her wait on the quay like a conspicuous fool. With her anger rekindled, Morgana lifted her fist and banged forcefully on the door.

"Who's there?" The question sounded like an animal's growl.

"Morgana."

"Begone."

Morgana narrowed her blue-eyed gaze on the door as if the offensive portal had ordered her away. She stood in indecision for one long moment, then opened the door and stepped inside the chamber.

With his back to the door, Willis placed the last of his possessions into his leather satchel and buckled it closed. Glancing over his shoulder at her, he scowled darkly and said, "I told you to leave."

"What's wrong?" Morgana asked, standing two feet

inside the room. She'd never seen the charming baron in so foul a mood. That fact, coupled with a feeling of foreboding, kept her from walking across the chamber.

Willis turned around and faced her. "Lady Luck played me for an April fool, but I mean to best her yet."

"I don't understand," Morgana said, becoming alarmed. "What has happened?"

"Even as we speak, your father is on his way downriver to fetch Devereux and transport him home," Willis told her. "Elizabeth has eased her dear unhappy Midas's imprisonment to house arrest."

"'Tis good news."

"That bastard leads a charmed life," Willis snapped. Almost instantly, he realized he'd let his facade drop, and he advanced on her, saying, "You should never have come here, my dear."

The coldness in his voice and the unholy light shining from his eyes frightened Morgana. She backed up two paces and reached for the doorknob. "I—I'll leave now," she said.

"Sorry, angel." Willis grabbed her upper arm in an iron grip and whirled her around. "Ruining my future is a thing I cannot allow you to do."

Morgana wet her lips, gone dry from fear. The baron had apparently lost his mind, and she needed to escape.

Willis reached into his doublet, withdrew a yellowed parchment, and waved it in front of her face. "Remember this?" he asked, arching a brow at her.

Morgana recognized the marriage certificate she'd found in the Talbot family Bible, the damning document proving that Henry and she were ducal bastards. "You said you'd destroyed it."

Smythe smiled coldly, cruelly. "'Tis an exceedingly valuable document."

"Destroy it this minute!" Morgana demanded, trying to grab it out of his hand. "'Tis valueless to you."

"On the contrary, angel." Smythe hid the parchment

inside his doublet. "It guarantees me control of two fortunes—Devereux and Talbot."

"What do you mean?"

"You cannot be as incredibly simple as you sound," Willis said. "I plan to snatch your *legitimate* sister. When Richard tries to escape Devereux House to rescue her, Dudley's men will kill him. As Richard's best friend, I'll wed the grieving widow. When your father later suffers an untimely accidental death, I possess the proof that the Talbot fortune rightfully belongs to Keely."

"You cannot get away with that!" Morgana cried, trying to pull away from him. "I'm telling."

Willis whirled her around and pressed her back against the door. "So beautiful," he said, "but so incredibly stupid. Did you actually believe you'd leave this chamber alive?"

"Help!" Morgana screamed.

With both hands, Willis grabbed her throat and began to squeeze, but her seeming lack of resistance disappointed him. "Even Jane struggled more," he muttered.

Desperate for air, Morgana raised her leg, and with as much strength as she could muster, she kneed his groin. Pained surprise forced him to release her for a fateful moment.

"Help!" she shouted. *"Murder!"*

Recovering himself, Willis grabbed her again and squeezed the life's breath from her body. As Morgana lost consciousness, someone in the corridor pounded on the door.

"Open up!" a boy's voice ordered. "Open up, or I'll call the guard!"

"Help me. The door's unlocked," Smythe called, hurrying to place Morgana down upon the bed.

Twelve-year-old Roger Debrett barged into the chamber, saying, "I heard a woman scream."

"Lady Morgana suddenly became ill and swooned," Willis lied, gesturing toward the bed. "Sit with her while I fetch the leech."

Roger hurried across the chamber. He sat down on the edge of the bed and peered at the lady's bluish-white face. "Sweet Jesus!" he cried. "She looks dead. Her throat—"

Wham! Smythe struck Roger on the back of his head, and the boy slumped unconscious across Morgana's body.

Willis grabbed his satchel and started to leave, but paused in momentary indecision at the door. Should he take the time to finish the job and kill the brat? No. Even now, Richard could be leaving the Tower. He needed to finish his business at Devereux House before Richard returned home. With that in mind, Willis quit the chamber.

Roger swam up slowly from the depths of unconsciousness. He opened his eyes and tried to sit up, but the room spun dizzyingly, sickeningly around. Roger snapped his eyes shut and waited for the nausea to pass. His head pounded ferociously, but he realized he had to get help. Baron Smythe had murdered Morgana Talbot.

And then Roger heard it—a faint, whimpering moan from the dead woman's lips. He opened his eyes and stared at the lady for a long moment. She wasn't dead at all—only in need of reviving.

Roger rose unsteadily and staggered across the chamber to the table. A full basin of water sat on top of it, and he dunked his face into it, the startling cold water clearing his head. Roger carried the basin back to the bed and poured the cold water onto the lady's face.

Morgana sputtered and opened her eyes. "Smythe tried to murder me," she said in a hoarse, breathless voice. "Find my stepmother!"

"Lady Dawn?" Roger was surprised. He'd never heard this one refer to the duchess as her stepmother. "You mean Ludlow's wife?"

Morgana nodded.

"Rest here while I call the guard and a leech," Roger ordered, starting to turn away. "Afterward, I'll find Lady Dawn."

With surprising strength, Morgana grabbed the boy's wrist and jerked him down on the bed. Nose to nose with him, she rasped, "Listen, idiot child. Smythe is downriver by now. He plans to abduct *my sister. . . .*"

"Soon, my daughter," Keely cooed, caressing her swollen belly. "'Tis ten days to Beltane, and then your father will be home with us. *Por tous jours*—for always."

Following her usual afternoon routine, Keely strolled leisurely around her husband's garden. May and June nagged her to nap, but Keely enjoyed her afternoon walks, loved to witness the seasons passing. Today she roamed the garden's far perimeters and admired the startling changes that the month of April had lavished upon the landscape.

Nature's new life emerged wherever she looked. Robins, trailing thin strands of grass from their beaks, flew to familiar haunts in the maples and built their ancestral nests, while bees foraged for nectar within the trees' blossoms. A blanket of purple violets covered the ground beneath the window of the earl's study. Yellow bordering daffodils nodded gaily at their friends, the brilliantly blooming yellow forsythia, in the rear of the garden.

Home. Like a siren's song, the mountains and the glens of Wales called to her.

Keely closed her eyes and imagined the woodlands and the meadows of her native land, her own ancestral nest. White bloodroot blossoms and red trilliums would even now be greeting the spring as the scent of lilacs wafted across the crisp clean air. The recently born lambs would be frolicking together in the meadows beneath the sun's warming rays.

Keely sighed. Someday she would take her children to visit the land of her birth, that special place called home.

Wandering across the garden, Keely stood at the sacred sight where the birch, the yew, and the oak conversed. What the earl needed was a sanctuary garden, and this appeared the perfect spot for it. Come next spring, she would plant a garden to honor the Goddess for gifting her with the daughter she carried within her body. Lady's slipper, maidenhair fern, and moon vines—flowers revered by the Goddess—would grow here.

Keely smiled to herself and pictured the scene in her mind. Each day, no matter the season or the weather, Keely would sit here with her daughter and teach her the Old Ways, pass the Golden Thread of Knowledge to her. *Exactly as Megan had done.* Thus the spiral circle of life would continue through all of eternity.

Other daughters and sons would surely follow this one; each would be special in her or his own way. Lovingly would she share the knowledge she possessed. Her single worry stemmed from her pragmatic husband. Keely prayed that the earl's inability to see beyond the horizon wouldn't be too negative an influence on their children.

"Countess?"

Startled, Keely gasped and whirled around. Willis Smythe stood there, his dark presence blocking the sun like an angry storm cloud. Aye, Baron Smythe was dark and dangerous—and something even more sinister.

"I do apologize," Willis said, an easy smile touching his lips. "I never meant to frighten you."

"No man frightens me," Keely replied stiffly, unable to mask her dislike of him. "Being yanked out of my meditation makes me uneasy."

"Meditation?"

"I've been contemplating nature's glory," Keely said, gesturing at the garden. "Do you not see the beauty surrounding us?"

Willis flicked a quick glance at the grounds. "Very pretty, indeed," he said.

"From where did you come?" Keely asked, cocking her head to one side. She hadn't heard his approach, nor had Jennings announced him.

"Hampton Court," Willis answered, misunderstanding her question. "My barge docked next door at the dowager's quay."

"Is aught wrong with Richard?" Keely cried, panic rising in her breast, her hands protectively touching her swollen belly.

"Richard is well," Willis assured her. "Though I do carry an urgent message concerning him."

"Come into the house."

"No. 'Tis best we avoid any possible eavesdroppers."

Keely cast him a puzzled, questioning look. The baron's presence made her uneasy. The familiar aura of untimely death again surrounded him like a shroud, and the black cloud that hovered above his head seemed larger and more threatening than ever. In a flash of total awareness, Keely knew the baron was a walking corpse. Death would soon embrace Willis Smythe.

Willis lowered his voice and said, "Richard plans to escape the Tower this evening——"

"Escape?" Keely exclaimed. "How? Why?"

"Please, madam. Your questions do waste precious time," Willis said, putting the proper amount of sternness into his voice. "Will you listen to me without interrupting?"

Keely nodded. She didn't want to endanger her husband.

"Several days ago, Richard transferred his lodgings from Beauchamp Tower to Cradle Tower," Willis explained. "Built to accommodate the direct hoisting of boats up from the river, Cradle Tower is lower than the other towers. Under cover of night, the earl's men from Basildon Castle will approach on a barge, dock at the wharf below the tower, and throw him a rope. Then the barge will take Richard upriver, beyond the gates of London and Devereux House, where a fast horse provided by his parents will be waiting."

Keely couldn't fully credit what he was telling her. Why would England's favorite son destroy his future at court by escaping the Tower and thumbing his nose at the Crown's justice? Elizabeth would never forgive him.

She opened her mouth to question the baron, but he hurriedly spoke up. "Meanwhile, you will accompany me to Smythe Priory," Willis went on. "I have horses waiting in the dowager's garden. From there, your husband and you will travel to Monmouth, where one of his ships waits to carry you to France. Your mother-in-law is French, you know. One of her brothers will harbor Richard until Elizabeth recovers her senses and the danger has passed."

Keely doubted such a plan could work. Would her husband truly endanger his firstborn by demanding she travel to France? But what alternative did they have? If the queen kept him locked in the Tower, their daughter would never know her father.

And then Keely remembered the Goddess's revelation: Richard and she would be together forever on Beltane. What the Goddess foretold had come to pass.

"Fetch the horses," Keely said, turning away. "I'll tell Odo and Hew to prepare themselves."

Willis grabbed her forearm. "Your cousins cannot accompany us. Shall we announce our intentions to the world by parading out of London?"

"I see what you mean," Keely agreed reluctantly, the prospect of traveling alone with him troubling her. "Fetch the horses while I pack a change of clothes."

"We haven't the time for that."

"I cannot leave without my pouch of magic—I mean, my valuables."

"Make haste," Willis said. Giving in required less time than arguing. "Share our plans with no one."

Keely hurried inside the house. She saw no one and, gaining her chamber, packed two changes of clothing and her pouch of magic stones into her satchel.

Before leaving the chamber, Keely paused and touched the dragon pendant she always wore. "Mother, protect my husband and my unborn child," she whispered, then fled out the door.

When she returned to the garden, Baron Smythe stood between two horses. "I'll help you mount," he said, stepping forward.

"I cannot ride this horse," Keely insisted. "'Tis sidesaddled."

Willis opened his mouth to argue with her, but Henry Talbot chose that moment to appear in the garden. Smiling like a satisfied tomcat, the boy sauntered toward them.

"Henry, run to the stables," Keely called before Willis could warn her to silence. "Tell Odo or Hew to bring me my saddle." As an afterthought, she added, "Baron Smythe is entertaining me today with an afternoon ride."

Henry glanced at Willis, then dropped his gaze to the satchels. Hiding his alarm behind an unwavering smile, he called, "I'll be back in a minute."

"Each second we delay endangers Richard's life," Willis snapped, knowing the two Welsh giants would never let her out of their sight. "Get on the horse, and be quick about it."

Keely worried her bottom lip with her teeth and nodded. Danger threatened all of them, else the baron would not be so nervous.

Smythe helped her mount and then leaped onto his own horse. Together they left Devereux House and rode west in the direction of Shropshire.

"Keely!" Odo raced into the gardens in front of Henry and Hew. "Where are you, little girl?"

"Son of a flat-chested bitch," Henry cursed. "He's got her!"

"Maybe the baron did offer to entertain her with an afternoon ride," Hew said.

Odo reached out and cuffed the side of his brother's head. "Packed for traveling, you blinking idiot?"

"Why would Keely send me to fetch her own saddle and then disappear with Smythe?" Henry asked. "She harbors no fondness for the baron, and I don't trust him."

"How will we ever find our little girl?" Hew whined, turning to his brother for guidance. "We don't even know which direction they went. And there's four of them but only three of us."

"*Directions!* North, east, south, and—" Odo's slap silenced Hew.

"Four what?" Odo asked, confused.

"If his intent is evil, the beast will take her to his lair," Henry said.

"Where's that?" Odo asked.

"Smythe Priory, in Shropshire."

"Saddle the horses," Odo ordered Hew. "I'll gather supplies."

"Saddle three horses," Henry said. "I'm going too." When the two Welshmen turned to him, he insisted, "I *am* her brother."

"His Grace—"

"His Grace isn't here to approve or to disapprove," Henry interrupted Odo.

The giant grinned and said, "Make haste, my horny young marquess. Our little girl needs us."

Twenty minutes later, the two Welsh giants and the fledgling marquess mounted their horses and rode west toward Shropshire.

"Welcome home, my lord," Jennings said, a warm smile of greeting upon his usually solemn face.

"Thank you, Jennings."

Richard grinned at the man as he crossed the foyer. Behind him walked Duke Robert and Hal Bagenal, his stepfather.

"Send my wife to the study," Richard instructed his majordomo, "but don't tell her who's here. I want my homecoming to be a surprise."

Jennings nodded and started toward the stairs. At this

hour of the day, his mistress either napped or sat near the window in her bedchamber to gaze at the changing sky.

Richard led his father-in-law and stepfather into the study. The two older men sat down in the chairs before the hearth, but Richard remained standing, facing them and the door. He wanted to see the expression of surprised joy on his wife's face when she walked into the room. All morning he'd been anticipating the coming night in each other's arms, and now the moment was almost upon them.

Richard planned to get rid of Duke Robert and Uncle Hal as soon as possible, then pass the remainder of the day and the night in bed with his wife. Tomorrow was soon enough to begin the tedious task of correcting the embarrassing errors he'd made on the queen's personal accounts.

Five minutes passed. And then ten. Where the bloody hell was Keely?

The door opened slowly, and Richard pasted his most devastating smile on his face. One second later, his smile drooped.

"Where is my wife, Jennings?"

"She's *gone*, my lord."

Richard jerked to attention, as did his stepfather and father-in-law. "What do you mean?" he demanded.

"My lady isn't in her chamber," Jennings explained, his worry apparent in his expression. "I checked the gardens, but she isn't there either."

"Ask May or June if Keely is visiting with her cousins at the stables," Richard ordered.

"They haven't seen her since before she went outside for her afternoon walk in the gardens," the majordomo replied. "June is quite certain she saw Odo and Hew ride out with the young marquess. That was several hours ago, and Lady Keely wasn't with them."

Richard started for the door. "I'm going to look for her," he said.

Duke Robert and Uncle Hal bolted out of their chairs.

Both men placed a restraining hand on the earl's forearms.

"Attempting escape is unwise," Duke Robert cautioned.

"If the guards kill you," Uncle Hal added, only half joking, "your mother will dice my innards with a dull blade."

"My pregnant wife is missing," Richard snapped, trying to shake them off.

Loud voices and hurried footsteps sounded in the foyer, drawing their attention. When Jennings opened the door to see what was happening, three people brushed past him into the study.

"Thank God you're here, Tally!" Lady Dawn cried.

"Chessy, what's wrong?" Duke Robert asked, alarmed.

"Papa, 'tis all my fault," Morgana sobbed, flying into his arms.

"Tell me what the problem is," the duke said.

Morgana lifted her chin several notches and exposed her neck. The three men gaped at the angry bruises circling her throat.

"Willis Smythe tried to strangle my poor darling," Lady Dawn told them.

Richard slid his gaze to the duchess. That Cheshire labeled Morgana *my poor darling* proved that something was terribly wrong. His world had suddenly tipped upside down.

"I saved Lady Morgana's life," Roger piped up from where he stood near the door, his pride evident in his voice.

"You're safe now," Duke Robert calmed his daughter, holding her protectively close. "When I find Smythe, I'll kill him for this."

"Smythe could be the one who dispatched Lady Jane," Uncle Hal suggested.

Richard snapped his head around and stared at his stepfather. Never would he believe that his best friend had become a demented monster who strangled defenseless women. Morgana had somehow provoked Willis into losing his temper. Her testimony proved his guilt less than his own dagger found at the crime scene.

Compelled by loyalty to defend his friend, Richard said, "Willis has no reason to——"

"Listen to me," Morgana interrupted, turning within the circle of her father's arms to face the earl. "Willis tried to murder me because I discovered his plan to abduct Keely."

No one spoke. All eyes riveted on the earl.

Richard stared at Morgana but looked through her. Every nerve in his body erupted in a wild riot, and a blinding fury etched itself across his features. An unholy gleam shone from his emerald eyes as the pieces of this puzzle fell neatly into place. *No one could locate Keely. His best friend had snatched his pregnant wife.*

Without a word, Richard turned away and marched purposefully toward the door. He would retrieve his wife, even if it meant hacking the queen's guard into tiny bits of flesh in order to leave Devereux House.

"Stop him!" Morgana screamed. "'Tis part of the baron's scheme. Willis *wants* the guard to kill him!"

Enraged beyond hearing, Richard yanked the door open.

Roger reached out and grasped the earl's wrist, saying, "If the queen's men lay you low, my lord, who will rescue your lady-wife?"

Richard paused, and his gaze slid to the boy's face. Long tense moments passed before his eyes cleared and focused on his wife's favorite page. Cold logic seeped through the red haze of unreasoning fury, and releasing that fury depleted him of excess energy. Almost imperceptibly, he sagged and then nodded at Roger, who removed his hand from the earl's wrist.

Slowly, Richard turned around to face his father-in-law and stepfather. "Any ideas?" he asked.

Everyone in the study relaxed. Roger reached behind

Richard and quietly closed the door, then sidestepped to stand in front of it, lest the earl lose control of his emotions again.

"I have a plan," Lady Dawn spoke up.

Her husband cast her a sidelong glance. "Chessy, strategy falls into a man's domain," he warned.

Lady Dawn arched a perfectly shaped auburn brow at him and asked, "My love, who knows more about strategy than a woman who's managed to trap four men into marriage?"

"Let her speak," Richard said. "I have good reason to believe in her strategic ability."

"I do appreciate your confidence," Lady Dawn replied. "We need a bit of feminine subtlety here. Our problem is to escape Devereux House without bloodshed or discovery. To that end, cook will prepare a delicious supper for the guards, a hearty stew liberally laced with a sleep-inducing herb. Thus, instead of hacking your way to the stables, all you'll need to do is step over a few prone bodies. No one gets hurt, and later, no one gets axed for committing cold-blooded murder."

"It could work," Richard said.

"What herb?" Duke Robert asked, unable to keep the suspicion out of his voice.

Lady Dawn's smile was feline. "Tally, my love," she purred. "I would never use such knowledge against you. 'Tis the herb I slipped my second husband—a nasty brute of a man—whenever he drank too much."

"Very well, duchess," Richard said, a smile appreciative of her ingenuity touching his lips. "We'll do this your way." Assuming command, he turned to Roger and ordered, "Accompany Jennings to the scullery and eat. When you're finished, go to the stables and saddle two horses. I want them ready to ride when I am."

Roger grinned and saluted his idol, then followed the majordomo out of the study.

Next, Richard rounded on Lady Dawn and his stepfather. "Duchess, supervise the preparation of this stew.

Uncle Hal, return to perch at court. When Dudley discovers I've flown the cage, he'll be demanding my head on a pike. I need you there to help Burghley calm Elizabeth."

Lady Dawn and Uncle Hal left together.

Richard crossed the chamber to stand before Duke Robert and Morgana. Gently, he tilted Morgana's chin up and stared at her shockingly bruised throat.

"You need never fear Willis Smythe again," Richard promised.

" 'Tis my fault my sister and you are endangered," Morgana said, a sob catching in her throat.

Her use of the words *my sister* surprised both men. Neither had ever heard Morgana sincerely refer to Keely as her sister, only as a bastard.

"Do not shoulder the blame for Smythe's misdeeds," Duke Robert said.

"Willis also threatened you," Morgana told her father. With tears rolling down her cheeks, she added, "I know about Keely's mother and you."

"What do you know?" he asked, a puzzled expression on his face.

"I'll leave you alone," Richard spoke up, deciding this was a private matter between father and daughter.

"Stay," Morgana ordered. "My knowledge concerns your wife."

Richard recognized the pain in his sister-in-law's expression, and in spite of the trouble she'd caused him and his wife, his heart ached for her. Pampered and spoiled, Morgana was considerably less stout-hearted than his wife and decidedly incapable of coping with life's problems.

"I know Keely is legitimate issue," Morgana announced. "Henry and I are the *real* Talbot bastards."

Her simple statement hit both men with the impact of an avalanche. Duke Robert paled and stepped back a pace as if he'd been struck. Richard gaped at her as if she'd suddenly, unexpectedly grown another head.

"I found your certificate of marriage in the Talbot Bible," she continued. "In misery, I showed it to Willis, who swore to destroy it. He lied. When I confronted him today, he said he wanted two fortunes. Once the guards killed Richard, he planned to wed Keely and then arrange for you, Papa, to suffer an accident. Willis wanted control of both the Devereux and the Talbot estates."

"I'm sorry you've been hurt," Duke Robert said, pulling her into his embrace. He planted a kiss on the crown of her head and said, "I commend your bravery, my golden angel. Go upstairs now and rest awhile. Mention this to no one, not even Henry."

When the door shut behind Morgana, Richard fixed a frigid glare upon his father-in-law. "What about my wife's pain?" he demanded. "Keely has lived her entire life branded a bastard."

"Aye, I deserve your anger," Duke Robert replied, holding his arm up in a conciliatory gesture. "Before the day Keely arrived in my hall, I never knew she existed. My father told me Megan had died miscarrying a babe eighteen years ago, and I believed him. Good Christ, how could I doubt my own father's word? With the news of Megan's passing, the heart in my existence died, and I cared about nothing. Like a dutiful son, I married my father's original choice for a bride—Letitia Morgan—and produced the requisite heir. You know the rest of my story."

"Keely stepped into your hall seven months ago," Richard reminded him, unmoved by the duke's apparent pain, his voice colder than the bitter north wind in winter. "My wife deserved—no, needed—to know of her legitimacy. Bloody Christ! Living in that Welsh dragon's household has scarred her almost beyond repair! You saw her at court. She walked about with her head hung low, as if she were the basest, most unworthy woman in England. How dare you keep this balm from her?" Contempt replaced anger when he added, "*What kind of a man are you?*"

"A simple man who loves *all* of his children," Duke Robert answered, his voice bleak. "When Keely dropped into my life, I vowed to do all I could—acknowledge her and find her a loving husband. *Which I did.* Yet I was unable to name my only son a bastard." He fixed a bleary-eyed gaze on Richard and asked in a voice choked with raw emotion, "Tell me, Basildon. How does a man choose which of his children to destroy?"

Staring into his father-in-law's violet eyes, so much like his wife's, Richard felt the duke's unspeakable pain. It was as tangible as the carpet beneath his feet. He placed a comforting hand on the older man's shoulder. "Though Henry and Morgana are innocent of your mistake, Keely must be told," he said.

"Aye, 'tis past time for the truth," Duke Robert agreed. "My lands and my fortune rightfully belong to Keely and, through her, the child she carries."

"Your possessions mean nothing," Richard said, shaking his head at the older man's lack of understanding. "My wife wants a place of loving refuge, a home where she belongs."

"And what do *you* want?" Duke Robert asked pointedly. "If Keely decides to keep her legitimacy a family secret, what will *you* do?"

"Nothing."

Duke Robert gave him a skeptical look. "As my daughter's husband, you have the right to petition the queen for her inheritance. I would not contest it."

"Your Grace, I am the richest man in England," Richard reminded him. "If I wanted your estate, I would have proposed marriage to Henry."

That remark brought a reluctant smile to the duke's lips.

"I married a penniless, Welsh bastard because"—Richard smiled, recognizing the depths of his emotion—"*I love her.*"

*   *   *

The sun died in a blazing fire as it did each day, and dusk aged into evening. An hour after supper, two black-clad figures peered out the door that opened onto the courtyard. The Earl of Basildon and the Duke of Ludlow stepped over the prone bodies of the queen's sleeping guards and walked down the path toward the stableyard.

"I'd hate to be wearing their boots when Dudley discovers I'm gone," Richard whispered.

"All men have a cross to bear," the Duke of Ludlow replied. "Too bad this is theirs."

Roger grinned when he saw the earl and the duke walk into the stable. "I'm going with you," the boy announced, gesturing to the three horses he'd saddled.

"No, you're not," Richard said.

"I can help," Roger replied. "I did save Lady Morgana from certain death."

"No."

Roger stubbornly refused to give up. "I am indebted to Lady Devereux and cannot chance losing my business partner."

Richard cocked a copper brow at the boy. Did the brat doubt his fighting ability? He ought to box his ears!

"Your lady-wife floated me the gold I needed to invest in the Levant," Roger explained. "'Tis a long story, which I'll relate as we ride."

Richard placed a hand on the boy's shoulder. "I do appreciate your loyalty, but if anything happened, your father would demand our heads on a pike. Besides, who will protect Lady Dawn and Lady Morgana in our absence?"

A wholly disgusted look appeared on the boy's face. He shrugged the earl's hand off his shoulder and said, "With all due respect, your words are naught but condescending cow shit."

Duke Robert chuckled at the boy's impertinence. Richard frowned. The boy spoke the truth; he was condescending to him.

"Let the fledgling ride with us," Duke Robert said.

Richard whirled around. "Have you lost your senses?"

"He'll follow us if we leave him behind," the duke replied. "Won't you, boy?"

Roger grinned and nodded.

"The boy is safer between us than behind us," Duke Robert said.

"When trouble starts, ride to Ludlow Castle," Richard instructed the boy. "Do you understand?"

Roger bobbed his head. "How do you plan to kill the baron?" he asked, excited.

"Very slowly," Richard answered. "And with great pleasure."

The Earl of Basildon, the Duke of Ludlow, and the queen's page mounted their horses and rode west toward Shropshire.

Chapter 19

Where, in the name of the Great Beyond, is Richard? Keely wondered, staring out the second-story window in her chamber at the Smythe Priory. The western horizon blazed with the dying sun, but Keely took no notice of nature's glory.

Her husband had disappeared.

Because of the swiftness of traveling by barge, Richard should have been waiting for her when she arrived at the priory. Had he fallen to his death from the Cradle Tower? No—she would know with her Druid's instinct if he'd passed into the Great Adventure. Had he been captured and returned to the Tower? Only the Great Mother Goddess knew the answer to that.

Fetching her satchel, Keely withdrew the black cloth bag and emptied the holy stones into her hand. From these she chose one white agate for spiritual guidance and eight purple beryls for breaking bad luck. Then she pulled her tiny sickle of gold from the pouch.

Keely walked to the center of the room and made a makeshift circle, keeping only the agate, one beryl, and the golden sickle in her hands. Entering the circle from the west, she closed it with the last beryl and said, "Allowing thoughts remain outside."

Walking clockwise around the inside of the circle, Keely pointed the golden sickle at its invisible periphery and fused it shut. She walked to the soul of the circle, faced the west, and dropped to her knees.

"The Old Ones are here, watching and waiting," Keely whispered, touching the dragon pendant that contained her mother's love. "Spirit of my love, Spirit of my journey, guide me. Spirit of my ancestors, guide me to hear what the trees say. Spirit of my me to hear what the wind whispers. Spirit of my tribe, guide me to understand what the clouds foretell. Open my heart that I may see beyond the horizon."

Long moments passed. And then it happened, images floated across her mind's eye. . . .

Swirling mist, revealing a magic circle. . . . A fiery-haired tinker, symbol of the white magician, locked in mortal combat with the black dragon, symbol of evil. . . . In a flash of movement, the tinker raised his mighty sword and, against all odds, slew the dragon to vanquish the evil. . . . Slowly, the tinker whirled around and called, "Keely, where are you?"

The image dissolved into the reality of a man's voice, asking, "Keely? Are you ill?"

Keely looked over her shoulder and for the briefest moment stared in a daze at the baron. "Stay where you are," she ordered, raising her hand to ward him off. "Breaking the circle is forbidden."

Willis Smythe cast her a puzzled smile and set a supper tray on the table near the hearth. He folded his arms across his chest and watched her.

Keely whispered a silent hurried thanks to the goddess and broke the enchanted circle. Looking at the baron disturbed her, so she avoided it as long as possible by collecting her magic stones and putting them away.

Finally, Keely faced the baron and gave him a nervous smile. The black cloud over his head appeared more forbidding than ever; death hid in the priory's shadows and waited for the predestined moment when he could step forward to claim what was his.

"What were you doing?" Willis asked.

"Praying for my husband's safe arrival," Keely answered.

"Within a circle of stones? Are you a witch?"

"Something like that," Keely said with an ambiguous smile. Another simpleton, she thought, who lived a shallow life of spiritual ignorance. Holy stones, but this England was filled with them!

Willis returned her smile. She was as stupid as her sister, he decided. Forcing her to his will would be easy.

The baron crossed the chamber and stared out at the night sky. The window's old-fashioned shutters caught his eye, and he turned around, saying, "I ought to modernize the priory. One of my daughters can have it as a dowry."

"Do you plan to marry?" Keely asked, surprised by his remark.

"Very soon now." Willis grinned. "I intend to sire a dozen little black-haired Smythes."

Black-haired Smythes.

Keely frowned. His hauntingly familiar words echoed in the distant corners of her mind. Black-haired Smythes . . . black Smythe . . . blacksmith!

"Beware the blacksmith." Megan's prophetic warning slammed into her consciousness.

"What have you done to Richard?" Keely demanded, heedless of consequence.

And the baron dropped his civilized mask.

"Perhaps you're not as stupid as I thought," Willis said. "I await news of your husband's untimely demise at the hands of the queen's guard. Afterward, the village cleric will marry us."

Keely felt the earth move beneath her feet. She clutched her swollen belly and reached for the edge of the table to steady herself.

"Are you ill?" Willis asked in alarm, hurrying across the chamber. If she or the babe died, his scheme died with them.

He reached out to steady her. Repulsed, Keely shrank back from the evil about to touch her. His expression of alarmed concern became sinister.

"I plan to get my heirs on you," Willis told her. "Better accustom yourself to my touch."

"Why are you doing this?" Keely asked, beginning to panic. "You're supposed to be Richard's friend."

"Betraying my closest friend does pain me, but I'll survive the guilt," Willis answered. "The future of two fortunes sits upon your delicate shoulders. Whoever possesses you controls a vast empire of gold, greater than the queen's."

"I don't understand."

"As stepfather to Richard's heir, I will control the Devereux fortune," Willis explained. "And once your father is dead, the Talbot estates become yours."

"Gaining the Talbot fortune through me is impossible," Keely replied. "Henry is the duke's heir."

"Unfortunately for Henry, bastards cannot inherit," he said.

"What do you mean?" Keely asked, confused.

Willis smiled. "Morgana and Henry are the real Talbot bastards."

His revelation stunned Keely. "Are you saying I'm legitimate issue?"

"Precisely."

Keely shook her head in disbelief. "My mother would have told me," she said.

"Did she tell you otherwise?"

Keely looked away. Megan had never said she'd been born out of wedlock. In fact, her mother had always advised her to turn a deaf ear on Madoc's bitter grumblings. Baron Lloyd, she'd always said, wouldn't recognize truth even if it tripped him.

"Well, did she?" Willis persisted.

Though it disturbed her to do so, Keely stared him straight in the eye and said, "His Grace would have mentioned it."

Willis chuckled, its sinister sound sending a ripple of unease skittering down her spine. "Do you actually believe the Duke of Ludlow would name his only son a bastard? I think not, sweetheart."

"Words prove nothing," Keely said. "I will deny your lies."

"Deny it all you want," Willis replied, reaching inside his doublet. He withdrew an old yellowed parchment and held it up. "I hold the proof of your legitimacy in my hand," he said.

Keely stared at the parchment and worried her bottom lip with her teeth. Could it be true? Had both of her parents lied by omission?

"May I see it?" she asked.

Willis passed it to her.

With badly shaking hands, Keely unfolded the parchment and stepped closer to the hearth to read it by the fire's light. Unshed tears glistened in her eyes as she read the document.

She *was* legitimate issue. She *belonged* somewhere.

And then Henry's handsome face shimmered in her mind's eye. Her noble brother would bear the burden of this. She'd lived her entire life carrying the stigma of her bastardy, but never could she lighten her own load by setting the heavy mantle of bastardy upon her brother's shoulders.

Keely knew what she had to do. In a flash of unexpected movement, she held the proof of her legitimacy to the hearth's flames, which burned not only the parchment but her fingertips.

"No!" Willis shouted, leaping forward to grab her hand.

Too late. His dream of wealth disintegrated into smoldering ashes.

Clutching her burned hand to her chest, Keely dashed across the chamber to the open window and shouted, "Somebody help me!"

One step behind her, Willis whirled her around and slapped her hard. He grabbed her upper arms in a punishing grip and shook her violently.

"My baby," Keely cried.

With a disgusted oath, Willis shoved her away from

him. Keely fell to her knees. Her burned hand clutched her belly protectively while the other grasped the window ledge.

"This changes nothing," Willis growled, towering above her. "Richard is dead, or soon will be. You will proclaim your legitimacy after we marry, and your father will not deny you."

Willis crouched down beside her. Grabbing her throat in a bruising grip, he yanked her face close and threatened, "Do as I say, or that brat you carry will be food for the worms. Do I make myself clear? *Do I?*"

Unable to speak, Keely managed to nod once.

Willis released her, then stood and stared down at her for a long moment. Finally, he quit the chamber and locked the door behind.

"Mother, help me!" Keely moaned, touching her dragon pendant.

Keely looked down at her injured hand, and the sight of her own burned flesh made her gag dryly. Regaining her composure, she stood and slowly crossed the chamber to sit in the chair before the hearth.

Her throbbing fingertips pained her less than her aching heart. Would her husband die? Would her brother's existence be shattered? Without her cooperation, the baron's scheme would disintegrate as surely as the proof of her legitimacy had. Suicide would assure her brother's future, and her husband—if he lived—would find a more suitable wife.

Keely couldn't do it. Leaping from the window to her death also meant killing the innocent babe she carried within her womb.

And then Keely recalled the Goddess's promise: *Once in a blue moon, and forever when the fires blazed.*

The fiery-haired tinker in her vision would slay the black dragon. . . .

Along the west side of Smythe Priory, a thick hedgerow grew between the house and the surrounding woodland. Three figures crouched behind this greenery and peered up at the second-story window where the baron held Keely prisoner.

"He struck her!" Henry exclaimed in a loud whisper, surging to his feet.

Two massive hands on either side of him hauled him down to the ground. Henry looked from one hulking Welsh giant to the other.

"Do you want to get yourself killed?" Odo asked, his voice hushed but angry.

"No one hits my sister and lives," Henry announced with all the bravado of an adolescent marquess.

"The baron did strike her and should die," Hew agreed with the boy. "I saw it too."

"Am I blind?" Odo snapped, reaching around the young marquess to slap his brother. "Smythe will suffer for touching our little girl, but we need to bide our time until she's out of harm's way."

"How will we get her out?" Henry asked.

"My lordship, you are about to become a hero," Odo told him. "Hew will stand on my shoulders, and you'll climb up us to stand on his. Reach for that gutter, then pull yourself onto the roof, then—"

"'Tis impossible," Henry argued. "My reach exceeds my grasp."

"What did he say?" Hew asked, scratching his head.

Odo ignored his brother. "Then Hew will give you a boost. We'll catch you if you lose your balance. Won't we, brother?"

Hew nodded.

"Wrap the rope around the chimney nearest the chamber and knot it tightly. Then lower yourself down the side of the priory to her chamber," Odo instructed the boy. "We'll get her out through the window, and the baron will never know we've been here and gone."

Henry gazed for a moment at the priory and its roof, then smiled and said, "I'm game."

"Once inside, don't frighten her," Odo added.

"Or she'll scream," Hew warned.

Meanwhile, Keely sat in the chair in front of the hearth. Her aching heart and her throbbing fingers conspired against her. Teardrops rolled down her cheeks, and her stomach churned with nausea. In an effort to calm herself, Keely closed her eyes and tried to conjure pleasant thoughts—her beloved forests in springtime, the birth of her daughter, her husband's devastating smile. She opened her mouth to scream, but a hand covered her mouth.

Unexpectedly, someone grabbed her from behind. She opened her mouth to scream, but a hand covered her mouth.

"'Tis Henry," whispered a familiar voice. When she relaxed, the hands dropped away.

Keely bolted out of the chair and rounded on him.

"Thank the Goddess," she exclaimed. "But how did you get here?"

"On wings of brotherly love," he answered, then flashed her a wicked grin.

Keely arched one ebony brow at him.

"Odo and Hew are waiting below," Henry said, gesturing to the open window.

Keely slid her gaze to the window and saw the rope hanging down the side of the priory. "Is it safe?"

"Safety is a relative thing," Henry replied. "Would you prefer remaining in the baron's company?"

"No." Keely lifted her satchel off the floor and hurried toward the window.

Henry reached for the rope.

"Wait." Keely cocked her head to one side like a doe sensing approaching danger.

Heavy lumbering footsteps sounded in the corridor.

"Under the bed," Keely whispered, closing the shutters to block the sight of the dangling rope.

As her young brother slid beneath the bed, Keely tiptoed to the chair before the hearth. Her heart pounded frantically, but she forced a serene expression onto her face. Hearing the clinking of keys and the door being unlocked, Keely suffered a powerful urge to turn around and verify that Henry was out of sight. She won the war with herself, but the battle cost her in composure. She trembled almost uncontrollably, and her stomach churned with a combination of fear and nausea.

Ever so slowly, the door creaked open. Carrying a basin of water in his hands, the baron advanced on her.

Willis set the basin down on the table and ordered, "Soak your fingers in that."

Keely submerged her hand in the water. Its coolness soothed the throbbing sting, and from beneath the fringe of sooty lashes, she peeked at her captor.

Willis slabbed a thick piece of cheese onto a slice of bread and held it out, ordering, "Eat this, or I'll force it down your throat."

Keely did as she was told.

The baron lifted her hand and examined her fingers. "Keep your hand up," he ordered, then lifted the strips of linen draped across his forearm and began dressing her burns.

"Why are you doing this?" Keely asked, hoping the baron's redemption was still salvageable. After all, the man stood poised on death's threshold, and if unrepentant, he would be severely punished for his misdeeds.

"You're worth nothing if you sicken and die," Willis said baldly. He quit the chamber then and locked the door behind.

Keely sat statue-still as she listened to the baron's footsteps receding down the corridor. Deeming it safe to move, she leaped out of her chair and hurried across the chamber to the window.

Henry crawled from beneath the bed. "What's wrong with your hand?" he asked, his gaze on the bandages.

"I burned my fingers."

"How did you do that?"

"I stuck them into the fire."

"But why?" Henry asked, staring at her in horrified surprise.

Keely vowed to hide the truth from her gallant young brother forever. Since she couldn't think of a plausible reason to put her hand in a fire, Keely took the only path left open to her—an irritated offense.

"Is this a social call?" she shot back. "Or had you considered rescuing me? If so, we had better hurry because the baron could return at any moment."

Henry cast her a measuring look and then opened the shutters. "Give me the satchel," he said. "I'll carry it."

Keely passed him her bag, then hesitated. She looked at him through eyes filled with obvious fright.

"'Tis the same as leaping from the earl's yew tree," Henry assured her, putting the rope into her hands. "Hold this tight, and keep your feet against the wall for balance. Don't scream if you slip; Odo and Hew will catch you."

"'Tis easier said than done," Keely replied.

Henry helped her onto the ledge and held her waist until she moved into position. He nearly laughed out loud at her expression of fright as she slowly lowered herself to the waiting arms of her cousins. Then he went out the window too.

"Are you well, little girl?" Odo whispered, gathering her into his arms.

Keely nodded, then turned to hug Hew and Henry.

In silence, the four of them hurried toward the safety of the surrounding woodland. Tethered to the trees, three horses stood ready to ride.

"Keely can ride with me," Hew said.

"No, I'm taking the girl up with me," Odo informed his brother.

"Keely is my sister," Henry reminded them.

"She's only your half-sister," Hew argued, "but our full-blooded cousin."

Henry gaped at the giant's incredible stupidity. Odo reached out and cuffed the side of his brother's head.

At that moment, Keely was incapable of riding anywhere. Her five-month pregnancy and her throbbing fingers conspired to hinder her quick escape. Her head spun dizzily. She dropped to her knees and gagged dryly while her rescuers crouched down to steady her and to whisper words of comfort.

"The ride to London will kill my babe," Keely said, her eyes swimming with tears. "Find a place to hide me while you return to clear my husband's name."

"We're bringing you home to Rhys," Odo announced.

"My husband—"

"—will blame us if anything happens to you," Hew interrupted.

"The idiot and I will ride to London as soon as you're safe in Wales," Odo promised.

"I'll remain with you in Wales," Henry offered. "Your brother can hold me hostage until Elizabeth releases Richard." This had been the best adventure in his young life; returning to his boring tutors at Ludlow Castle frightened him more than Willis Smythe.

Keely nodded and tried to rise, but her knees buckled. With a soft cry she fell in a dead faint.

Odo caught Keely before she hit the ground and cradled her in his arms like a baby. "She's riding with me," he said.

"Will she and the babe survive the trip?" Henry asked. Odo nodded, saying, "She'll be well-padded on my lap."

"Too much excitement weakened her," Hew said. "She'll regain her strength with a bit of rest."

The three of them mounted and turned their horses west in the direction of the Welsh border. Hew and Henry rode on either side of Odo. In case of a surprise attack the brigands would need to go through them to get to Keely.

"After we've seen to the girl's safety, we'll stop here on our way to London and kill the baron for daring to touch her," Odo told his brother.

"Sounds reasonable to me," Hew replied.

"Brother, you wouldn't recognize reason if it jumped up and bit your rear end."

"'Course not," Hew shot back. "Do I have eyes in the back of my head to watch the crease in my arse?"

Henry bit his lip to keep from laughing, then remarked, "I never crossed the border into Wales."

"'Tis like stepping through the gates into heaven," Hew told him.

Odo cast the unimpressed marquess a sidelong glance. "The prettiest women this side of paradise live in Wales," he added.

"Aye," Hew agreed, winking at his brother over the boy's head. "And there's nothing these ladies love more than a hero."

Henry mentally rubbed his hands together and shifted in his saddle. Anticipation was already hardening him.

"You'd better wipe your noble chin," Odo teased him.

"Aye, you're drooling," Hew added.

"From both ends," Henry admitted with a rueful grin.

The two Lloyd giants dissolved into deep rumbles of laughter.

"'Tis there." Richard halted Black Pepper and pointed at the two-story stone priory in the distance.

The earl, the duke, and the queen's page paused within the shelter of the woodland cover and gazed at Smythe Priory. The house appeared an idyllic picture of impoverished gentility, and the slanting rays of the afternoon sun fingered the priory's facade with light and shadow as if angels plucked the strings of a harp. The serenity of spring, the season of life's yearly renaissance, ranged beyond the horizon; yet the three on horseback sensed the invisible threat of death wafting through the air.

"How innocuous," Duke Robert remarked.

"Aye, no one would ever imagine the Devil himself lived inside," Roger added his own opinion.

Instead of charging toward the priory as every fiber of his being screamed at him to do, Richard moved Black

Pepper forward at a slow but steady pace. The Duke of Ludlow and the queen's page rode slightly behind him on either side. They halted their horses beside the priory's eastern border of hedgerow and dismounted.

Richard drew his rapier and led the way around the priory to the front. "Wait outside," he ordered the boy.

Roger opened his mouth to protest, but then clamped his lips together. The grim determination in the earl's expression discouraged argument.

"I'll shout if I need your assistance," Richard said, then added to soothe the boy's pride, "Draw your dagger, and be ready for a fight."

Roger nodded gravely and stood tall, the earl's confidence in him a balm to his boyish pride.

With rapier in hand, Richard stepped toward the door. He could have merely tried to open it first, but cognizant of the watching boy, he chose a more dramatic approach. He lifted his booted foot and kicked the door open.

"Who's there?" called a voice.

Richard, followed by Duke Robert, marched in the direction of the baron's voice. Both men paused inside the entrance to the priory's common room, a not-so-great hall.

Willis sat alone in a chair in front of the darkened hearth. He stood in surprise when they walked into the hall.

"Richard, is it really you?" Willis greeted them, pasting a smile onto his face. "How did you escape the Tower?"

With cold contempt etched across his features, Richard stared at him for a long moment and then shouted, "Keely?"

Silence was his answer.

"I'm alone here," Willis told him, an expression of bemused confusion appearing on his face.

"She could be locked away," Duke Robert said. "I'll check the bedchambers." At that, the duke raced up the stairs two at a time.

"What's this all about?" Willis asked, smiling as he advanced on the earl.

Richard lifted his rapier and pointed it at him, warning, "Stay where you are."

Willis lost his smile. He stopped short and held his hands up in a conciliatory gesture.

"She isn't here," Duke Robert called, returning downstairs.

Richard fixed his gaze on his former friend. Murderous rage, barely held in check, shone from his emerald eyes. "Has your wife left you?" Willis asked, feigning innocent surprise. "You cannot possibly believe that she and—"

"The game is finished," Richard interrupted, his voice mirroring the violence surging through his blood. "Roger!"

With his dagger drawn, the queen's page ran into the priory. The boy appeared ready to duel with the Devil.

"Recognize him?" Richard asked, his gaze never wavering from the baron's.

Willis stared coldly at Roger.

"You murdered Jane and dropped my dagger beside her body," Richard said.

"Then you tried to strangle Morgana," Duke Robert added.

"Both the lady and I still live," Roger informed the baron. "'Tis time to pay the piper for your crimes."

If looks could kill, Roger would have dropped dead on the spot. "I should have taken that extra moment to silence you permanently," Willis sneered at him. "Meddling brat."

"Where is my wife?" Richard demanded.

"The damned *taffy* escaped," Willis answered, a bitter edge to his voice. "If I'm under arrest, give me five minutes to pack a bag."

Richard cocked a copper brow at him. "I haven't come to arrest you, Willis."

A smile of surprise spread slowly across the baron's face.

"I intend to kill you," Richard told him.

Willis lost his smile.

Richard flicked a glance at the boy and ordered, "Roger, leave."

"I said, get out!"

Reluctantly, Roger turned away and left the hall. Allowing the two combatants space to fight, Duke Robert backed away and waited in the hall's entrance.

"Why did you do it?" Richard asked.

"For money, of course."

"Sick greedy bastard."

"'Tis an easy life for a man like you, who never lacked funds," Willis said in an accusing voice.

"You never lacked for anything either," Richard shot back. "And where's Ludlow's marriage certificate?"

"Destroyed."

"Liar."

"That sneaking witch you married stuck her own hand in the fire to be certain I couldn't salvage it," Willis told him.

"You actually expect me to believe my wife burned the proof of her own legitimacy?"

"'Tis truth. With that paper destroyed, there's no need for either of us to get hurt."

"The minor matters of abduction and murder need settling," Richard replied. "Didn't I warn you never to look at my wife? Your final hour is here, baron. Better say your prayers."

"Would you slaughter an unarmed man?" Willis asked.

"Draw your sword, baron."

Willis inclined his head and reached for his sword, then advanced on him. The two friends began circling each other.

Willis made the first move. He leaped at Richard suddenly, and their swords kissed with a metallic clang.

Equally matched, Richard and Willis swung and parried with deadly expertise, and neither could gain the advantage. Though the baron was stronger and heavier, Richard possessed a predator's agility. Within minutes, the hall was a shambles of overturned table and chairs.

Unexpectedly, Willis tripped over a fallen stool, and his sword slipped from his hand. Richard thrust his blade forward. The baron rolled to the right, sprang to his feet, and drew his dagger.

Richard drew his own dagger and then tossed his rapier toward his father-in-law for safety's sake.

"Interesting piece," Willis remarked as they began circling each other again.

"Scottish dirk, a gift from my brother-in-law," Richard replied, smiling coldly.

"Death by dagger is so intimate," Willis said. "A fitting end between friends."

In a flash of movement Willis leaped closer and flicked the point of his blade across Richard's cheek, drawing first blood. Then he quickly danced out of the arc of the return swing.

Again and again, Richard and Willis clashed and separated. Only their occasional grunts and the whoosh of their blades broke the silence inside the hall.

Attempting to draw more blood, Willis jumped inside the arc of his friend's reach. Richard sliced at him but missed, and Willis hastily stepped back to safety.

Richard went after him. Willis anticipated such a movement. With one leg, he swiped Richard's legs out from under him.

Caught off balance, Richard went down, and the baron fell upon him in an instant. Gleaming death aimed for Richard's throat, but he grabbed the baron's wrist and strained with every ounce of strength he possessed to keep the dagger at bay.

Savagely, Richard fought back. He kneed the baron's groin and pushed upward.

Willis grunted and toppled backward. Glinting steel

sliced the air as Richard drove his dagger into the baron's heart. In one swift motion Richard rolled to the left and sprang to his feet, ready to block any further attack.

Willis Smythe was beyond fighting back.

Richard dropped to his knees beside his fallen friend and gently closed his eyelids. "God rest your soul," he whispered as a sob of raw emotion escaped his throat.

A strong hand clasped his shoulder.

Richard gazed through tear-blurred eyes at his father-in-law and said, "I once loved him like a brother."

"A friend's betrayal is always heartbreaking," Duke Robert replied. "Only time will soothe the pain."

"You heard what he said about that marriage certificate?" Richard asked, wiping his eyes and his bloodied cheek on his sleeves.

Duke Robert nodded.

Slowly, wearily, Richard stood and scanned the hall as if bewildered by all that he saw. "Keely!" he shouted, his voice mirroring his despair. "Where are you?"

"We'll find her," the duke promised, placing a comforting hand on his shoulder.

"My lords, Lady Keely didn't escape alone!" Roger cried, dashing into the hall. "Someone rescued her! A rope dangles from the chimney to the ground along the west wall of the priory."

"Her cousins?" Richard said, glancing at his father-in-law.

The duke nodded. "Probably Henry too."

"Dudley will see me axed if I return posthaste to London," Richard said.

"Then we'll stay here," Duke Robert replied. "Chessy will send us word when Keely returns to Devereux House."

"What do we do now?" Roger asked, eager for more adventure.

"Can you stitch?" Duke Robert asked him.

"Stitch?" Roger exclaimed. "Sewing is women's work."

"Ah, but there aren't any women on the fields of battle to stitch a man's flesh together," the duke informed him.

"I never thought of that."

Duke Robert nodded sagely. "First, find me needle and thread so I can stitch Devereux's cheek. Afterward, we'll bury Baron Smythe."

"And then?" Roger asked, turning to the earl, hoping for something more exciting.

"We'll cook ourselves supper, fledgling, and do what all warriors do in between their battles," Richard answered.

"Which is?"

Richard winked at the boy. "We wait."

Chapter 20

"Holy horse shit!" Roger exclaimed.

Standing outside the priory, the boy shielded his eyes against the sun's glare and stared off in the distance. A small contingent of men on horseback advanced on the priory, and Roger recognized the two men in the lead.

"Earl Richard!" he called, running back inside the priory. "Soldiers from London approach. 'Tis Dudley and my father!"

Both Richard and Duke Robert grabbed their swords and hurried outside. Behind Dudley and the Earl of Eden, Roger's father, rode six men.

Richard flicked a worried glance at his father-in-law. Was Dudley here to arrest them, or did he carry the news of Keely's safe arrival in London?

A week had passed since that fateful day when he'd confronted Willis. By now, his wife should have reached London and explained who really murdered Lady Jane.

"Sheath your sword," Richard said, recognizing the man who rode directly behind Dudley. "Uncle Hal rides with them. Keely must have reached London."

"I cannot trust Dudley," Duke Robert replied, sheathing his sword reluctantly. "Debrett fares no better in my regard. No offense, Roger."

"None taken," the boy said. "My father fares no better in my regard either."

Robert Dudley, Simon Debrett, and Hal Bagenal halted their horses and dismounted, as did the five soldiers who rode with them. At Dudley's nod, the men-at-arms drew their swords.

"I told you so," Duke Robert whispered.

Richard flicked a questioning look at his stepfather.

Appearing decidedly unhappy, Hal shrugged his shoulders in an apparent apology. In that instant Richard knew that Dudley had somehow forced his stepfather into revealing where he'd gone.

"Richard Devereux and Robert Talbot, I hereby arrest you by the order of Her Majesty, Queen Elizabeth," Dudley announced. "You have willfully thwarted the Crown's justice *and*, in so doing, have abducted young Roger Debrett, heir to the Earl of Eden."

"'Tis a lie!" Roger shouted. "I forced them to take me along."

"Incorrigible brat," Simon Debrett muttered. He reached out and slapped his son so hard, the boy toppled backward and landed on his rump.

Both Richard and Duke Robert growled and took a step forward to protect the boy. Five swords pointed at their chests persuaded them to remain where they were.

"Where is Baron Smythe?" Dudley demanded. "He is under arrest for harboring fugitives."

"Smythe lies with his ancestors in the family vault," Duke Robert told him.

Dudley hastily stepped back three paces and asked, "Was he diseased?"

"We dueled," Richard answered. "I won."

"You murdered Smythe too?"

"'Twas *execution*," Roger defended the earl. "Not murder."

"Keep your lips shut," Simon Debrett snapped, giving his son a rough shake. "You'll regret this when I get you home."

"Dudley, I already explained that Smythe abducted Richard's wife," Hal spoke up. "'Tis the reason he escaped house arrest."

"Then where's the lady in question?" Dudley asked.

Richard turned a worried gaze upon his stepfather. "Keely hasn't returned to Devereux House?"

Hal shook his head.

Where is she? Richard wondered. Where had Odo and

Hew taken her? Could brigands along the road have attacked them? Good Christ, his pregnant wife had disappeared! And judging from the hatred shining in Dudley's eyes, he wasn't going to get a chance to search for her.

"Well, Devereux. What have you done to your lady-wife?" Dudley sounded almost pleased. "Perhaps we would do well to look inside the Smythe vault."

"Think what you're saying," Richard argued, appalled by his rival's sickening insinuation. "Would I murder the woman who carries my heir?"

"A demented monster like you is capable of anything," Dudley replied. "Drop your weapons. Slowly."

Surrendering to the inevitable, Richard and Duke Robert dropped their swords on the ground and then their daggers. Richard flicked an accusing look at his stepfather, who had the good grace to flush.

"I'm sorry, Richard," Hal apologized. "Dudley convinced Elizabeth to hold Louise, Cheshire, and Morgana hostage in the Tower until you surrender and explain your actions. I rode with Dudley to assure your safe arrival in London."

"You put *my mother* in the Tower?" Richard exploded. Rage surged through his body. He expected no mercy from his bitterest of rivals, but abusing his gentle mother infuriated him beyond reason.

Heedless of consequence, Richard shoved one of the soldiers out of his way and lunged at Dudley. He grabbed the other man's throat and began to squeeze. Two of the guards grabbed Richard and dragged him off their lord, but he continued to struggle, which forced them to keep a tight hold on him.

Taking his cue from his son-in-law, Duke Robert sprang at Dudley. His fist connected with the Earl of Leicester's jaw.

Two other guards leaped to their lord's defense. They fought to control the enraged Duke of Ludlow.

"Craven bastard!" Roger shouted at Leicester, breaking free of his father's grasp.

The boy landed a vicious kick on Dudley's left shin. The last of the earl's guard grabbed the boy.

"Control your brat, Eden!" Dudley snapped.

Debrett stepped toward the boy, but Hal Bagenal placed a restraining hand on his forearm and asked, "Would you beat your own son for exhibiting loyalty to a friend?"

"Basildon, I've waited a good, long time for your downfall," Dudley said as he drew his fist back to strike.

"Enough, Leicester," Uncle Hal shouted, drawing his sword and pointing it at the earl. "Strike my stepson, and you'll answer to me."

"Debrett, disarm the traitor," Dudley ordered.

The Earl of Eden looked from Robert Dudley to Hal Bagenal. He had no part in Leicester's grudge, yet he refused to borrow another's trouble by aligning himself with an enemy of the Crown. Debrett did nothing for a long pregnant moment and then judged Dudley to be on the winning side of this argument. He reached for the hilt of his sword.

"Don't none of you fine and mighty lords move a muscle," a voice nearby ordered.

"Moving means death to you," a second voice added.

Everyone froze for a fraction of a second, then looked at the two Welsh giants advancing on them. Richard stopped struggling and watched in relief as Odo approached the Earl of Leicester and prodded the man's back with the tip of his sword.

"Greetings, cousins," Richard said with a grin. He was so glad to see his wife's kinsmen, he could have kissed them. On the lips.

"Tell your men to release them," Odo ordered Dudley.

"And then discard your weapons," Hew added, the tip of his sword teasing the Earl of Eden's back.

"The punishment for obstructing the queen's justice is severe," Dudley warned. "I guarantee you'll hang at Tyburn Hill."

"What do you think, brother?" Odo asked.

"Let's kill the lot of them," Hew answered. "Then the bastard can't squeal to the queen about how we obstructed her justice."

"If you value your continued good health, Dudley, do as they say," Richard advised, watching his stepfather use the tip of his blade to caress Leicester's cheek. "When Uncle Hal gets nervous, his hand shakes. A sword scratch would mar your handsome face."

"Very funny," Dudley sneered. Then: "Discard your weapons, men. Debrett, too."

The five men-at-arms released their prisoners and then dropped their swords. Dudley and Debrett also disarmed themselves.

"Sit down against the wall of the priory, and keep your hands up in the air," Hew ordered.

When the seven men did as they were told, Hew stood guard beside them. "Move one muscle," he warned, "and I'll hack you into tiny pieces."

"Where's Keely?" Richard asked Odo.

"Safe with Rhys in Wales."

Thank you, God, Richard thought. Relief surged through his body, and he placed a hand on the big man's shoulder, saying, "Thank you, cousin."

"You're welcome," Hew called before his brother could say anything. "The young marquess is with her."

"Keely sent us back to clear your name," Odo said. "We decided to stop here first and kill the baron for daring to strike her." The giant turned to the duke and added, "'Twould seem Henry's been a hero waiting to happen. He risked his life to bring our little girl outside to safety."

"Thank you for sharing that with me," Duke Robert replied. He grinned and puffed his chest out with pride. "I always believed he'd eventually take after me."

"We can detain Dudley for a few days while you fetch Keely," Uncle Hal suggested to Richard, who nodded.

"What about me?" Roger asked, flicking an anxious glance at his father.

Richard looked from Roger to the obviously irate Earl of Eden. He smiled at the boy and said, "Fledgling, His Grace and I would never consider leaving without you."

"Let's take their horses," Duke Robert suggested.

"'Twill save us the time of saddling ours."

"No, we'll ride our own," Richard replied.

"One moment, my lords." When they turned to him, Odo blurted out, "Rhys is holding Keely and Henry for ransom."

The Earl of Leicester and the Earl of Eden looked at each other and hooted with derisive laughter.

"My brother-in-law holds my wife for ransom?" Richard echoed, flushing with embarrassed anger.

Odo nodded.

"How much?" he snapped.

"Rhys don't want your money," Odo answered, then turned to the duke. "Baron Lloyd desires the gentle and b-b-beauteous—I think 'tis the word he told me to use— the beauteous Lady Morgana in honorable marriage."

Duke Robert smiled. "Baron Lloyd is welcome to my daughter *and* a handsome dowry."

Richard and his father-in-law started walking in the direction of the stables. Realizing the boy wasn't beside him, Richard called over his shoulder, "Are you coming, fledgling?"

Roger grinned and hurried to catch up.

"Get back here, son!" the Earl of Eden shouted, though he dared not move with the giant's sword poised to pierce him. "Obey me, or I'll beat you within an inch of your life. I'll disown you!"

Richard stopped short and turned around slowly. Placing a protective arm around the boy's shoulder, he said, "Roger has more integrity in his little finger than any ten nobles put together. Touch even one hair upon his head, and I'll see you paupered before Midsummer's Eve."

"Is that a threat?" the Earl of Eden challenged.

"Consider it a promise."

The Earl of Basildon, the Duke of Ludlow, and the queen's page turned and headed for the stables. As they rounded the corner of the priory and disappeared from sight, their voices drifted back to the others.

"Why don't we take their horses?" Roger asked.

"Fledgling, always anticipate your opponent's next move," Richard instructed the boy. "If we take their horses, Dudley will try to persuade Elizabeth to hang us for horse thievery. . . ."

Twenty-five miles northwest of Smythe Priory, the Lloyd keep nestled in a secluded mountain valley south of Lake Vyrnwy. Spring always arrived late in these mountains of Wales, but that particular day had dawned cloudy and unusually cold in spite of the fact that the first of May was virtually hours away. Winter seemed to be reminding the world of men that he hadn't yet been vanquished.

Keely wandered into the Lloyd great hall just before the noontime dinner hour. She carried a heavy woolen cloak slung across one arm and one of her mother's old Beltane baskets. Setting these on the high table, Keely sat down beside her brother.

"You're beginning to look like you swallowed something whole," Rhys teased, winking at her. "How is your hand?"

"Much better." Keely glanced down at her swollen belly and blushed, but then an expression of worry shadowed her features. "Do you think Odo and Hew arrived safely in London?"

"If you were a brigand," Rhys countered, "would you attack two giants?"

Keely shook her head. "But how long do you think 'twill take to free my husband?"

"That depends on the English queen," Rhys answered. "Wales is your home, sister. Remain here as long as you want. Forever would please me."

"Thank you for that." Keely smiled at him. With Madoc dead, she did feel that she belonged at the Lloyd keep. No one called her a bastard. In fact, all the Lloyd clansmen and retainers seemed friendlier than they'd ever been. Perhaps they'd really liked her all along but had feared Madoc's wrath.

"I cannot stay here indefinitely," Keely said. "My husband and my baby need me *and each other*. Though he is terribly flawed, I love Richard."

Rhys cast her a sidelong glance and asked, "In what way is the earl flawed?"

"His Englishness prevents him from seeing beyond the horizon."

Rhys bit his lip to keep from laughing in her face. His sister was delightfully illogical. After all, the only people he'd ever known who were farsighted enough to see beyond the horizon were Megan and Keely. Others hereabouts believed his late stepmother possessed special powers, but Rhys himself was more pragmatic by nature. Keely scanned the hall's occupants and asked, "Where's Henry?"

Rhys winked at her. "Communing with his newest best friend, Elen of the big teats."

Keely rolled her eyes. She really ought to have chaperoned her younger brother, but in view of the fact that he'd saved her life, she hadn't had the heart to keep him from celebrating their survival with his own brand of fun.

"I must gather the Beltane branches," Keely announced, reaching for her basket and her cloak. "I intend to visit Megan afterward."

"'Tis a tad chilly today," Rhys told her. "Don't stay outside too long, or 'twill sicken my nephew."

"You mean your niece," she corrected him, and then left the hall.

Outside in the courtyard, Keely breathed deeply of the pure Welsh air. A low overcast colored the sky a depressing gray, but tiny pockets opened occasionally and allowed sunlight to filter down to the earth. Gazing at the drooping clouds, Keely knew that winter struggled in vain to retain its grasp on the land and its people. With her Druid's instinct, she saw beyond the horizon—spring was hiding behind those threatening clouds.

Keely drew her cloak tighter around herself and walked into the woodland surrounding the Lloyd keep. With her Beltane basket hooked over her left forearm, she foraged for the nine types of wood branches needed for the sacred Beltane fire.

First, she chose oak and birch, representing the God and the Goddess, symbols of fertility. Branches of rowan to protect against evil followed those into her basket. Next came hawthorne for purity, hazel for wisdom, berry vine for joy, and fir for rebirth. Last and most important, Keely selected apple wood for the magic of love. Beltane celebrated the sexual joining of young lovers, and the apple wood was the most sacred ingredient on this particular holiday.

With her task completed, Keely returned to the clearing in the valley and headed in the direction of her mother's grave. She passed the hallowed ground of the Lloyd graveyard and walked toward the grassy incline where three gigantic oaks stood together like old friends. The solitary grave beneath then faced the east, the sacred direction of the rising sun.

"Good day," Keely greeted the three majestic oaks who, like sentinels, guarded her mother's eternal resting place.

Keely knelt in front of the grave and recalled happier times. No matter the season or the weather, Megan and she sat together on this very spot. Here her mother taught her the Old Ways, passing the Golden Thread of Knowledge to her.

Feeling a presence beside her, Keely looked up. "Papa!" she cried, surprised.

"Thank God, you're safe," Duke Robert said, then knelt beside her. He drew her into a sideways hug and planted a paternal kiss on the ebony crown of her head.

"'Tis Megan's grave?" he asked, glancing at the marker.

"Her body lies here," she answered, "but her spirit is enjoying the Great Adventure."

"An arrogant English pup—who thought he knew everything—traveled to Wales eighteen years ago," Duke Robert told her, a soft smile of remembrance touching his lips. "He fell hopelessly in love with a beautiful magical woman, a descendant of ancient Welsh princes, and married her. Life intruded upon their love and separated them for a time; the pup proved a very great fool who believed his father's lies. . . You are my legitimate heir, Keely, and I intend to acknowledge you as such."

"I lived my whole life a bastard," Keely replied. "Condemning my brother to suffer what I did serves no purpose. Besides, I am a bastard no longer—I am the earl's wife."

"I had a feeling you'd say that," Duke Robert lifted her bandaged hand and gently kissed it. "You are Megan, both inside and out."

"Thank you, Papa," Keely smiled with love at the English duke who had become her father in truth. "Please try harder to persuade Elizabeth to release Richard. I know he doesn't really love me, but I cannot allow my daughter to live without her father. Experience has taught me how heartbreaking 'twould be for her."

"Elizabeth did release your husband to house arrest, merely hours after Smythe convinced you to leave Devereux House," Duke Robert told her. He removed his dragon pendant and placed it in her hand, saying, "Richard loves you more than life and deserves to wear this as a symbol of the love you share."

"If that's true, why did he send you to fetch me?" Keely asked, unable to mask the misery swelling in her breast. She felt relieved that her husband was finally safe, but—

"If you look over your shoulder," Duke Robert said,

"you will see a man whose love incited him to risk the queen's wrath by escaping house arrest."

Keely whirled around. Her husband stood at the bottom of the grassy incline and watched her.

Richard had come for her.

"I need a moment alone with Megan," Duke Robert whispered close to her ear. "Go to your husband, child."

With the assistance of her father's steadying hand, Keely arose and started down the incline toward her husband. Unaccountable shyness slowed her step, and then she recognized the love shining from his emerald eyes.

Richard opened his arms to her. With a cry of joy Keely lifted her skirts and sprinted the remaining distance to him.

Richard crushed Keely against his body as if he would never let her go. His mouth captured hers. He poured all the love he possessed into that single stirring kiss.

"I love you," Richard vowed. "*Por tous jours.*"

"And I love you *for always*," Keely whispered. She glanced at the dragon pendant in her hand, then placed it over his head, saying, "This belongs to you."

"Thank you, dearest." Almost reverently, Richard touched the gleaming dragon pendant. "I will cherish it and your love forever."

"Can we stay for the Beltane celebration?" she asked, her violet eyes sparkling with excitement. "'Tis the day young lovers leap over the fire."

"Aye, and we'll join their celebration," he answered, pulling her against him. "I'd leap over a thousand fires for you, my love."

Keely turned within the circle of her husband's arms and watched her father sitting at Megan's grave. He appeared a lonely and sad figure of a man.

"Mother, he loved you so," Keely whispered, giving voice to her thoughts. "Send him a sign."

A sudden rumble of thunder rolled across the horizon. Tiny pockets opened in the cloud cover, and thin fingers of sunlight reached for the world. Huge delicate snowflakes fluttered down from the yawning clouds and laced the air.

Surprised, Duke Robert glanced up at the sky. A serene smile touched his lips and banished the melancholy expression from his features.

" 'Tis thundering and sunning and snowing," Richard said. "All at the same time."

Keely gazed up at her husband through violet eyes wide with wonder and asked, "Did I do that?"

"No, dearest. *Megan did it.*"

She arrived on the tenth day of August, and they named her Blythe.

Six weeks later, on the twenty-first day of September, English hedges and gardens misted with purple Michaelmas daisies. Their strange fragrance wafted through the air, announcing the full Harvest Moon and the autumnal equinox, when day and night balance perfectly.

At midnight, London's Christians had already eaten their St. Michael's Day feast, and the farmers in the countryside had celebrated their Harvest Home. England was a sleeping land—except for one of the great mansions in the Strand.

"You're satisfied with a daughter instead of a son?" Keely asked the tall white-robed figure standing beside the cradle.

"I'm actually *relieved*," Richard admitted, turning around to smile at her. "I love Blythe and you too much to want a tour of duty in Ireland, and I'm too proud to tell Elizabeth I've changed my mind." He gazed at his sleeping daughter again and complained, "Bloody hell, though. I cannot like the look of her."

"Yea, Blythe is uncommonly beautiful," Keely said, crossing the bedchamber to stand beside him. "She's the nectar of our love."

"Aye, 'tis God's vengeance upon me for seducing so many—I'd rather she'd been blessed with a plainer face."

"Why?" Keely asked, surprised.

"England has too many glib-tongued rakes whose sole purpose in life is stealing a maiden's virtue," Richard answered.

Keely smiled at his anxiety. "Is this the man no woman could refuse?" she teased.

"One did, and I fell in love with her," Richard said, pulling her against the side of his body. "Which doesn't solve the immediate problem of keeping those handsome young swains away from Blythe."

"Immediate problem? She's only six weeks old."

"Being prepared is always wise," Richard told her.

"Darling, you cannot stop the bees from tasting the flower's nectar," Keely said.

"Let them taste someone else's nectar—not mine."

"Do you plan to worry about this for the next fifteen years?"

"Probably."

In the great hall below, both family and friends waited for Richard and Keely to appear with Blythe. Twelve of them wanted to participate in the magic night ceremony when the Goddess would bless baby Blythe. Duke Robert and Lady Dawn spoke quietly with Richard's parents before the hearth. On the other side of the chamber, Henry and Roger shared sweet memories of their stay in Wales with Elen. Odo and Hew stood with their wives, June and May. Jennings, the earl's majordomo, had insisted upon being included in *his* little Blythe's special night. With Jennings stood Mrs. Ashemole, whom Keely had recently hired to help with Blythe and whatever children followed.

Except for Richard's three sisters, who lived in foreign countries, Keely's stepbrother and half-sister were the only absent family members. Morgana Lloyd, heavy with a difficult pregnancy, was unable to travel from Wales; and her adoring husband, Rhys, refused to consider leaving her behind in that delicate condition.

After pulling up the hood of her ceremonial robe to cover her head, Keely handed each of her guests a candle.

The various colors of the candles signified the personal traits she desired for her daughter. Every quality from health and courage to true love and great fortune were represented in those candles.

While her husband waited with their daughter cradled in his arms, Keely lit each loved one's candle. In silence, she led the procession outside to the garden where the birch, the yew, and the oak stood together.

Keely used her holy stones to form a large circle, leaving only the western periphery open. Between each of the stones she set wild berries of elder, whortle, sloe, and damson.

Everyone filed into the circle from the west, and Keely closed it behind with the last holy stone, saying, "All disturbing thoughts remain outside."

Keely led Richard and Blythe to the center of the circle. Their loved ones held their candles high and formed a circle around them.

At his wife's nod, Richard lifted Blythe toward heaven, and Keely called, "Great Mother Goddess, fierce guardian of all your children. Behold Blythe, the jewel of my life, conceived and born in love. Bless and protect her. Keep her feet planted solidly in the earth, while her spirit soars upward to seek the wisdom of the stars."

Keely took Blythe from her father's arms and cradled the infant against her breast. She closed her eyes and whispered, "Open my heart, that I may see beyond the horizon into my precious one's future."

Long silent moments passed. A satisfied smile touched Keely's lips and then vanished.

"I thank the Goddess for passing her wisdom through me," Keely said, ending the ceremony.

Keely handed Blythe to Duke Robert, then walked to the circle's western periphery and broke the enchantment. "Mulled wine and spiced cider will be served in the hall," she said as the invited guests left the sanctity of the circle.

Everyone but the proud parents started back to the

house. While Keely walked around the outside of the circle and collected her holy stones, Richard wandered down to the edge of the fog-shrouded Thames and waited for her.

"What do you see?" Keely asked, slipping her arm through his.

"Beyond the horizon."

Keely smiled. "You must possess the incredible sight of a soaring hawk."

"I'll need hawk eyes to keep the rakes away from our daughter," Richard said.

Keely giggled. "Darling, you're about as sensitive to the invisible as a brick."

"'Tis the reason I married you," Richard replied, laughter lurking in his voice. "You keep me from tripping over things I cannot see."

"You are very funny."

Richard drew her into the circle of his arms and kissed her thoroughly. "I do love you, dearest," he murmured against her lips.

"And I love you," she vowed.

He lifted her up, and she entwined her arms around his neck. As he carried her across the lawns to Devereux House, Richard asked, "What did you see in Blythe's future?"

"One brother," Keely answered. "And six sisters."

Richard stopped short. "Seven maidenheads to guard?"

"Holy stones! Don't drop me!"

"I will never let you go," Richard promised with love shining from his eyes. "*Por tous jours.*"

"For always," Keely whispered, then pressed her lips to his.